FRIENDSHIP'S BOND

MEG HUTCHINSON

Friendship's Bond

HODDER &
STOUGHTON

First published in Great Britain in 2010 by Hodder & Stoughton
An Hachette Livre UK company

1

A CIP catalogue record for this title is available from the British Library

ISBN 978 1 4447 1384 8

Typeset in Plantin Light by Hewer Text UK Ltd, Edinburgh
Printed and bound in the UK by CPI Mackays, Chatham ME5 8TD

Hodder & Stoughton policy is to use papers that are natural, renewable
and recyclable products and made from wood grown in sustainable
forests. The logging and manufacturing processes are expected to
conform to the environmental regulations of the country of origin.

Hodder & Stoughton Ltd
A division of Hodder Headline
338 Euston Road
London NW1 3BH

www.hodder.co.uk

For my husband who is, and always will be, part of me

ACKNOWLEDGEMENT

I am very grateful to Pierre Gilliard for his wonderful book *Thirteen Years at the Russian Court*, which has proved an invaluable source for my research.

I

'*So what is it the Lord decrees? You are His self-appointed spokes-man, the one chosen to carry His word, to interpret His will to those less favoured, so tell me: is it the Lord's will I turn Alec from this house, that I leave him friendless and alone in a land foreign to him? Is that God's decree or is it yours?*'

As she stared into the cold grey deadness of an empty fire grate Ann remembered these words, saw again the pinched mouth of Thomas Thorpe tighten, making his thin lips disappear while his pale eyes glittered with the displeasure her retort had aroused.

'*I am simply telling you what the people are saying; they think it wrong that a young man and woman who are not of the same blood are living together under the same roof.*'

'*The people! The people think it is wrong!*' she had replied quietly. '*And you, Mr Thorpe, how did you answer the people; did you, as you so frequently do, quote the Scriptures? Did you remind them of the words Jesus spoke, words which tell us to love our neighbour as ourself?*'

Had she hoped her words would touch the man's conscience, have him retract what he must know to be untrue? Perhaps. Ann pulled her worn coat closer in an attempt to ward off a shiver, not so much because of the cold of an autumn morning as at the remembered icy gleam of his narrowed eyes. Thomas Thorpe's sharply pointed nostrils had flared at her perceived reprimand.

'*The congregation,*' he had snapped, '*the congregation is concerned that chapel property, namely this house, is being put to misuse.*'

She had understood the implication of his words but had deliberately raised a questioning eyebrow. Whether self-elected bearer of the congregation's misgivings or, as she suspected, the vessel of his own spite-filled intentions, Thomas Thorpe was going to be made to put his accusation into words.

Had she not challenged him, not confronted him in so direct a fashion then maybe Alec and herself would not now be homeless; but her indignation at the falsity of the allegation had swept away any thought of caution.

'*Misuse? What exactly is the nature of the misuse the congregation fears? But then it is unfair of them to let you bear the brunt of their dissatisfaction; I cannot let you be their sole spokesman while they remain in the background. Therefore I shall meet with them in the chapel, I shall demand they say outright what they mean.*'

She had seen the result of that, the quick flicker of alarm flash across his eyes, the sudden uneasy twist of a stone-hard mouth; she had seen Thomas Thorpe's guilt and he . . . ? He knew it had been observed, that he stood condemned by his own reaction; but the flare of recognition vanished as swiftly as it had come. Staring straight at her he had laughed, a low victorious laugh.

'*That . . .*'

His laugh had become a snarl.

'*That will not happen. You see, the congregation have expressed the wish you no longer be allowed to worship there.*'

'*The chapel is a House of God, no one can deny me the right to attend divine service.*'

'*Indeed,*' he had answered, '*and as a responsible member of the Church I pointed out the same at the meeting.*'

2

Ann's heart flicked as it had on hearing those words. There had been a meeting, one kept secret so as to afford her no chance to defend herself against any scurrilous allegation; and on whose instigation? The answer had been clear to read in those sly fox-like eyes: Thomas Thorpe's.

'*I reminded them of that.*'

The snarl had softened, his confidence of success lending a smarmy obsequious note.

'*I said that while they might exclude you from their company you could not be refused entry into the building though I feel, given you are no longer welcome there, it would prove less painful for you should you choose to worship elsewhere.*'

No longer welcome! He had smiled with vulpine malice on hearing her sharp catch of breath at those words. Thomas Thorpe had been extracting revenge for her refusal to be flattered by his attentions; she had told him the advances he pressed were unwelcome, that she had no desire for a relationship other than that which existed at present. Was this why the meeting had been held without her knowledge? Had Thomas Thorpe's vanity been so injured he would see her not only excluded from the chapel but shamed and humiliated in the eyes of its congregation, with her reputation sullied by unsavoury gossip? Or was there yet another reason, one even more important to Thomas Thorpe than revenge?

Watching him in this room yesterday she had felt supposition harden into certainty. The man was afraid of his own reputation being brought into question. Given the opportunity of coming face to face with her fellow worshippers she might denounce him, inform the people of the true characteristics of their so-pious lay preacher. Seeming to guess her thoughts he had gone on.

'*You were aware when offered the tenancy of this house that it is the property of the chapel. As with that building, the congregation bought and now maintain it with their offerings and therefore their wishes as to its occupancy must as a courtesy be observed.*'

'*And that wish is?*'

He had shuffled his feet, glanced at the hat held in his hands in a show of discomfort but the instinct which had told her his fears were for his own standing in the community had told her just as definitely there was no regret. It was no more than pretence, a fabrication designed to mask the spite he really felt, which could only be sated by seeing her thoroughly discredited.

'*I'm sorry . . .*'

Had he smiled on saying that? Had the slight clearing of the throat been a suppressed laugh? A moment later those animal-sharp eyes had met hers with all the triumph of the victor about to deliver the final blow.

'*. . . you understand I am simply the messenger, had I any influence . . .*'

She had wanted to scream at the hypocrisy she discerned beneath that self-absolution but instead had interrupted calmly.

'*Was it not your influence which secured me this house, did you not recommend me as a tenant?*'

The question had disconcerted him but his recovery had been swift. Thomas Thorpe was too certain of his own superiority in the eyes of the people he claimed to represent to allow any question of hers to frustrate what was plainly his purpose, yet even so she had persisted.

'*You were aware at that time of the relationship between Alec and myself. Surely you shared that knowledge with the others so why is it only now they find that relationship to be unacceptable?*'

4

He had drawn a long breath as if to bolster himself for the delivery of sorrowful news but the gleam in his eyes had proclaimed only elation. '*Miss Spencer, I can only say what I have been requested by the congregation to say; that is to inform you the tenancy of this house can no longer be extended to you. Having received this due notice you will vacate the property by noon tomorrow.*'

'*What you have been requested to say . . .*'

She had repeated the words calmly but disbelievingly. Then at his threatening glance she had continued.

'*. . . while you of course tried to convince them their concerns were unfounded; you told them how your own attempts to seduce their tenant had met with rejection and with her having refused such a moral, upright man then assuredly she was too virtuous a woman ever to think of indulging in wrongdoing with a boy. Or is that something else I should put to the congregation?*'

Her refusal to become his mistress might as she had surmised have punctured the man's pride but the barb she had cast at that moment had driven deeper. Staring into the fireplace she had cleaned so meticulously Ann watched the shadows of yesterday dance in its emptiness.

Thomas Thorpe had drawn a vicious-sounding breath, emotions darting in rapid succession across his tight-drawn features while his eyes, never wide, had at that instant closed to mere slits, leaving no doubt: Thomas Thorpe cared only for Thomas Thorpe. He would do whatever it took to prevent any stigma marring his reputation as a caring religious God-fearing soul anxious only for the well-being of the community. So what of Alec's well-being? Thomas Thorpe's pale spite-filled eyes had said as clearly as ever words could that this was yet one more question which required no answer. To a man such as he, the welfare of a twelve-year-old was of no consequence and so she had not asked.

5

'*Be advised . . .*'

His words seemed to echo from the starkness of the fire-place, to slither across the room as they had slithered the evening before, to hiss again in her ears; the poison of a man refused as a lover, a man so enamoured of himself it seemed vengeance was the only thing that would assuage his damaged pride.

'*Be advised,*' she heard in the silence of her mind, '*any accusation made against me will rebound upon your head. You will become the victim of what will be seen as baseless claims, a woman caught in depravity seeking to extricate herself by the devious method of shifting blame on to the shoulders of another. The people will not believe and Thomas Thorpe will not forget; so again be advised, leave the chapel and the town with a silent tongue.*'

He had turned on that last word but even as he opened a door on to the small space separating house from chapel she had said quietly, '*I pity you, Mr Thorpe, the sewers of the town you profess to safeguard are sweeter than your mind; if you are the representative of God, the spokesman of the chapel congregation, I want no part of them and no part of the religion they follow.*'

As the door banged shut behind her unwelcome visitor Ann had felt tears of despair rise in her throat.

The House of God and the house of man.

Both had been denied her.

Bailiffs sent by Thomas Thorpe had come to see her out. Ann glanced towards the door when she heard a loud rap. It was no person from any neighbouring house; they had come to accept her as one of their own, approaching her as they did neighbours of long standing by pushing open the scullery door and calling as they entered, 'It be only me wench,' followed up by a woman's name. Apart from Thomas Thorpe collecting the weekly rental no man had visited. She had smiled at the answer given to her query about that; 'Eh wench,' Dolly Horton had said, 'a man don't go a doin' o' such, be there a need to call at folks' 'ouse then that be left to the woman, men meet at their place o' work and should aught need a sayin' then it be said there.'

A sharper second rap demanded attention and Ann rose to her feet. She had hoped Alec would have returned before they were evicted but like any young boy, promises to be home at a given time were lost on him once he was outdoors. But the house was to be vacated and even if Thomas Thorpe himself was at the door she would not ask to be allowed to wait inside one more minute. The chapel did not own the street; she would wait at the side of the road until Alec showed up.

'I were a wonderin' be you goin' to answer of my knock.'

Since she was expecting to see a bailiff probably accompanied by one, possibly two men, the sight of a short slight figure dressed entirely in black with a small bonnet on top of a severe grey bun surprised Ann.

'I sees I don't be what you reckoned to find standin' at your door.' The grey head swung side to side.

'No, I . . . I was expecting . . .'

'I knows who it be you was a waitin' of.'

How could the woman know? They had not met before, of that Ann was positive. Had it been otherwise she would surely have remembered; not so many people attended the chapel that she would not recognise one of them and certainly this woman was not an immediate neighbour. Taught from childhood it was rude to stare Ann glanced across the woman's shoulder then with a brief smile invited her unexpected visitor to step inside.

'I won't be a doin' of that thought I thanks you kindly.' The head swung again, this time in vehement denial. 'I won't set no foot 'neath that roof nor any other to which them chapel folks gets theirselves, not so long as Thomas Thorpe be among 'em I won't!'

The very mention of the name made Ann quiver and it seemed from the look crossing the lined face that this woman experienced the same. But not surely from the same cause! Thorpe was a vile man but despicable as he was he would not make advances to a woman so much older than himself.

They were strangers to each other, the woman would not step inside the house; so who was she and why had she come here? Ann looked again at the figure standing resolutely beyond the open doorway. The lines on her face, her callused hands holding a worn shawl tight about her shoulders were not all due to age; as for so many in this town, life had shown this woman little kindness.

Suddenly aware she had given no response to her caller's forceful statement Ann apologised and enquired what she could do for the woman.

'Ain't what you can be doin' for me brought me to this doorstep, no wench, it be more what Leah Marshall can do for you, allus supposin' you be of a mind.'

Be of a mind for what? Ann frowned. The appearance of the woman, her worn face and hands, her plain dark skirts, the shawl which had obviously served long and well, all pointed to a life of toil affording little reward and certainly seeing nothing left over for charity.

'I knows what you be a thinkin'.' The woman's slightly stooped shoulders lifted in a shrug. 'What can it be a perfect stranger thinks to offer? Well, though Leah Marshall be not known to y'self her be known to the folk of that chapel and to many in Wednesbury along of 'em. It be the way in this town as I 'spects it be in others, folks' tongues wag an' it be a bit o' that waggin' come to the ears of Leah Marshall, talk which says of you and a lad bein' turned from this house, of bein' put on to the streets for reason of the lad bein' no blood relative. That be a reason I finds hard to accept but I be askin' no other, all I be sayin' is this: Leah Marshall's house don't be property of no church nor chapel, it don't have no landlord to say who can or can't bide beneath its roof. Small it be and holds naught grand in the way o' furnishin' but what it is belongs to Leah Marshall alone and should you and the lad care to lodge there then you be welcome.'

A lodging . . . this woman was offering a place to stay. Relief swept through Ann, but the welcome offer raised questions. Why would she take two people she knew nothing of into her home?

Leah noted the swift tinge of pink rise to colour Ann's wan cheeks. She had not believed the gossip surrounding this girl, whispers uttered behind her back. That practice never sat well with Leah Marshall, even less so when it came from that particular source. The lies had no doubt been brewed by one who was a master at covering his own doings.

'Thank you, but I . . .' Ann stumbled over the reply which would make the woman withdraw her offer, yet it had to be said. 'The purpose of my being evicted, what the people believe of me . . .'

'You don't say no more.' The bonnet, tied on with a bow almost as large, bobbed precariously. 'Leah Marshall be a body likes to make her own decisions regardin' folk and that be what I'll be a doin' along of you and the lad should you choose to be teken my offer.'

Meeting the steady gaze Ann felt something she had not felt in many months, a quick indefinable lift which said Leah Marshall was a woman she could trust.

2

Leah Marshall watched the various emotions chase across the face of the young woman accepting her offer of a home. She knew very little of her except for the odd snatches of gossip overheard in the market place and those were no sound basis for judgement, but she did know enough of the world to see it had not treated Ann in the best of ways and the weeks spent in that house had in all likelihood played a part.

'I'll bide 'ere 'til y' be ready to go.' Leah took a step back from the open doorway of Chapel House, a determined pull of the shawl draping her shoulders a clear indication of her intent.

The woman was no longer young; she should not be asked to stand in the open. Uncertain as to how to phrase this concern Ann hesitated.

Leah had read the look. 'Set y'mind to rest. Leah Marshall don't be so old her can't go standin' for a few minutes nor her legs so weak her be needin' of a chair.'

'I'm sorry, I did not intend any slight.'

She would find no disagreement in that. Leah acknowledged the sincerity of the apology. 'There be none teken, so like already be said I'll bide 'ere while you gathers of your belongin's.'

Ann glanced to where a small bundle lay just inside the room. A change of underclothing was all it held. The thief who had taken her suitcase had left nothing behind. The small amount of money she had thought safely hidden beneath her clothes, the cheap trinkets her grandmother had purchased for her at the town fair and even the photograph of her mother, the one she had freed from the clutch of her dead father's hand, all had been stolen. Alec had found the photograph. Partly damaged by being ripped from the frame it had been thrown mindlessly aside yet even though the horror of robbery had numbed her, she had thanked God for the mercy which had saved for her the one memento she had of the mother she so loved. She sighed at the memory, took up the bundle and said quietly, 'They are already gathered.'

Tucking the ends of her shawl beneath her breasts Leah turned again to wondering what was the background of the girl she was taking into her home. From the few possessions she had it could be thought she followed the way of the gypsy wandering the roads to wherever they led yet her speech, her dress, the very look of her said nothing of the Romany. So where was she from? If the lad she spoke of was not a relative then who was he and how come they were so close?

Such questions she would not ask yet. Leah nodded towards the house. 'Then if there be naught of you or the lad left inside I suggests you be closin' o' that door and we waits of him along of the street.'

Thomas Thorpe had insisted the key be handed over imme- diately and had taken it away with him. Fears of his return, of another ordeal such as the one she had been subjected to being repeated, had kept sleep away, every sound of the night, each creak of roof timbers, every sign of branches tossed by a gathering breeze setting her nerves jangling. Thankfully the hours had passed uneventfully. She had told Alec nothing of what had happened, saying instead that a minister might be appointed quite soon and so they must leave. Why had she lied? As at so many times since departing from St Petersburg this was one more thing she would keep to herself.

Ann shut the door firmly and turned to join the waiting Leah.

Please heaven, the night just passed would be the last of her nightmares.

'*They trusted me, they trusted me as they would no other man.*'

Seated at the window of the bedroom Leah Marshall had provided for her use, Ann stared at a high slow-moving moon.

'*I gave my word and they honoured me with their trust; they asked I take into my keeping their most precious possession with the prayer it be kept safe, and now ...*'

In the night silence it seemed she heard again the rough rattle of hard-fought-for breath, heard the gasp which followed, felt the clutch of the hand grasping at her arm.

'*... do it ...*'

It had been a whisper, words breathed even as pleading eyes were glazing over.

'*... do it for me child, keep ... keep my promise for me.*'

He had died in her arms, the father she loved yet had barely known.

His employment by the Foreign Office had involved her parents in much travelling and so they had decided their daughter would stay with her grandmother, be educated in England and in due course rejoin them wherever they might be. That place had been St Petersburg.

But it had not been the happy reunion she had dreamed of during that long sea voyage.

A bank of cloud drifting over the golden orb of the sky plunged the small room into darkness, as that terrible day had plunged her world into darkness. Ann's fingers tightened in her lap.

She had arrived to find her father a heartbroken man. The love of his life, the wife he adored, had been struck down with some mysterious illness, one which had swiftly claimed her life.

The burial had been over and finished before the ship had docked, the approach of winter meaning the ground would soon be too hard for the digging of graves. Her father could not stand the thought of his wife's coffin being stored, as was the practice, in some frost-bound 'Waiting House' which every city, town and village in the whole of Russia had to keep in order to house the dead until the coming of spring released winter's iron-hard grip on the land.

He had not meant to be distant. Tears traced Ann's cheeks. He had been used to a home where his wife had been his sole companion, so a daughter he had not seen in the twelve years since leaving her in the care of a grandmother had in the darkness of his sorrow been . . . no, not ignored. Ann shook her head at the thought, her father would not have deliberately ignored her, yet how could she deny even to herself that during those long lonely days it had seemed that for her father she might not exist?

They were to return home to England.

Beyond the window cloud retreated, allowing the brilliance of moonlight into the bedroom again but in her memory Ann was standing once more in the small sitting room of a poky little house in an unfit back street of St Petersburg. The embassy did not house its less important members in grandeur and the post of clerk was least grand of all.

She had found the note lying on a narrow table jammed into a hall which begrudged it every inch of space. The paper, folded once across, bore one word, 'Priority'. The handwriting had caught her eye. Delicate yet also strong, letter flowed into letter, each joined to the other, in beautiful copperplate style. She had not seen it before that moment; the letters she had received at her grandmother's house had always been in the tight, almost bunched hand she knew to have been her mother's.

Was the paper something he had meant to take with him? Had he put it there on the hall table then forgotten to pick it up? Ought she to read it? The business of the embassy was not meant to be seen by those not employed in its service! But surely 'Priority' indicated the paper was of some importance, so maybe her father would be in trouble with his superiors for having left it behind. This thought decided her. Whatever might be written on that solitary sheet, it belonged with her father. She had donned her coat and fur hat then fastened a scarf about her shoulders; the ends of it had brushed against the note sending it fluttering to the floor. Had her gloved fingers been clumsy as they retrieved it, was that how suddenly the note was opened?

It bore no salutation, but was, clearly meant for herself.

The premises will be vacated in two days' time. Have all luggage ready for collection at two p.m. on the fifteenth.

There was no one else living in that house, no one that brusque instruction could have been left for.

No name! Ann breathed deeply as tears squeezed beneath her tightly closed lids. He would barely acknowledge her presence in the short time it took to eat the evening meal she prepared against his return from work; there was no smile on seeing her, no 'goodnight' as he left the dining table to shut himself away in his room and definitely no kiss. When had her father last kissed her? When had he last held her in his arms? She could not remember when!

He had left those instructions for his daughter, a daughter for whom he had no love. She had tried to put his behaviour down to grief at losing his wife, but she too had been lost and unhappy. With a smothered sob Ann turned from the window. She must not blame him, a man so unused to having a child about him, a man who during that child's whole lifetime had spent no more than a few hours in her company because the demands of his work were his priority.

Priority! As she slipped into bed the word danced in Ann's mind. It was one she would not forget.

She was gone, she and the lad along with her. Thomas Thorpe stared about the neatly ordered living room of Chapel House. Grand though the name the congregation had chosen for the property their hard-earned coins had bought was, it was simply a two-up and two-down cottage at the rear of the chapel itself. For some of the worshippers parting with pennies and halfpennies would mean going without a meal, yet he had not discouraged the offerings, quite the opposite. Thomas Thorpe smiled to himself.

His sermons on the selflessness of giving, the blessings the act of charity brings, had proved quite an inducement, a practice that he had followed until the tumbledown house had been restored by the free labour of male chapel members, their womenfolk providing cloth which they had sewed into curtains, covers and even linen for the beds. A home fit for the minister they hoped to see appointed. But that day had not arrived; it appeared no man was eager to come to the smoke-ridden town of Wednesbury. This suited Thomas Thorpe. So long as the position remained unfilled then this house was virtually his, the congregation happy to leave the question of occupancy to him.

The smile died, leaving in its wake an expression of displeasure. He had sold them the idea of letting the place to that woman, had them accept it as easily as they had accepted his exhortations on the rewards of charity. He had fully expected the reward for that particular act to be his. The woman was alone except for a young lad, there was no husband, no father, in fact no man to bring bread into the house. She was in need of a friend who could not only help with the problem of where to live but also with finding work. Help of course would give rise to gratitude, to appreciation.

He had played the friend, careful in the presence of others not to be overindulgent towards her, never ready with more care or advice than he offered elsewhere. But with every meeting the attraction she had held for him since first seeing her in the chapel grew a little stronger. Even so he had waited until Fate presented him with the perfect opportunity.

She had been alone in the house, a fire of a few sticks almost dead in the grate, a candle in place of the paraffin lamp lending barely enough light by which to see. Most telling of all, he had detected no smell of food cooking in the fireside oven. He had deduced the reason immediately. Employment of the sort she looked for was not easily come by in Wednesbury, the few residents wealthy enough to engage others to wash and sew for them already having domestic staff covering those duties.

He had seen her hand linger over the rent book placed ready on the dresser, heard the quickly stifled sniff of threatening tears as her glance had lighted on the coins laid neatly beside it.

This was the moment he had watched and waited for, the chance he had ached for, and now it was his, he had only to grasp it.

His body had quickened with that awareness, his flesh thickening with the promise at hand yet despite the flare of emotion he had picked up the book, marked the weekly payment then had let the coins lie. She had queried this omission with a puzzled frown.

Had it been those eyes that had banished all caution? That soft velvet look, blue as sky after summer rain? Had that caused him to toss the slim volume aside and catch her to him, his body pressing close against hers?

In his memory he felt again the hard jerk, the drive of tautening flesh that had ripped through him when at last that enticing body had touched his own. He had heard the soft cry as she came into his arms, felt the quiver running through her as his mouth closed over hers become stronger as his hand closed about her breast. He had begun to release the buttons of her dress, the tremor rippling along her spine a silent testimony to the pleasure of his touch.

'*There is no need of money,*' he had released her mouth just long enough to say, '*payment in kind is much more satisfactory.*'

There had been a tangled moan as his mouth again took hers, a sound he had taken to be that of acquiescence.

But it had been no sign of compliance.

Snatching up the rent book he stared at it, anger coursing along his veins. Her words throbbed in his brain, adding to the resentment of rejection.

'*Get away from me ...*'

She had twisted from his arms, almost running to the far side of the cramped room. An obvious shudder had shaken her whole body as she looked at him.

'*Take the money and go, don't . . . don't ever come here again, I will bring the rent to the chapel every week.*'

But that would have given rise to talk, speculation as to the reason why she would give up the tenancy of a comfortable home when she had nowhere else to go. What had decided her on such a move? Such conjecture might conceivably become enquiry and that he could not allow.

And so he had lied and she had been evicted.

He had thought that would be an end to it, the threat of what she knew gone along with her from the town.

Except she was not gone from the town. A fresh wave of anger surged hot but beneath it there was another feeling, a slow ebb tide of anxiety.

Ann Spencer and Leah Marshall. His fingers tightened about the slim book, screwing it up into a tube. Two women sharing one house; two women either of whom could cause the downfall of Thomas Thorpe.

3

'Let the lad find his own way, it'll go easier for the both o' you if he don't feel tied down.'

'But farm work is heavy and I don't think he is used to that.'

'Hmmph!' Leah's snort echoed along the whitewashed walls of the small outbuilding she had turned into a dairy. 'He won't never get used to it neither lessen he be given the chance. Seems to me the lad has more'n a fair share o' common sense, should a task prove too much then he'll say it do.'

But would he? Ann gathered wooden pats she and Leah had used to shape rich golden butter into small rectangular blocks and carried them into the house. After placing them in the scullery's shallow brownstone sink she went to fetch the kettle from where it hung above the living-room fire. When she reached for it a spurt of steam gushed from the spout, the same pressure setting the lid clanging noisily, and in the instant she was back in Ploschad Morskoy Slavy, the great Square of Maritime Glory in St Petersburg, the harsh cry of horns announcing the arrival and departure of ships, the steam from their funnels hissing like enormous terrifying sea creatures of fairy tales. That dreadful scene had however been part of no fairy story but a frightening reality.

The Russian language had proved almost impossible to learn, so that her trips to the market to purchase food became a daily struggle to make herself understood; the walks she had taken around the city to alleviate the loneliness of that tiny house got her lost many times, including that day walking to the seaport in order to save what she could of her money.

Ploschad Suvorova, Aptekarsky, Bolshoi, Prospekt, names difficult to interpret in themselves made the more so by many of the Cyrillic letters appearing what to her was the wrong way round. It had proved virtually useless to ask direction of people hurrying about their business; most had shrugged, shaken their heads and moved on, others had simply walked past without a glance. So it had taken what seemed like hours but at last she had found her way.

'*Sankt Peterburgsky Morskoy Vokzal,*' a guttural voice had muttered at her as she stood staring about a wide square whose right side was graced with a pair of small identical crown-headed towers. '*Morskoy Vokzal.*' A lined face had frowned beneath an astrakhan hat, a gloved finger pointing towards an impressive archway inscribed on which were more mysterious letters.

She had thanked him, though his information had done nothing to help, then the sound of a horn blasting the air made her realise he had been telling her she was standing at the entrance to the port. The man had hurried on his way but she had stood, suitcase in hand, while a sound other than those of the streets and the port surfaced in her mind.

'*... they asked I take into my keeping their most precious possession ... do it ... keep my promise for me.*'

Her father's words. Ann swallowed hard. He had made a promise but could not keep it; his dying words entreated her to do it for him. She had not been able to tell him she would, but she had murmured it as she held his dead body close. In the days which followed she had searched each of the rooms of that small house but found nothing she would remotely have termed precious. Maybe the officials at the embassy would be able to help, perhaps the item her father had been requested to take charge of had been deposited there, so he could bring it away with him when his service finally ended.

Oblivious to the hiss and clatter of the kettle, Ann walked again through wide streets flanked by buildings fighting to outdo each other in architectural splendour.

How long had she walked? Time had ceased to exist, the beauty and grandeur of the city sweeping everything else from her mind until the bells of the many churches and cathedrals filled the air with a symphony of music.

The medley of chimes had released her from the narcotic pull of her surroundings but where was she? Despite the strangeness of the lettering she managed to read a sign placed high on a wall. 'Suvorova'. She had seen that word before. Think! She had urged her brain to function but it was not until her eyes lighted on the gigantic statue of a classical warrior complete with plumed helmet, raised sword and shield that recognition dawned. The statue was a dedication to the celebrated General Suvorov of whom she had read in those many hours spent alone in the house.

Suvorova Square. Relief had rushed in a warm flood along her veins. Those same books had told her this was where she would find the British embassy. She had caught her breath at sight of a building entirely occupying the further side. She had also read of this and now she was looking at it, the Saltykov Palace. She had been in no way prepared for what greeted her, for the sheer resplendence of such a vision in stone.

Confident in their own cream-white beauty, a façade of graceful arches topped with enormous windows each intersecting with elegant semi-circular double columns of the same white stone stared majestically back at her.

How different to the Angliskaya Embankment where people like her father, the porters, postal workers, clerks and lower administrative staff in the employ of the embassy were housed. No doubt those buildings too had once been the elegant homes of nobility but being subdivided as they now were had robbed them of that former glory.

It had taken several moments to gather courage enough to approach and a few more to tug that heavy iron bell pull. Beyond an ornate railing the door of a small gatehouse had opened.

'Them pots don't be like to wash theirselves! Be you a goin' to stand maudlin' all day, wench?'

'What!' Ann frowned.

'I says be you goin' to stand all day admirin' o' that there kettle!'

Ann struggled with a voice which did not fit the body stepping from the doorway, a shape fading even as it spoke again.

'There be cream pans a waitin' to be scalded and benches to be scrubbed and they won't bide while folks stands daydreamin'.'

Turning to find Leah and not a uniformed figure watching her, Ann blinked the last remnants of mist from her mind. 'I ... I'm sorry,' she said as she reached for the kettle and hurried with it into the scullery, 'I was miles away.'

Leah hooked her own large pan of water to the iron trivet then swung it above the fire, saying as she returned to the scullery, 'We all gets carried away betimes wench, me no less than many, but it don't do to go a wanderin' the lanes o' memory when reaching forra boilin' kettle.'

Leah was right of course. When the older woman had gone from the room Ann bent to the task in hand. But how did you prevent the memories returning? How did you banish words and pictures that had you long for sleep which came only with the dawn?

Leah was as well-meaning as she was kind. She had taught Ann many things since bringing her to this house, had answered many questions, but even she could not answer that one.

How was it a young woman and a lad had managed to travel so far? Not that she knew the number of miles separating Russia from England. Leah looked up from yet one more cloth she was sewing to cover an increasing number of cream vats, letting her glance rest on the boy sitting at the table.

Worry rested heavy on the shoulders of the lad, that was obvious in the way he scanned the newspaper, but far from home and family as he was then it was only natural he would fret.

What of his family? Leah returned to her sewing but her mind stayed with Alec. He himself, though friendly in conversation, never made mention of parents, of brothers or sisters. Was that because of some dreadful happening that had robbed him of all his kin? An event so awful he had closed his mind against it? That was something she had seen in several men repatriated from the front, their bodily injuries only one part of the harm this dreadful war had done them, while other more terrible injuries had been done to minds so filled with horror they had withdrawn into themselves like men hiding from life.

This lad surely could not have been called up into any army, he were barely of an age to be gone from school. But then who could say what policy other nations abided by. Glancing again at the figure, tow-coloured head bent over the newspaper,

Leah silently repeated the prayer said so often in the privacy of her bedroom.

Lord, may the light of Your mercy shine on all who be sufferin', may the comfort of Your love ease grief and heart-ache, Your grace rest on them who seek to ease the pain of others and for the many who have been taken by this terrible war, I ask You gather them into Your loving arms as I knows You have gathered my own sons.

After she finished, Leah held her breath tight to prevent a sob, but she hid her reaction as Ann rose from the chair asking if Leah would care for a cup of tea.

'That'd be welcome and mebbe's Alec would like some hot milk, I brought a jug fresh from the last milkin' and there be a spoonful or two of cocoa left in the tin.' She smiled across at the boy carefully closing the newspaper. 'I knows y' be partial to a sup o' cocoa.'

A smile had accompanied his reply but Ann had seen the hint of tears glinting in the soft light.

Ann mixed cocoa powder with sugar she knew Leah delib-erately declined to take so there would be a little extra for Alec. She felt her heart twist in sympathy for the boy she had come to care for as she might a younger brother. He was hurting inside; much as he tried to mask it he was not always successful, and though many times she had hoped he would confide in her, tell her how he had come to be at Morskoy Vokzal that day, so far he had not. She had wondered if she should ask whether he and the man with him had been intending to board ship at the sea terminal only to be swept along with her in a different direction.

Ann poured hot milk into the cup and stirred the creamy brown contents. She had often hoped he would say, but tonight as so many times before she would not ask.

★   ★   ★

26

'Our brave men are fighting, God bless them, are suffering grievous injuries, many of them giving their very lives to keep this country free, to ensure their loved ones can sleep safely in their beds. How many of you have known the heartbreak of that ultimate sacrifice?'

Thomas Thorpe paused, his face creasing with sympathetic pain at the broken sobs of women, the shuffling of the few men, the old, the repatriated or those who for whatever reason had been deemed ineligible for combat in this conflict with Germany; a war now involving so many countries it was fast being described as a world war. The men cleared their throats, swallowing tears the pride of manhood forbade them to shed. But the tears he wanted to see would not be shed in this chapel, although that did not mean the cause of them would not originate here. Beneath the veneer of compassion the need for revenge dripped its venom. Ann Spencer and Leah Marshall both would regret crossing Thomas Thorpe; the sorrow they would feel would long outlast any war.

He surveyed the seated congregation, allowing his voice to throb with subdued emotion.

'How many mothers will never again hold a son in their arms, know the pleasure of his kiss against their cheek? How many fathers will never again shake the hand of the lad they reared with love and pride, that same pride filling their hearts as they watched their son march away to face the danger threatening his homeland? But danger does not exist solely on foreign shores. The ambitions of the enemy can spread far beyond those borders crossing even the shores of England.'

He could see fear mounting on the faces of women suddenly clutching children to them, men frowning in bewilderment. This was not going to prove difficult.

'We have all heard of spies,' he went on, 'of people living in our towns and cities, folk that are liked and trusted yet who in truth serve the enemy by passing on to them knowledge of defence measures as well as vital information regarding places of production of armaments.'

'Be you saying we 'ave such 'ere in Wednesbury?'

Thorpe shook his head at the question. 'No.'

'Then why be you a sayin' it? Such talk serves to frighten women.'

''Old on Zeke,' another man's voice cut across the protest, 'the pastor don't be meanin' to frighten folk.'

Pastor. Thomas Thorpe's blood warmed at the term. He was already recognised as leader of the congregation, the man who conducted religious service and now he was being referred to as 'Pastor'; a few more uses of the title and talk of having a properly ordained minister would be forgotten.

'Don't 'e!' Though seventy years old, Ezekial Turley's voice rang firm round the small unadorned chapel. 'Then what do 'e be meanin' of?'

'Zeke be right in what 'e be askin', what do you mean Mr Thorpe, ain't been no strange man not in these parts, 'ad there been we . . . well, we would 'ave noticed.'

Mister! Elation which had briefly soared hot in Thorpe's veins tumbled to a cold hard stop.

'So goo on,' Ezekial Turley urged, 'tell 'er, tell we all what be back o' this talk o' spies? What be the reasonin' when like Mary says there ain't bin sight o' any strange man, not here-abouts there ain't.'

The demand, assisted by a wave of speculation fluttering among the assembly, afforded him time to mask his displeas-ure at being addressed as plain Mister. Thorpe looked at the woman who had called her question, a woman now clutching protectively at the arm of a lad beside her.

A woman and a lad! A lad appearing to be much of an age as the one who had shared Chapel House!

A lad of much the same age. He must remember to thank heaven for its bounty.

'Mrs Slater . . . Mary.' He smiled indulgently. 'It was not my wish to cause concern but simply to remind us all of the need for vigilance. We have to remember the enemy may not always act as we would expect.'

'Meanin' what?'

The question again put by Ezekial gave further assistance to the plan formulating in his mind. Thorpe kept his tone placatory.

'You have all heard Mary and Ezekial attest to the fact that no strange man has been seen in this area, and I agree with them . . .'

'So why all this hoo-ha?'

'You says y'self you agrees wi' Zeke an' Mary, that there be no cause for we to go a' worryin'. So why talk o' spies if there don't be none?'

A rumble of questions was beginning to rise on all sides, questions he quickly dismissed as a fuss over nothing.

Evening service had ended some minutes since and the women especially would be wanting to be home putting their youngsters to bed. He had to speak now for once the congregation was on its feet the advantage would be lost. Thorpe floundered, then a sudden loudly called query rekindled his determination.

'Wait!' The ringing voice made every head turn in its direction. 'Wait, all o' you. Mr Thorpe don't mek no habit o' sayin' what don't need the tellin' an' for meself I says we should listen, let 'im put his point, an' again for meself,' a man's glance swivelled to fasten on the figure still standing in the plainly wrought pulpit, 'I asks you, Mr Thorpe, to explain what were meant by the enemy not always actin' as we would expect?'

The chance might never come again! Thanking his good fortune Thorpe grasped the moment.

'Friends . . .'

He lifted both arms in what he hoped would prove a calming gesture as he repeated the call and when the hubbub subsided lowered his hands to his sides, a brief diplomatic smile flitting across his narrow features.

'Friends, we are all weary of war, weary from the pain and heartache it brings, but we must not let weariness close our eyes to what I can only call a danger from within. I said a moment ago the enemy may not always act as we would expect.'

He paused as silence affirmed his audience's attention.

'I said also I was in agreement with those of you claiming no strange man has been seen here in Wednesbury, but seeing no threat we look for none and that complacency is our country's inner danger. The enemy is aware we would suspect a man.'

A deep frown furrowed his brow as if the next words were a bitterness on his tongue. His head swung slowly side to side as he breathed deeply before saying almost to himself, 'But a woman, a woman perhaps with a youngster, that would raise no question.'

Saying God bless to each of the people, watching them shuffle into the darkness of night, Thomas Thorpe congratulated himself. He had left off at just the right moment. He had made no specific accusation; leaving people to dwell on what he had said would prove the wiser way. Mothers with sons at the front, wives who feared every waking moment might bring news of their own man's sacrifice, they were the means by which the seed he had planted would be nourished.

He locked the door of the chapel, slipping the key into a pocket of his coat. They would talk, those women, in the market place, in the home, in their place of work, talk over what had been said in the chapel, discuss the possibilities Thomas Thorpe had put forward. If a woman with a child was a spy in the pay of the enemy, she would add to the danger their own sons and husbands were in; and their attention would turn to the one newcomer to their midst with only one result. Ann Spencer and the lad along with her would be driven from the town.

4

Three years. Taking a framed photograph from the mantelshelf above the fireplace of her tiny immaculately neat front parlour Leah Marshall looked through gathering tears at the portrait of two young men, whose faces reflected the pride they took in the uniform they wore, in answering their country's call.

Three years on this day, since her world had crashed about her.

'*But y'be scarce growed.*'

Leah pressed the photograph to her breast as she relived the past.

'*I be growed enough.*'

Tall and strong, the image in body and mind of the father lost to a collapse of the coalface deep beneath the surface of Brunswick colliery, Daniel smiled back at her sharp reply.

'*No, no you ain't . . . you ain't growed enough!*'

The pain of that moment struck Leah as deeply as on that morning. Daniel, her youngest son, had taken her in those strong arms.

'*Mother . . .*'

In her mind that beloved voice spoke again.

'*I don't be no child; there be lads wi' less years than me already gone to the front.*'

'*Less years!*' she had cried. '*Y'be nobbut a lad.*'

A deep and carefree laugh sounded from the vale of yesterday, Daniel's reply ringing after it.

'*A lad y' says, I be near enough eighteen.*'

'*Six months short is what you be, six months short of that eighteen y' boasts of; no Daniel, y'be too young, I won't 'ave you follow in the wake of your brother, one son be too much to give to the Army. I refuses to give another.*'

As she clasped the photograph Leah heard the quietly spoken reply.

'*You might think me no more than a lad, Mother, but don't prevent my being a man.*'

And so as he had done from his first days of walking Daniel had followed in the footsteps of his brother, followed nineteen-year-old Joshua into the army. And three months later he had followed him into heaven.

On this day in nineteen fifteen had come the notification: 'Killed in Action'. The three words had torn her world apart.

Leah heard again the voices of her sons, saw their smiles, felt their kiss on her cheek then in her mind's eye watched two straight figures march proudly from her sight.

'*We won't be gone long.*'

Leah touched the photograph with her lips.

You don't be gone my dear ones, you don't never be gone; you be in the air I breathe, you be the blood that flows in my veins, your names be the beat of my heart and your sweet faces the light of my soul. You live where you 'ave ever lived, in the love of your mother's heart.

Leah returned the photograph to its place, her glance going to one set beside it. Housed in a matching oval mahogany frame, lovingly polished, a ringleted young girl demure in ribboned lace rested her hand on an ornate jardinière and smiled from gentle doe-like eyes. Her heart felt this time it must break; Leah snatched the frame to her, holding it so tightly she could hardly breathe.

'Deborah . . .'

Tears she could not hold spilled silently over her lined cheeks.

'Deborah child, my dear love, why . . . why?'

Sounds from the scullery pulled her back to the moment. she replaced the photograph then looking to another placed opposite murmured quietly, 'Watch over our children, Joseph, watch over them until I come.'

'*I add to your burden Ann . . .*'

Alec's quiet words spoken as they had walked together beside the small cart with its several empty milk churns reverberated in Ann's mind.

'*I have taken advantage of your friendship, of your kind generosity for too long, it is time I leave and give you back your freedom.*'

'*Leave!*' She had stopped so abruptly the horse drawing the cart had whinnied disapproval at the drag of the bit against its mouth.

Alec had smiled that shy smile she had seen so often but today it had not reached those blue grey-eyes, nor added any sign of pleasure to those chiselled delicate features.

'*Yes,*' he had nodded, '*I have known almost from that day in the Ploschad Morskoy Slavy, the great square in Petrograd . . .*'

There had been pain in his voice, a deep sense of hurt as he had spoken the new name for the city of St Petersburg.

'*. . . known,*' he had gone on, '*that I should not be a responsibility to you yet I had not the courage to do what I should, to have left you in Morskoy Slavy, left the moment . . . but I did not, I allowed myself to be frightened by the noise of shouting, frightened as only a coward would be.*'

'*No, Alec*.' She had caught at his hands. '*You were no coward; like everyone else in that square you were taken by surprise*.'

'*I ran away, Ann*.'

'*No*.' Her sharp reply had rung on the morning air blessedly quiet beyond the sounds of factory and workshop. '*You did not run away and I ask you not to do so now. It would be a worry to me, Alec, wondering were you well, were you safe; please, I know this is hard for you, that you want to return home to your family, but until this dreadful war is ended that has to wait*.'

There had been no more discussion. Rinsing the butter pats Leah often referred to as 'wooden hands' Ann's thoughts remained with Alec. They had walked on in silence but she had seemed to feel the turmoil in his mind, asking why the relatives he had spoken of, those who were to meet him in England, had not been there at the dockside? Why in all his months in this country there had been no word?

Her fingers were now slippery with water and one of the several metal ladles she reached for dropped against the stone of the sink. Ann gasped, a sudden fear ripping through her at the hard dull sound.

Vivid in its clarity, graphic in every detail, a picture flooded into her mind, a scene taking place in that Great Maritime Square.

There had been a rumble, a sound like distant thunder. She had glanced at the sky; it was clear, a blue promise of a day free of snow.

Ann saw herself turn to glance along the length of that vast square, undecided as to whether she had tried hard enough. Should she return to the house? Search again for that 'most precious possession'?

Once gone from Russia there would be no further chance to preserve the honour her father had spoken of, no chance to keep her own promise given at the moment of his death. She had glanced towards the huge arched entrance to the seaport; the ship – if she missed her ship!

It was not only overhead, that rumble of thunder. Alive in her mind it sounded as it had on that day, coming nearer, a constant repetitive drumming . . . and the people. Caught up in the confusion of finding her way and then in her indecision about whether to return to search those rooms again, she had taken little note of people scattered around. Then loud above the throb of still-distant sound had come shouts, men calling to others emerging from doorways or running from side streets; tall, short, young and old they had come together in groups, their faces set in expressions of anger, some waving fists as they shouted. But she heard too the cries of women, frightened cries as they were pushed from the way of the assembling men, screams of fear from children knocked accidentally to the ground, echoed by mothers hauling them to their feet only to push desperately through what had become a solid line fronting the port entrance.

What was happening? Where had all these men come from? Why were they shouting?

She had tried to ask but they had not understood her questions nor she their responses; yet their gestures, the rough hands pushing her away could not be mistaken: she should leave the square.

But they would not let her pass. With arms locked together, the chain of figures refused to give way. She had decided to wait in the shelter of some doorway; whatever this protest was about it would soon be over, the men would disperse and she could enter the port, enquire after the next ship leaving for England.

She had taken one step, one step only before being caught by the arm.

A stillness had settled over the crowd. Their cries had died away but not that other noise, that pounding pulsating beat, bouncing from wall and stone paving, echoing and re-echoing until like a great net of sound it closed over the square.

'*Forgive please my rudeness . . .*'

It had come like a gift from heaven. The man now releasing her arm had spoken in English. Relief flooded through her. '*Please, I am trying to get into—*'

She had got no further; his words spoken quickly as her own brushed aside her intended request for assistance.

'*My friend, Mr George Spencer . . .*'

'*George Spencer!*' Her exclamation had carried above the din yet he had continued as though she had not spoken.

'*. . . we worked together at the British embassy.*'

He worked at the embassy! She had felt a slight flicker of suspicion. That day she had visited she had seen no person dressed like this man and the boy who stood beside him. They were not attired in the smart clothes she had seen there, these two like the mass of men blockading the entrance to the port wore rough shabby coats and caps, threadbare trousers tucked into worn-through boots: garments seen in the poorer parts of the city.

Had the threat of demonstrations, maybe of violence, been a factor in her father's decision to leave Russia?

'*I would not ask this of you but my friend he made a promise.*'

He would not ask what of her? Her attention had been distracted from what the man had been saying; she had been about to apologise when a sudden roar had erupted, a volley of noise making her turn to look again at the lines of figures at her back all of them now with raised arms waving and shouting towards the entrance to the square.

'*Please . . .*'

Once more her arm had been caught and this time a sharp tug whipped her round to face the man but with a gasp she had glanced beyond the pair confronting her, looking instead at a troop of mounted uniformed men with sword and pistol at the ready, horses' hooves striking sparks from the flagstones as they dragged to a halt.

'*Please . . .*'

The hand had shaken her arm demandingly but her attention had focused on the figure at the head of what had to be a body of soldiers. Astride a huge black horse, sword held above his head, the bemedalled figure called to the demonstrators.

The words had passed over her head but not so the defiant answer rising to meet them.

'*Niet . . . niet.*' That word she understood. '*No . . . no!*' Loud in its defiance it had sounded along the square.

'*Please, the promise of my friend, it was . . .*'

'*Niet!*' The crowd's rising anger had drowned that one voice, the one she should have listened to.

She stared at the ladle lying in the shallow well of the sink while regret stabbed at her with sharp fingers.

The man had named her father, was about to tell her the promise which had been given. But even as he had tugged at her arm, had tried to shout above the din, her eye had caught the flash of a sword sweeping downward and with it the crack of a pistol shot. His hand had slipped slowly down her arm, over her hand, sliding away from her fingers. As though in some terrible nightmare she had watched the figure slump to the ground, watched it fall on to its back and a stream of scarlet blood spurt from the open mouth while the dying eyes tried vainly to finish its message.

5

'Hill Rise be a long walk for legs ancient as mine so I be askin' you brings your answer along of my 'ouse.'

'Get along with you Leah Marshall, you should be ashamed fishing for compliments.'

'Compliments you says, be long past time for them.'

'There you go again.' Edward Langley's laugh rang across a wide earth-packed yard. 'Incorrigible is what you are, incorrigible but pretty so I guess I can forgive you.'

'Forgiveness is it!' Tartness did not quite mask the fondness in Leah's tone. 'It be y'self should be a beggin' o' the Lord for that, y'self askin' Him forgive the lies you speaks.'

The man lifted his brown eyes to the sky for a few moments before returning his attention to Leah, whose head was shaking at what she obviously expected to follow her censure. 'You see,' Edward Langley's smile spread across handsome features deeply tanned by exposure to all weathers, 'no lightning . . . that is clear proof the Lord agrees with me Leah Marshall is a pretty woman.'

Leah released a snort of feigned disparagement but her heart warmed as strong arms caught her, whirling her several times before setting her down. All three had greeted her that way from becoming young men. Leah left the yard, full of memories. First would come Joshua, his laugh ringing as he swept her up; tall and strong even at fifteen years of age he could lift her easily as he might a doll; then would come Daniel, close as a shadow on the heels of the brother who was his sun, determined as ever to do exactly as Joshua. But then neither was to be allowed to outdo Edward. He too would catch her up, hold her as he might his own mother, the mother taken in childbed when he was eight years old. The boy had hidden his grief from his father realising even at such a tender age that the man already carried a heavy enough burden of sorrow. But in her home, the house of his best friends, he had cried with his young face hidden in her lap, sobbed at the pain of losing his mother.

Had she tried to become mother to Edward? Leah shook her head at the thought. She would never do that.

Disturbed by her approach a trio of rabbits darted across the heath, tails bobbing white among the dark green bracken. A trio! The scampering rabbits became three young boys racing one after the other. Joshua, Daniel and Edward. As infants they had played together, as children they had attended school together until the age of eleven, when they could each leave to work full time for their living, Edward on his father's dairy farm and her own sons on the plot given her as compensation by the colliery following Joseph's death. The long hours of toil had not been sufficient to part the three completely for their few free hours had seen them walk and talk in these very fields, though often when he was visiting, Edward's eyes had rarely left Deborah.

She had hoped. Leah blinked against gathering tears. She had asked the Lord could the pair come one day to marry, could the affection of children become the love of a man and a woman? But then war had called all three. They had wept together, she and Deborah, shared the sorrow of seeing brothers and friends march away, sat together in the long soul-numbing hours when those brief messages had informed them Joshua and Daniel would never come home, would never again sweep mother and sister into their arms.

She had mourned her sons, longed for them, prayed for them as so many mothers in this and other lands trapped in the bitterness of war, yet had thanked God for the mercy that had let Edward Langley return from that horror. He had suffered a bullet wound to the leg so was to be repatriated. She had thought Deborah would, if not dance with joy, at least be full of smiles. But Deborah had not smiled.

Her daughter had reached for her coat. She was going to the chapel but had shaken her head when Leah said they would go to give thanks together. She had not pressed Deborah nor had she followed. Overcome at the news of Edward's safety, Deborah had needed a little time alone to thank the Lord for His bounty.

A little time! Leah gasped at the pain cutting through her heart. Noon had given way to evening, the yellow sunlight of afternoon becoming emblazoned with the gold and crimson banners of sunset before ceding to the purple-grey of night. It was then she had gone herself to the chapel. Deborah was not there. She had frowned in confusion on being told her daughter had not been seen there by wives and mothers who in breaks between shifts at their places of work would slip into the chapel to pray for husbands and sons fighting at the front. But of all the women she had asked none had seen Deborah go into or leave that building in Queen's Place. She had asked the same question of folk as she had looked for her daughter in the adjoining Queen Street, the busier Holyhead Road and almost every other street of the town, then when she returned home to find Deborah was not there she had repeated the process; asking, searching until the market place had emptied of customer and trader, the beer houses had closed their doors for the night and the last street lay empty and deserted. She had walked the long dark hours of night going from town to heath where the open coal shafts lost in the depths of shadow held less terror for her than the fears beginning to build in her heart.

Men exchanging shifts at coal mine and steel foundries had shaken their heads at the woman out on the heath before dawn had lightened the sky and all had answered the same.

No one had seen Deborah!

No one had seen her pass on the road, or cross the waste ground off Lea Brook, no one had watched her come to the bridge spanning the water, no one had seen her fall in.

Leah herself had found her child. A fast-flowing current had thrown and then held her daughter among the thick reeds hiding its verge from the bracken and low bushes of yellow flowered gorse that grew on open land.

She had almost passed by without seeing. With tear-swollen eyes and numbed by hours of unrelenting anxiety she would have walked by, never have seen . . . never have found! But she had seen and she had found.

She recalled the scene in all its detail as her fingers twined in the soft cloth of the shawl, reaching for the comfort which never came.

She might have been beyond that spot, might never have witnessed that horror, but Fate had decreed otherwise. It was not to be given to Leah Marshall that she be told her one remaining child had been found by another, that she see her only when washed clean and laid in her coffin.

With a shuddering pain-filled breath Leah stared into yesterday.

Night was at last surrendering to dawn; the first beams of the rising sun flashing scarlet defiance over the narrow river had gleamed across a tiny island of colour, highlighting the patch of peacock turquoise.

For a moment it had felt her feet were fastened to the ground yet tired as it was her brain had recognised what lay there trapped in the inky water, had recognised the material of the coat Deborah had so loved to wear, a coat of an almost identical colour to her lovely eyes.

But those lovely eyes had been closed, their fringe of long lashes resting on cheeks the colour of marble, and the long fair silken hair was now threaded with slime-covered weed, weed wrapped round the floating figure clutching it. Every eddy of water threatened to rip the body from her grasp; but in that it had failed.

She had cradled her dead child. There in the birth of a new day, alone beside that river, she had held her daughter close, had crooned softly the lullabies she had sung to her as an infant, rocked that cold, cold body as she had when pains of croup or fever had resulted in restless nights, had in the lonely silent dawn kissed that lifeless face gently as at every bedtime.

Her words a mere whisper, Leah murmured to a daughter she could not see. 'It were only goodnight, child, it were not goodbye for I can never say that word; it be as it is along of your brothers and your father, you don't be gone for you bides 'ere in my heart where you will ever be.'

Why had Deborah not gone to the chapel? How come she had gone instead to the river? And how in God's name had she come to fall into the water?

Walking on, Leah remained with her thoughts. The years had provided no relief from heartbreak and certainly none from the agony of a question carried in her most secret heart.

She had put that question to no one, especially not to Edward Langley. His face had been alight that day he had come to the house, happiness at the prospect of seeing the girl she had known he loved apparent on every feature. That happiness had died as painfully as Leah's own.

Edward! Even in her remembered sadness Leah smiled. War had left its mark on him as it would leave it on many yet, but he remained the same honest, trustworthy man she had watched grow from the cradle, a man so different in every way to the one she would speak to next.

Holding her shawl about her shoulders, ignoring the quick March breeze tugging playfully at her bonnet, Leah retraced her path across the open expanse of heath and meadow which bordered a heart of iron and coal.

The Black Country. She let her glance rove over the vista of chimneys rising like a huge flock of crows black against the skyline.

The Black Country was how this very heart of England was described, a term well justified by the pall of smoke overlying the town, a perpetual veil of grey shutting out much of the beauty of daytime skies and then cloaking the majesty of stars spread across the night void. A forest of chimney stacks belched foul black breath from iron works, collieries, steel and brass foundries. Street upon street of tight packed houses huddled close to each other, and to the grudgingly spared communal yards with their shared outhouse and privy. From every roof rose the smoke of coal fires, the one weapon with which families fought the damp of old dilapidated homes, their every brick robed in black soot.

No building escaped. Not even the House of God. Leah's glance rested a moment on the church of St Bartholomew.

Black as any other building it gazed down from its hilltop on the town it had served for centuries.

She sighed heavily. How Wednesbury must have changed during those hundreds of years; how it had changed from the days of her own childhood. It had been so different then. Yes, parents must have found it hard raising a family just as now in this soot-ridden town, but for her as for the children she had played alongside worries of that nature did not exist. She had run with others barefoot across fields, she had gambolled and tumbled among stalks of wheat tall as herself, had danced among stately rows of barley.

So many happy reminiscences, so many cherished memories, but none were so treasured as the recollections of when as a young woman she had walked with Joseph.

'We shouldn't go walkin' amid the crops, a farmer's labours be hard, it be unkind of folk to go destroyin' o' what he works long to produce.'

Joseph, her ever thoughtful Joseph. Even as a young man his actions had been considerate of other folk before himself. So they had taken their strolls here on the heath, his hand shyly taking hers only when they were beyond the sight of houses.

Feeling the brush of bracken against her boots she was again with Joseph, who was laughing at a young girl dressed in her Sunday best gown, her sliding feet hidden among deep drifts of daisies while her cream cotton skirts caressed the heads of kingcups and rich purple clover.

Leah sighed. Where was the golden wheat speckled with scarlet poppies? It was gone, never to gleam again, buried beneath stretches of earth blackened and scarred by the ravages of coal mining. The colour-strewn heath and meadows, once-lush pastures, all that delight was now swallowed beneath an ever-expanding dark sea called industry. The ache of losing it felt almost physical. Standing a moment, she stared ahead. There had been so many changes, and Wednesbury groaned beneath the insatiable demand.

Ugly, noisy, a cancer on the beautiful face of nature; those buildings were all of that but . . . Leah sighed with acceptance. Objectionable as was their presence, the twenty-four-hour ceaseless clang and clamour, the perpetual pall of acrid smoke, those workplaces produced many of the materials with which this country was fighting for its life.

So much had already been given to that fight. How many scars had been left on the hearts of families robbed of their menfolk, and how many yet would be called to face that terrible sorrow?

'How many more? Lord, how many more before the world comes to its senses?'

Maybe she should have stayed in Darlaston, tried to find a home for herself and Alec there, but how would she have found a place without money to pay for it?

That had been the final straw, the blow which at that moment had drained her will, swept away the determination that had kept her going despite all the trials and tribulation of getting back to England.

'*Eh wench, your gran be gone these many months,' 'er died but a few weeks after y'self 'ad left to be wi' y' parents along o' that foreign country. Weren't aught could be done, there be no cure for tumour o' the stomach. With you gone an' no other kin a'bidin' wi' 'er the house were given over to another family.*'

She had longed for her grandmother, the one person in the world she thought remained to her, who would take her in her arms, welcome her home. But there had been no grandmother, no home.

With no more deliveries to make, with nothing to hold her concentration, memories crept like wraiths into Ann's mind.

''Er be laid along o' St Lawrence churchyard.' The voice of the neighbour went on relentlessly. 'There were naught but what the penny a week insurance policy paid an' that barely saw 'er decent into the ground so there be no 'eadstone to mark where 'er lies but there do be a wooden cross wi' 'er name, my 'usband seen to the mekin' o' that.'

She had thanked the woman for having overseen the burying of her grandmother, asked that those same thanks be passed to all of the houses in the street because the folk would have contributed halfpennies and pennies in order to purchase a wreath; then she had walked to the churchyard.

There, kneeling beside a patch of earth bereft of any enclosing stone border, of any gift of flowers beneath the rough wooden cross with its name traced in white paint, the last of her resistance had crumbled leaving her crushed beneath the weight of guilt for not having been there when she was needed.

'I should have known.'

The words had sobbed from her.

'I should have stayed here with you ... Oh Gran, I should have known.'

'You can't blame yourself.'

Alec had knelt alongside her, his arm about her shoulders, his whisper gentle against her ear.

'If your grandmother had told you she was ill you would not have left her. That much I know of you, Ann, and hearing you speak of her it is my belief it was her love for you made her insist upon your going, a love so strong it wanted to protect you from her pain.'

'*Was it that, Gran? Was that the true reason? Is Alec right in what he said?*'

'I don't know about Alec being right in whatever it was he said, but I was certainly right in thinking to find you here; really, you should vary your route if not the days of making your deliveries.'

Dragged from the darkness of sorrow to the deeper dark of the fear to which she still woke in the blackness of night, Ann felt the blood chill in her veins.

'I see from your expression you welcome my company as much as on previous occasions but I shall not let that deter me, in fact it increases my determination we become . . . how to put it nicely . . . we become intimate friends . . . *very* intimate friends.'

The unwelcome encounter was enough to snap the invisible bond holding Ann in darkness. Blood which seconds before had been stilled by fear now raced hot with revulsion as she stared at the figure blocking her path.

'Mr Thorpe.' She paused, swallowing the distaste for that name on her tongue, then went on icily, 'I have no desire for friendship with you.'

'Friendship.' He laughed. 'That does not appeal to you therefore I forgo that aspect of our association, but as for that other word you used – desire – that I cannot forgo; you see, Miss Spencer, I desire you and what Thomas Thorpe desires he makes very sure he gets!'

He pulled her hard against him, the force of it pushing the breath from her body. For a moment he held her there, the fingers of his free hand twined in her hair to prevent her from turning her head away from the mouth brushing her own.

'Here!' He spoke thickly, his breath hot and rapid. 'Shall I take it here, take my payment for what I did for you, the reward you thought to deny me?'

'Please!'

'Please.' He laughed again, an exultant laugh. 'Oh I shall be pleased, Miss Spencer, be assured of that, I shall be pleased many times over.'

He meant to rape her! In panic Ann twisted her head away from the hot breath, the sickening touch of a tongue flicking against her mouth, pleading to be let go even as she was brutally forced once more to face him.

'Let you go!' The reply snarled against her lips. 'Oh I intend to let you go, in fact I shall make it my business to see you gone from Wednesbury, you and the brat you brought with you; but of course I cannot allow that until I deem your debt fully repaid.'

'I am not in debt to you, I paid the required rent, I—'

'Not in debt!' Thomas Thorpe snapped away the reply. 'Not in debt to the man who secured you a place to live, the man who argued against his friends, against the very congregation he tries so hard to serve, that it would be no more than Christian charity to let you have the tenancy of Chapel House.'

Disgust overcame her fear, making Ann's response lash like wind-driven hail. 'Christian charity!' She held the pale eyes with a look of pure contempt. 'Is it in the name of that same charity you would force a woman to lie with you, does Christian charity include rape? And once you have taken what you see as your due will you inform those friends, that very congregation you try so hard to serve, will you tell them about the extra payment? Payment demanded by their so-caring layman!'

Layman! She had taken pleasure in using that word, highlighting the fact of his non-clerical status. A mistake, Miss Spencer. A very grave mistake ... and one which the grave alone would rectify. He had thought to drive her from the town by use of slander but now that must change. There would of course be no enquiry; Ann Spencer and the boy had chosen to leave Wednesbury to go who knows where. Nobody would care enough to ask and certainly not to suspect murder.

Thomas Thorpe glanced to where in the distance a solitary building stood opposite the Monway Sidings, a pair of rail tracks conveying the products of Monway Steel to the main London and North Western Railway for transport across country. One house and nothing more than open heath until Hobbins Street marked the edge of the town's miserable housing. He could take her here. He released Ann from his arms yet fastened a grip on her wrist while he contemplated the idea. There was little chance of being observed, but any chance of being watched detracted from the enjoyment of the act, from the pleasure of stripping away each garment, the delight of laying that naked body beneath his own, the ultimate satisfaction of thrusting deep between parted legs. No. He turned along the track worn between bracken and yellow-crowned gorse. That entertainment would be the more gratifying taken in the privacy and comfort of Chapel House.

6

There had been no reply.

Leah glanced at the window of a house set amid a long row of dark-stained tight-packed terraced houses each joined to the other like so many peas in a pod. A shake of her head emphasised an inward snort of disapproval. Tight-packed they might be but peas were pleasant to look at. She glanced again at the line of buildings, faceless in their unanimous drabness. She knew well the interior of those houses; hadn't she once lived in similar? Two bedrooms upstairs, a living room and scullery downstairs and three children. How much less space for families she knew were housed here, families with six and seven children who along with three other households shared the use of one privy and one brewhouse set in a tiny cramped communal rear yard.

Cross Street! She drew her shawl tightly around herself. Like so many dwellings in this town these had not been built for the comfort of tenants but the expediency of industrialists concerned more with the business of profit than with other people's comfort. Jam houses cheek by jowl and you got more of them, more families with men and boys to labour in your mines and factories.

Except war, as with so much else, had changed a deal of that. Sparing one more glance at a lace-curtained window she turned away. War demanded not only men and boys, some barely two years out of school, but women and girls also to operate its factories, to fill so many of the jobs once done by their menfolk while those not called to fight continued the heavier labour required in the iron and steel rolling mills or underground in the coal mines.

Yet not every man. Leah felt the savage touch of anger. There was one who avoided both factory and fighting. Thomas Thorpe had been skilful at this, as he had been in refusing to answer the knock at his door. But if he truly was not in that house, then where?

The chapel. The answer loud in her mind Leah walked in the direction of Queen Place. The sly little toerag was probably swanning around indulging in his fantasy: minister, indeed! Thomas Thorpe could pretend all he liked, spout the Scriptures 'til he was blue in the face, but the Lord God knew the truth of the man. He recognised Thorpe had no faith other than in himself, his only creed being a belief in his own infallibility. But that was folly and though heaven might sometimes be tardy in its dealings it never failed in its justice.

Coming in sight of the chapel Leah made the sign of the cross on her breast, whispering a plea for forgiveness should her thoughts be displeasing to the Almighty.

She halted at the front of the building darkened as much with time as with soot. What justice had been done for a young girl pulled dead from that river? Accidental death had been the verdict of the official inquiry but she had known with every fibre of a mother's being that Deborah's drowning had been no accident.

Leah seemed to see again the pale reed-covered face, to feel the inert body cradled in her arms. The death of her daughter had been no accident, nor were it suicide neither!

She forced the scene from her mind as she walked on, nodding the time of day to the few women who like herself were not called to work in one of the factories or workshops. She wondered why their replies were clipped, why they turned so abruptly from her, ushering the children they minded quickly away.

Those women all shared one blessing which would never be visited upon Leah Marshall; the little ones they had care of. Some were infants still suckling, while others, not yet three years of age and so not attending school, had been left with grandparents thus releasing younger women to war work.

War had snatched that blessing from her, war had taken her sons and with them her hopes of grandchildren, and Deborah? While her death had not occurred on the battlefields of Ypres yet this war and nothing else had been its cause.

The content of many prayers whispered in the long lonely hours of night rose again.

You knows I be right. Silent on her tongue, the words rang in her heart. You knows what I says be truth, Lord; my wench be dead of this war surely as if her'd bin shot by them same bullets which took 'er brothers. It were war an' naught else had Edward Langley leave this town, it were that an' that only would 'ave him leave my girl an' that leavin' be cause for her dyin', won't none in 'eaven turn my mind from that an' none'll keep me from repayin' be I given chance even though the doin' sees my soul damned.

Immersed in thought, she had not registered the turn to the left which had taken her into School Street. Now, halfway along its length, she paused at the opening which gave on to Queen's Place. The one she had come to see might well be inside that chapel or yet in the house at its rear; but neither building would see her enter. Leah stood resolutely on the narrow footpath. Sooner or later someone would come or go from chapel or house, someone who could tell her if either held Thomas Thorpe.

So many of them had said the same thing, spoken so nearly the same words it might have been rehearsed.

Butter she had first carefully weighed then fashioned into four-ounce blocks was placed neatly on a well-scrubbed wooden board. Ann carried the whole across to the cold cupboard set on one wall of the dairy.

'*I don't be a wantin' of you comin' no more . . .*'

Hard as stones the words had seemed to strike at her.

'*. . . y'can be a tellin' Leah Marshall should 'er be wantin' to sell 'er butter an' cheese then 'er'll 'ave to be a deliverin' of it 'erself.*'

She had attempted to ask the reason, to ask had she in some way annoyed the woman and if so to offer apologies, but the door had slammed shut before the chance was given.

Bewildered, she had moved to the next house only to meet with the same sharp ultimatum. '*I don't be a wantin' of you comin' no more.*'

What had she done wrong? Many times she had asked herself that question while walking back to Leah's house, going over again in her mind the previous deliveries to those women, yet try as she might, she could not recall any incident which might have given rise to the animosity which had greeted her today.

Ann stared blindly at the interior of the cupboard where butter set along its shelves gleamed like golden drops of summer sun.

'*I won't be a tekin' of no more lessen it be fetched 'ere by Leah 'erself.*'

'*Don't you go a comin' 'ere no more . . .*'

'If'n Leah don't fetch it 'erself then 'er can find another to send it wi' cos I don't want you a comin' of this 'ouse no more!'

'But why? Please tell me what I have done,' Ann answered out loud. 'If I have displeased you . . .'

'You'll certainly displease Leah should you hold that cupboard open much longer.'

'Alec, the women they—' The words died as Ann saw who it was at the entrance to the dairy.

'Not Alec I'm afraid, but then neither am I the bogeyman, at least I hope that isn't how you see me.'

'No, no. I . . .' Ann stared at the figure outlined by the glow of setting sun.

'Glad to hear it.' Edward Langley smiled.

'I'm sorry, I was thinking of . . .'

Of what? Even from that distance he had seen the dread sweep across the face of the girl who had instinctively backed against the wall and whose fingers clutched white against the board laden with butter portions. Something definitely had Ann Spencer feared. Or should that be some*one*?

'Here,' he smiled again, covering the awkward pause left by Ann's unfinished sentence, 'let me help with getting that lot into the cold cupboard. I'm not afraid of hobgoblins or things that go bump in the night but when it comes to Leah Marshall and her butter, then I admit to being a real coward. I'd sooner face the Kaiser and the whole of his army than stand in Leah's path should her dairy be threatened so let's tuck this batch away before she comes to check everything is as it should be.'

As it should be! Ann turned the phrase over again and again, each time wondering how Leah would react to being told of what had transpired on today's delivery round, when so many customers had said they would only buy if Leah herself brought the butter and cheese. Would Leah place the blame with her? It had to be something *she* had done, but what?

'Phew!' Closing the cupboard door on the last of the butter Edward laid aside the board then made a play of mopping his brow. 'Safe from the wrath of the tyrant!'

'Oh, an' just who be the tyrant you be safe from!'

'You!' Edward's reply rang along the lime brick walls. He caught Leah up and whirled her around, laughing. 'You, my dear Mrs Marshall, you be the tyrant has my heart sing its fear.'

'Your 'eart be it?' Leah gasped against the mad whirl. 'It'll be your ears a singin' o' their sting wi' my boxin' 'em the moment you sets me to me feet.'

'Then in the interest of my personal safety as well as my personal pleasure I must hold on to you.'

Hard put to keep tenderness from her voice, Leah pushed against strong shoulders. 'Put me down!' she snorted. 'Put me down you niggen-yedded nawnypump.'

Coming to an abrupt halt Edward's face assumed an injured look. 'You heard that, Miss Spencer, you heard that defamation: I ask you, is it a reasonable assessment of a man's character?'

'It be reasonable on account you be a stupid nincompoop an' one as don't be so growed I can't leather y' backside wi' one o' them there butter pats.'

Holding a red-faced Leah firmly in his grasp Edward shook his head slowly. 'Now a threat to give a hiding to a poor simple-minded man; does that not show you Miss Spencer, does it not prove to you the tyrant Leah Marshall is?'

Twinkling eyes belied the asperity of her tone as Leah retorted, 'Ar, 'er 'eard what it be were said an' you y' great lummock will see what this 'ere tyrant can do wi' a butter board lessen y' sets me to me feet right now.'

'The butter board!' Edward pursed his lips musingly. 'That, Mrs Marshall, is a far more serious threat; to set you to your feet is, for me, risk to life and limb and that truly would be stupid so,' he hitched her higher in his arms, 'I see no other solution than to keep you where you are. Do you not agree, Miss Spencer?'

Leah pushed harder against his relentless shoulders. 'No 'er don't, not unless it be agreein' you be a barmy 'apporth; now you let go o' me this instant!'

Edward looked at the face of the woman he held dear as a mother, saying teasingly, 'Not until you say you love me.'

'Hmmph!' Leah sniffed derisively.

'Admit it Mrs Marshall.' Edward chuckled jubilantly. 'Admit you love me and I might be persuaded to let you go.'

'But I won't be persuaded against fetchin' you the lea-therin' y' deserves should y' be tardy gettin' y'self gone from my dairy.'

Edward released Leah and cast a dejected look to Ann. 'Ordered from the door, turned away into the night; take note Miss Spencer, take note of the cruelty of this woman.'

Leah looked smiling at the tall man, his shoulders drooping with pretended misery.

'Did you come all this way just so y' could clog up my dairy?'

'No.' His mischievous smile returned as Edward reached into a pocket of his jacket. 'I came to bring what it was you walked to Hill Rise Farm to collect then forgot to bring away with you.'

'Eeh!' Leah's head swung. 'I swears I 'ave a brain like a sieve these days; I thanks you for the bringin' lad, milk wouldn't form no curd wi'out the usin' of a bit o' salted skin from a calf's stomach an' I be near to usin' the last o' what be left.'

'So I see.' He appeared to glance to where a tiny piece of dried skin was nailed to the wall, a square of newspaper preventing its touching the limewash, but instead Edward looked at the face of the girl beside the cold cupboard, a face pale as the milk poured into the shallow stone vats. The dread he had seen flash across it had now become a fear of a different kind. It was not fear of himself, her continued presence indicated that, and it certainly was not fear of Leah, so what had made those features so drawn? What fear haunted Ann Spencer?

'Be you hurried to get back to Hill Rise? There be fresh scones and the kettle be to boilin'.'

'It be well for fishermen it's a dairy you have and not a boat for with your method of baiting the seas would be empty within a twelvemonth.'

The answer had come quickly but Leah caught his glance at Ann, one asking the questions she so often asked herself. Edward Langley too wondered what lay behind that drawn expression, but did his interest end there or did he have other feelings for the girl, feelings he had once had for Deborah?

She turned from the dairy, calling as she crossed the yard, 'I teks it that be meanin' you'll tek a bite o' supper so you mek y'self useful helpin' wi' the carryin' of them there ladles an' such along of the scullery for washin'.'

Edward smiled. 'Best do as I've been told, I learned very young it doesn't do to give Leah cause to tell a body twice.'

'Mr Langley . . . has . . .'

A pause, a tremor as though she was afraid to voice a question! Collecting pats and ladles, dropping them into the pails, Edward Langley showed no sign that he had detected the anxiety preying on this girl's mind. He surmised that to press any question of his own might well have her retreat again behind that barrier of silence so he simply continued with the gathering of implements.

'Mr Langley . . .'

Ann spoke quietly, seeming as yet still unsure if she should be speaking at all.

'Did Alec return the empty churns?'

Was it the boy she feared for? But the lad wasn't sick, he wasn't simple in the mind, so why would she worry for him?

'Delivered them same time as usual, he's a very dependable lad.' He answered lightly but again wondered as the reply darkened eyes already shimmering with unshed tears.

As she placed butter boards one on top of another Ann felt the reply chill her. Dependable! So why was it Alec had not come home?

7

'Alec!'

Tight with horror, her voice trembled in the darkness.

'Alec . . .' The cry died on her lips. Ann stared at a figure with one arm held viciously across the boy's throat, the free hand raising a club. Some inner sense warned her that to call out would have the weapon smash against Alec's head. Ann's next words were a strangled whisper.

'Please, please let him go.'

For a moment it seemed there would be no answer then the man snatched Alec so close the savage tug made him gasp for air. The stranger's voice grated on the night.

'You give,' it snarled, 'you give!'

Money! The man holding Alec wanted money. But she had none.

'Go Ann . . . leave, you can't—'

Another callous press to the throat cut off Alec's call. The man's head turned slightly, a sudden shaft of moonlight glittering on cold eyes.

'Give,' he rasped, lifting the club above Alec's head, 'give or he dies.'

'No!' Ann stepped towards the boy but was halted by the thick club swinging savagely inches from her face.

'Please.' Helpless, Ann could only beg. 'I have no money.'

'You give.' The words slithered on the darkness; then in a

tone like the hiss of a snake ready to strike he added, 'You give now.'

How could she make him believe she was telling the truth?

Though she was trembling in every limb, fear for Alec drying her mouth, Ann knew she had to try. 'Please,' she swallowed against the stricture in her throat, 'please understand I have nothing to give. I have no money nor has Alec, please . . . !'

She pressed her hands against her mouth as she watched the club rise higher above Alec's head, the ice-cold glittering eyes of his captor watching her as it began to descend.

'He doesn't want money.'

Across from Ann the club halted in mid-air, the head of the shadow-shrouded figure whipping round to meet a new voice.

'He isn't asking for your body either, though I have no doubt he would not refuse given the opportunity.'

'But he demanded payment, he said give.'

'I heard what he said.'

Quiet, less strident, the second voice answered Ann though the figure stepping from a darker ring of shadow looked directly at the man brandishing the club. He was not so stockily built, less of a block against the weak light of the moon, his tread making no sound as he stepped closer to the one still grasping Alec around the throat.

'I heard . . .'

It was repeated softly but Ann detected the threat, the razor sharpness of steel hidden beneath velvet.

'. . . now it is his turn to listen.'

Afraid to take her eyes from Alec in case any second that heavy stick came down on his head Ann was not sure if the movement at the corner of her eye was real or imagined.

'Release the lad. Be certain that it is the only time I tell you.'

64

That she had not imagined, neither the words nor the underlying warning.

'No!' The guttural, defiant reply was hurled towards the opponent. The man tightened his arm about Alec's neck, ignoring the gurgle as the boy fought for breath. 'Not until I am given . . .'

'Then I must be the one to give.'

Even as he spoke Ann caught the movement of the second man's hand, caught the glint of moonlight on metal . . . saw the gun aimed directly at the boy.

A muffled click exploded like thunder in her brain and she watched the body of Alec topple to the ground.

'No . . . oooo!' Ann flung herself forward, catching the falling figure of the boy, sobbing against the unmoving head. 'I'm sorry, Alec, I'm so sorry I . . . I had no money to give.'

She heard movement in the darkness, a shuffling drag followed by what could have been the soft splash of something being lowered into water, but though her ears caught the sounds they did not register over the horror dulling her senses.

'Alec,' she murmured against the boy's face, 'Alec, I could not make him believe I have no money.'

'He did not want money.' From the blackness of shadow a man's voice spoke.

Caught in a nightmare Ann clutched the silent figure even more tightly, her words a whispered sob. 'He said give, he kept saying I must give!'

'But not money.'

'Then what?' Ann looked towards the voice but saw only shadow.

'He came for what you carry with you, that which you brought from St Petersburg, the precious possession passed to you.'

'Nothing was passed to me, you are wrong. I carry nothing but what I brought with me from England.'

From deep within the obscuring darkness a hand fastened on her shoulder; a hand pulling her free of Alec.

'No! I have noth—'

'Ann . . . Ann.'

'No!' With the cry Ann's eyes shot open.

'It's all right wench, it be only me.' Leah's soft words betrayed none of the concern the freshly lit oil lamp showed gleaming in her kind eyes. 'You be 'avin' of a bad dream, ain't nuthin' more than that.'

'Alec!'

'Alec be fast asleep in his bed.'

'But he, the gun . . . the shot!'

'Ain't no gun nor be there any shootin', all it be is a dream.'

Ann pushed herself to a sitting position. Though still shaky she leaned against the pillows, the glance she cast about the bedroom showing fear was not altogether gone.

'I . . . I'm sorry I woke you.'

'No 'arm done, wench, be time I were a stirrin', cows'll be callin' to be milked in an hour.'

It had been a nightmare. Ann stared at the door which had closed on the departing Leah. A nightmare that would never go away.

'I had searched my father's house.' Ann held a mug of hot tea between her cold hands while she continued with the explanation Leah had protested was not necessary. But it was necessary, Ann had decided when getting dressed; an explanation was long overdue. 'I had asked at the embassy if he had left anything there for safe keeping, but there was nothing; yet at the port when that man was shot his last words were of a promise made by my father, a promise involving "a most precious possession". But if there was any such thing I found nothing of it.'

Leah was silent for several seconds before saying, 'Somebody thought you did, what otherwise could account for what that fellah said about some precious possession? But all o' that be behind you, the pair o' you be safe in England. As for the bad dreams they be a consequence o' what you've gone through an' though they be fearful when they comes they'll fade given time.'

'*Fade given time.*'

The words lingered in Ann's mind after Leah had left to milk the cows.

But time had no end and neither did the nightmare. She had briefly told Leah of what had followed the uprising in the Ploschad Morskoy Slavy, of the onrush of armed horsemen causing panic in the crowds and how she, without conscious thought, had grabbed the boy and pulled him with her as she turned to run. But that was all she had told.

Ann set a pan of water above the fire Leah had lit then reached for a jar containing porridge oats.

'*I have to get ship for England.*'

She watched the oats she had poured into the pan swirl in the stirred water; it seemed she saw again the panicked crowd, the terrified faces of women, the fearful countenances of men all rushing to get away from the threat of horses' hooves, the sabres of their riders; a mass of people with no mind to listen to a girl even had they understood her words.

It had been as if she was caught in a great tide of people carrying her along, carrying her with them aboard ship; only then had she realised she still held the arm of a complete stranger, a young boy who had gasped in disbelief as he saw his companion shot dead.

Disbelief they had both shared!

Somehow she had found a corner with space enough for herself and the boy to sit, then as her nerves quieted enough for her to think with reasonable clarity she had decided to request she be shown her cabin.

'*Niet . . . niet.*'

This was the response to her every question; people pushed her away, their own troubles obviously enough to deal with. At last she had found a man in uniform, the gold braid of what could signify a senior officer adorning a heavy jacket.

He had shaken his head at her question.

'*Niet.*' It had come with a flourish of the hand together with a rapid spate of words which though unintelligible to her were clearly emphasising his denial.

'*But I have reserved a cabin!*'

Desperation had her flourish her ticket but it had simply resulted in yet another curt 'no'.

The boy had explained. He had followed her and now interpreted what had been said.

She had no cabin.

In darkness which had fallen rapidly as a lowered curtain she had stared at the lad, seeming to hear from a thousand miles away his quiet, '*You have no reservation. This ship does not sail to England, this is the ferry going to Finland.*'

The panic, the dash for the entry to the docks: in the madness of it she had been carried not in the direction of the ocean seaport but in that of the local ferry.

The boy's words had stunned her. How did she find her way home from there, a country she had never set foot in? How long had she stood on the deck, the splash of waves against the hull of the ship not registering, her only feeling that of numbness until . . .

The remembered shock made her tighten her fingers about the spoon.

. . . until returning to the corner where she had sat! Cloud over the pale moon had added to the darkness so at first she had not noticed, then as a filter of moonbeams cast pallid light she had seen her suitcase lying open, its contents gone. She had dropped to her knees, her distracted mind asking only one thing. Where was the photograph of her mother? Alec had found it, handing it to her with quiet sympathy.

Ann stirred the contents of the pan but saw only pictures of the past.

She had been clutching at the photograph, her head bent low over it, so she had paid no attention to the boy until a startled cry made her glance up then slowly, disbelievingly, rise to her feet. With one arm across the boy's throat and the other encircling his body a man dragged him to stand against the ship's rail.

Who had that man been, what was it he had demanded she give, and who was the one who had shot him then tipped the body overboard?

'I reckon that porridge be cooked, or be it you intends 'avin' the bottom outta that pot?'

Leah's return to the living room whisked her back to the present. Ann fetched bowls from the dresser but even as she spooned porridge into them the questions she had asked herself remained just below the surface.

'*All o' that be behind you, the pair o' you be safe in England.*'

In England, yes.

But safe . . . why could she not believe that?

Dreams, especially the unwanted sort, left a troubled mind in their wake.

After she returned to the dairy Leah pondered the look she had glimpsed on the face of the girl cooking porridge.

Last night had not been the first time Ann had cried out in her sleep. It wasn't to be questioned that the shock of being robbed of that which you held dear sent its terrors to haunt you nights; hadn't she suffered the same on being robbed first of her sons then of a cherished daughter?

Sleepless nights were nothing new to Leah Marshall and though the cause of them might differ the fear was the same. She had seen the shadow of it on Ann Spencer's face, the mark left from robbery, from finding herself practically penniless in a land she knew little of and whose language she could not speak; that ordeal would scare any woman.

But time and the balm of God's mercy reduced if not the hurt then at least the fear it brought with it, so why did the shadow never quite leave that girl's eyes? Why did it cast a deeper shade across her face when she thought herself alone? She had told of one reason; but what other nightmare haunted Ann Spencer?

8

First she removed the small piece of dried salted calf stomach from water it had soaked in overnight, then Leah poured the resulting liquid into milk Edward Langley had delivered fresh from Hill Rise Farm, adding it to the yield from her own small herd. He had not been his usual cheerful self this visit, in fact he had not been anything like the Edward she was used to; the hug had been there and so had the smile, but neither held their customary warmth.

While she stirred the contents of the stone vat with a wooden paddle Leah considered the whys and wherefores underlying such a change in behaviour.

Had it been Ann Spencer's conduct of the evening before? She laid aside the paddle in order to reach for a stone jar glancing as she did so to where Ann was removing butter from the cool cupboard and setting the portions carefully into shallow trays lined with muslin. It was obvious Edward Langley was taken with the girl and she in her turn had shown no dislike of his company. Until last evening!

After adding a helping of salt from the jar to the creamy milk Leah stirred again, her thoughts circling like the eddies produced by the paddle.

The girl had refused the offer of help in the scullery, a swift shake of the head her only reply when Edward said he would wash out the churns in which he had delivered the evening's milking; as before she had uttered no word of thanks when he had said he would carry the metal churns to the scullery.

It took time to scour so many landles and pans, the sieves and pails needed at every stage of butter- and cheese-making, but the girl had taken more than was necessary, so much so Leah herself had bundled her from the scullery with an irate, 'Be you a wantin' Edward Langley a thinkin' we be wi'out manners!'

Leah glanced again at the slender figure now carrying the last tray of butter from the cold store.

Ann Spencer had blushed at the reprimand, had apologised to Edward for her curtness, but the atmosphere had been less than easy.

The wench had seemed far away . . .

Leah turned her attention to milk which the evening before had seen the addition of water treated with calf's stomach skin, using both hands to break the resulting solid mass of curd into small chunks, but her thoughts remained with the events of the previous evening.

Her features had been pale and drawn, her eyes worried. Edward Langley too had caught that look.

Of course Alec not being home by his usual time would account for some stress; Ann was fond of the lad and it was natural she fret when he was extra late, but that should have ended completely when Edward Langley had brought him to the house not five minutes after saying his goodnight.

Even as she had thanked Edward for walking the lad to the house after finding him the worry had by no means left the girl's eyes.

Placing the broken curds in muslin Leah tied the corners of the cloth together.

There was something biting at Ann Spencer, something more than a lad coming late home.

Could the reason for the wench being so drawn into herself be one and the same as that which had seen herself go looking for Thomas Thorpe? Had the wench heard the tittle-tattle Leah Marshall had overheard while in the market place?

'*. . . why other would a foreigner be 'ere?*'

'*But he be naught but a lad.*'

'*A lad ar!*'

Jinny Jinks' sharp note of reproof had caught Leah's attention.

'*But one as don't be blind nor deaf neither, nor be 'e puddle in the 'ead.*'

'*That be as you says Jinny, but in all charity I can't say I sees the lad's bein' 'ere for the purpose it be put to.*'

'*Charity!*' Jinny had snorted again. '*What good be that to the men bein' killed in this war? Men and lads we knows and them we don't; what we needs to look at be the 'arm we be a doin' by the harbourin' of a foreigner.*'

Lottie Hopcroft had frowned and shaken her head at that.

'*It be all well an' good what you be sayin' but Ezekial reckons—*'

'*Ezekial Turley be a man who's seen more 'n most in this town but he ain't seen everythin' and he ain't been every place!*'

Jinny's sharp retort cut Lottie's protest.

'*So common sense has it Ezekial Turley don't 'ave the knowin' of everythin': though I believe what he said as to that there Kaiser Bill bein' a sly 'un, that there be naught he wouldn't try to see Germany a winnin' of the war . . . and to my mind that includes the sendin' of a young lad for to spy.*'

'*But the wench who be along of 'im I hears her grandmother lived along of Darlaston.*'

'*So what difference do that mek?*'

Lottie's reply was hesitant.

'*Well . . . stands to reason, the grandmother be English so*

73

the wench'll be an' all, an' wouldn't no English go 'elpin' of no Germans.'

'Stands to reason do it!'

Jinny Jinks had snapped like a terrier.

'Then so do this stand to reason: a wench who be turned out of a house on account of 'er bein' no better than 'er should be wouldn't be shy of tekin' money along of 'elpin' a spy!'

'Eeh Jinny, you 'eard what Mr Thorpe said, her give up tenancy of Chapel House to go look for work cos none were to be got along of Wednesbury.'

'Oh ar we all 'eard Mr Thorpe but then we all knows his 'eart be too soft for 'im to go tellin' of the true reason ... and another thing, if'n that wench needed to leave in search o' work why be her still 'ere livin' along of Leah Marshall?'

'Be no business o' your'n why her be livin' at Leah Marshall's place.'

As the women burned to face the sharp admonition, their cheeks had flushed pink.

'We ... we was just a sayin' ...'

'I 'eard what you was just a sayin' Jinny Jinks. Now you 'ear what I be a sayin': should it be you goes spreadin' any more of your muck then it'll be Leah Marshall will be a fillin' of your mouth with the same, 'ceptin' her won't be a usin' of words when good honest cow dung can serve the same purpose!'

She had walked away leaving both women open-mouthed.

'... we all knows his 'eart ...'

She smiled a grim smile. Thorpe! It could only be his hand at the back of all this, that congregation knew only what he chose to tell them. She had determined to find out if she would be told the same, but a visit to his home and then the chapel had failed to locate him.

A soft exclamation recalled her to the present. Leah looked

to where Ann was staring down at a pat of butter on the ground, her hands pressed to her mouth.

Leaving the board to lie where she had placed it she moved to the girl's side saying briskly, 'Don't give no mind to that, won't go wastin', old Betsy likes a dab o' butter.'

She scooped up the soft mound and dropped it into a bucket of whey drained from an earlier pressing of curd and put aside for feeding to the pig housed in a sty set alongside the privy at the furthest end of the yard.

'I thinks we could both be doin' wi' a cup o' tea.'

After she had cleaned her fingers on a scrap of cheesecloth Leah touched Ann's arm. 'Go you put the kettle to the pot while I teks old Betsy her treat.'

The wench had gone on the round as usual but her smile had made no appearance.

When she returned to the dairy Leah placed a series of weights on top of the wooden board covering the muslin-wrapped curds then, leaving them to drain, turned her attention to milk left overnight in a shallow stone vat to settle. She scooped the cream from its surface to transfer it to a wooden barrel-shaped churn banded about with brass and attached to a trestle. A few drops from a bottle of carrot water added a richer colour to the resulting butter. She locked the lid of the churn before turning the handle to rotate it, all the while her mind dwelling on Ann.

Leah watched the steadily rocking churn without seeing it. That it was a different matter to the one spoke of – a murder in that Russian square – left it plain to see there were fears other than that plaguing Ann Spencer, for her were sensible enough to know them happenings were in the past, and naught of them could follow her here to Wednesbury.

But was it here in this town had come cause for fresh worries? Was it the wench had heard for herself the backbiting being mouthed by Lottie Hopcroft and that snipe-nosed Jinny Jinks?

Leah's hand tightened its grasp, setting the churn to rock unevenly.

That woman had a tongue sharp enough to clip branches from a tree.

Straightening, Leah pressed a hand to her aching back.

'Ar,' she murmured aloud, 'Jinny Jinks, you be a ranter when it comes to preaching the faults of others regardless whether or not them faults exists but one thing you don't be, you be no mullock when it comes to your own well-bein', you knows that to clip one more branch from Ann Spencer's tree will 'ave you answerin' to Leah Marshall an' that meeting be liable to put an end to your well-bein' for many a bright day.'

Once the churning was finished Leah removed the golden yellow curds, washing them to remove any trace of buttermilk, then using the broad 'Scotch Hands' patted it for several minutes to clear it of any excess moisture. Finally she set it aside for later shaping into blocks.

Leah stood for a moment, feeling weary. She could take a few minutes, make a cup of tea, sit beside the fire while drinking it; but sitting never got jobs finished.

The advice, though sound, would not ease the tired ache of her bones. She turned back to the cheese curds draining beneath their weighted board. She unwrapped the chunks, sliced them thinly then worked them between her fingers until they resembled fine breadcrumbs. Then she sprinkled on a little more salt and tied them in fresh muslin this time banding them with a metal hoop which would allow the cheese to take on its rounded shape on being returned to the sieve.

But the process was not finished; like the butter she had just patted the cheese crumbs needed to have the last drops of whey pressed out.

With a long drawn sigh she placed the large sieve on a rigid perforated board beneath a 'queedle' – a strong plank Joshua had planed himself before bolting one end firmly to the dairy wall. This had been the part of cheese-making she had enjoyed most; so had her sons, and when his work at home allowed Edward would come and together they would sit on the loose end of the queedle bouncing it up and down like a see-saw, all the while pressing the cheese against the perforated board, each of them boasting it was he pressing out most of the whey.

Drawn back in time Leah watched three young boys each jostling for position on the plank.

'*You don't be no heavier than a fly, it be best you stands lookin' out for the whey bucket, see it don't get turned over.*'

'*You stand watchin' over the bucket! I be as strong as you, Joshua, I can bounce good as you!*'

'*Your tongue be all you can bounce, don't the teacher at school be forever tellin' you so.*'

'*That don't be true, now you admits that don't be true Joshua Marshall!*'

Leah had watched as many times Daniel pushed the teasing Joshua backwards off the plank. Deborah stood beside her laughing at her brothers' antics, then she had smiled as Edward hauled his grinning friend to his feet and nimble as a kitten slipped into the space Joshua had fallen from, saying as he settled:

'*The way these two go on they have no need of a queedle, they be like to do the job with the seat of their pants so mebbe it be better I sit between them wouldn't you say Mrs Marshall?*'

'*I would say, Edward, seein' as how I would 'ave that cheese set into a moulding press afore next Mickelmas.*'

Her smile belied the reproof and provided Joshua with a fresh chance to tease. Taking two wooden butter pats he turned to the seated two.

'*Right the both of you …*'

He clapped the butter pats loudly together.

'*I warned what would happen should there be any larkin' about … now seeing neither of you paid any consequence to my words I be goin' to have to put them a mite stronger.*'

Again it was Edward who had answered. With his lips pursed in typical contemplative manner he had asked quietly, '*What say you to that, Daniel?*'

Leah smiling, watched again her youngest son. Ever agile as a cat he leapt from the queedle.

'*What do I say, Edward?*'

He had raised his hands to his hips.

'*I says him and whose army!*'

'*Do them three rogues be a playin' you up, Leah?*'

Joseph! Leah's whole world lit up. Joseph was home.

'*Leah?*'

Leah listened to the voice of her husband but as her name came again it seemed her breath caught suddenly inside her.

Joseph was not come home; like her sons and her daughter he would never come home again.

'Leah.'

Yet it was there again, his voice calling her name!

'Leah … for God's sake are you home?'

Sharp as a dousing of iced water the call cleared all her bemusement. She crossed the dairy as quickly as her tired legs would allow then at the doorway stopped dead in her tracks.

It had been Edward Langley who had called her name, Edward Langley who stood in the yard, a figure carried in his arms.

With a cry of fear Leah saw for a single instant the body of a slender youth in soldier's uniform, saw her son being carried from the raging hell of the battlefield.

Edward's voice broke the nightmare.

'There has been an accident, it's Alec. I'm afraid it's bad.'

9

She had dropped the butter because her hands had been shaking. Deliveries finished, Ann walked beside the small horse-drawn cart. Maybe she should have told Leah last evening what her customers had said with regard to purchasing any more butter or cheese but perversely she had decided to make one more delivery herself, to explain to those women how Leah could no longer manage to make the dairy products and deliver them too. Yet what if her explanation fell on deaf ears?

Ann gave herself to her thoughts.

It was a risk; if customers should still refuse to buy that would spell the end for the dairy, for Leah's living, and the fault would be Ann Spencer's. If she had refused to come to live with Leah then none of this awful business would have happened. But what was done was done.

Earlier, when she had glimpsed Leah trudging across the yard to the pig pen, Ann had determined the woman must not be made to suffer for what had been a kindness.

She had placed the last of the butter and cheese trays on to the cart. She *would* make the deliveries, she would apologise to each and every customer and promise that Ann Spencer would leave the house of Leah Marshall, and the town, the very next day. But Alec, what of him? In her concern for Leah's welfare she had given no mind to his reaction. What would he think of her leaving him behind; would he consent?

Ann felt herself pulled in opposite directions. They had shared so much, lived through times of fear supporting one another like brother and sister.

But he is not your brother!

No, Alec Romney was not her brother. He had no call on her and she none on him; he had kin here in England, relatives who should he be forever on the move would have that much more difficulty tracing him. He had settled so well with Leah and it was evident the woman had love for the lad she had given a home to. For him to leave would hurt them both; and then there was the friendship he had found with Edward Langley.

It had been Leah who had first taken Alec to Hill Rise.

'Walk'll do you good an' the company of a smart-lookin' lad be pleasin' to an old woman.'

Leah's words echoed.

That was what Alec had brought to Leah; to deny her his company now would be almost like making her lose her own sons all over again.

She would not be the cause of that!

A note addressed to the both of them? Ann dismissed the idea. Leah and Alec deserved better than that, they deserved to be told face to face she needed to move on alone.

Was that what Alec and Leah truly merited?

Ann felt again the sting of divided loyalty.

Did they deserve to be lied to? That was what such an explanation would be; but to say otherwise would serve only to prolong the situation and that in turn might mean more encounters with Thomas Thorpe.

'I was certainly right in thinking to find you here.'

He had grabbed her wrist. Breathtaking in its clarity the scene returned. A stretch of open ground, no building other than a small house in the distance. She had been returning from taking a basket of butter, cheese, eggs and milk, a gift from Leah to the elderly couple living there, the husband ill with a sickness of the chest.

'*. . . really you should vary your route . . .*'

Thomas Thorpe's voice grated in her mind.

It seemed he stepped from nowhere, the menace of him blocking her path, and his eyes had glittered with that same threat they had held when he had grabbed at her in that house, the threat of rape.

He must have observed her over the days, noted the times of her deliveries, and waited for the perfect chance to waylay her.

'*. . . what Thomas Thorpe desires he makes very sure he gets . . .*'

It had seemed he would take what he wanted there and then, but with a sudden change of mind he had released her though he kept a grasp on her wrist, saying thickly he would savour the pleasure more so in the comfort of Chapel House.

He had laughed at that, a low obscene sound dark as the pall of factory smoke enshrouding the sky above the approaching town. Please . . . she had prayed silently with every step, please don't let this happen, please let someone be crossing the heath. But no other person had appeared. Then as the drab huddle of Hobbins Street came into view she had glanced away across to where the Holyhead Road bisected heathland and pasture, looking to where Leah's house stood. Maybe she would be in the cow field, maybe she would hear a call.

'*Don't think it!*'

Thomas Thorpe's grasp had hardened, his fingers biting into the flesh of her wrist.

'*I've waited long enough for what be due so in case you be think-ing to speak with anybody we pass then remember this, should I fail to get what is owed by one then I simply take it from the other; male or female, woman or boy, either is acceptable. You understand me?'*

It had been said quietly but the implication had screeched in her mind. Should he not have the satisfaction of raping her then he would violate Alec!

The horror of it had so overriden even the screaming in her mind that she had not seen the man stepping from an entry running between the line of blackened houses, his stick waving in the air as he called, *'I were 'opin' forra word wi' you Mr Thorpe, p'raps y' would spare me a minute or so since y' be passin'.'*

Thomas Thorpe's intake of breath had been one of irritation. The pressure of his fingers reminded her of his threat before he released her.

'I gave Miss Spencer my word I would see her safe home, the heath can be daunting for a woman walking alone and especially so given the times we be living in; I mean it is not always easy to distinguish who is a friend from one who is in the pay of the enemy.'

Thomas Thorpe's reply had carried an underlying note which seemed almost a vindication of some former assertion.

'Be right in what y' says Mr Thorpe.'

Ezekial's head had nodded, Thomas Thorpe's thin-lipped smile had appeared.

She could have protested then, could have thanked Thorpe telling him she had no need of further company. Ann's memory of that moment triggered a fresh sickness in her throat. She could have refused and she would have except for the words which had held her tongue silent: *'Woman or boy, either is acceptable.'* She would not risk Alec's safety in exchange for her own and so she had said nothing.

'*Ar it be right good o' you a mekin' o' the offer to walk the wench 'ome.*'

Ezekial's stick had waved in the direction of Leah's house but his eyes had fastened on her own.

'*. . . be a Christian act Mr Thorpe.*'

Had Ezekial read the fear in her glance? Could that have been the cause of his continuing?

'*But then a body can see clear to Leah Marshall's place an' naught atwixt 'ceptin' for the 'oss road, an' both y'self an' me can watch the wench safe across . . .*'

He had smiled at her then, his tone apologetic.

'*If it be you wouldn't 'ave objection to the goin' on alone, wench, then my old bones'd be spared the 'avin' to tek the walk along of the chapel or else to Mr Thorpe's 'ouse for to 'ave that word.*'

Thorpe had realised she could not but consent to Ezekial's request; but his eyes had told her there would be another time.

And there would. Only by leaving this town could she be truly free of Thomas Thorpe. And then what of Alec? Should he elect to stay then, if only out of revenge, Thomas Thorpe would do as he had threatened. Somehow or other he would harm Alec. Ann bowed to the truth of her heart. Freedom demanded a high price; one she could not pay.

'Miss Spencer.'

Thorpe! Ann's heart missed a beat. He had not waited long.

'Miss Spencer, I was hoping to meet you.'

Ann forced herself to look to where the call came from, then stared as Edward Langley went on.

'An accident . . . Leah . . .'

'*An accident . . . Leah . . .*'

She had not waited to ask what or how, she had not thought of horse or cart with its empty trays and milk churns nor had the dreadful memory of being waylaid by Thomas Thorpe remained any longer as her mind suddenly filled with new anxiety. Had Leah suffered a fall? Was it the queedling, had the handling of that heavy plank caused her an injury? Could it be one of the cows had pushed against her, the weight of it knocking her to the ground? One after another the questions had raced while she had run breathlessly all the way to the house.

Leah had not been in the living room, the chair she favoured close to the hearth had been empty. At that moment Ann had frozen with dread.

'... *an accident* ...'

It had clanged like a bell.

An accident which had taken the life of one woman who had proved a friend?

Looking at the figure lying in its narrow iron-framed bed Ann could not lock out the memories.

She had stared at the chair numb to all but the terrible feeling of emptiness; the silence of the tiny room drawing her deep into itself and closing her from everything, letting her drift away on a soft cloud of comfort.

'*Is everything all right?*'

There had been words coming from a distant place, from a world she did not know.

'*Miss Spencer ... Miss Spencer ...*'

Floating in that gentle calm, wanting only to be left to its peace, she had let it carry her away from all disturbance.

'*Miss Spencer ... Ann ...*'

The tone was sharp and demanding; a sudden force grabbed her arms holding, shaking, snatching her from that benign serenity until finally the voice of Edward Langley again calling her name had returned her to her senses.

'*Ann, what's wrong, what is it?*'

It had tumbled from her. '*Leah … an accident, she … she is dead.*'

'*Dead!*' His grip had softened but not relinquished its hold. '*Leah is not dead.*'

'*But you said …*'

'*What I would have said if you had waited long enough to listen was it is Alec who has met with an accident, not Leah, and before you go careering off again let me tell you he is also not dead.*'

His hands had remained a few moments on her arms then she had turned from him, the clatter of her boots on the well-scrubbed tread of the narrow stairs matching the drumming of her racing heartbeats.

As she sat beside the sleeping figure Ann heard again in her mind those questions which had come in the quiet hours at Alec's bedside. Had it been her imagination that Edward Langley's hold on her had been more than the touch of re-assurance? That the look vanishing from his eyes almost at the moment she noticed it had held more than sympathy? Had she wanted it to be more? In those same quiet hours had come acknowledgement of her wish that she had not simply imagined it.

Embarrassment made her blush slightly as she shifted self-consciously in her seat.

Catching the sound, Leah turned from the tiny washstand tucked into a corner of the room.

'The lad be restin' an' so should you be; best y'be away to your bed, ain't no sense in sittin' the night in that chair.'

Ann shook her head. 'Just a little longer, if Alec should need anything.'

'So he calls, ain't neither o' we so far away we wouldn't 'ear 'im.'

Leah had not seen him on that other occasion. The colour which thoughts of Edward Langley had brought to her cheeks drained away as Ann reached an involuntary hand to the boy. Leah had not seen Alec in those days after they had been turned away from that ship.

'I was so afraid.'

'I 'ave to be admittin' to fearin' meself,' Leah answered. 'When I seen the lad in Edward's arms I feared of there bein' more than broken bones but Edward said as there couldn't be no such cos of the lad a movin' around normal like after fallin' from that cart; said he done naught but bump against the wheel but then after an hour or so Alec were limpin', that were when Edward insisted he be allowed to look for hisself what 'urt had been done; said the lad's leg showed sign o' bruisin' as were to be expected but when the limpin' got worse he thought it better the lad be fetched 'ome. It were Edward put him to bed then called of the doctor. He agreed no bones were broke, said bruises be natural after a knock, they be unsightly but that be due to a slight bleedin' 'neath the skin, certainly naught to worry on.'

'*Naught to worry on*'. Ann caught at the words. If only she could be sure.

Leah placed a fresh cloth beside the jug and bowl on the washstand as she went on.

'Lads be always tumblin'; I raised two o' my own and bruisin' of a limb were a daily 'appenin' but they does no real hurt. So like I says you be away to bed an' no more worryin' for it be all over, the lad be all right.'

Ann glanced again at Alex, seeing the angry flush rising over the pale face, hearing the soft moan mingle with short rapid breaths, and her whole body tensed.

'No Leah, Alec is not all right. It is not all over . . . it is only just beginning.'

10

Ezekial Turley, the old fool, had robbed him of a pleasure already too long anticipated! Entering the chapel Thomas Thorpe breathed hard against a searing flush of anger, the same which had burned since that meeting.

Turley might have known what had been in store for Ann Spencer and that knowledge might have caused him to ask what he had on purpose, knowing full well any refusal on Thomas Thorpe's part would have flown about the town on wings an eagle might envy.

Irritated further by the thought, he flung it away. Turley didn't have second sight, he couldn't know and neither could anybody else.

He collected a pile of hymn books from a table placed near the door. A few more minutes were all he had needed, a few minutes would have seen them inside Chapel House and Ann Spencer would have been right where he had wanted her . . . and exactly *how* he wanted her, naked and spread-eagled on the bed, tied there if need be. But Thomas Thorpe had not been given satisfaction, all due to Ezekial Turley wanting a word.

But why had the man insisted they talk right then, why had he used the excuse of 'old bones' when those same old bones carried him about the town with little apparent difficulty? Why, unless he knew?

Exasperation added to his irritation. He slammed the books hard on to narrow ledges of pews kept cleaned and polished by women who, despite the combined pressures of long hours of factory war work and the care of homes and families, still found time to keep the chapel spick and span.

Retrieving a book which had slipped to the floor, he stared at it.

Hadn't he taken great care to keep all activities which had taken place in Chapel House entirely secret?

He breathed more easily. The old man hadn't known or their conversation would no doubt have followed a different path.

'*Mark what I says . . .*'

Turley had waited until the girl had been out of earshot.

'*. . . there be a fomentin' along o' some folk, a brewin' o' trouble that less'n it be checked could lead to more'n the throwin' o' words.*'

He had concealed his impatience, had controlled his urge to push Turley aside, telling him gossip and its 'fomentin'' was the only amusement open to many in Wednesbury, an enjoyment which rapidly lost all appeal once the next item reared its juicy head.

But the allure of being lay preacher at the chapel had proved too strong. It was his firm intention to continue in that position, one which had afforded many past pleasures taken in the house at the rear of the building and which would allow many more of the same. To tell the man he was a fool then walk away and leave him standing would not go down well with other parishioners. It might even mar that ultimate aim of becoming the permanent preacher.

'*I been a 'earing talk . . . talk among some o' the women wi' regard to that there wench . . .*'

Talk! It had stopped the breath in his lungs. Was this the reason Ezekial Turley had asked for a word? Did the gossip he referred to involve Thomas Thorpe? Had knowledge of what had passed between him and Ann Spencer reached other ears? He had remained tensely unmoving while the old man had gone on.

'. . . *seems they no longer be partial to the 'avin' o' butter'n cheese teken 'em along of 'er . . .'*

Butter and cheese! Turley was talking of butter and cheese!

'*But why?*' He had masked his relief with a half laugh.

'*I asked o' that reason, turns out they don't be a wantin' o' no truck wi' somebody who be 'arbourin' of a spy.*'

With both hands resting firmly on his walking stick Ezekial Turley had looked him straight in the eyes, saying quietly:

'*I 'as no cause to be askin' where it be that idea were mooted for we both knows where, same as I be thinkin' to know who be wieldin' of the spoon that be stirrin' o' that particular pot so I be sayin' to you what I answered o' them women: think long an' hard afore layin' trouble to Leah Marshall's door for though her meks a sturdy friend 'er meks a stronger enemy.*'

Turley had left it at that; with a brief nod he had turned back along the passageway leading to his home. But what he had said had lingered in Thorpe's mind.

He walked slowly along the aisle to the pulpit where he mounted the three shallow steps to stand within it.

'. . . *think long an' hard afore layin' trouble to Leah Marshall's door . . . 'er meks a stronger enemy.*'

Perhaps he might follow that advice. Leah Marshall was already no friend of Thomas Thorpe and would not hesitate to demonstrate the fact should she be given reason to think he threatened Ann Spencer.

He laid the hymn book on the pulpit, hands spread one each side of it as he cast a long look about the room. Leah Marshall's leaving the congregation so abruptly had, though they had not said so, left some asking themselves why. And to have that woman voice any accusation could have them ask that same question again, this time openly.

Deborah Marshall! Hair more gold than brown glistened in the light of candles, eyes starlit with tears gleamed in a face pretty as could be wished, and the body . . .

He breathed deeply to suppress the fierce pull at the base of his stomach.

Breasts high and firm, a tiny waist above gently rounded hips, her body held the very essence of desire, desire which had throbbed in him that evening she had been alone in the chapel.

'*I'm so afraid . . .*'

She had turned to him, her eyes gleaming blue crystal.

'*I'm afraid Edward will die, that he will be killed the same as Joshua and Daniel have been killed.*'

He had drawn her to him, holding her gently as a father might, but the feeling which pounded in his loins had not been that of a father.

'*I fear each morning I wake that a telegram will come, that it will say Edward is dead.*'

She had sobbed against his shoulder, the trembling of that delightful body adding to the throb of his own.

'*We will pray together . . .*' he had murmured, fighting the urge to fondle the breasts he could feel against his chest.

'*. . . we will pray the Lord protect Edward and comfort us with His mercy.*'

Anxiety or the tenderness of years? Either way, Deborah Marshall had been easily duped. She had complied without question with the suggestion they go to Chapel House, where she might feel more comfortable free from the possible embarrassment of explaining the reason for her tears to anyone taking a moment after work to ask the Lord's protection for loved ones away at war.

They had gone to the house not just on that evening but several more, the sympathetic touch of his hand on her shoulder when she left being gradually replaced with the touch of lips first to her forehead and later her cheek. He had played his hand carefully and she had not suspected.

Then had come the dreaded telegram. Edward Langley was 'missing, presumed killed in action'.

She had come to the chapel as had become her practice, to seek consolation and support, and he, as had become his practice, had taken her to the house there to pray together, to seek the comfort of the Lord.

And comfort had been given . . . to Thomas Thorpe.

Wrapped up in her grief she had not been aware of the buttons of her dress being loosed, of the hand he slipped inside to caress her breast. She had stayed unaware that he was pressing her backwards on the couch, lifting her skirts, pulling away the cotton bloomers; only the touch of his fingers brushing the cleft between her legs alerted her to what was happening. By that time it had been too late; with a hand over her mouth to deaden her scream he had snatched open his own clothing and thrust his pulsing flesh deep into her.

'*It would be unwise to speak to anyone of this.*' He had caught her wrist, holding her as she made to run from the house. '*Think of what people will say not only of you but of your mother? What will they say of a woman who allows a sixteen-year-old daughter to visit a man alone and at night? They will say that she encouraged you to come here, to seduce with pretended tears.*'

'*Folk would never say that, they know my mother.*'

'*Better than they know their preacher?*' His reply had cut away her words. '*I don't deny that, but they also understand the limits of a man, a man enticed beyond endurance, teased and tormented by a girl, the flaunting of her naked body finally snapping the power of his will.*'

In the silence of the empty chapel Thomas Thorpe felt again the exultant rise of the laugh with which he had greeted her denial.

'*Go then,*' he had released her, '*go tell your side of the story. I'm sure folk will listen with interest same as they'll listen to a man broken in spirit by the wickedness of a girl and a mother set upon trapping him into marriage; and one thing more I can be sure of, they will believe the word of their preacher, the man who has helped and served the community in every way he could. That belief will destroy the reputation of your mother and of you, Deborah, you will be ignored by any you called friend, forced by their disgust to leave Wednesbury. Think of it . . .*'

He had snatched her hard against him, revelling in the gasp of fear as she had felt the hard rise of flesh against her thigh.

'*Think of your mother already desolated by the loss of two sons, think what the shock of another ordeal will do to her.*'

It had been enough; he had seen the flame of defiance die in her eyes. Deborah Marshall had crumpled before that argument. But she had not come alone again to the chapel, not until the arrival of a letter to say Edward Langley had been found, that he was recovering from a wound and would shortly be repatriated. She loved Edward, she loved him and wanted to be his wife.

'*Please,*' she had pleaded, '*please promise he will never learn of . . .*'

'*Of you being a whore, that you lay willingly with me.*'

With his hands pressing hard against the smooth surface of the pulpit he smiled inwardly at the girl staring back with horrified eyes; felt the elation of mastery and side by side with it another equally satisfying sensation: the prospect of pleasures his promise could demand.

'*There will be no need of Edward Langley learning anything . . .*'

He had paused, allowing Deborah Marshall a moment of relief, before continuing, '*That is of course so long as you agree to resume our relationship, shall we say once a week.*'

He had sneered openly at her gasp of abhorrence.

'*Why should marriage make any difference? Lying with one man need not prevent you lying with another.*'

But she had not seen it that way. Sobbing that she would rather both her mother and the rest of the town know what he had done, what he further demanded, she had turned away.

The threat of exposure flashed like a lightning bolt in his mind. Grabbing the heavy metal cross from the table which served as an altar, he had followed her and brought the object smashing down on her head as she reached the door. She had dropped to lie without a sound yet he feared she might not be dead.

His glance travelled to the spot where she had fallen as he breathed again the fear of that moment.

It seemed he had stared an age at the crumpled figure, its turquoise-coloured coat rapidly staining with the crimson of blood seeping from a second blow, staring until the clang of metal striking stone as the cross dropped from his hand had recalled him to what he had done and to what must yet be done.

He could not take her to Chapel House; the woman cleaning there would not yet have left and it was too light to risk leaving a body among the bushes bordering the building where anyone passing along the street might spot it.

Panic was beginning to race in a new flood along his veins when his eye had rested on a cupboard set in an alcove near the door. It was used only to store bucket and mop, utensils which would not be needed for several days to come. It had proved an adequate hiding place. He had left the body there, locked the chapel on the last parishioner then taken the short walk to Foster Street. Enoch Phillips had worked as a wheelwright and in his younger days had built himself a small trap which along with the horse kept in his back yard he would generously lend for chapel business, namely that of the 'minister' paying visits to sick members living on the outskirts of the town.

'O' course y' can 'ave the borryin' o' it, gie me a minute an' I'll 'ave the 'oss in the shafts.'

It had all been so easy; the old man falling over himself in eagerness to facilitate *'the goodness o' you Mr Thorpe, a goin' of seein' folk after a long day a workin' in that there foundry an' then more hours along o' the chapel, y'be a fair blessin' to folk an' no coddin'.'*

If only the old man had known the 'coddin'' he spoke of had been his own in believing the reason for loaning his horse and trap. But he had not known and neither had anyone else.

The remembered fear of a moment before melted in the warm glow of self-praise as Thorpe gazed expansively about the small room, its only ornament the metal cross.

He had driven back to the chapel where it had been the work of minutes to transfer the body to the trap, relock the building and drive away again. He had seen no person in the adjoining street yet tension at the possibility had not eased until he turned the vehicle on to the Holyhead Road, where a trap would be unremarked on a highway busy with carts and trams.

He had chosen well.

Halfway along the rise of Holloway Bank it had been necessary to bridge narrow but fast-flowing water in order for traffic to continue on into West Bromwich; no one would notice a traveller leaving his vehicle to answer the call of nature beneath the shelter of its arch.

During a lull in the traffic, blessed by the dark of a moonless night, he had lifted the body from the trap to hurry with it down the embankment.

It had felt almost weightless in his arms, so light the rush of water might carry it away. But the wound to the head must be made to look like an accident should the girl be found here. Again the bridge had solved his problem. Hitting her head against the buttress would give rise to the theory she had fallen from the parapet, striking her head in the process.

Yes, he had chosen well.

As he had hoped the body had been carried along, finally being caught in weeds further along the valley where the Tame doubled back on itself, and of course the verdict had been accidental death.

Deborah Marshall had denied him but the loss of that pleasure had soon been recompensed.

Taking the hymn book back into his hands Thomas Thorpe smiled at the young girl entering behind an older woman.

Yes! He stepped from the pulpit.

He was most definitely being recompensed.

11

'It be only just beginnin'!'

With a frown Leah met the worried glance of the girl seated beside the bed.

'Alec,' Ann's reply trembled, 'I think he has a fever?'

Leah shook her head. 'Fever, Lord, wench, whatever give you that idea, fever don't come from no fall, it be tiredness 'as you imaginin' things . . . now y'be goin' to do as told an' get y'self to your bed an' no more worryin'.'

'Please Leah, I know it sounds strange, but this is what followed once before, he became hot and feverish with nothing to account for it other than a fall.'

Leah's protest was arrested by a soft moan. She moved quickly to the bedside, her own fears mounting as she looked at the flushed, perspiring face contorted with pain. The lad had no broken bones, no open wound, naught apart from bruising of the leg and no bruising she had ever known had given rise to fever, yet signs of that were showing clear.

'The time y' spoke on, did the doctor say the cause?'

Reaching for Alec's hand, holding it as pain twisted his body, Ann replied tightly that there had been no doctor.

Leah's bewilderment deepened. So how could the wench know the lad had suffered fever? Same as you be knowin' it! Leah answered herself abruptly. It be marked on the lad's face plain as a pikestaff, just as it be plain y' needs do somethin'.

Perhaps Edward had missed some small cut when putting Alec to bed . . . perhaps the doctor had been overhasty in his examination. Leah gently turned back the bedcover, a sharp catch of breath held as she saw the spreading mass of bruises.

'*Bruises are simply bleeding 'neath the skin.*' The doctor's words could have been her own, hadn't she learned that from dealing with her sons; but this was something she had not witnessed before. The spread of darkening purple showed this was no slight bleed.

The doctor? He could take an hour to come. An hour's delay meant so much more internal bleeding, a loss which the lad might be unable to survive. But to attempt to treat him herself . . . if it should fail . . .

A low moan banished her indecision and Leah turned again to the wash stand. If she failed she could be counted a meddler; if she didn't even try she would be branded heartless.

Wringing out the cloth she had soaked in cold water she placed it across the hot forehead.

'Hold you that,' she instructed Ann brusquely, 'it'll help cool 'im; wring it out again when need be.'

'But I should fetch the doctor!'

'Later,' Leah's reply floated after her departing figure, 'first we 'as to do summat about that bleedin'.'

Leah stirred the sleeping fire to new life beneath the kettle, then carried the oil lamp into the scullery using its light to show a variety of bottles and jars lining a cupboard. She had needed to make her own medicines and cures as the children had grown and now gave silent thanks it was a habit she had continued, though her ointments and salves were now mostly requested by neighbours who found difficulty in paying the two shillings and sixpence doctor's fee.

Would there be sufficient for what she needed to do? Holding the lamp closer, reading labels she had affixed to every container, she ran a finger along the shelf stopping before a tightly corked bottle. Arnica. She read the faded lettering. This had eased the pain of bruising both with Joseph and the boys, it had helped stem the under-skin bleeding, so please God it would do the same for Alec. But his fever needed to be brought down too.

Lifting down the bottle Leah continued to scrutinise other handwritten labels.

'Mullein,' she murmured, 'that be for the curing of coughs. Coltsfoot?' Again Leah shook her head. 'That be for the soothing of joints plagued by the rheumatics; Platain,' she read on quickly ascertaining the use of each remedy until her eye lighted on a pot-bellied jar whose label stated it was Fenugreek. This had proved its worth in calming fevers in many a child and with the blessing of heaven it would prove so now.

She took both bottle and jar into the living room, setting them on to the table before returning to the larder. Still by use of the lamp she searched its cool dimness taking honey and apple cider vinegar. She slipped a tiny box that caught her eye into her apron pocket.

The kettle was singing softly on its bracket. Leah stared at the ingredients and utensils collected on a table which years of daily scrubbing had made gleam pale as the cream from her cows.

Was she doing the right thing? Should she do nothing except wait for the doctor?

These were questions to which no answer came. She closed her eyes, placed the palms of her hands together then murmured quietly:

'Lord you knows all things, what be in every heart, therefore you knows I wouldn't never do no 'arm to the lad who 'as found a place in mine, that bein' so Lord I feels I can ask you let of your Holy Angel set a hand over mine, to guide it in what that same heart be a sayin' I must do; I prays that through that blessed angel your loving grace and mercy bring relief an' comfort to a sick child.'

After crossing herself Leah opened her eyes. She had asked the help of the Almighty; now she must use it.

With a deep breath to steady her mind she took a handful of dried leaves from the pot-bellied jar, crumbling them into smaller pieces before adding a small amount of water from the kettle. Covering the basin with a cloth she set it aside. The herbs would take several minutes for their essence to seep into the water; that time would allow for the making of a poultice.

Pouring a generous measure of apple cider vinegar into a pan, setting it above the fire, she reached for the bottle labelled Arnica. The contents gleamed pale gold in the soft glow of lamplight. She had picked the bright yellow flowers during long lonely summer evenings, had lightly bruised the silky petals, covering them with her own home-made apple vinegar, and once every day for two weeks had gently stirred the pot. Then once the beneficial properties of the petals were drawn out she had carefully sieved the mixture before bottling the resulting liquid.

While she stood in the small living room with the gentle hiss of the pan above the fire the only sound in the silence, Leah seemed to see again a patch of heath. Not yet fallen victim to the spread of factories it blazed with a carpet of vivid yellow.

Leah pushed the picture to its place in the past. Daydreams were pleasant but they could not help her now.

She glanced once more at the bottle then poured a small amount of the pale translucent liquid into a separate basin.

Arnica made for a powerful tincture; those few tiny drops would be sufficient for her needs. Quickly she re-corked the bottle and lifted the pan from the fire, pouring the bubbling contents into the basin, stirring once before turning her attention to the leaves left soaking in water; pray God they had steeped a sufficient length of time.

She took one of the several pieces of clean white cloth gathered in readiness then spooned the mush of leaves on to it, folding it to form a pad which she dropped into the arnica mixture. Essence of fenugreek still present in the leaves would seep through the cloth to mix with the arnica adding to the potency of the poultice. But there was still the fever remedy to complete.

Leah frowned as her fingers brushed momentarily against the pocket of her apron.

She had forgotten a most valuable aid to reducing the effects of shock!

Chiding herself mentally she transferred the fenugreek-infused water to the pan adding honey, one cup of apple cider vinegar and finally from the small box a barest pinch of her prized cayenne.

It needs to simmer gently . . . the herb needs time to mix with the honey and vinegar.

Leah used the minutes to collect all that was needed on to a wooden tray then once the potion was ready she carried it upstairs.

Please let Leah return, let her be home before the process has to be gone through again. Leah had to be back . . . she had to!

Glancing at the boy, his eyes shut, his hand limp in hers, Ann strained to hear the sound of footsteps but heard only the tick of the tin clock Leah had brought into the room.

Why could the woman not have permitted her to go fetch the doctor?

'*Where be the sense in that? You don't yet be knowin' the town so well darkness won't 'ave you take of a wrong turn; best I goes, a body who has walked these streets so many years needs no light of day to show the way.*'

Leah's dismissal had been brusque as had that other given on bringing her mixtures upstairs.

'*Ain't no time for blartin', you can sit an' cry later if you must but right now you needs 'ave clear eyes as well as a clear mind!*'

It had not been intended as a reprimand. Ann acknowledged the anxiety behind the sharpness, which had been due to her worries for Alec.

'*Watch well what be done.*'

Leah's voice had softened yet the instruction accompanying each ministration had been firm and precise.

'*The poultice needs be squeezed but not so tight it takes out all of the moisture. Wrap the pad quickly in another piece of cloth so it keeps in the heat then use a strip of cloth to bandage it to the leg.*'

Lowering the bedcovers into place Leah had smiled down at Alec, taking a moment to press his shoulder gently. She had returned the basin, standing it beside the fire lit the moment Alec had been put to bed.

'*Remember, wench, that poultice needs be kept moist. Touch it every 'alf hour or so, if it be dry against the fingers then soak the pad again but take care the lotion be warm, settin' it stone cold against the skin can only add more shock to the system so be sure you sets that bowl along of the hearth, that way will 'ave it ready for the next usin'.*'

Ready for the next using! Glancing at the clock Ann's nerves tripped. It had been almost thirty minutes since Leah went for the doctor. She had not strictly stipulated the time of reapplying the poultice, the 'or so' could allow a little extra . . . a few minutes and the doctor would be here to . . .

A spasm of the fingers held in hers swept the rest of the thought away. Ann felt fear bite at her throat. Alec was trying hard not to voice his pain but it was only too visible in his eyes.

'*That poultice needs be kept moist . . .*'

'I can't, I can't . . . if I should cause more pain . . .'

'Ann.' It was a whisper answering that which had slipped from her own lips. 'Ann, you would not willingly cause me pain, we are friends and friends trust each other so please . . .'

Alec grimaced with pain and his words trailed off, leaving the plea only in his eyes.

Glancing at him, his eyes closed against a further spasm, Ann felt the answer swell in her heart. Alec was saying he trusted her, he was asking she attend to his injured leg.

'*Watch well what be done.*'

Ann brought the bowl from the hearth, her fingers shaking. Had she watched well enough!

He had not cried out, he had not jerked away from the pad being replaced nor the bandage being wrapped. Afterwards Ann's mind seemed suddenly empty. Beside her on the shelf above the small fireplace the tin clock murmured its rhythm.

Tick . . . tick . . .

It sang softly, unobtrusively.

Tick, tick, one two.

Tick, three . . . tick, four . . . tick, five.

Why stop there? Why did the song not pass five?

Five! For a moment it hung meaningless, then recognition dawned.

Leah had emphasised the number while carefully measuring from a cup kept apart from the bowl in the hearth. '*Five drops, no more'n that; give it to drink in a spot o' water an' it'll help bring fever down.'*

The uncertainty she had felt had transmitted itself to Leah and now the woman's answer calmed as it had then.

'Should y'be unsure wi' the drops then a teaspoon o' the mixture be their equal.'

After following the instructions Leah had given, Ann returned to sit at the bedside.

Only then did she let the tears of nervous exhaustion slide down her cheeks.

12

'*They trusted me as they would no other man.*'

The lad drifted into sleep. Ann, holding his hand, let her mind wander slowly into the past.

'*They asked I take into my keeping their most treasured possession . . .*

'*Do it for me, child.*'

Behind closed eyes Ann saw the figure of her father buckle and slide to the floor of a drab soulless room, saw the framed photograph clutched in one hand, the entreaty in eyes already glazing, heard those last dying words.

'*Keep my promise for me.*'

Across the room half-burned coals settled deeper into their cast-iron bed but no sound penetrated the depths of Ann's mind.

What was your promise, Father? How could I keep it when I didn't know what it was? I tried . . .

I searched the house not once but several times for the precious possession you spoke of, and when I found nothing I enquired at the embassy but the official I spoke with said nothing of yours remained; there was nothing more I could do, yet even as I went to the port to take ship for England I felt I should try again but . . .

Drawn deep into bygone horror Ann lived it again. In her head echoed the screams of terrified women, the shouts of angry men, shouts suddenly subdued by the drum of galloping hoof-beats. With them came mental images, flashing, rolling, tumbling together, picture upon picture rapidly sweeping one from the path of another: uniformed men, swords glinting silver streaks as they struck out at others running away. A man clutching her sleeve . . . a boy, his face drawn with disbelief . . . a shot . . . a man falling dead at her feet . . . now a room . . . an unhappy soul-less room . . . a figure slumping to the floor, a figure clutching a silver-framed photograph. Relentlessly, as if on some macabre carousel, her inner vision returned the picture of her dying father, his lips stilling on the murmur: '*Do it for me, child.*'

'I couldn't!'

Ann bent her head to the hand clutched in her own.

'I couldn't do it . . . I failed you as I failed Alec.'

'*I failed Alec!*'

The words drifted across the room and held Leah in stunned embrace. The girl had said she couldn't deal with the dressing of the lad's leg; her hands had trembled when passing the wrappings, her mouth had quivered at being told the care which must be taken to keep the fever mixture distant from the bruise potion.

Leah's nerves jolted sickeningly as she stared at the figure bent across the boy lying motionless in the bed.

Weakened by shock and fever, he would not have been able to fight against the effect of arnica, a herb so potent in its natural form it must never be given internally as a medicine nor used on cuts and open wounds.

Was that what had happened? Had Ann been so flummoxed, so feared of what she had been left to do, she had mistakenly dosed the lad, wrongly given him arnica to drink instead of honey and fenugreek?

Had it already proved too much? Blame could only lie with Leah Marshall; it was her had disagreed with the wench's fetching of the doctor, Leah Marshall who had gone herself leaving a wench with no knowledge of herbal medicine to treat a lad ill of fever.

Leah crossed to the bed. She alone would do what must be done. Hesitating for the briefest time she touched Ann's shoulder.

'Be no fault o' your'n,' she said quietly. 'Come you away wench, I'll see to the lad.'

'Leah!' Ann looked up. 'Oh thank goodness you are back, the doctor—'

'Doctor won't be comin',' Leah interrupted, 'we won't be seein' of him for some hours, not if Leah Marshall be any judge.'

Ann took a second before asking, 'But why? He must surely know you wouldn't go for him in the middle of the night unless it was serious?'

'Ar, he would've knowed,' Leah nodded, 'and he would've come along of me 'cept he were called to Clara Jeavons not five minutes afore I reached his 'ouse. Clara don't birth none of her kids easy, last one took nigh on a full day afore it come an' I reckons this one could be doin' of the same. That be why I says it's like to be a few hours of the doctor comin' here.'

Hours! Ann lowered the hand she was holding back on to the bed. Hours in which Alec could grow worse.

'Leave me with the lad, I'll do what need be.'

Ann looked at the boy who had come to mean so much to her, then rising to her feet turned to the woman who had befriended them both.

'No.' She smiled palely. 'We will do it together.'

She had glanced at the clock, told herself the time then fetched the bowl from the hearth! Inside of herself Leah felt the strong pull of pity. The wench thought to carry on with the dressin' of the lad's leg, her thought him to be still living.

A soft sound from the bed arrested the thought. Leah glanced at the slight figure, at the eyes opening, at the smile touching the mouth. Her own eyes reflected relief as she scolded herself internally. You be a daft old fool Leah Marshall, a daft old fool to go a thinkin' as you did.

Ann heard Leah sigh and looked up from the bowl she had uncovered.

'Alec, is . . . is he? Have I done something wrong?'

'No wench.' Leah smiled, placing a light hand to the boy's brow. 'You've done all the way as should be, the fever be broke, though there'll be need of poultice and mixture for a while longer.'

'*You've done all the way as should be . . .*'

Wanting to cry, wanting to smile, not knowing which emotion was the stronger, Ann carried the bowl across to the tiny table beside the bed.

'I thought maybe you would be needing a bit of help so I've seen to the girls and let them out to play.'

'A man's hands a touchin' of 'em will have that lot frisky for days . . . mind you,' Leah looked at the man sitting at the table of her small living room, 'I can't go a blamin' of them for that, nor do I reckon there be a wench in Wednesbury wouldn't feel the same should it be Edward Langley come a courtin'.'

'Shame on that frivolous tongue.' Edward smothered the laugh gathering in his throat. 'Shame . . . and you knowing the only girl I would go a courting is yourself!'

Leah spooned porridge into a dish with a decided plop then returned the pot to the trivet drawn alongside the fire.

'I'll thank you not to let my girls go hearin' you sayin' of such.' She fetched a jug of cream from the scullery and placed it on the table. 'They gets fierce jealous and when that 'appens they gives less milk.'

'In that case I will just have to go on hiding my feelings, at least until you get new girls.'

'Ar, you do that.' Leah laughed, scalding a fresh pot of tea, adding as she poured it into stout earthenware mugs, 'It were good of you, lad, doin' of the milkin' and seein' my cows into the field; I heard them callin' but couldn't see to them until I'd seen to the lad.'

Edward looked up from stirring sugar into his cup. 'How is he? Is there anything I can do?'

Leah declined his offer and relayed the happenings of the night finishing with, 'I give no thought to the wench mebbe havin' no truck with the usin' of herbs, of her p'raps never seein' the usin', it were daft of me to go leavin' of her to treat the boy, I should've known the risk.'

'You knew the risk of her taking a wrong turn in the darkness, the harm that might come were the doctor delayed; you trusted her to carry out your instruction. That was the wisest path to take, and as you say no harm has come of it.'

When he saw the young woman entering the room from the staircase the words resounded in Edward's mind. Her care of the boy, her watching through the long hours of night, her refusal even now to rest had made her features pale and drawn and though she might not realise it the hands holding the large enamelled bowl shook with what could only be fatigue.

'Alec is sleeping . . .' Catching sight of Edward seated at the table Ann paused then with a fleeting smile said quickly, 'I did not thank you yesterday Mr Langley for coming to look for me, it was most ill-mannered.'

Edward returned the brief smile. 'Fear be a chaser of manners, as for thanks they are not needed.'

'You may not feel the need of them, Mr Langley, but I need to express them both for myself and for everything Leah tells you did for Alec. I am sure when he sees you he will thank you for himself; I hope you will visit soon.' Suddenly conscious of the personal nature of the invitation Ann's cheeks flared with a rush of colour. Her next words she stammered confusedly. 'I . . . that is we . . . with Leah's consent . . . I'm certain Alec would appreciate your calling to see him.'

Alec would appreciate? Or was that rather Ann Spencer would appreciate? As Ann disappeared hurriedly into the scullery Leah took a fresh apron from a drawer of the dresser, exchanging it for that she had worn in the sickroom. Next she wrapped a square of white cloth about her head, tucking a straying strand of grey hair firmly beneath it.

'Lad be washed and sleepin'.' She glanced at the clock, now back in its familiar place on the mantelshelf. 'I reckons there'll be time for me to get that milk into the butter churn afore I needs set fresh dressin' to his leg.'

Emerging at that moment from the scullery Ann put in quickly, 'I can do that, please, you need to rest.'

'Ar wench we both does but . . .'

Sounds from the yard caught everyone's attention. Edward rose from the table.

'That will be the doctor,' his glance met that of Leah, 'I reckon he will want to know what has been used to treat Alec. Perhaps Miss Spencer would rather you explained all that.'

Ann's quick agreement coincided with the short sharp rap to the street door. Leah nodded, saying over her shoulder as she crossed into the parlour to admit the man waiting on the pavement, 'Them milk pails be heavy, you waits 'til I can be there to help with the liftin' of 'em.'

'The yard can be mucky what with fetching the cows in and out,' Edward explained. 'Wouldn't be wanting him carrying mud to the next place he might need to call; this town spreads enough soot and dirt on folks' houses without the adding of a bit more, apart from which,' he smiled, 'bringing him through the parlour gives Leah chance to show off her pride and joy.'

'Shh!' Ann glanced at the couple re-entering the small living room. A tall slightly stooped figure dressed in black swallowtail coat, grey pinstripe trousers and top hat carrying a somewhat battered Gladstone bag followed Leah to the door giving on to the stairs. Returning the man's quiet 'good morning' she turned to see Edward had already left.

Standing alone Ann experienced a surge of disappointment, an emotion she knew she had no right to feel. Edward Langley had come to this house to help Leah, to speak only with her. With Leah gone from the room it held no more interest for him.

She helped herself to an apron and headsquare, as Leah had done, then went out to the dairy.

'I did this with Daniel and Joshua when we were kids.'

Edward's words as she entered the low-roofed whitewashed building, said without a glance in her direction, made the feeling of rejection rise again in Ann.

'We would compete for who lifted the most pails, the loser being landed with the job of turning the handle of the butter churn, Joshua . . .'

He paused and it seemed to Ann he looked past her, that his smile was directed at someone else.

'Joshua.' He laughed softly. 'You were so determined it wouldn't be you turning that handle, but Daniel knew your tricks.'

A squawk of hens quarrelling in their pen dispelled the moment. He lifted a brass-bound pail, emptying the still warm milk into a setting dish.

He had talked not from friendship but because he felt he ought to, that it was the well-mannered thing to do. Ann placed fresh muslin in the several large sieves ready to receive the curd Leah had left to set overnight, then glanced at the figure lifting pails like they were paper cups. Edward Langley had gone out of his way to help with Alec just as now he had left his own farm to come and help Leah by milking her cows. But pouring that milk into the setting dishes was taking advantage of good nature, it was work that should be done by her. She must thank him yet say firmly she could manage alone. How to do that without seeming ungrateful or impolite? He could think himself unwanted here, but that wasn't true, she wanted . . .

Once the last pail had been emptied Edward glanced up, the flick of a frown drawing his brows together as he saw the flush of pink colouring Ann's cheeks.

'Leave that!' he said abruptly, 'you need rest as much as does Leah; there is nothing here I can't do.'

He had mistaken the rise of colour to be a sign of tiredness. Thankful for the misunderstanding Ann hid her relief behind a shake of the head, saying quietly, 'I am sure there is not, Leah has told me of some of the antics you and her sons got up to while professing to help; but you need to be returning to Hill Rise and your own animals. I thank you for all you have done but truly, Mr Langley, I can cope with the rest.'

He had collected the empty pails and without a word carried them across the yard to the scullery. Ann felt a stab of conscience. He had taken what she had said to be a rejection.

I didn't mean for it to imply you are not wanted! Ann gathered the soaked curd, breaking it before spreading it in the sieves she had prepared, then gathering the corners of the muslin tied them securely together. When she reached for the board used to press the semi-solid mass she was startled by it being taken sharply from her grasp.

'Antics might be the way Leah described to you . . .' Edward Langley was already lifting the heavy weights on to the wooden board, '. . . but "useful as a clock with a limp tick and no hands" was the way she would say it to us, though it came rather more strongly the day a whole pail full of milk was spilled. Joshua was so set on not being the one to do the churning he didn't quite empty his pails. Daniel, seeing what he was up to, collected the leavings into one pail, then when Joshua claimed he was finished pouring before us showed him the amount he had "inadvertently" left in the several pails. This of course led to a rumpus, the three of us laughing and rolling on the floor; laughing that is until Leah arrived. It was those few seconds of her saying nothing, of her staring at the milk spreading across the floor from the knocked-over pail scared us most. We didn't know what to expect, then when she grabbed a butter pat . . .' he paused to smile, then went on '. . . she held it like the sword of an avenging angel saying, "The good Lord has given me the knowin' of the curin' of many an ailment but naught as'll put sense where there be none, so I be goin' to try a remedy of my own, one which you noggin' 'eads deserves . . . a good belloilin' wi' this here pat!" '

He fetched an empty bucket in place of that half-filled with whey. 'That was one time Leah did not live up to her word, we neither of us got the threatened spanking,' he chuckled.

It had felt almost like sharing memories with a friend. Ann smiled, a smile which died at Edward Langley's call from the yard.

'I'll just feed this to the pig then I'll give you a hand with putting deliveries on to the cart.'

13

'There is nothing more I can tell you,' Ann answered the doctor. 'I have no knowledge of Alec's family; as I explained, we met during some unrest in St Petersburg.'

'That was where the boy experienced the same illness?'

Ann shook her head. 'No. It was several hours later. We had been put ashore. The wind had whipped the water, showering us with spray. I thought that had caused Alec to catch cold and that was why he was feverish.'

As he took the hat and gloves Leah held out to him the doctor glanced at Ann. 'I see . . . and was your supposition confirmed by medical examination?'

'A man did come but I . . . I could not understand what was said, we could neither of us speak the other's language.'

'But you must have understood the treatment, what needed to be done for the boy, the medication prescribed.'

'No.' Ann met the statement positively. 'Alec was cared for by a woman in whose home we stayed. I cannot tell you what she applied to the bruise on his arm and shoulder or the medicine she gave him, but she did time those treatments by the clock as does Leah.'

The doctor's tired face showed a brief smile as he turned to Leah. 'Obviously a woman with your skills; the boy has much to be grateful for.'

'We be beholden for your comin' right on after bein' to

deliverin' Clara Jeavons, her and her new babbies be all right?'

Taking up the black medical bag, nodding once in Ann's direction, the doctor preceded Leah through the parlour to the street door. 'Mother and twins all well, as that boy will be thanks to you, Leah. It is your hand has saved him. I could have prescribed lotion and fever cure but what you would have got from Jackson the Chemist would contain only the ingredients you are using. Carry on as you have been doing, three more days should see the boy well on the road to recovery, but should you have any worry at all then send for me.'

'. . . *it is your hand has saved him* . . .'

The words echoed in Leah's mind.

Crossing to the gleamingly polished fire grate she touched the framed photograph in pride of place on the mantelshelf.

'We both knows that don't be so, Joseph,' she smiled at the silent face, 'we both knows there were more than my hand tended that lad. Thank Him for me Joseph, thank the Lord's Holy Angel for placing his hand over mine.'

She had stood like someone caught in a bad dream. When the evening milking was done Edward loaded the full churns on to the cart.

He had fed the bucket of whey to the pig, thoroughly expecting Ann Spencer to have, if not finished setting butter portions into the trays, at least to have begun the process but instead she had remained as if rooted to that same spot; when he had shaken her arm to free her mind, she had jumped like some startled jackrabbit.

Why? The question had stayed with him much of the morning, a question it seemed had been answered by women taking delivery of cheese and butter.

He had offered to make those deliveries along with his milk round saying he knew Leah's customers as well as he knew his own but Ann Spencer had shaken her head.

A silent refusal!

A wry smile accompanied the thought. He called to the horse then as the animal moved obediently let his mind return to the scene in the dairy.

She had turned away without so much as a glance, in fact she had barely glanced his way during those few minutes in the house before the arrival of the doctor and the half dozen words spoken in the dairy had been forced.

It could not be clearer if it were painted in letters six foot high. Miss Ann Spencer had no liking for Mr Edward Langley.

But then she had no cause to fear him yet he had caught the tremor of her lips as she turned to the cold store, the shaking of the hands placing the butter and cheese on to the trays, heard the quiver of breath when Leah had come to fetch her back to the living room and accepted his offer with a grateful, 'Thank yer lad, Ann and me both 'preciates it.'

'*I sees Leah Marshall 'as teken notice . . .*'

'*. . . what were said needed the sayin' . . .*'

At almost every house where he had called on behalf of Leah women had made indirect remarks, which it seemed they were not prepared to enlarge upon. So what was it Leah had taken notice of? Was Leah in some kind of trouble which had provoked the suggestion she had put forward on her visit to Hill Rise? He quickly dismissed the notion. Leah Marshall had many characteristics, some of which might not always sit well with women of the town, but no one could challenge the honesty and fairness of her dealings, he least of all; there would have been nothing untoward in her proposal that he take her herd, combine it with his own: unless – he drew a quick sharp breath – unless she was ill, an illness threatening her life! That she would not have mentioned at Hill Rise. 'Pride keeps a still tongue.' The saying often used by his father brought a coldness in its wake. Leah's pride, her very independence, would keep her from revealing any threat to her well-being.

Anxiety made him tighten his fingers on the rein. He urged the horse to a trot. This was one time Mrs Leah Marshall's pride would not stand in the way.

'I be sorry for the troublesomeness of it, I knows it'll cause a bother but ain't no other way ...'

Troublesome! Thomas Thorpe smiled to himself. That Ada Clews was no longer able to continue with the twice-weekly cleaning of Chapel House had had the very opposite effect; far from being an inconvenience it had become a veritable pleasure.

'... the extra hours I be called to do in the factory don't leave no time 'ardly for anythin' else. I don't be sayin' it be the fault of them works managers, be none to blame 'ceptin' the Germans and their Kaiser; I knows what I'd be a sayin' to that one was I to meet 'im ...'

Me too Ada. I would say thank you for the recreation your war has afforded Thomas Thorpe.

'... I feels bad about lettin' you down ...'

The woman's apology sang in his head.

'... and wi' things bein' the way they am, I means wi' every woman bein' in the same boat as meself so to speak, well it ain't goin' to be no simple matter findin' one wi' time enough to spare for the cleanin' of one more 'ouse along of their own.'

It can't be helped, Mrs Clews, don't worry about it, I'm certain someone can be found to give a couple of hours a week.

The words had been on his tongue but thanks to some watchful fate they had remained unsaid, Ada Clews running on quickly. '. . . *so I been a thinkin', my Sarah be excused them extra hours along of the factory seein' 'er be a twelve month short yet of seventeen so . . . allus supposin' it be suitable to y'self . . . then her could tek over the seein' to Chapel 'Ouse, y' wouldn't 'ave no worries as to it bein' kept proper, Sarah be a good little wench wi' a mop and a polishin' rag, 'er can do all I done meself.'*

Oh yes. She did all that her mother had done; and much that Ada had not.

He once again thanked that watchful fate which had allowed a childhood chest infection to keep him from the Army and also from the foundry floor; the doctor's opinion that the heat of furnaces, the dust and smoke of iron and steel smelting, would further irritate his lungs had led to a position as wages clerk, one not requiring extra hours. More favourably still, being office staff meant he left the workplace before day shift ended and night shift began, thus benefiting from unlit near-deserted streets. This added to the chance of his going unseen the evening he went not directly home to Cross Street but to Chapel House.

But then soon Chapel House would be *his* home.

The thought warmed him like mulled wine. They had no idea! Those letters the congregation asked be written requesting a minister were of course dutifully done by himself, then read aloud there in the chapel for the approval or otherwise of the members who then entrusted the sending to him.

A reply? Contempt thickened in his throat. How could they have a reply to letters never posted! But nobody questioned whether they were sent just as nobody enquired into the management of Chapel House; Thomas Thorpe was their trusted preacher, the friend of everyone. He was just a little more friendly to some . . . like to the daughter of Ada Clews.

He returned the farewells of other clerks while pretending a last-minute check of the wages ledger ensured he was last to leave the office and so could avoid any offer of a companion on the walk home.

He paused at the entrance to the yard with its wide green-painted gates boasting the title 'Patent Shaft and Axletree' to turn up the collar of his jacket then pull the flat cap more firmly down on his brow. The evening had turned brisk; no one would give a second glance to a man buttoned against the cold; another advantage for one who did not wish to be recognised.

With a glance behind to check the watchman had withdrawn into the warmth of his hut, he pushed his hands into his pockets then with head bent low walked quickly along the narrow alleyway between a row of tight-packed houses, tension easing only when he reached St James' Street, a less direct route to Chapel House. He acknowledged the diversion to himself. But with the church and graveyard occupying almost the length of one side and the rectory and school filling the other, it positively guaranteed he be unobserved; after all, a cemetery was the last place folk would choose to be on a dark night. Yet even going this longer way meant having to follow some short distance along the more frequented Holyhead Road, but the traffic of carts, wagons and trams had local people avoid it wherever possible and that suited his purpose admirably; as admirably as specifying the two evenings a week when there was no chapel meeting as the times when the Clews girl should clean the small house set at its rear.

As always his proposal was accepted and as always no question was raised regarding his satisfaction with her activities. '*I 'opes as how my wench be a doin' all as 'er should Mr Thorpe, that 'er work be pleasin' to y'self.*'

As he slipped into Queen's Place, moving silently past the darkened chapel, Thomas Thorpe's scathing reply laughed loud in his head. Yes thank you, Ada, your wench is proving very pleasing.

'I had to be certain it were you, I can't never be sure as it ain't me mum or one of the kids sent to walk me 'ome.'

Did she always have to say exactly the same thing! Dissatisfaction he had felt grow over the weeks reared in Thorpe as he looked at the girl smiling back at him.

Mousy hair, its dullness unrelieved by any forgiving gleam of copper or bronze, was shackled with pins coiling it tight into the nape of an overlong neck, that same severity causing her brow to appear wider while in contrast her mouth was small, the lips thin and uninviting.

No Deborah Marshall by any stretch of the imagination!

Cynicism added to his dissatisfaction.

Sarah Clews had none of that girl's prettiness or grace of manner . . . but then neither did she have Deborah Marshall's objections.

He locked the door he had closed behind him.

He had managed the whole business very well, he congratulated himself. He removed cap and jacket, placing them in a cupboard the size of which dominated the tiny entrance hall. He had bided his time, allowing mother and daughter to settle comfortably to the situation, remarking to Ada after each Sunday evening service how well the girl had done, what a good teacher her mother had proved to be.

The compliments had flattered the woman as intended. She had talked with friends, evidently enjoying letting them hear the praise being accorded herself and her daughter, how the girl *'be trusted wi' the run o' the place'*. But those later compliments paid directly to the girl the times he went to lock the home had not been heard by Ada.

'. . . *such lovely hair* . . .'

'. . . *what an attractive smile* . . .'

'. . . *you are such a pretty girl* . . .'

Lies, but they had resulted in considerable enjoyment.

Again he had played cautiously, a hand lingering on her arm, his glance holding hers a little too long each time she left for home, one devious ploy after another, deceptions sweet to her ear as honey to the tongue, drawing, luring her ever more surely into his web. When her whole attitude showed victory was his for the taking he had cast the final dice.

'. . . *as happened with your mother my own hours of employment have been extended, consequently* . . .' He had smiled ruefully. '. . . *we will have to discontinue the present arrangement; I'm sorry, Sarah, you can no longer come to Chapel House.*'

Crestfallen, she had stared a moment then almost sobbed, '*You mean y' don't want me.*'

'*No Sarah, I don't mean that at all, I do want you* . . . *I want you* . . . *very much!*'

This last was said in a low almost breathless tone. He had caught both of her hands in his, holding them while the look on his face had been deliberately despairing.

'*So why do you be sayin' we can't be goin' on? That arrangements be no longer suitable?*'

Gently, the perfect facsimile of an older brother reassuring a younger child, he had drawn her to him, his arms firm yet not imprisoning.

'*Sarah,*' he had murmured, his lips brushing her cheek, '*you have to understand the changes in my hours at the foundry mean I can only come to carry out my own duties in this house when you are here* . . . *and that is out of the question.*'

'*Why?*' she had snuffled against his chest, '*why be it out of the question?*'

With a soft laugh he had answered quietly, '*Your mother, Sarah, she would never hear of it.*'

She had drawn her head back to look at him, her eyes bright with defiant tears.

'*Then 'er won't hear of it cos we won't tell 'er, what Mother don't know won't 'urt 'er none.*'

'*Sarah . . .*' His hold had tightened, pressing her body close against his own, his broken reply a masterly art of barely controlled ardour. '*Sarah you . . . you would trust me . . . but can I trust myself?*'

As he followed her into the bedroom Thomas Thorpe's inward laugh was one of pure contempt. The rest had been child's play. She had believed that first time that his moral values made him loth to lie with her, that his hesitancy, his trembling breath, denoted a continuing struggle against the emotions of love.

Watching the cheap dress slide to the floor, petticoat, bodice and long-legged knickers following, he fought the desire to laugh out loud. This poor fool had believed him in love with her, so believed she had given herself, as she would go on giving for as long as he wished.

14

'What gives you that idea, lad?' Leah looked at the man standing in the doorway connecting living room to scullery, placing a pot on the table as she did so.

Would she tell him if he asked, would she admit to being unwell? Edward Langley felt the worry of the day pull even harder at his nerves. If Leah Marshall had a failing it was pride; would that pride prevent her telling of something being wrong?

Leah breached the interval saying firmly, 'There be groats and barley in this pot, there be carrot, parsnip and 'tater along of a nice piece o' beef cheek, what don't be in it is Edward Langley's tongue, in which case I'll tek it considerate if you was to answer when you be asked of a question.'

Experience had taught him that that tone of voice meant no more prevaricating yet anxiety about what her answer to his question might reveal made Edward hedge. 'Beef cheek ... mmm, acceptable, though I was fancying a nice dish of tongue.'

'Y'won't be fancyin' of this ladle about your shoulders but that be what I'll be dishin' out to you should y'be tryin' to pull the wool over my eyes so y'best set to words what it be I sees in your own.'

She had not been deceived; but then she had always been able to detect duplicity, and the years had not clouded that ability.

He said quietly, 'You gave me that idea, you've looked so tired these few days. I wondered were you . . . is there anything wrong?'

'Be you askin' am I sufferin' some illness then the answer be no I ain't, but tiredness, that I don't deny; the nursin' of that lad, the hours of sittin' through the night teks toll of a body young as well as old, it's teken it of Ann Spencer same as meself but illness,' Leah smiled, 'no lad, ain't neither the wench nor me be sufferin' no illness.'

Ann Spencer was not ill. Edward watched the delicious-smelling meal being ladled on to a plate. That was as maybe but he had seen more than tiredness on that face, and with the boy on the mend it could not be attributed to anxiety on his behalf. So what was the worry he could see sitting on her shoulders?

'Oh there y'be wench, I were about to ask Edward go call you in . . . the meal be the tastier for not bein' left to go cold.'

He had not heard her come into the scullery. Standing aside for Ann to enter the living room Edward noted the brevity of the nod she accorded his greeting. Leah Marshall was not easily deceived but neither was he; it was easy to see where he stood in Ann Spencer's esteem.

'I've got a meal ready at home.' It wasn't the truth but it would spare Ann Spencer the onus of his presence.

'Since when were a slice of bread and cheese preferable to a plate of beef cheek!' Leah looked up sharply from the plate she had set on her ancient wooden tray. 'You'll sit there my lad and eat of that meal, hmph! Bread and cheese indeed!'

The bang of the spoon and fork on the tray emphasised that she would brook no argument. Leah returned the pot to the hob, saying as she did so, 'I'll tek a plate to the lad.'

'No.' Ann reached for the tray. 'You have done enough today. Sit and talk with Mr Langley, I will take Alec his meal.'

'Be good of you wench.' For a moment it seemed Leah would take advantage of the offer but with a characteristic lift of the head she went on. 'But like I were sayin' a minute since, you've been on the go as much as me and though y'be many years the younger y' gets every bit as tired.'

'I can rest later.'

'We both can rest later!'

Leah's dogmatic retort brought a quiet chuckle from Edward. 'A word in your ear, Miss Spencer. Leah Marshall is a hard woman, she will argue the sun out of the sky simply to get her own way. Take my advice, and admit defeat while you have strength left to talk.'

'There be one more bit of advice needs be given.' Beside the fireplace Leah was rolling back her sleeves. 'Comin' the old buck gets a lad a leatherin' and big as you be Edward Langley you ain't too big to get your arse smacked!'

'What did I tell you, Miss Spencer.' Edward sighed in mock despair. 'Not only is a man accused of impudence but he's also threatened with a hiding.' He reached for the tray Ann was holding. 'Please let me take Alec his supper, help me get out of this room before my rear end becomes too sore to sit on.'

'Cheeky young sod!' Leah shook her head fondly. 'I swears young 'uns today don't 'ave no respect.'

Eyes that glinted with laughter locked momentarily on Ann's, then Edward pleaded in a theatrical whisper. 'Show a poor man a kindness miss, spare me any more of the woman's chuntering.'

'Chunterin'!' Leah's hands went to her hips. 'Now it be me askin' of you wench, let that rogue tek of that tray afore I gives 'im the true length of me tongue.'

Listening to the footsteps going upstairs Leah lowered herself wearily into a chair.

'He be a good lad.' She smiled over the plate Ann set before her. 'Kindness be Edward Langley's middle name.'

'You love him don't you?'

Leah nodded. 'Like a son. He were always that for me, more so after his mother were teken, God rest 'er. Oh, John Langley were a good father but the heart died inside him when he lost Miriam, then with news of Edward bein' missin' in action the man just give up the ghost. He were dead afore we got word Edward were found wounded but livin'. Deborah and me took on the seein' to Hill Rise 'til the lad were able to do it for hisself, I'd ever hoped him and Deborah . . .'

'I'd ever hoped him and Deborah . . .'

Ann poured the jug full of water in which a small piece of dried and salted calf stomach had soaked overnight into the evening milk Edward had emptied into the vat, hearing again as she did so those quietly spoken words in her mind. Sympathy ran like a tide in Ann. Leah had hoped for her daughter and Edward to marry – and he? She stole a glance at the tall figure carrying empty churns across the yard to the scullery. Edward Langley also must have wanted that marriage. His feelings for Leah's daughter, did they still run deep? Had love for her kept him from forming a relationship with another girl, might it prevent his ever doing so?

The last query stung so sharply it made her catch her breath. Ann stared at the swirl of milk. Such a question should not have her senses react in that way . . . it must not be allowed to affect her in *any* way. Thought of Edward Langley choosing to marry or not to marry could be of no concern to her.

No concern!

Ann met the smile of the man returning across the yard.
So why did it hurt so much?

'I'll be along in the morning to see to Leah's girls.'

The emotion of the previous moments prevented Ann from replying.

The lady wanted no conversation! Lifting churns he had helped scour on to his cart Edward smiled grimly to himself. Leah Marshall had been and still was like a mother to him. He loved her dearly and had been happy with the prospect she had put to him. Joining her holding to Hill Rise, becoming joint business partners would have provided him with a way of taking care of her. But Ann Spencer's presence in this house was already doing more for Leah than ever he could; she was a daytime companion Leah could talk with whereas he after completing his milk round was out in the fields until gone dark; and then in the evening and especially the long night hours the presence of that girl and the lad lent Leah the security of knowing she was not alone in the house. That was a security Edward Langley could not supply. He heard the words he knew Leah would say: '*A young lad unmarried! Livin' in the 'ouse of an older woman who be no relative! Whatever would folk say? Well I tells y' this Edward Langley, they won't be sayin' it of Leah Marshall.*'

Once the last of the churns was in place Edward felt the obvious truth of the situation. Ann Spencer could take the place of a daughter but with her aversion to him he must relinquish the idea of replacing a son. He bolted the tailboard of the cart into place, then took the horse's bridle, saying over his shoulder, 'Be sure to tell Leah I'll see to the girls.'

No goodnight, no smile? But was that not understandable? Sympathy rippled through Ann. Seeing a perfect stranger where his beloved Deborah should be. That he came to the house at all must demonstrate great strength of mind but nothing had power enough to keep that sadness completely hidden from his face.

'Leah's girls, does . . . does she always refer to cows in that way?'

It had come quickly. Ann blushed, knowing she had spoken not for the want of an answer but to have him turn to her before he left.

'Not all cows.'

He had turned to look her way but there was no smile.

Her question provided an opportunity for a few moments longer in her company. But though she had asked she had not looked at him, had not spoken with warmth. Edward told himself it would be less stressful for her and a whole lot less painful for himself to let that brief reply suffice, to leave without further word. But watching her now, the shadows of dusk kissing her cheeks, Edward Langley knew that was advice he could not follow.

'Leah has seen every one of that herd born right here on her own patch, named each even before it stood on its feet for the first time. I reckon they have helped her face the pain of losing a family, that talking to them while milking eased the loneliness. She looks on them more as friends than animals, p'raps that is the reason of her calling them "the girls"; but now you and Alec are here with her Leah isn't lonely though it's my belief she'll go on speaking of those cows as "girls".'

But I won't be here! The answer flashed silently in Ann's mind. Alec is well enough to be told . . . tomorrow I have to do as I promised those women.

Taking her silence and failure to lift her head as further proof Ann wanted only his departure Edward clucked softly to the horse, then as it began to move off said, 'Tomorrow, after the cows have been put into the field, I'll load the butter and cheese, give you more of a break before you set about deliveries.'

'I won't be making any deliveries, I have to leave.'

Barely a dozen yards from her the cart stopped abruptly making the animal whine a protest.

'You have to leave!'

Ann's fingers closed painfully about the wooden ladles. She had not meant her thoughts to be said aloud; but they must have slipped out without her realising.

'Why?'

No movement accompanied the word, the very stillness of the tall figure intensifying a silence already crushing Ann.

'I asked why?' It snapped like the crack of a whip. 'Why are you leaving?'

It felt wrong to be telling him before speaking with Leah, it felt like she was deceiving a woman who had been so good to her. But wasn't it better Leah heard a lie from her than hear from her customers they would no longer buy her dairy foods?

'You don't wish to give reason to me, that I can understand, after all it's no business of mine, but out of consideration for Leah p'raps you will tell me when it is you intend to leave so that I can adjust my work to fit with hers. I take it you have told Leah?'

He had turned towards her, the purpling shades of the evening accentuating the strong line of his clean-shaven jaw, emphasising the sudden tautness of the mouth, eyes bronzed by red-gold shafts of sunset gleaming with overt accusation.

It was obvious what he thought of her, every line of his tightly held body shouted condemnation. But he didn't know . . . he didn't know! Ann's glance dropped away.

'I see. You have not spoken to Leah, you prefer instead to just walk away, to turn your back on the one person who offered help when nobody else would; so yes, Miss Spencer I agree you should go, for with a friend such as you Leah certainly has no need of an enemy.'

Strange how words said so quietly could make her smart so much. Ann swallowed against the rise of emotion in her throat. But whatever Edward Langley might think, his words of reproach could not be allowed to sway her judgement. Leah's living must take precedence over all else.

Edward continued to stare. 'And the lad? What of him? Is he to go with you or do you plan to play the same dirty trick on him?'

'Alec, he . . .' Ann's cheeks flamed at this fresh accusation, '. . . he is not ready.'

'Which all fits rather nicely.' Edward's scornful jeer was harsh as that other had been soft. 'So he must stay here. In other words you can leave him to Leah. I wouldn't have your conscience Miss Spencer, but there I go making another mistake in thinking you have a conscience.'

The sting of that remark choked her for several moments. Ann made no reply then at his snort of derision lifted her head, her glance meeting that brown-gold stare. Coldness was her only defence against the savagery of his comments, a barrier holding back the press of hot tears, so she forced her answer to come calmly.

'Yes,' she nodded, 'you have made another mistake, the first being to assume I would go without explanation to Leah, the second that I would leave Alec behind, both quite without foundation. But allow me to point out yet one more of your mistakes. You presume insightful knowledge of the charac-ter of someone you have spoken with no more than a dozen times, an assessment, Mr Langley, I feel reflects clearly upon your own character.'

Shot with your own bullet, Edward Langley! Beneath the encroaching shadows of night Edward smiled admiringly. The girl was not without spirit, she was not afraid of hard work as hours in the dairy and then walking the streets of the town making deliveries had amply proved, yet she was ready to forgo the companionship of a trustworthy woman, give up the security of a roof over her head, the true reason for which she doubtless would not disclose to Leah.

He had provided the perfect opportunity for Ann Spencer to relate what instinct increasingly told him must have been said to her during her delivery round yet she had chosen to say nothing despite his deliberate provocation. There could be only one answer. Ann Spencer would not risk alienation between Leah and her customers, a situation which would harm not only Leah's income but friendships. That had to be the reason Ann Spencer was keeping silence even though it would result in homelessness for herself and the lad. His regard for her deepened. He called after the figure walking towards the house.

'Miss Spencer!' As she halted he went on, 'I should not have spoken as I did. What you choose to do or not to do is none of my affair but I take the liberty of believing Leah Marshall is. Her happiness and well-being are to me a prime consideration and though I may be judged guilty of more presumption I venture to say it is the same with you.'

Ann turned to look at him, smiling briefly as she replied, 'In that you have made no mistake.'

'Nor, I believe, will I be mistaken in what I say next.' He almost felt her stiffen with apprehension. Edward continued, 'A few moments ago I asked why you were leaving; you refused to give a reason so now I will give it for you. You would rather go from this town than have Leah's livelihood put in jeopardy by you and Alec remaining here.'

'How—'

'How do I know?' Edward's interruption was sharp. 'I might pretend to be a poor judge of character but I won't pretend to be a fool! A man with naught but muck for brain would have worked out what was meant by the words of almost every woman coming to my cart today, remarks I feared then alluded to something being amiss with Leah's health, an idea you and I both know to be wrong.'

Veiled in that strange half darkness of dusk, a shadow moved across the slightly open doorway to the scullery, unobserved by those it watched.

'. . . *I sees Leah Marshall 'as teken notice* . . .'

'. . . *what were said needed the sayin'* . . .'

Sheltered behind a half-closed door the dark shadow listened, its form shifting, pulling upward at Edward's words drifting across the yard.

'You recognise the meaning behind those words and so do I. They were the result of threats those women had made, warnings they would take their custom away from Leah unless you and Alec leave Wednesbury altogether. Is that not so?'

Wooden ladles clicked against each other in her tightening fingers as Ann glanced across to the house where a yellowed gleam of lamplight filtered from an upper window. Leah would be there in Alec's room; might she have heard what had just been said?

No sound issued from the building, no movement could be detected at the lighted window. Her suspicion was groundless.

Ann returned quickly, 'Leah must not know, she must never know! Please, I ask you Mr Langley . . . promise you will not tell her.'

No, he would not tell Leah. In a yard left empty after the girl darted into the house Edward's resolve echoed in his mind. He would not break the promise he had given Ann Spencer and neither would he break the one made to himself. Somehow, some way, he would find a means of keeping her in this town.

15

It was regrettable that his little enjoyment could only be indulged twice a week. Standing at the junction of Cross Street and the wider Holyhead Road Thomas Thorpe watched for the Clews boy who would call at Chapel House to walk his sister home. He would see the lad cross to the chapel and a few minutes later he himself would arrive, making it appear he came directly from the foundry. The ruse worked perfectly. Then why wouldn't it? Wasn't he the people's trusted preacher, the man who helped yet asking nothing of anyone in return? Well, perhaps not everyone. With a smile he moved to stand against the smoke-blackened wall of an end-of-terrace house as the boy he watched for came into view. When he was no longer to be seen Thorpe began the walk which would bring him to Chapel House. There had been no need of asking.

She had been eager as a bitch in heat and like any dog he had been ready to serve, as he would continue to do until a more desirable playmate came along. She would not be happy giving place to a prettier girl. The next one must be pretty; she must compensate for the times he had of necessity lain with the plain-faced Sarah Clews; and when he no longer wished to avail himself in that direction?

When that more attractive replacement was at his disposal Sarah would be told her 'bedroom' services were no longer required; as for her finer feelings? What did they matter? The girl was of no consequence.

A rumble of sound caught his attention; he glanced in the direction of the shrill clang of a bell then stepped back into a well of shadow cast by the line of terraced houses as a bus rattled to a halt. The one alighting passenger, a man dressed in flat cap, moleskin trousers tied about the ankles and a muffler looked neither right nor left but walked quickly the few yards to the Dartmouth Arms disappearing as rapidly through the lantern-lit doorway. A foundry man imbibing a nightly pleasure before going home.

Satisfied he had gone unnoticed Thorpe resumed his own short journey, his thoughts slipping back to pleasures of his own.

The girl was of no consequence. Meantime he would continue to 'sup the broth' which had been so conveniently made available, though it would be desirable were the 'broth' served more frequently. But a request for the girl to come more often could cause someone to enquire why with that house used only an hour or so a week for the purposes of chapel correspondence, it needed so much cleaning.

Correspondence! He almost laughed aloud. Letters written yet never sent, questions asked yet never relayed to church authorities. Coming into Queen's Place, staring at a building black against the deep grey of night, his pulse throbbed with an almost painful surge. He, Thomas Thorpe, was the ruling body of this chapel! That was the way it would remain as it would with the house; that would be used only by him, his private domain where he would continue to enjoy Sarah Clews' 'extra services'. As he had enjoyed them an hour ago.

Standing in the pool of deep shadow cast by the chapel walls it seemed he saw again the girl he had followed into that small bedroom, watched the garments slip one by one to the floor in a faded patched heap gathering about her feet, saw the openly inviting smile as she kicked away the repellently ugly bloomers.

Long gone was the shy casting-down of the eyes, the blush which said she knew what she was doing was wrong, the trembling breath, the uncertain half pull away as he touched her; now she stood naked, her arms stretched out for him.

Thinking it would add to the romance of the moment she had freed her hair of its pins but it hung in lank dull strips like dried wounds across breasts he found overlarge for his liking; Sarah Clews had nothing to his liking but then you didn't look on the shelf while poking the fire. And afterwards? Since her brother called to collect her it meant there was no time for 'afterwards'. It all worked well insomuch as the girl was willing and he had the use of her body.

Therein lay the fault!

He moved soundlessly around the side of the chapel pausing again as the small house came in sight, a lamp-lit window verifying the girl was still inside.

It was ease without satisfaction, the kind of satisfaction he would have had from lying with the prettier, infinitely more desirable Deborah Marshall. But she had thought herself too good for him. Too good! The daughter of a woman scratching a living from some half-dozen cows thinking herself above associating with the chapel minister! Well, she had paid for that lack of judgement.

But Deborah Marshall was not the only one who had made a mistake; Sarah Clews also held a wrong opinion. The fool! He snarled irascibly, the sound bouncing back from shadowed walls. She believed him in love with her. He stared at the house cocooned in the velvet dark of night. He held no more feeling for her than he might for a pig.

How long before he brought the girl's ridiculous fantasy to an end?

'Be that you Mr Thorpe?'

After replying to the lad come to walk his sister home Thomas Thorpe silently answered his own question.

He would indulge Sarah Clews' foolish misconception just as long as it took for someone better to come along.

So they would buy her cheese, continue to take her butter and cream only supposing she give Ann Spencer and the boy their marching orders.

With lips set in a tight line Leah Marshall tied the ribbons of her black bonnet.

There were conditions, requirements which must be met if custom was to be kept. No doubt Jinny Jinks were back of that, her and Lottie Hopcroft and Lord knew how many more were making demands. But Leah Marshall knew the answer those demands would receive.

She had not been meant to hear. It had been as she had come from seeing the lad settled after taking him supper. She had needed neither lamp nor candle to light her through a scullery she had spent half a lifetime in so her approach had gone unseen by the couple talking in the yard. It had not been her intention to listen, but as she was about to step outside she had heard Edward's words coming clear on the quiet of evening.

'*I sees Leah Marshall 'as teken notice.*'

'*What were said needed the sayin'* . . .'

Had curiosity made her hesitate at the threshold of that open door? Or was it rather an intuition that should the subject of discussion be something which would hurt her own feelings then in order to save her hurt neither Edward nor Ann would repeat it? With that thought in mind she had made to leave the scullery when once more Edward's words halted her.

'*I see you recognise the meaning of those words . . .*'

Meaning? She had frowned. Why would the wench recognise what were meant? Unless they had been said to her.

'*. . . they were the result of threats those women had made . . .*'

Threats! The word had held her motionless, only her brain whirling with its questions. What threats? Who had made them? Why when it concerned Leah Marshall had no woman approached her?

Edward had supplied the answer.

'*. . . warning they would take their custom away from Leah unless you and Alec take yourselves away from Wednesbury altogether . . .*'

So it weren't all due to the lad's illness. Of course that had the wench tense with worry but with her return from making yesterday's deliveries there had been a quietness about her, which was still there.

'*Leah must not know, she must never know . . .*'

The reply had reached to the scullery, the sound of quick footsteps running across the yard following her as she had returned upstairs to the boy's room.

Anger bottled up so long inside threatened to burst to the surface. Leah smoothed an irate hand over her long dark skirts. She had asked no question of Ann Spencer and none of Edward Langley nor would she ask any of Jinny Jinks or any other buying the products of her dairy . . . but that didn't mean those women would be left in any doubt as to the reason of Leah Marshall's visit.

Turning towards the cupboard from which she had taken her bonnet Leah looked at a woollen coat, instantly recalling the day she had purchased it from John Kilvert's pawn shop.

The sky had been leaden, great banks of grey cloud rolling together obliterating every vestige of blue, and the rain, herald of a storm, had held a softness, each drop gentle as the tears her children had wept. Joshua, not quite fourteen yet already tall and straight, walked to her right trying valiantly to hold back that outward sign of heartbreak. To her left Daniel, not yet so tall but as ever copying his brother, kept his stare resolutely forward while like his brother he was unable to stem the trickle of tears that slipped down his face: only Deborah, clinging fearfully to her mother's hand, had wept openly as they had walked behind a horse-drawn hearse. But she had not wept, not then. All that day she had bitten hard on the grief which had racked her since hearing her husband was dead, held the tears which for the sake of her children she had forbidden to fall as her life's love had been lowered into the grave.

She had hung the coat away. When the children were sleeping, when the house lay silent, she had hung it here in a cupboard of the bedroom she had shared with Joseph. Only then, crumpling to her knees, had the flood of grief overwhelmed her. When the pink light of morning had filled the room she had at last forced herself to her feet, to face a life without the one man she had loved, a life which for their children must be lived.

'*Stay beside me Joseph,*' she had whispered into the dawn, '*stay close my dearest love, let your strength help me raise our children, to see them safely wed.*'

She *had* raised them. Leah's fingers closed on the soft cloth of the coat. But Heaven's grace had not allowed she see them wed. Three more times she had donned the coat she had vowed that morning never to wear again. Leah closed the door of the cupboard. Three times more she had followed behind a hearse, had felt her heart shatter as her loved ones had been placed in the earth. Pray God He would not have her do so again. Perhaps if she had got rid of the coat after Joseph . . . maybe keeping it had tempted Fate and that was why . . .

Stop that, Leah Marshall! Glaring at her reflection in the mirror Joseph had hung above the small wash stand Leah admonished herself. That be superstitious twaddle an' you knows it! Weren't no coat responsible for the loss of Joshua an' Daniel, it were bullets fired by Germans!

Leah sighed heavily.

Joshua and Daniel, both killed by soldiers quite possibly as young as themselves, lads who were also fighting a war they had no likin' of; young men whose mothers lived as she lived, in the heartbreak of knowing they would never again hold those sons in their arms.

But it were no war had taken Deborah.

The swift stab in her chest made Leah try to block further thoughts but silent as predators they stole into her head.

No gun had been fired, no bullet had ended her daughter's life.

'*Drowned following a fall. Death by misadventure.*'

The verdict of a coroner . . . but not the belief of a mother!

Voices from across the tiny landing brought her back to the present. Leah breathed a long stabilising breath then, composing herself, left the bedroom.

'I be goin' along of Spring Head.' She turned to Ann who had followed her down the stairs.

'I, that is Alec and myself, we . . . we need to talk with you, there is something we have to tell you.'

'I be naught of a betting woman but I'd lay odds I knows what it be you an' the lad feel need of discussin'.' Leah tied the corners of her shawl beneath her breasts, answering at the same time, 'Well lessen it be vital important I'll ask y'waits 'til I be back, there be a bit o' business I wants to see to an' this evenin' be the best time.'

The wench had said no more of the matter, which Leah felt certain would prove to be her intention of leaving both the farm and the town.

Crossing the market square, dark and empty of stalls, the shops lining each side closed as was usual on the Lord's Day, Leah walked quickly. Although she no longer took part in the services held at the chapel in Queen's Place, she had not turned her back on the Lord. Prayer said in her bedroom would she knew be heard as readily by her Maker as those said in any building yet tonight she would speak to God in His own house.

Having turned left to enter the equally darkened street of Spring Head she paused before the imposing edifice of the much larger chapel there, beams of candlelight playing across its tall arched windows to flicker on the steps of an ancient horse mount block positioned against its front wall.

She would ask no blessing. What she planned to do later this same night would deserve none. Lifting the shawl to completely cover her head Leah walked into the building; she would pay the Lord the respect of admitting to the sin of revenge.

She had chosen to sit at the very back of the wide semi-circular room. Like the chapel in Queen's Place this was unadorned by the plaster effigies and carved stone statues contained in churches of other denominations, but held just a plain golden cross placed in the centre of an equally plain altar. But unlike its sister chapel this boasted a balcony which skirted both sides of a strikingly majestic organ.

What would Thomas Thorpe give to be minister of this place?

Immediately she crushed the thought and followed the familiar service. As it neared the end she had slipped quietly away, retracing her steps across a deserted market square, going now not home but to Queen's Place.

Thomas Thorpe was never one to miss an opportunity to spout forth. The last amen was barely said before he was up the steps of that pulpit like lightning, sermonising, moralising, playing the preacher for all it was worth. Leah snorted contempt. Where was the morality behind the talk of a young lad being a spy for the Germans? She need not look far for the answer. Thomas Thorpe's 'guidance', all his talk of serving the community, was no more than a way of planting ever more deeply the idea of him as minister. But he didn't fool Leah Marshall nor would he be fooling the Lord and where one could mebbe never call Thorpe to book the other most surely would.

But tonight she was grateful for the self-importance which would have the man delay the congregation those minutes longer, treating them to the benefit of his 'wisdom', minutes which had allowed her to arrive in time.

At the door of the familiar chapel Leah lowered the shawl covering her bonnet, then with a deep indrawn breath to bolster her resolve flung the doors wide.

16

Alone in Leah's tiny living room, a muslin cheesecloth she was sewing lying forgotten in her lap, Ann's mind replayed events following the older woman's departure on her visit to Spring Head.

She had not meant to sit with Alec. Although he was recovering well from his accident rest and sleep were beneficial. Knowing this she intended to chat while he drank the nightly cup of cocoa Leah ensured was always there for him but then as she reached to take the emptied cup his hand had caught her own.

'*Ann.*' Blue-grey eyes had looked up at her, concern bright in their depth. '*Ann, what is wrong? Why are you unhappy?*'

She had laughed a short brief sound, denial already on her lips, but before she could speak Alec had shaken his head.

'*No Ann.*' He had not released her hand. '*Do not tell me I am mistaken, I see in your eyes that there is something troubling you. Ann . . . is that something me?*'

She had been so caught up in her own problems she had not seen what was happening with Alec, had been blind to the look on that young face which silently asked again that same question: Is it me? She had shaken her head, saying quickly:

'*Alec, how could you . . . ?*'

'*Think such?*' He had smiled but there had been no laughter in those wide eyes. '*Ann, I am not of your family, yet I have allowed myself to depend upon you too long. I fear that is the source of the unhappiness I have seen on your face these past days.'*

'*Then you fear wrong!*' Her retort had come sharply yet even as she made it she had recognised its implicit indignation was really directed at herself, for being so preoccupied she had not seen what must have been there.

At her reply he had released her hand then as she had turned to leave he had spoken again, a quiet determination ringing in every word.

'*Ann, I am not a man but I ask you do not treat me as so young a child, do not shield me when doing so causes ill feeling between yourself and other people.'*

'*There is no ill feeling.*' She had tried to sound light but her lowered glance betrayed the falsity of tone. Alec had seen it too and suddenly in that benevolent smile she had felt as if she was the child and he the gentle understanding adult.

'*That is not the truth, Ann. Nor I think was the reason you gave for us vacating Chapel House. Had it been as you claimed, that you wished to move on to a different town, you would not so readily have accepted the offer to come here.'*

On the instant she was back in the living room of Chapel House. The room was in darkness, the one candle she had left scarcely challenging the deepening shadows while the fire of a few almost burned-out sticks made no impression on the chill of approaching night. She and Alec had walked the town all day asking at every likely house for employment for herself but nothing had been offered. Now Alec was in bed and she sat alone staring at the last of her money, coins glinting in the flickering candle flame.

Had there been a tap at the door which she, locked in despair, had not heard? Or had Thomas Thorpe simply walked into the house uninvited?

Ann watched the lean figure write an entry in the rent book, saw the lift of sly vulpine eyes, the thin lips drawn back. Then the book skimmed away and in the same moment a swift darting movement caught her into his imprisoning arms, that mean tight mouth crushing hard on hers, while the hand – she shuddered – the hand was on her breast squeezing, kneading and then . . . Oh God! It was clawing at her clothes!

'*Ann.*'

It had seemed to call from some faraway place she could not reach.

'*Ann!*'

Someone was calling her name. It had to be Thomas Thorpe. Nausea foamed like a tide in her veins, every atom of her wanting to be free of the threatened horror. She had pulled away, movement making the cup tumble from her hands.

'*Ann, I'm sorry, what I said was wrong. I have no right to speak that way.*'

Alec! It had been Alec calling her name. With a sob of relief she had pushed at the last lingering tendrils of fear though her reply as she retrieved the fallen cup had held echoes of its presence.

'*That was clumsy of me.*' She had tried to smile. '*Thank goodness it was empty. Leah would have wondered what was going on if her sheets were stained with cocoa.*'

'*Ann,*' Alec had called quietly as she turned to leave the room, '*why did we leave that house, was it truly a matter of money or was it the man who called to collect it? I know failing to find employment was a cause for worry but on the days he was due to call that worry became fright. Why, Ann? Was it that he threatened you in some way? Could it be he threatens you still?*'

That last word had halted her in mid step. Alec had said 'still'! Did that mean he had heard, might he know what

Thorpe had said to her in Chapel House . . . even worse, had he perhaps seen the man paw at her body? Shame had flooded her as she had turned to meet his penetrating look.

Seeming to stand outside of herself, Ann watched the figure at the foot of the narrow iron-framed bed, saw the glance drop to the fragments of pottery, the finger position and reposition the pieces, saw the boy propped against the pillows, his own gaze steady.

'*Mr Thorpe threatening me!*'

The figure she knew to be her own yet strangely felt to be no part of her had at last answered. '*That is absurd, Alec, why on earth would he! Of course being unable to find work was stressful, I was anxious there would not be money enough for future payment of rent which was why I was eager to accept Leah's offer. It meant both a home and employment, that is the only reason we came to live here.*'

A wisdom beyond his years shone in the boy's clear eyes, the reply he gave attesting to it.

'*In Russia also we have words for stress and for horror. I understand the meaning of both as I understand the difference. It was not simply unease I saw in you the days Thomas Thorpe called at the house, it was fear; it could only have been fear of him.*'

Had the look in her own eyes betrayed her? The pictures faded back into the vault of memory as Ann stared at the needlework in her lap.

Alec was young and not without courage. Like all boys he could act without thinking. Were he to find how accurate had been his assessment of Thomas Thorpe he might well confront the man.

'*. . . should I fail to get what is owed from one then I simply take it from the other; male or female, woman or boy, either is acceptable.*'

Thomas Thorpe had not spoken these menacing words merely to frighten, he had meant every one. He would vent his spite on Alec and that spite would take only one form. Rape! Nothing less would slake his desire for revenge.

Ann, shuddering, did not feel the needle prick into her thumb.

She had seen the way Alec had looked at her. He doubted the truth of her response that Thomas Thorpe posed no threat to her; in all probability he might ask Thorpe the same question directly to his face.

That could be disastrous. She could not stand by and let Alec walk headlong into the danger that was Thomas Thorpe.

As she stared into flames dancing beneath a quietly bubbling kettle Ann confronted one more difficulty. How, if Alec chose to remain behind in this house, was a meeting with Thomas Thorpe to be avoided?

The whole room had fallen silent, the entire congregation turning as one to stare at the figure in the open doorway. Leah's glance, though, rested only on the man in the raised pulpit.

Why was *she* here? Thomas Thorpe's pulse quickened. Ann Spencer! Had she told Leah Marshall that he molested her while she lived in the house behind this chapel? Had she spoken of the threat he had made against herself and the boy? Was that the reason Leah Marshall now stood at the door? It would not be unlike her to face him with it, to challenge him as to the truth in front of the whole congregation. Question, reason, cause, effect: like a maelstrom in his mind thoughts circled, each adding to the drumbeat pounding along every nerve. Should he speak, or would it serve him better to have the woman break the silence? Should he leave the pulpit, go to meet her? No, from here he could look down on the unwelcome visitor. She must come to him.

From the well of the room murmurs began to rise, increasing in volume as people voiced their own speculation, accompanied by enquiring glances in his direction. To say nothing would likely lead them into thinking as he had, that Leah Marshall was here to question what had happened in Chapel House.

Concealed behind the pulpit he drew a handkerchief surreptitiously from his jacket pocket, wiping palms moist with nervous apprehension.

Any mention of what he had said to Ann Spencer, any claim that he had tried to force himself on her, could be denied, dismissed as no more than malicious lies.

But most people in this room had known Leah Marshall all of their lives and those who had known her less long were all acquainted with her reputation: forthright, outspoken but honest for all that.

Mud sticks to the cleanest of clothes! Though accusation may not be believed the stain of it remains! He wiped his hands a second time. The slightest whiff of doubt could very soon become the pungent stink of gossip, tittle-tattle enjoyed regardless of its victim, and if Leah Marshall had come to denounce him he would be that victim.

A cold bead of perspiration trickled along his spine. He locked glances with the woman, who as yet had not spoken. Leah Marshall could destroy him, could have him replaced as lay preacher, and with that would go any chance of his becoming permanent replacement for the hoped-for minister. She had to be forestalled. She had to be prevented from damning him. But how?

'Come you in Leah, y'be welcome to a seat.'

154

'I thanks you kindly Ezekial, but my word stands now as when it were spoke, I'll set no foot across this threshold so long as Thomas Thorpe be among the congregation. But it don't be him has the bringin' of me here tonight.'

She was not here to speak of him! Relieved, Thorpe returned the handkerchief to his pocket.

He breathed thankfully watching Leah's glance move from him to sweep the seated assembly.

'It don't be just one will 'ave the hearin' of Leah Marshall's words.' Shawl held across her breasts, Leah continued loudly. 'They'll be listened to by all they hold meanin' for and though there be some among you for who they'll mean nothin' I meks no apology; this way, everybody hearin' the same leaves no room for addin's on and no tekin' away when it be talked of among y'selves. There be women here tonight who reckon to tek no more from Leah Marshall's dairy lessen it be delivered along of 'erself.'

Waiting for the buzz of whispers to die completely, she continued.

'I'll be namin' of no names though them who be responsible be well known to me. Mekin' conditions be their privilege, I owns to that; but it don't be theirs alone. Now they be goin' to hear what be the rights of Leah Marshall. There'll be not one ounce of cheese goes to them from my dairy though the keepin' sees it turn green wi' mould . . . not a single pat of butter nor a gill of milk will go from my house to theirs . . . what don't be fed to the pigs will be thrown along of the drain though the doin' of it brings the wrath of heaven down on my head.'

'Hey, 'old up Leah wench, y' can't go a doin' the like o' that.'

Ezekial's exclamation was immediately followed by a chorus of the same.

'Ezekial be right, Leah, y' can't refuse . . .'

' 'Er can't do such . . .'

'That be naught short o' wickedness . . .'

Then a woman was on her feet, her voice carrying over the rest.

'What Ezekial Turley says, what be said by all o' we, be Leah Marshall don't 'ave cause to threaten nor do her 'ave the right to deny folk, to refuse the sellin' of butter an' cheese; tell her, Mr Thorpe, tell her that don't be no proper thing to go a doin'.'

''Ar preacher, you tells her, you tells Leah Marshall her can't go doin' what her said, tell her it don't be proper.' A second woman championed the plea then dropped away as Leah turned a glance to the man standing in the pulpit.

'Well!' Leah met the silence. 'Don't you be goin' to do what be asked, don't you be goin' to tell Leah Marshall what be right? After all with you bein' a paragon of all that be proper who better to do it?'

She had afforded him no courtesy of title, had not addressed him as Mister nor referred to him as a representative of clergy. Beneath the veneer of calm an icy anger swept through Thorpe's entire body. Those words, 'a paragon of all that be proper', were a taunt, a deliberate attempt to draw him into a discussion, in which she doubtless intended to accuse him of abusing Ann Spencer. That was a trap he must avoid yet not to answer when the whole room was turned to him would very well bring its own accusation.

Caught in the crossfire of indecision Thomas Thorpe glared at the woman who was as much a source of fear as she was of irritation.

17

Leah Marshall had chosen her moment well. Timing her visit to coincide with the end of Sunday evening service, when every member of the congregation would be in the chapel, was well thought out; the perfect opportunity for her to place the facts of Ann Spencer's departure from Chapel House before them.

Facts! Facts were something she could not prove, but proved or otherwise, any accusation would be of no advantage to him.

'Answer 'er, preacher.'

The call of a man anxious for his supper-time ale was followed by another from someone equally eager to be gone.

'Ar, goo on Mr Thorpe, give Leah answer.'

He had to speak. A breath helped to allay the anger inside, the barest hint of a smile flicking his mouth. Thomas Thorpe looked across the room. 'I'm sure,' he paused, the bile of anger burning his throat, 'I'm sure Mrs Marshall cannot really intend withholding the produce of her dairy, I think—'

'Oh I intends all right!'

Thorpe's clenched hands relaxed. Intentional or otherwise the woman's sharp intervention had drawn attention away from himself, the call for him to answer forgotten by the people now watching Leah Marshall. That was how he would let it remain.

'Leah wench.' Ezekial Turley tapped his stick on the stone floor. 'I don't be knowin' what bee you 'ave a buzzin' 'neath that bonnet o' your'n but surely you be tekin' the catchin' of it a mite too far.'

'A mite too far you says Ezekial,' Leah answered immediately. 'And what of demandin' a wench leave the only place her can call home, demandin' her leave this town altogether and to tek a young lad along of her; threatenin' should that wench refuse the doin' then Leah Marshall's livelihood will pay the price: tell me now Ezekial, is that bee you talks of still tekin' too much catchin'?'

From his chair at the far side of the room Ezekial Turley answered, several shakes of his grey head lending emphasis to his quietly spoken words. 'Think Leah wench, goin' on as you say won't be of no benefit to you, the refusin' to sell what be med alone of that dairy'll gain you naught but 'ardship.'

Silent for a moment in which her glance played over the entire meeting before coming to rest on the woman as yet on her feet, whom she knew to be one of several responsible for the threat made against Ann Spencer, Leah replied with quiet determination.

'Then I must suffer it.' She stared hard at the eyes meeting her own. 'But the loss won't be all my own. I tells folk who knows my words be for them, try buyin' your butter and your cheese from William Rowbothom or John Craven or maybe Melia's grocery shops along of the market place, you might even try the Home and Colonial, but I thinks you'll find their answer to be, "sorry . . . we only have enough for our regular customers." Then there be milk an' cream . . . be it you visits Robert Hastilow's place in Oakeswell Street, Jeredik Slate in Upper High Street or mebbe Charles Babb across the way in Holyhead Road they all be dairymen though I'll wager you'll get no more than was got from them grocers; so then ask along of Samuel Spittle, he deals in butter an' eggs but were I you, I wouldn't be tekin' of no basket. But then it don't only be dairy food you be like to find your families havin' to do without, there be the question of meat. Y' see there'll be none of Betsy's litter of ten will go to Hollingsworth's slaughterhouse so it follows there'll be less pork, less bacon, less sausages an' less of all the rest that be got from a pig going to their shop in the town, and I don't have to go a tellin' you how many meals that be. Of course Hollingsworth butcher shop don't be the only one in Wednesbury. You can go along to Charles Hinton or John Field and if not them, then Thomas Mason, they all be close in the market place, but y'be like to find their answer also will be "Sorry, nothing to spare." What you seemed to forget when mekin' of your demands be the fact war has foodstuff less easy come by since so many men be called to the front . . .'

'Seems to me you've forgot a few facts!' An irate Jinny Jinks was again on her feet. 'Seems Leah Marshall be the one forgettin' we be fightin' a war, that things be 'ard enough for folk havin' their men killed wi'out her addin' to their worries.'

'Leah be acquainted with that. Sorry Jinny, her lost both sons to the war.'

'So her did!' Jinny's angry glance shot to the old man, his gnarled hands resting on a walking stick. 'And I don't be disputin' the pain o' that, but it be pain shared by many, Ezekial, some of who be grievin' for folk killed not on foreign soil but right here in Wednesbury, the night them Zeppelins dropped their bombs. You all remembers . . .' Jinny's look swept her audience. 'You remembers January the thirty-first.'

'Remembers clear.'

'Were a terrible night.'

'King Street, nobbut a stone's throw from this very spot, were all but demolished.'

'Ar, and the Crown Tube Works flattened, put men out of work did that.'

Fluttering like the wings of so many startled birds the mutterings grew.

'Tekin' work be bad but the tekin' of the lives of innocent children . . .'

When a sob ended another woman's lament Jinny Jinks grabbed the opportunity to continue.

'We all of we remembers that don't we Leah!' Her look flashed to the open doorway. 'None of we be like to forget Jemima Smith along of King Street, of her leavin' the house on hearin' a loud explosion; thought it were an accident inside the factory but when bombs started to drop behind of her, bombs comin' from a Zeppelin her seen shinin' clear an' silver in the sky, her run back home, Jemima run back to find the 'ouse naught but rubble. The bodies of Nellie, just thirteen years old, and Thomas, eleven, along of their father Joseph were brought out of the ruins that night but her youngest, Ina, barely past her seventh birthday, weren't found 'til next morning, found where her little body had been thrown by the blast of that bomb on to the very roof of the James Russell Works. But that don't be all of the folk who died that night, them bombs took ten more from this town as well as folk from Dudley, Tipton and Walsall.'

'Won't nobody'll go forgettin' that night,' Ezekial put in solemnly. 'But it were nineteen sixteen them raids was carried out, some two years gone, and ain't bin no other since so where be the point in rakin' over cold ashes?'

'Point!' Jinny pounced on the word. 'The point be them Zeppelins d'ain't go droppin' their bombs on no empty 'eath but right where them Germans knowed to be coal mines and factories, and how did they know? Cos they was told, told by a spy right here among we, a spy who'll do the same lessen we does summat about it; he'll 'ave them Zeppelins back to tek the lives of more poor folk.'

Ezekial rapped his stick impatiently. 'That be naught but scaremongerin'. We knows who it be Jinny be talkin' of an' I says her be wrong, that lad weren't in Wednesbury at the time them there airyplanes come.'

' 'Ow does you know!' The bit firmly between her teeth Jinny rounded on her opponent. 'Cos he d'ain't live here at the time don't mean he couldn't know of them mines, the iron and steel works; there do be buses and trains, he could've easy got hisself in an' out of the town.'

'A spy!' Derision vibrated in the snapped words as Leah turned a long deprecating stare towards the pulpit. 'I don't needs ask who it be helped Jinny reach them findin's same as I 'ave no need of askin' who it be set minds to thinkin' the young lad under my roof be a spy.'

She looked back to the quietly whispering assembly, glancing at each face in turn, as she continued. 'Leah Marshall won't be wantin' of no help with *her* findin's for they be already med and they be this. The lad and the wench along of him be remainin' at Leah Marshall's place so long as they be minded; so . . .' She glared intensely at the woman whose implied accusation had caused such a stir '. . . that bein' the way of it Jinny Jinks then you and any other folk holdin' any argument with that best bring it not to Ann Spencer nor yet to Edward Langley but to me. You all knows where I live.' Gathering the corners of her shawl Leah held them, her glance shifting from the suddenly silent onlookers to the lone figure in the pulpit.

'You all knows Leah Marshall's place,' she repeated, her look unwavering, 'but should it be Jinny, Lottie Hopcroft or any other feels the need of help putting thought into word then I be certain Thomas Thorpe'll be ready to give advice, ready as he ever is to fill folks' minds and mouths with whatever be useful to Thomas Thorpe.'

The last words provoked a series of sharp gasps around the room. Leah lifted the shawl, draping it to cover her bonnet, then turned and walked away.

'*There be summat I needs tell the pair of you.*'

Leah had looked up over her cup of tea.

'*I waited of you comin', Edward, for I wouldn't 'ave you thinkin' Ann had talked of that which her begged you say nothin' of. But it 'appened neither of you needed break no promise for I 'eard for myself. Don't be Leah Marshall's way to go listenin' to other folks' conversation but what drifted across that yard when I were comin' through the scullery, what you said about women no longer wantin' to buy from my dairy, then I considered it to be my business to listen cos I knowed rightly not you nor Ann would've said a word of it to me.*'

Leah had known yet had made not the slightest mention of the fact. Ann felt again a feeling almost of guilt at hiding something from the other woman. Even Edward's glance, his quick smile as if to say, 'I could have told you so; you can never hide anything from Leah,' had not entirely compensated.

As she fastened the buttons of the calico nightgown conscience burned warm again in Ann. On the first evening in this house Leah had brought her to this room, had taken the nightgown from the dresser. For a moment she had held it close to her breast, seeming to tremble, then she had turned but though the trembling had been mastered the pain in those gentle green eyes had not.

'*I couldn't 'ave the sendin' of these to the pawnshop.*'

Leah had smiled as she spoke but tears had sparkled and again it had seemed the ache inside would be too strong to let her speak. Then she had held out the nightdress.

'If it be you 'ave no quarrel with the wearin' then the things you'll find in this room be your'n an' welcome.'

She had left then, her quick footsteps on the wooden stairs seeming to Ann to be the drum of heartbreak she had glimpsed behind the threatened tears.

Her fingers pausing on the last of the row of tiny buttons Ann looked at her reflection in a small mirror. How much pain had it caused Leah to part with the belongings of a cherished daughter?

Now, Ann Spencer was adding to that hurt. Her own eyes seemed to accuse her from the mirror. It is right I should leave, Ann cried silently, staying here can only bring more unhappiness to Leah.

And what of Ann Spencer? The reflected eyes asked their own silent question. What of her unhappiness?

She would not think of that, she would not think any more of what had passed earlier in the evening.

Ann climbed into the neat iron-framed bed but even as she turned off the pretty blue-globed lamp memories began to live in her mind.

'There you 'ave it!' Leah's voice seemed to rise in the stillness. *'I told it plain, Alec and y'self bides in this house for as long as you be minded.'*

'We both know your kindness and we thank you for it ...' Ann heard her own reply. *'But Alec and I are agreed we cannot be the cause of any loss to your business.'*

Behind closed eyes Ann saw Leah shake her head.

'Loss!' Loud in the silence of the sleeping house the words returned. *'I won't be sufferin' no loss of business. Them women be*

easy led, they don't always 'ave the thinkin' of what be the outcome of what they say afore they says it, but they'll 'ave sense enough to realise that feedin' of their families be preferable to listenin' to rumours. Mark my words, that cart won't be bringin' back a smidgeon of cheese nor a scrape of butter; there won't be a soul among the lot of 'em will be refusin' to buy.'

Nobody would refuse! Ann opened her eyes on to the moonlit shadows of the room. Leah could not be certain her customers would not refuse her dairy food; she could not be positive the ultimatum given to the people gathered in the chapel would have the desired effect, also she could not manage both the work of the dairy and the delivery round on her own. Hadn't she said as much?

Should Ann stay the dairy would lose trade, should she leave then the dairy might be closed; either way Leah's living was threatened. Could she risk either happening to the woman who had been so kind?

Ann stared resolutely at the shadows dancing about the walls. Leah's livelihood would not be threatened by her leaving. There were girls right here on the woman's doorstep, the daughters of neighbours she could train in the dairy, girls already familiar with the streets and alleyways of the town. They would have those same deliveries made that much more quickly; and Edward Langley would also be here ready to help.

Lifting an arm across her face Ann tried to blot out the pictures from her mind but still they came. Darkness was no barrier to the light of memory; she watched the girl she knew to be herself carry the bowl to the yard, saw her empty the contents into the open channel feeding into a drain then stand, bowl in hand, her gaze going across the field where Leah's 'girls' grazed contentedly. But here in the silent solitude of her bedroom Ann knew it was not the cows that glance had sought but the tall figure of Edward Langley moving in the distance.

He had come bringing the evening milk yield from his own herd as usual, then stayed on to assist in the dairy, a practice not usual before Alec's accident. But now with Alec being well enough to move on would that practice stop?

The attempt to shut out the past failed to halt either picture or word, so Ann lowered the arm flung across her brow.

What mental imp of mischief had urged she ask that question when in her heart she well knew the answer? But she had asked it.

Her glance had followed the figure, watched it disappear beyond the gentle swell of land that was the beginning of Hill Rise Farm while the result of her question replayed vividly.

Edward Langley had turned from hoisting a freshly scrubbed milk churn on to his cart and for an instant it had seemed there was a pleading in those clear brown eyes. Then turning again he had resumed the task of loading the cart.

Her head pressing into the pillow Ann felt the sting of what had followed bite at her afresh.

She had thought the silence following her question to mean he would not reply but with the last churn in place and the tailgate of the cart safely bolted he had turned to face her a second time, his eyes now holding a very different look. Any plea she might have seen was gone, replaced by a detachment hostile in its coldness.

'*Miss Spencer . . .*'

His icily indifferent words again brought the chill they had produced when they had been said. '*Leah Marshall managed well enough before you came to live here and she will manage well enough after you are gone, a move I think would be best for all concerned were it done sooner rather than later.*'

There had been no handshake, no word of regret at a friend's leaving the district. He had not even smiled. A sadness such as she had not expected to feel had risen, bringing the choke of swift tears. Edward Langley had been so aloof, so impersonal in his attitude. But then what could you expect! Leah Marshall was as a mother to Edward Langley and he stood as one of the family she had lost; they were virtually mother and son so any feeling of regret must be for Leah, for her being let down by a woman she had befriended, taken into her own home when others of Wednesbury had turned their backs. That was how he viewed the matter; she, Ann Spencer, had let down the woman who meant so much to him and for Edward Langley that was unforgivable.

But there was no other way! The cry in her heart had winged silently after him. He had taken himself completely from her; whatever friendship might have built between them was over.

'*I think would be best for all concerned were it done sooner rather than later.*'

Edward Langley had made it perfectly clear. He would feel no loss at her going. But she? Ann closed her eyes against the surge of hot tears. She already felt loss, an emptiness that yawned like a deep dark well at the pit of her stomach.

18

He wanted her gone, out of this town, wanted the complete assurance none of this would be taken from him, something only her leaving Wednesbury would give.

Thomas Thorpe glanced about the small study, drinking in its simple orderly neatness, the well-polished shelves which would hold his books, the comfortable chair drawn to the equally cared-for table which would serve as his desk.

His! Chagrin burned in Thorpe's veins. This house, the chapel, and all that went with it belonged not to any stranger but to him. Thomas Thorpe should live here, Thomas Thorpe preach in that chapel, he and only he deserved to be minister. And he would be. Taking a long calming breath he glanced again about the room. With Ann Spencer gone there would be nothing to challenge his security.

He had intended she be spurned by those women, driven away as a result of their notions, ideas sown by him. Now the harvest was being reaped. But he would have preferred the process to take a while longer thus allowing time for him to reap his own reward, to enjoy in reality that which plagued his thoughts almost constantly: his rape of Ann Spencer.

But Leah Marshall's little tirade had taken that delight from him; her saying she would supply nothing to women demanding her lodgers be sent packing might have seemed like a threat which would make Jinny Jinks and the rest withdraw their own ultimatum but on reflection she would have realised the real threat was against herself. Without custom there was no business and without either business or family to support her it would be Leah Marshall would suffer most, and for all her championing of the homeless the loss of her own was something the woman just could not risk: and so Ann Spencer and the brat she had with her were probably even now well away from Wednesbury. A pity – he reached for the oil lamp lighting the small room designed to be the minister's study – but then where one delight was denied another was often given in its place. He would not now revel in feeling that girl's fear, seeing the hope die in her eyes as she realised resistance was in vain. Oh yes, he smiled to himself, Ann Spencer would recognise her master, she would do exactly as she was told. He would have her undress, slowly, one garment after another until she stood naked, then after his gaze had travelled over every trembling limb, after he had drunk in every inch of that desirable body he would have her remove his clothing, while his fingers would trace unhurriedly over those tantalising breasts, play for delicious moments with firm cherry nipples then, almost lazily, one hand would slide from between those firm little mounds down, oh so pleasurably down, to that enticing vee.

The picture imagination painted was clear and vivid. Thomas Thorpe's breath rasped in the silence but his ears heard only the quiet pleading sobs of the woman caught in his arms, the woman being pressed towards the bed . . . the alluring form spread-eagled . . . the tear-filled eyes begging then . . . Thomas Thorpe's veins sang a wild triumph . . . his own naked body lowering, his legs forcing those trembling ones even further apart. He dragged again at the air, a raucous grating sound, as his inner eyes watched himself drive deep between slender thighs.

Passion jerked his hand against the glass lampshade and snatched the vision abruptly away.

That was all he would have of Ann Spencer, that self-induced illusion of what had so very nearly been his!

His fist slammed down on the table, making the lamp rock precariously, but in his anger of frustration he ignored it.

It was all Leah Marshall's doing. She would be made to pay!

Revenge would be the salve easing the sting of disappointment. He would see her apologise, see her humbled, the pride of the woman destroyed.

Where would he require that recompense be made? He stared at the gentle glow of the lamp, a smile playing on his lips.

Where but the very place the warning of reprisal had been given? Leah Marshall would make retribution in the chapel.

But not from the doorstep!

She would be made walk the length of the chapel, stand at the very front of the room. There below the pulpit, the pulpit in which Thomas Thorpe stood, she would confess remorse to the entire congregation for her hasty behaviour.

An eye for an eye. Having that woman humiliated would go some way towards making amends but sweet as that would be it provided a poor substitute for that desire which even now dragged at his loins, a desire those evenings spent riding the panting unattractive Sarah Clews did not lessen.

There was another way to make Leah Marshall pay, one he would hold in store.

He turned off the lamp then walked out into the tiny hallway.

A means of ensuring the woman pain no apology could ever alleviate, not that Thomas Thorpe would ever have any intention of apologising.

The smile which had hovered on his lips deepened to a laugh in his throat.

Opening the door, he stepped into the night.

Thomas Thorpe would experience the sheer elation of telling Leah Marshall just how her beloved Deborah had died.

Thomas Thorpe froze, with the key in the lock. There was something nearby, something which did not wish to be seen. Breath snagged in his throat. Or someone? There had been no meeting at the chapel nor was this an evening when Sarah Clews came to clean the house so there was no reason for any member of the community to be here. An animal? He listened for sound, rejecting the idea when none came. A dog or a cat would have moved again, yet there had been no second movement.

He had been mistaken; it was no more than a trick of the mind. Those past few minutes, the thoughts he had enjoyed before leaving the study still had him a little unsettled.

They had been very pleasurable, especially— A sound close by made him glance towards the hedge. Was that a mistake?

Tension once more caught his breath as he stared harder into the line of the hedge. There it was again! A little further along branches swayed as from a sudden push, the movement sprinkling moonlight like silver sequins on to leaves night had painted black. However it was not that delicate moonlit ballet which held Thomas Thorpe transfixed but fear, cold and stark.

It was no animal moved among those bushes. The metal of the key bit hard against the pressure of his fingers but he ignored the sting.

No animal, so a person. But who? And why hide in the hedge? It seemed he rocked back on his heels when the answer came thudding into his brain.

Sarah Clews! The stupid cow of a girl must have told of their affair, spoken of what took place in this house the evenings she came to clean. After all he had said! A blade of anger twisted inside him. How many times had he said it must remain hidden, that she must not speak of it to anyone until he said she might? With each telling he had coated the subterfuge with the sugary lie that their love was so special he would have them keep it to themselves a while longer. But the dolt of a girl had not kept it to herself.

Love! The word snarled in his head. Sarah Clews was as much fool as she was whore to believe Thomas Thorpe in love with her.

But was she the fool he thought? Had she after all seen through his lies? Had she guessed at the true reason why he had insisted she tell no one? Had she recognised that she simply served the purpose of satisfying his lust and so to make sure of him had revealed all?

Stupid bitch! He swore silently. Sarah Clews was stupid as she was plain but her parents would not be so easily taken in, they would want wedding bells and that figure stepping from the shadowed hedge was Arthur Clews come to make certain they would ring.

He had pretended the key had fallen from his fingers, had bent close to the ground as though retrieving it but instead his hand had closed over a sizeable stone bordering the strip of flower garden. The figure had continued to come towards him, the crunch of feet on the gravelly ground matching the grinding beat of his nerves, yet somehow he had controlled the urge to run, had forced himself to prolong the pretence of searching for the key. Then, when the figure was almost at his side, he had sprung to his feet, in the same instant swinging the stone hard against Arthur Clews' head.

Run! His mind had turned in wild circles as the figure had dropped to the ground. Then as the stone had fallen from his hand caution took the firmer voice. *No*, it had said quietly, *no use to run, Clews knows who struck him, he'll come after you.*

Come after you ... come after you ...

It had rolled like thunder in his head and between each boom had come the thought, *He can't come for you if he's dead.*

Like a douche of ice water it had steadied his panic, letting him think coldly and rationally.

There would be no one who could point the finger of blame at Thomas Thorpe; he had not seen the man, he had not been at Chapel House that evening. He must remain calm, let that be the answer he would give to any enquiry made by the police.

And to the chapel community?

He smiled at the answer springing at once into his mind.

Mr Clews had maybe gone to the house in order to discuss the job of erecting an extra kitchen shelf but seeing no light from the window he had realised Thorpe was not there. Then a sound had possibly caught his attention so he had made to investigate, and that was likely when an intruder had attacked and killed him.

It was feasible, as was the next thought entering his mind.

Should Mrs Clews try to press the same demand he would see her hailed as a liar, a woman so determined to conceal the misdeeds of a wanton daughter she had concocted a story she hoped would trap the one man compassionate enough to offer the girl marriage sooner than see her disgraced.

He would not stand in the pulpit, he would not speak from before the altar table but sitting at the centre of the group, one with the people he served.

He saw the picture in his mind, heard his own soft, halting, forgiving voice.

With hands clasped together in his lap, his head lowered but not so much as to hide the pucker of distress furrowing his brow, he would whisper he would bring no charge against Ada Clews, that terrible though the lie was the girl's predicament was worse still, that he would pray heaven forgive her sin and forgive that of her mother.

Caught in the moment Thorpe's smile broadened as he watched the brilliantly clear picture in his mind.

Oh Lord forgive! Lord forgive!

The low cry was consummate deception, treachery that laughed in his ears as would the rest when 'heartbrokenly' he would murmur seemingly to himself, was Ada Clews by way of accusing him regarding the girl's licentious behaviour? Was she seeing in their caring lay preacher a man so charitable he would accept all blame? A man merciful enough to marry a girl who would otherwise be the object of shame?

People who knew him – or rather who *thought* they knew him – would swallow every word. He wallowed in his own ingenuity. Ada Clews and her less than becoming daughter would have their allegation thrown back at them while Thomas Thorpe was applauded for the generosity of his forgiving, he—

A low moan interrupted the illusion, a cry which when repeated louder shattered his fantasy. No one must know of his being here tonight.

But Arthur Clews knew!

Drawing one long breath he picked up the stone.

19

She had tapped several times at the door, thinking at first Alec had overslept. They had talked together long into the night when she repeated again that it was not because of him they were leaving Leah's house, but despite her assurance his demeanour as well as his own argument had indicated he believed otherwise.

'*I believe that is the very reason, Ann.*'

As she stood at the bedroom door words he had spoken the previous evening returned to her mind.

'*I also believe the same will happen wherever we might go together. I am a foreigner and as such cannot be accepted.*'

She had denied that, pointing to the fact Leah, Edward, Ezekial Turley and some of the people they had delivered dairy food to had accepted him. Besides, she had added with what she had hoped to be a convincing smile, you will find the people of Darlaston will not be so prejudiced. She had gone on talking quietly so as not to disturb Leah sleeping in the next room, talked of her childhood with her grand-mother, how the folk there would remember her and make them both welcome. At that he had smiled and closed his eyes and she had gone to her own room praying earnestly while preparing for bed, imploring heaven it would be as she had said; yet even as sleep touched her eyes she had feared it would not.

When a second slightly louder tap brought no response a frisson of alarm flicked at her senses. Perhaps those hours of discussion had overtired him; he had given himself hardly enough time to recuperate from that fever, perhaps he was ill again. She had opened the door then, calling his name, allowing a minute before stepping into the bedroom, in case he was dressing. But there had been no reply.

Standing in Leah's small yard Ann stared across the field dotted here and there with grazing cows, their brown hides gleaming polished mahogany against grass whose lush emerald hue shone with dewdrops glittering like a million diamonds.

Busy coaxing the sleeping fire to a glow, setting the porridge pan over it, Leah had dismissed any cause for concern with the reminder that Alec liked to spend time with the horse, to brush and feed the animal before the start of the day's work.

'*Leave the lad to his pleasure, it's been days since he were out there so let him enjoy it while he can.*'

Leah's words had sounded again in Ann's mind. Ann had felt the heartache beneath the smile, the same sadness which had underlain last evening's discussion in which Leah had declared it was to be Alec's and her own choice that they left.

But it was not by choice. Neither she nor Alec wished to go but for Leah's own sake they must.

Every second spent setting bowls, spoons and milk on to the table had seen her worry build until she had almost run from the room to call Alec to breakfast.

She had seen at a glance he was not in the yard. The cows, having been milked, were drifting steadily from patch to patch of the meadow, the milk cart though standing ready beside the dairy had no horse harnessed to it, even Betsy and her piglets had seemed strangely quiet. She had stood waiting in the hope that he would suddenly dart into view then with a flick of alarm she had begun to run.

She had gone to the stable, knowing as did Leah the boy's affection for the horse; it was there he would spend time when feeling particularly down, talking to the animal as though it understood. She understood. In an instant Ann was back in St Petersburg, in her father's drab little house. Drawn back to her own unhappiness Ann seemed to watch again the silent figure sitting opposite a young woman at the dining table of a poorly lit room, the fire in a stone grate barely alive; watched as the man ate then rose and left without a glance at his companion. Her father had been in his own kind of hell. Ann stifled a sob. But she too had walked its dark halls, known the misery of loneliness, of being unwanted by the one who should have loved her most. That had been heartbreaking but she had hoped her father would eventually 'see' his child, talk with her, allow her to be the daughter she so wanted to be; with his death hope had also died and in place of heartbreak had come utter desolation, and with it a fear of the unknown, the harrowing distress of being entirely alone in a country whose language you could neither speak nor understand. The assurance of coming home to the comfort of a loving grandmother had been her mainstay, the one beacon in the gloom of misery: yet even that had been snatched away, leaving her feeling empty inside.

Was that how Alec felt? Was he feeling empty, isolated from all he had known, so desperate to find his own family again he had run away?

I tried, Alec, I tried to be a sister to you. Ann's cry was silent on her lips; friendship could not replace love of a family.

Yet she had grown to love the boy whose hand she had clung to during that terrifying attack by armed horsemen, the boy she had held close so many times during the journey to England, and though she knew he held regard for her she recognised that deeper feeling which must be drawing him home.

'Be the lad there in the stable?'

Leah came from the dairy with a pail of whey in her hand. She frowned at the look she saw on Ann's face as she walked back to the yard, a shake of the head her answer.

'Don't be like him to go leavin' the house wi'out a word.'

Leah shifted the pail to the other hand. 'Like as not I'll find him chattin' away to Betsy an' her brood when I teks this along to the pig pen; he'll be sayin' of his goodbyes to the place. I knows cos . . .' she breathed a quick deep breath, 'cos that were what my own two lads done afore leavin' for the Army.'

Watching the woman walk across the yard, dark skirts almost brushing the ground, button boots crunching the pitted surface, her body bent to one side beneath the weight of the heavy pail, Ann felt her own heart trip.

That Leah Marshall had genuine affection for Alec was beyond question. It showed in her face when she looked at him, in her every action towards him. Had he come to mean the same to her as did Edward Langley? Was he, like Edward, helping ease the hurt of losing her own children?

If only she had known! If she could have guessed the bond which would form then she and Alec would not have come to live in this house, to bring its owner fresh grief.

Alec had not returned to the house. Ann stared dejectedly across the expanse of open heath. Her body felt like she had walked for a lifetime, her feet and legs aching from the hours of searching streets and alleys, her throat dry from the enquiries made of everyone who would stop and speak with her. Not one of the few said they had seen a boy answering Alec's description.

She had refused Leah's suggestion, made after an hour of waiting for Alec to return, that they go search for him together. Leah needed to look to the dairy; cheese and butter did not make themselves and though maybe not so many folk would be visited by the delivery cart there were some that would, people like Ezekial Turley. He had been sorry to hear of Alec's disappearance and had even gone so far as to express the same on hearing that she and the boy planned to depart from Wednesbury.

'*Fools!*' The old man had spat his contempt. '*They all be no more'n fools thinkin' as they does; why even a body wi' no eyes could see that lad be no threat, not to nobody he don't!*'

Not foolish, only afraid. As they had every right to be. Leah had talked of those dreadful Zeppelins, of the fear which had grabbed people by the throat, mounting to terror as one after the other bombs had dropped. Then with the raid over and the giant aircraft gone a silence had seemed to settle, a silence the last fall of brickwork, the crackle of flames had not penetrated. Shock, utter and terrible, had lain like a pall over the streets until . . . Leah had hesitated as though to speak more of that awful evening was too much. But after a few moments she had gone on to say that the cries of Jemima Smith finding her family lying dead among the heap of rubble which only minutes before had been their home, cries echoed again and again as others discovered their home destroyed, their loved ones killed were more freezing to the blood than even the thud of bombs. But fear had not ended with the departure of that Zeppelin for at around midnight a second one had passed over the town dropping more bombs.

'*There be no understandin' of it,*' Leah had repeated. '*That there Kaiser be a relative of our own King, it ain't like he be out and out foreign; ehh! There be no trustin' of some folk.*'

Alec too had listened to Leah's account of those raids and in his mind must have concluded foreigners were not to be trusted.

'*I am a foreigner and as such cannot be accepted.*'

That was what he had said last night and that was why he had left by himself.

'That can't be true of everywhere, we would have found a place!'

Ann's sharp cry sent a flurry of crows winging into the air cawing loudly and censoriously, black wings flapping like the dark cloaks of some approaching menace. Beneath the clamour Ann whispered, 'Where are you Alec . . . where are you?'

'It be good of you to come lad, I knows how busy you be seein' to your own place.'

'Never too busy to come to see you.' Edward Langley watched the woman pouring tea into stout earthenware cups, cups which reflected her character. Leah Marshall had always been strong-minded but with that came integrity and honesty; she would never call a teaspoon a shovel just to have something suit her purpose.

'I hear you made the rounds yourself this morning.'

'Then you d'ain't hear no lie.' Leah handed a jug of fresh milk across the table. 'It were best I took the cart meself, that way I got to hear first-hand any comment Jinny Jinks and others wi' the same judgement might have to say.'

'And did they have anything to say?'

Cup halfway to her mouth Leah smiled grimly. 'Well it certainly weren't "thank you", not from some for they got naught from the cart; but sayin' naught to my face don't mean them women be lost for words the minute my back were turned. It be my bet their tongues'd be red hot afore I got back here.'

Gossip was something Leah would pay little thought to but her livelihood was something she couldn't afford to ignore. Edward stirred milk into his cup while thoughts which had occupied his mind while walking here from Hill Rise recurred. Leah was steadfast in her sense of fair play and though that was admirable it could not be allowed to deprive her of a living; yet – he sighed mentally try – telling her that and he could find himself turfed out of the house with his ears ringing.

'I looked in on Betsy as I came up.' Tact took him on an indirect route. 'She's looking to her young ones well enough; they'll soon be of a size with their mother.'

'Betsy be a good sow,' Leah agreed, 'her litters proves that, they be allowed a fair share of the whey I pours into the trough.'

'Speaking of which I wouldn't mind a few minutes' ride on that queedle.'

Leah placed cups beside the ancient brown teapot on her equally aged wooden tray, staring down at it as she did so. Edward Langley had not walked here simply to take the evening air nor because he fancied queedling cheese curds; he had come out of concern for her, concern no doubt aroused by hearing from his own customers the fact of Leah Marshall's reduced sales. In that case there was no use in beating around the bush, not that she indulged in that practice at the best of times, so better to say what had to be said. Leah followed her own advice saying determinedly:

'Be no queedlin' needs doin' tonight nor none tomorrow night and to save you the askin' I'll tell you it don't be no fault of the "girls", they've given good a yield as they always does.'

The cows were giving their usual amount of milk! The whey he had seen Betsy and the piglets nose deep in! No queedling pointed to one thing: no queedling so no cheese-making. Anxiety flicked along Edward's veins. Had today proved the work of dairying too much? Had it caused Leah to admit to herself what she would not admit even to him? That she had been given no help since early morning when he had loaded trays of butter and cheese on to the cart, that she alone had done all the rest needed no putting into words; lines of fatigue etched on her face expressed the fact clearly enough. So his ears might ring! He pushed away from the table, but if he said nothing, if he let things continue as today then conscience would clang louder.

He took the tray and carried it into the scullery, saying as Leah followed, 'You say the "girls" have produced their normal amount of milk which if my eyes haven't deceived me Betsy and her brood have enjoyed the majority of and if there are no curds to be queedled then it seems likely the milk from Hill Rise has also gone into the trough. I've never known you to waste a single drop, yet here you are feeding gallons to the pigs. Why? It can't be a couple of days being down on sales is the cause.'

'Ain't no use to mek what don't be like to sell.'

The exasperated bang of the tray on to the wooden board by the shallow brownstone sink took her by surprise. It seemed in that moment Leah looked into the face of her husband, heard the chiding tone his voice held whenever he feared she had worked too long.

'That's an excuse and you know it!'

'Joseph,' she reached out a hand, 'no cause to fret.'

'Leah!'

'Joseph.' Her reply came as a murmur. With a smile soft on her lips Leah stepped into gentle shadow, into the arms of the man she loved.

Had he come this way? Ann stared across the heath, its wide spaces falling captive to the dusky vanguard of night, imprisoning it in its own dark secretive world.

Had Alec crossed the heath despite Leah's warnings that the whole area was riddled with disused gin pits, shafts dug into the ground by men mining coal only to be left unmarked and uncovered when they became too deep for a man to work alone? '*Nobody knows how many be sunk nor the places they lies, it only be known they waits 'neath a coverin' of bracken, waits for any poor soul steppin' in the wrong place.*'

Leah's warning echoed in Ann's mind. Had Alec fallen into one of those gin pits, was he lying out there injured, terrified?

Sheer desperation blinded her to danger as Ann forced her aching legs to move, forced herself to run until a straggle of bramble caught at her foot and tripped her to the ground.

This was not the way to search. The force of the fall cleared her mind, making Ann look at the foolishness of what she was doing. She had no more knowledge of the heath than Alec; she was just as likely to fall victim to a concealed gin pit and if that happened!

But it would not happen. After scrambling to her feet, brushing at skirts she could hardly see in the weakening light, Ann turned determinedly back the way she had come.

Alec was no more welcome to the people of Wednesbury than was she but however great their distrust they would not leave him frightened and alone. An organised search was required: she would knock on every door, ask every man, beg if that was what it took; somehow she would get them to scour the heath.

20

'How can you deny it? How can you deny you used Leah for your own ends, that you came here for one reason only. Miss Ann Spencer has concern only for one person: herself.'

'I had no intention . . .'

'Exactly!' Edward Langley banged a closed fist against the wall, setting an assortment of dishes and cups rattling in their places on Leah's plain wood dresser. 'The only purpose you had in mind . . . that you *ever* had in mind . . . was that of finding someone to take that lad off your hands, somewhere to leave him so you could go your own way; it didn't matter to you the woman you found was already burdened down with work that had her on her feet from sunrise 'til the early hours of the next day.'

'That's not true,' Ann broke in on the tirade, 'Leah knew . . .'

'Oh yes, Leah knew.' His clenched jaw stemmed emotions blazing in the depths of him. Edward turned, the very slowness of the action emphasising the effort it took to speak quietly. 'She knew you would not settle for life here, for the hard work that goes with running a farm and a dairy, but having that knowledge did not prevent her taking you into her home, nor has it prevented her risking the loss of her living: huh!' He shook his head in condemnation. 'Now you have the gall to come back after sneaking off without so much as a word. Why is that? Your next victim not so easy to find as you had thought?'

'I did not—'

'Enough! I don't want to hear! Your lies don't impress me.'

Ann's whole body stiffened. Head high, eyes like blue ice, she looked across at her accuser, her freezing reply cracking like hailstones.

'And your attitude, Mr Langley, does not impress me. I have no reason to explain my behaviour to you and I have a deal less reason to excuse it; I would ask you to remember what I do is my own business, it has nothing whatsoever to do with you.'

Edward stepped closer to the table. Leaning both hands on it he stared at the girl who aroused emotions in him he would not admit, his answer when it came spat from tight lips.

'Nor would I desire it to have. You, Miss Spencer, mean nothing to me where Leah Marshall means everything.'

'I love her too.'

'Love!' snapped Edward. 'If what you have displayed today is love then God save us from it.'

Ann hid the hurt she felt at his harsh words. She returned quietly, 'God is merciful Mr Langley, He hears all our prayers; but the one you make now will not require heaven's intervention for you will never be the recipient of Ann Spencer's love.'

The tension vibrating along Ann's every nerve quickened further as she caught his brief frown saw the shadow darken his bronze eyes almost to black, heard the swift intake of breath as though from a man in pain. Then as quickly as they had come each reaction was gone, leaving Edward Langley's features once more cold and impassive as he straightened up from the table then turned away to cross the small room to stand at the fireplace. The slight limp which marked his gait seemed more pronounced as though the pain she had imagined briefly etched on his face was somehow transferred to his wounded leg, and as he rested a hand on the mantelshelf, his head lowered to stare into the drowsy fire, Ann felt guilt twine with the fear which that encounter in the street had knotted about her stomach. If she had called at Hill Rise, told him she was searching for the missing Alec, explained it was with Leah's full knowledge and approval, then he would not have been subjected to even more concern for the woman he loved, or perhaps not been so angry with one he did not.

'Mr Langley.' Ann saw the hand touching the mantelshelf clench, the shoulders stiffen. Edward Langley was already rejecting any explanation, yet she went on, 'I left the house this morning . . .'

'Of course you did!' Edward's quiet intervention dripped condemnation. 'You left regardless of anyone or anything, you had no thought for Leah, or the fact she might need help.' He stared a moment longer into the fire then turned as he added, 'You can leave now with no further thought. Leah Marshall won't be needing your help any more.'

'The wounds of sorrow cut deep, they lay their scar across the heart . . . shadows lie along the path, sadness and fear wait in their depths.'

Words murmured by an old woman then interpreted by a priest crept silently back from the past into Ann's mind as she looked at the still figure lying beneath the smooth unruffled counterpane, the grey head barely denting the brilliant white pillow.

'*. . . sadness and fear . . .*'

How right those words had proved. The heartbreak of her mother's death, the misery of rejection by her father, the devastation on learning of her grandmother's death, the utter desolation which had come with being totally without family: all had laid their scars and now a new one cut its jagged path.

Ann dropped to her knees beside the bed. 'I wanted only to find him,' she murmured, 'but I didn't, I searched but there was no sign and now he is . . .' A sob caught in her throat as she covered her face with her hands, an almost silent whisper squeezing between her fingers. 'So many failures . . . Father, Alec, and now you; each put trust in me but I couldn't live up to it, I let everyone down and especially you, Leah; no wonder Edward is so angry with me. He is right to be but he is wrong in saying I care only for myself.'

Ann knelt a moment longer then pushed to her feet. She looked at the woman she had come to care deeply for, at the face time and unhappiness had painted with lines.

'*The wounds of sorrow cut deep, they lay their scars across the heart.*'

Ann listened to the echo in her mind. Leah Marshall's heart bore many scars; would Ann Spencer inflict one more?

'No . . . please, not that! I love you Leah, I never wanted to hurt you.'

The door opening on to the stairs was flung wide and Edward Langley heard in the stillness of the tiny living room Ann's heartfelt 'I love you Leah', words immediately followed by others which cut to the soul of him: '*You will never be the recipient of Ann Spencer's love.*'

At the sound of footsteps on the stairs he turned again to the fireplace, his own words silent in his heart. You will never know you have Edward Langley's love.

She had thought he had left for Hill Rise so could not prevent her quick gasp which she realised must have sounded more one of fear than of surprise. Edward Langley had noted the same; had that been the reason for the look in his eyes as he swung to face her?

Sitting fully clothed in the bedroom Leah had allowed her to use Ann stared blindly into blackness, the only sound in which was that of words spoken in her mind.

'*You best stay here; Leah wouldn't want you walking the streets at night.*'

'*Leah wouldn't want . . .*'

In a stillness so intense it seemed the whole world had somehow disappeared, leaving her in a void of silence, the words rang in Ann's brain and behind them the sting of his apparent lack of concern.

'*Things over at Hill Rise will take no harm 'til morning so I'll stay on; I'll milk Leah's cows then go see to my own.*'

He had dropped into the chair Leah kept drawn alongside the hearth, his eyes closing in dismissal, obviously wanting no more to do with the woman who had betrayed the trust of a friend.

But I didn't! Ann's heart cried its misery. I didn't betray Leah's trust, she knew the reason.

He could have known it too. Logic spoke coldly. She could have explained to Edward Langley, told him she had left to search for Alec.

'*. . . your lies don't impress me . . .*'

Was that why she had made no further attempt to explain? From fear of hearing that same rebuke?

In the shadows of the room it seemed to Ann she saw the face of an old woman regarding her across a bed in which Alec lay trying desperately not to cry out in pain.

Her body taut, her hands clenched tightly together, Ann tried to ward off the spectres of memory. A hand grasping her arm; an urgent 'the promise of my friend'; the crack of a pistol shot; then another followed by the plop of something heavy dropped into the sea; the disparagement of the officer who had brushed aside her protest at being told she must leave the ferry; the indifference of the sailor pushing her roughly on to a rowing boat; the cry of the boy at her side being snatched back then dropped into the boat as the same sailor knocked aside the hand grasping Alec's coat sleeve.

There had been no time to ask if the man reaching for Alec was a relative, someone who had been meant to meet him at the port. No time even to glimpse the face of the figure being swallowed by darkness.

Alec had landed in the boat, only her own swift action preventing him falling overboard into the freezing water.

They had huddled together, her arms holding him close, his face pressed to her shoulder as she leaned across him trying to protect him from wind-whipped spray flung like daggers of ice against the skin. It had seemed the crossing would never end, that waves tossing the boat like a cork must surely overturn it, throwing its occupants into the black depths. Then at last with the firmness of land beneath her feet she had thought the ordeal was ended, only to real-ise as each of the people ordered from the ferry melted rapidly into the darkness one more trial had been replaced by another.

Beyond the bedroom window a shaft of moonlight flashed its splendour across the room endowing it with silver brilliance, and in its glow Ann seemed to see two figures each barely able to stand against a wind screaming demonic fury, while others hurried away intent on escaping the savage frenzy.

Not one of those erstwhile passengers answered the query regarding lodgings, a place of safety for the remainder of the night.

They stumbled together up the steep incline leading from the water's edge. Ann watched them struggle against the force threatening to throw them back into pounding waves, watched as they came one by one to the dense shapes etched on its summit, unlit buildings where she got no reply to repeated knocks.

Ann lived again the horror of a night spent in the lee of what had proved a church, hours which had seen her slowly lapse into semi-consciousness, numbed into stupor by the freezing cold.

An old woman had saved her life. Transferred by memory to a room lit by a single oil lamp, the warmth of a wood-burning stove seeping into her bones, Ann listened to a bearded black-robed figure, a distinctive hat and heavy gold cross worn about his neck marking him as a priest such as many she had seen in St Petersburg.

'*You were both almost dead from cold . . .*'

The quietly spoken heavily accented words had been difficult to understand but the priest had been patient.

'*. . . praise to God Maija found you.*' He lifted a finger to head and breast. '*It is her practice to come each dawn to the church to give thanks for the life of her sons and pray for their safety while they are away fishing; it is her house you are in.*'

'*I . . we . . . were going to England.*'

'*England!*' He frowned then listened without interruption to the explanation of how she and Alec had boarded the wrong ship, then to her query as to why they had been forced off it and put ashore in darkness. He shook his head, his reply itself half questioning.

'*The ferry had many people, too many I think for safety; the captain he is responsible, he would be fined heavily also maybe his licence it is taken away so he avoids by putting people off ship.*

But this must not be seen. He must not use the ferry ports nor land them in places such as Hamina or Porvoo right on the coast that …' He nodded as though confirming to himself. *'Yes, that is the reason of rowing boats, they can come up the river Kyma, leave people here in Ruotsinpyhtää … then the ferry continues its journey without problems.'*

Without problems! Momentarily drawn back to the present Ann sighed deeply. It had not been that way for Alec or herself. He had been in so much pain and not knowing the language she had virtually been unable to help.

'Maija understands, she says you wash dishes very clean, that is enough of help and for the boy you should try not to worry; Maija she is skilled in the use of herbs, she trusts God will permit the child will be healed, we must also trust.'

The gentle words brushed away the darkened bedroom replacing it with soft gleams of evening sunlight shimmering on the surface of a river, its banks rimmed by a forest of tall trees sheltering a scatter of buildings. A forge, its timbers blackened by the smoke of its fire, stood in sharp contrast to houses and farm buildings, the rust red and white of their painted walls reflecting brilliant as gemstones on the velvet blue of water. In the centre of the tiny village as though cradled at its heart stood an ancient octagonal wooden church, outside of which a young woman removed a shawl from her head shaking loose a pale sherry-gold fall of hair. Then she draped the brightly knitted shawl about her slender shoulders as she began to walk away.

Ann watched the slight figure pass beyond the cluster of houses, watched as a breeze off the river lifted the hair in a silken cloud; watched the taller heavier figure of a man glance around then moving quickly follow in the same direction.

Muffled by the soft grass of the river bank, whisked away by a gathering wind, no sound of footsteps alerted the woman as she stood smiling at caps of silver cresting waves washing gently to the river's edge. But as callused fingers grabbed at her shoulder Ann cried a fear real as it had been that evening, a cry drowned beneath the beer-soaked breath of a mouth closing over her own. Her hands pressed hard against her knees as if she pushed again at the man. He had released her mouth. She had not understood one word of what he had said but the look in those bleary eyes, the press of a hand to her breast had needed no interpretation.

'Da . . . Da.'

Hoarse, guttural, the words sounded in her mind, leering laughing words seeming to imply she agreed with the man's intention. But she had not agreed. She had cried out, a scream coinciding with the man's loud, almost bestial howl, carrying it out across the river away from the village, away from any help.

He had held her for a moment at arm's length, beer-fogged eyes playing over her face before one hand clasped the back of her neck in the grip of a vice and the other threw away the shawl and ripped open her dress to paw at her body.

'Da.'

He had laughed that strange word again then as she tried to twist free had slapped her hard across her face, his own features now a dark mask of lechery. Releasing her neck he caught her arm in the same vicious grip.

Maija's shawl! Unconsciously Ann's hand reached now as it had then for the patch of colour lying vivid against the green-covered earth, the spread of it holding the promise of protection against the fear threatening to engulf her. Had that fear caused her to cry out like a child whose comforting toy had suddenly been taken away, a cry which like before had been swallowed up in a roar?

But the roar had ended in the savage low-throated growl of a predator whose prey was making a break for freedom.

In the shadowed darkness of the bedroom the hand Ann had stretched out for the imagined shawl, struck blindly at the face leering in her mind; she heard the enraged howl as her fingers clawed at the rough pitted flesh, felt the thud of his body against her own, his strange-sounding words hurling at her like so many stones.

There had been little chance of escaping that hold yet even as anger tightened it she knew she had to try. Squirming, twisting, her free hand lifting to strike again stubble-thick cheeks she had hurled herself backwards attempting to use her body weight to pull herself loose.

It might have worked. In the silence of the sleeping house Ann's hand dropped defeatedly to her lap. In the seconds after he released her, he raised a hand to the stinging scratches painting scarlet lines on the weather-browned canvas of his face and she had turned to run but in that same moment wind from the river had lifted her hair out behind her like a streamer, a ribbon her attacker had caught. He had snatched her back laughing as she cried out against the painful tug to her scalp, continued to laugh as he drew her close, her spine pressed against the hardness of him. His other hand had pushed inside her torn dress, scaly fingers rubbing rasp-like across the tender flesh of her breasts.

Then from the deepest recesses of her mind, rising above the fear, above the revulsion, had come one thought: relax, let her body rest against his, let the scream in her throat become the soft cry of enjoyment; smile as he turned her to face him, then the moment his guard dropped push with all her strength. He might not fall down but he would at least stagger back and that would give her time to run back to the safety of those pretty painted houses.

The thought had warmed her fear-frozen mind. He was heavy-set, his frame encumbered by thick clothing and sturdy knee-length sea boots where she was lighter and so able to run faster.

But the idea had crumbled, sinking with her into welcome darkness at the sight of the man's friends coming to join him.

21

Had she seen three more men racing in, one grabbing her round the waist trying to hold her back, to deny her the safety of her dark place, or had it been an illusion her brain had conjured out of its own terror?

Rising slowly into paler darkness she had tried to wrap herself in the soft velvet of its blackness so as to hide again in depths where pain and fear held no powers.

Yet darkness had withdrawn its shelter.

Light, yellow flickering light played over her closed eyelids; voices, low hushed voices brushed her ears.

Even though deep down Ann knew she was in Leah Marshall's house the memory of that moment jolted her senses.

They were men's voices! The men who had attacked her! Where had they brought her, what would they do with her once they had taken their pleasure? Would they leave her in this place? No! Leaving her alive posed a risk to themselves. They would not chance that. The river! She gasped as if already feeling the breath-snatching coldness of those deep icy waters.

'*Ann . . . Ann is awake.*'

Her gasp had caught their attention. She had tried so hard not to tremble. If she could lie still, hold her eyes fast closed, maybe they would leave her alone; they might even tire of waiting to take their sport and leave altogether.

'*Ann, Ann.*'

She would not answer, she would not.

Of a sudden she realised someone was speaking her name; had she in her fright cried it aloud, were these men now repeating it in order to trick her into wakefulness?

'*Ann.*'

Help me! she had prayed silently. Help me not to breathe!

'*Ann . . . Ann, it's Alec, please . . . please come back, don't stay in that dark place.*'

'*There is no one here will harm you.*'

A quiet gentle voice had added itself to the younger-sounding frightened one yet still her mind had whispered 'trickery'.

'*Do not be afraid,*' the deeper voice of a man had continued, '*you are safe in the house of Maija. Her sons rescued you. They were returning from their fishing when they spotted a shawl lying on the ground, and recognised it as belonging to their mother. Maija knits her special design into each garment she makes, it is a tradition with the women of the village; that way they identify their own kin should a fishing boat meet with disaster. Maija's sons were puzzled as to how the shawl came to be there but then they heard a cry, which came from a woman being half dragged along by a man. Fearing some mishap had befallen their mother they caught up with the man. It was not Maija but a young woman whose mouth was bleeding and her cheek marked with the scarlet weal of a blow. That told all.*'

'*It's true Ann, Maija's sons took you from that man and brought you here to their mother.*'

That was Alec's voice; he would not lie to her.

She drew a deep breath into her aching lungs, ending the pretence of being still unconscious.

Ann watched the tapestry of the past unfold, saw herself

lying on the narrow truckle bed Maija had provided for her use and beside it outlined against the pallid yellow light of an oil lamp the darker more solid shape of a robed priest lifting a cross from his chest to touch it with his lips.

'*The one who attacked you was not a man of this village, he is not of Ruotsinpyhtää, for that we thank God.*'

The quiet voice of the priest echoed this explanation while behind him Maija, Alec and Maija's three tall sons almost hidden in the gloom of the tiny house reverently marked the sign of the cross at forehead and breast.

'*He is of the crew of a Russian fishing vessel anchored at the mouth of the river. On occasion they come to Ruotsinpyhtää for to relax from the long days of their work and leave with no trouble; but that man drank not only Nelos Olut, a very strong beer, but also Salmeikkikoska, a spirit of high alcohol and then despite being advised against it drank several glasses of Koskenkova, a vodka that is even more intoxicating than the others; it was this, too much of drinking, had his mind fall to the wickedness of the Devil.*

'*Maija's sons are happy they were able to save you,*' the priest said with a smile, '*now they and I together must go to the church there to ask forgiveness of the Lord for the beating they gave.*'

Maija's sons! The scene faded as Ann turned to where the dawn light crept over the tiny windowsill. They had rescued her that evening in Ruotsinpyhtää, saved her from an evil that only hours ago had reared its head again.

'There you go ladies, it's been a pleasure.'

'Ar, an' a mite too much of a pleasure judgin' by old Daisy, her be fair skippin' along of the field.'

'Just you be sure it's only Daisy and her girl friends does the skipping and not you.'

'Me skip, eh lad, them days be long gone.'

'You know what I mean . . .'

'I knows you be worried for me lad but there be no need; now you get away and see to your own cows afore they suffers from bein' kept too long for the milkin', overfull udders be painful for a beast.'

'I'll be sure to apologise and ask forgiveness.'

Ask forgiveness. The priest! She must not let him leave without offering her thanks. Frowning in bewilderment Ann gazed across a room which moments before had been darkly shadowed but was now bathed in clear light, a room empty of anyone but herself. But she had heard him speak, had seen him, seen Maija and her sons! How could they not be here!

'You go rest, I'll be back in a couple of hours, the dairy work can wait 'til then.'

'Now look you 'ere . . .'

Maija. Ann smiled. There was the reason the room was empty, Maija and the others had stepped outside.

'. . . there be naught savin' a prison cell will keep Leah Marshall from her dairy so lessen you wants to see me put there for latherin' a man's backside you'll get yourself off to Hill Rise, Edward Langley, afore I fetches meself a pair of Scotch Hands from out of that very dairy!'

The words snapped Ann back to the reality of where she was. But it was reality tainted with confusion.

It was Edward she heard speaking in the yard, Edward speaking with . . . but it couldn't be . . . Leah was lying dead in the next room!

'You has my thanks lad, an' I be certain you 'ave that of Daisy and the rest of the girls; it's given a rare start to their day havin' a man whisperin' sweet nothings in their ear. Like many a wench they don't be averse to a bit of flattery.'

'Does that include Leah Marshall?'

'You try that, Edward Langley, and you'll find out what I can truly do with a pair of butter pats.'

It *was* Leah's voice, it was her down there in the yard! Bemusement vanishing, Ann raced from the room.

'It were naught but a bit o' tiredness.' Leah smiled as Ann asked for the third time if she was truly feeling all right.

'But Mr Langley said . . .'

'Edward Langley builds walls that don't be needed, though he builds 'em for reason only of kindness.'

'He loves you very much, he is concerned for your well-being.'

'I knows wench, I knows.' Leah nodded over the teacup Ann filled again. 'But like I tells him Leah Marshall be good for a few years yet, there be no cause for him to go a worryin' over what were no more than tiredness.'

Teapot in hand, Ann stared into a fire gleaming with life while in its heart it seemed she saw the face of a woman, pale and still, eyes closed against the world. Leah's face! Lined with weariness she should have helped prevent.

'. . . *you had no thought for Leah or the fact she might need your help* . . .'

The words Edward Langley had shot at her the previous evening rang in her brain. Ann set the teapot on the hob of the cast iron fire grate Leah's years of polishing had shined to a brilliant sable. He had been partly right, she had not given any thought to the amount of work to be done, to the effect it could have on an already wearied Leah. But I did not leave for the reason you stated, it was not so I could rid myself of Alec.

Ann lifted the quietly steaming kettle from its bracket, carrying it to the pump in the yard.

It would have done no good to have told Edward Langley that. It had shown quite plainly on his face as she had run from the scullery that he thought her embrace of Leah, her garbled thanks to heaven the woman was not dead as she had imagined, was a blatant display of lies to cover her own guilt.

So what would he say of her tonight? What would Edward Langley say of the woman who this time would leave without even the excuse of searching for Alec?

'Y'be welcome to the usin', Mr Thorpe, it be a kindness you goin' out your way to visit of folk too sick to be a gettin' o' theirself along o' the chapel.'

'*Y'be welcome . . .*'

Enoch Phillips had replied to the request asking for the loan of his pony and trap. But would the man have shown that same generosity had he the least notion of the real purpose for which his vehicle was borrowed? But he would not know. No one would ever find out, nor would they find the body it had carried.

He had thought the man coming from the hedge was Arthur Clews, he had held that same thought while bringing the stone down several times on the fallen man's head. But it had not been Arthur Clews.

Thorpe reached for the jacket draped carefully across a chair back then glanced at the black valise lying on the table taking pride of place in the cramped living room of his tiny terraced home, a home which soon would be exchanged for the more comfortable Chapel House. It was heaven itself choosing he become minister; he, Thomas Thorpe, and not the man who had carried that valise. But why had the fellow been among the bushes? Answering a sudden call of nature? He shrugged into the jacket. Whatever the reason he had been there, no one would be asking the question and certainly the fellow would never be giving any answer.

For a moment he had panicked. Someone would be sure to know Clews had come to Chapel House, if not his family then maybe a work mate. They might even be following on his heels right now!

Such had been his fears last night, fears which faded when he had seen the face and realised the man he had killed was in fact a perfect stranger . . . a perfectly *dead* stranger!

Dressed, ready to leave for work, Thorpe glanced again at the leather valise, its brass fastener gleaming against the dark leather. Should he remove it from the table, hide it away? He rejected the notion; he lived alone, he had no one come to cook or clean, and the house, unlike those of his neighbours, was always locked while he was away, therefore he had no need for secrecy. But there had been every need of secrecy when dealing with that body.

Walking quickly along Portway Road, nodding briefly at the greetings of others making their way towards Monway Steel Foundry, Thorpe's mind replayed what had followed the murder of a stranger.

The knowledge that the man was unknown to him and so likely unknown to anyone else in Wednesbury had helped calm the last tingle of nerves leaving his brain clear, his thoughts precise.

The body had to be moved; stranger or not a man with his head smashed in would give rise to every kind of speculation not least of which would be the question, 'What brought him to Chapel House?' There must be no such question and there wouldn't be if the body were not found here. The solution was clear, but the method? For a moment it had eluded him but then like a beam of light the answer had flashed in his mind: do with this body as he had done with that of Deborah Marshall. But here caution had intervened. This man must not be taken to Holloway Bridge, he must not be tipped into the brook lest the current not be strong enough to carry the body away; nor must it be left lying on the doorstep of Chapel House while he went to Foster Street to request the loan of Enoch Phillips' pony and trap. He glanced at the line of bushes. They were thick enough to conceal it given the cover of darkness.

A moment to get his breath; best not to appear flurried should he meet anyone as he left Queen's Place. That same inner voice cautioned him again to flick leaves and bits of twig from his clothes. Then first listening for any tell-tale sound on the path leading to the chapel he had left.

Had fate led him to choose to go by way of the narrow Queen Street and Cross Street rather than the more direct route crossing over the wider Holyhead Road?

He passed through Monway's large wooden gates, nodding good morning to the watchman lifting a gnarled finger to a dusty flat cap; Thorpe silently thanked the fortune that had smiled on him.

It had been halfway along Cross Street. He had emerged from an opening which allowed access between the streets, a dark empty patch of ground made darker by the otherwise unbroken fringe of soot-clothed houses, when a figure had hurtled into him.

'*I couldn't find him . . . I searched . . . I searched all day . . .*'

Breathless, half sobbed, the words had poured out as Ann Spencer told of her fruitless search for the lad Alec. But while her mind had been distraught his had functioned with ice-cold logic.

'*He is not on the heath.*'

Night had hidden the smile.

'*Alec is not lost.*'

'*Where? Where is he? Please tell me.*'

Though aware of the need for haste, he could not deny himself the gratification of having her plead.

'*Please . . . you must tell me where Alec is.*'

The tears in her voice had thrilled him. This was how he wanted this woman.

'*He is with me,*' he had replied, then before she could speak had continued, '*If you want him then you will come to Chapel House tomorrow evening at eight. You will come alone, after all payment of the sort you must make should be made in private. Oh . . .*' he had paused, '*I should tell you, the boy is not in that house; he is well hidden, so well in fact that should you refuse my invitation or inform anyone of what is said here your precious Alec will never be seen again.*'

He could have insisted that she go with him to Chapel House that same night, but common sense had advised he finish the business in hand. Besides, it had whispered again, the anticipation of a dish is a delight in itself.

He had left her there, his confidence she would not risk the boy's safety by calling on anyone's help lending a spring to his step.

'Y'be welcome Mr Thorpe, may 'eaven reward your doin's.'

Enoch Phillips' call following after the trap driving from Foster Street echoed in Thorpe's mind, adding its own warmth to the glow of satisfaction.

Heaven had indeed rewarded.

The body he had dragged into the hedge still lay where he had left it. Though the man was of slight build it had proved a struggle to lift the dead weight into the pony trap while every second fearing someone might decide to visit the chapel or come to the house at its rear. But nobody had come and despite the need for haste he had taken time to kick away the marks in the gravel left by hauling the corpse; and that had seen heaven once more bestow its favour.

Clouds which had veiled the sky had parted, allowing moonlight to bathe the house and to reveal an object lying near the doorstep; a bag he had not noticed the man carried. The valise now stood in his living room.

Seated at his desk with a ledger open in front of him Thorpe found that his brain refused to leave the scenes which played so vividly in it.

Where to dump the body?

Needle sharp, the question had pricked again and again.

Where? Where?

Then as he had driven from Queen's Place it seemed he heard the words repeated each time he left Ebenezer Spittle's house in Short Street.

' *'Ave a care a' crossin' o' the 'eath Mr Thorpe, that there Devil's Pool just be a waitin' to cop the unwary.*'

The Devil's Pool! Relief had swept over him. Disused, flooded as far back as memory could reach, the open pit shaft had been named for its black waters. Locals carefully avoided the place. But anyone not familiar with terrain pockmarked with abandoned pit workings could easily fall victim to its treachery.

It was fortunate no houses stood closer than Ebenezer's to that black hole, fortunate there had been nobody to witness that body being hauled from the pony trap, the pockets of its clothing being emptied of all means of identification before it was rolled into that black oily maw.

Then keeping to the way he had come, taking the path running behind St Peter's Church and on along the derelict ground that bordered Short Street he had returned animal and vehicle to its owner then himself to Cross Street all without the need to explain his late-night jaunt to anyone.

In the privacy of his own home he had opened the valise; in the silence of the living room he had been given yet one more blessing.

22

'I knows the cause of your goin' off the way you did and I understands; I be only sorry you didn't find the lad.'

'My behaviour was selfish and thoughtless, Mr Langley was right to say so.'

'No,' Leah insisted. 'It weren't for Edward to go chidin' you, he don't know the all of it.'

Nor do you. Ann kept the thought to herself. You don't know what I have to do to get Alec away from Thomas Thorpe.

Continuing the daily task of turning cheeses stored in the cool cupboard, inching each large round block a little further along the well-scrubbed shelves in order to make room for more, Leah went on. 'You an' the lad; time 'as you feelin' for one another as would brother an' sister, it be natural your worryin' for him same as it be natural for you to go a searchin' again today.'

'I won't be searching for him today.'

'Not search! Eh wench, don't go leaving off lookin' for the lad on account of me; what 'appened last evenin' were the fault of tiredness an' naught beside so you go look for Alec and pay no mind to aught but that.'

'I . . .' Ann stumbled over the reply building in her mind. It would be lying to the woman who trusted her but to tell Leah the truth could have Alec in terrible danger. 'I . . . that is Alec has spoken more and more of the people who were to meet him. I think he has gone to them.'

'But I thought he d'ain't know where it was them folk be livin'.'

Oh Lord, she was making things worse. Ann met the quizzical look as Leah turned from closing the cool cupboard. She strove for a plausible reply. 'A week or so back he said he was fairly certain he knew where to find them.'

'But to go off wi'out a word, slippin' away afore folk be up, don't seem the sort o' thing that lad would do.'

'It wasn't exactly without a word,' Ann countered, 'he has been leading up to it for a while now. He told me he felt unable to make the break the moment we arrived in this country. He would not admit to lacking courage to strike off on his own but I knew how it felt to be in a country where you knew no one, where everything was strange and different. Now I feel Alec has found the confidence he needed.'

'That be all well an' good but still he should have teken a bite afore goin', should have let me mek him a sandwich or two to tek along of him.'

What Leah was really saying was, why had he not at least said goodbye? Watching her now patting freshly churned butter into small portions Ann's heart tripped in sympathy for the obvious hurt the woman was feeling. That was a feeling she also knew well, the hurt those many times her father had left the room without a word, the times he had seemed not to notice or even care she was there at all.

'Alec did what he did for a reason. He loves you very much and feels you love him the same way; leaving secretly was his way of sparing you heartache.' Ann carried the tray of butter portions to its own cool cupboard, hiding the tears that threatened to fall.

'It would 'ave been hard.' Leah sniffed her own threatening tears. 'Like you says I'd come to think much of the lad; I prays God be alongside of him wherever he be.'

'*. . . he is not at Chapel House . . .*'

Where then? Where had Thomas Thorpe taken Alec? And would the man keep to his word, would he release the boy once he had raped her? Would one time be all he demanded?

Seeing from the corner of her eye the shudder rippling across Ann's shoulders Leah marched to close the cupboard saying as she did so, 'Bein' out on the heath as long as you was don't go doin' a body no good, it's put a chill to your bones; you go rest by the fire while I finishes up, ain't like there be so much to do 'ere.'

'I haven't taken a chill it's just . . .'

'Just?'

It had to be faced and now was the moment. 'Leah.' Ann swallowed hesitantly then more firmly. 'Leah, there is something we need to discuss.'

'If that be meanin' you 'ave summat to say then you best say it an' be done.'

'It . . . it's the matter of the dairy,' once started Ann rushed on, 'the fact of your producing so much less, that is all a result of my being here; you have to allow me to speak with those women, to apologise for the trouble I have caused them.'

While stirring rennet into the fresh milk it seemed Leah would make no answer; then she turned a tight look to Ann.

'Trouble!' she snapped. 'And what of the trouble they've caused you?'

'That doesn't matter.'

'Oh don't it!' Leah's indignant exclamation chased along whitewashed walls. 'Well it mightn't matter to you, wench, but it matters to me. I won't 'ave nobody a tellin' me who I can or can't 'ave bide 'neath my roof.'

'But look what is happening, the loss of customers means loss of income.'

As she turned off the tap draining the last drops of whey from sieves of muslin-tied curds, Leah lifted a sharp glance.

'That be my business and none of nobody else; but this much I'll tell: if the like of Jinny Jinks and Lottie Hopcroft think they'll see Leah Marshall come knockin' on their doors a beggin' of 'em to buy her butter and cheese then they'd be well advised to get theirselves good strong eyeglasses for they'll be older far than Methuselah afore ever that 'appens.'

'But making less butter surely means a lot of the milk going to waste.'

Leah cast a long searching look about the dairy. 'Waste?' She glared. 'I'll ask you the same as I asked Edward when he spoke as you've done: 'ave you seen other than the whey given Betsy an' her little 'uns leave this dairy, anythin' y'might call waste?'

'No.' Ann blushed at the accusation. 'But you can't go on making cheese, the cupboards are already full.'

'Ar wench, they be full.' Leah nodded. 'But come tomorrow they'll be empty. One thing you needs learn about cheeses: looked after properly they'll keep for years, the flavour improves along of the keepin' in a cool dry place and my cellar be perfect. Them there cheeses'll mature nicely and as for the whey drained in the mekin' of 'em you go look at old Betsy and them piglets then tell me does you still think aught be goin' to waste? So now if your enquirin' nose be nicely wiped you can help get these trays and vats scoured ready for Edward bringin' of milk from Hill Rise.'

★　　★　　★

He had barely spoken to her. It had been as though even to look at her had been distasteful to him. Filling the water bucket from the pump in the yard Ann glanced in the direction of the town. She had offered to make the delivery to Leah's customers but Edward Langley had turned his back, his refusal polite but unreservedly cold.

Ann carried the bucket into the scullery where she poured half of its contents into the shallow sink. Then she fetched the kettle from the living-room fire and added boiling water, the resulting cloud of steam condersing like tears along her eyelashes.

He had said Leah would have wanted her to stay overnight, Leah would have worried for her being on the streets. Leah would have worried! Ann blinked away the fringing moisture. Edward Langley had shown no such concern. Perhaps he would have preferred her to refuse to walk out of the house there and then; most certainly his look on seeing her run to embrace Leah, his attitude while unloading and reloading the cart had been that of cold antagonism.

She refilled the kettle then turned to scrubbing ladles and butter pats. Edward Langley had demonstrated clearly he found her presence here undesirable, his very silence had cried loudly he wanted her gone. Not to worry, Mr Langley. Ann rinsed the last of the scrubbed utensils in a bowl of Leah's own home-made sterilising solution of one part water to three parts white vinegar. Today will see you get what you want.

It would also see Thomas Thorpe get what he wanted.

Ann leaned heavily against the crude wooden board set against the sink.

It need not happen! She did not have to go to Chapel House, she need not submit to Thomas Thorpe's atrocious demand; she could walk away from this town and all it held.

'. . . *should I fail to get what is owed by one then I simply take it from the other; male or female, woman or boy either is acceptable.*'

That was why she could not walk away, no matter how tempting the prospect of freedom. Alec had said friends should trust each other; it was a trust she would not break. Alec was confined against his will where she was imprisoned only by her own. A prisoner of friendship! How Thomas Thorpe would laugh at that.

'I've went along of you today lad cos I wants to talk with you.'

'You are going to marry me, I knew I would break your resistance given time.'

'I've warned you afore, I'll be doin' time lessen you leaves off your daftness, time in one of His Majesty's prisons.'

Driving the milk cart into the yard of Leah's smallholding Edward turned to the woman beside him. 'I give in but I don't give up.'

'Ar well you never did 'ave sense enough to know when you'd lost,' Leah retorted, climbing from the cart. 'Now lessen you 'ave more fat to chew I'll away inside and show the kettle to the pot then we'll see to the washin' of them churns.'

Edward shook his head. 'Churns can wait, first you get your cup of tea.'

'I don't hold no objection to that lad,' Leah nodded agreeably, 'but I reckon after a pullin' of that cart all mornin' old Jess there deserves a drink and a nosebag afore pullin' it all the way 'ome to Hill Rise.'

'You've seen the way of it, seen for y'self the number of women no longer buyin' from my dairy, that be what I wants to talk to you about, that an' the business we talked on a week or two back. It be my thinkin' we should no longer consider bindin' of my place to your'n; with things the way they be that would be an unfairness to you.'

'Leah you don't have to worry . . .'

'Hear me out lad.' Leah glanced up from tea she had brewed while Edward had given his horse water and oats. 'It's been in my mind them folk havin' teken their custom elsewhere might 'ave no mind to bringin' it back and I won't hitch a failin' business to your'n.'

'They would be back tomorrow if not for your being so stubborn.'

'If I made Ann and the lad go! Say what you means lad, that way saves we both a march around the Wrekin.'

Ann. Edward noticed the easy use of the name. Leah had really taken to her pair of orphans; it would cause her real regret when they left but their staying might cause even more. Adding milk to his cup he watched the swirl of white and brown turn and twine drawing closer to each other. Like a man taking a woman into his arms, bringing her to him, holding, caressing, touching like lovers . . . A movement at the other side of the table broke the reverie. Edward stirred his tea vigorously. Thoughts of that kind were for moonstruck kids.

'You said to speak plain so I will.' He spoke tightly, the words addressed more to the young woman so constantly in his mind than to Leah. 'Things were going along fine until they came, now everything is cockeyed. The folk of the town are on edge and you . . . you are working harder than ever yet sales are cut by half. How long do you think you can go on this way?'

Swallowing a mouthful of tea Leah gave a moment to the pleasure. Tea had served her well in the past, been a comfort in long lonely hours; a quiet cup of tea had helped with many decisions since losing her family and would help again now.

'I shall go on as long as the good Lord sees fit to give me strength; as for what you an' them folk along of the town sees as a problem it don't be such for me. I won't pretend I don't be grieved at the lad's decidin' to go nor will I deny it'll cause me that same sorrow when Ann does the same but I've long learned to cope with losin' of them I loves.'

Leah had made it a lifetime rule never to interfere in other people's affairs, to afford them the privacy she expected in her turn. But, the argument she had dwelt on so many times since the death of Deborah rose again, wouldn't any mother try to help when she saw her child was hurting? Hadn't this man been like a child to her since the passing of his own mother? The answer was yes but did that accord her the privilege of speaking out of turn or would it be the ending of a friendship? Seeing him glance towards the scullery, knowing that in Edward's mind he looked further, into the dairy where Ann Spencer was working, Leah's decision was made.

'Edward lad.' His glance returned to her so Leah went on firmly. 'A minute since I said for you to speak plain, now it be my turn. I never was one to walk a mile when a yard would bring me to the same place so I speaks frank; be sure, be sure in your soul it won't be Leah Marshall alone will be heart-broke with that wench leavin'.'

She had said her piece. From at the door opening on to the yard Leah watched the tall figure, its stride hampered by a slight limp. She had thought in the seconds of loud silence following her words Edward Langley had taken offence but he had fastened her in his arms and said quietly, 'You certainly know how to hit a man over the head with a bargepole.'

But it seemed her blow had not been heavy enough.

Leah watched him load the churns Ann had kept ready and noticed him turning his hand quickly the other way as the girl came to the dairy entrance. As he led the horse from the yard without a word to Ann, Leah sighed. She had tried to put sense into his stubborn mind but as with everything else in Edward Langley's life the problem of Ann Spencer must be resolved by him alone.

23

Edward Langley had refused her offer to accompany him on the delivery round. Had he done so in order to avoid conflict with more of Leah's customers, women who would take umbrage at her still being in Wednesbury? Ann, folding linen, shook her head at the thought. It was more true to say Edward Langley did not wish her company. To try to explain only to have him accuse her as before would have been even more painful, so she had said nothing.

But wasn't she planning to do much the same thing? Wasn't it her intention to leave this house giving no reason? If only she could explain, go with Leah's blessing as she had with Maija's.

That also had been done in secrecy under the cover of night. Ann was suddenly whisked back in time, memory bringing her to a dimly lit room warmed by a black iron stove. Alec, his fair hair gleaming in the lambent glow of the one oil lamp, was taking the bowl of soup handed to him by Maija. It was as her hands touched his it happened, the same strange occurrence as twice before.

Maija's body had tensed, her breathing suddenly quick and shallow. At the rim of the lamp's yellow spill the priest, taking his leave, turned at the sound then, with Maija's sons at his heels, came to stand beside her. Telling Alec there was no cause to be afraid he nodded to the eldest son who gently lowered his mother to her chair.

'*Restlessness breathes over the land . . . death waits in the shadows . . . its hand moves . . .*'

The woman's unblinking eyes shone like polished stone as they stared at a scene no one else could see. Her voice, at first a trembling whisper, became almost a cry as she jerked forward and reached out her hands as if to hold something.

'*. . . the eagle . . .*'

Words the priest had murmured sounded afresh in Ann's mind.

'*. . . the eagle is pushed from its nest, its wings are broken . . .*'

What had it meant? Once more fully in the present, Ann asked herself the question she had put to the priest but he had supplied no answer, nor could she. Twice before she had seen the woman caught as by some unseen hand, twice watched as she seemed to look upon some other world, yet each time she had spoken of it to the priest the man had appeared reluctant to discuss the matter.

Did his religion forbid him to accept what her own grandmother had often referred to as 'the second sight'? Did he think perhaps Maija's senses were beginning to wander?

She took the folded linen to the chest of drawers, still dwelling on the events following rapidly on that evening, events which had her smuggled from the village of Ruotsinpyhtää in the hours before dawn.

The priest had called at Maija's home a little after breakfast the morning following the woman's strange behaviour. There were men, strangers to the village, one of whom Maija's sons recognised as the man they had beaten. They might want only to buy fish and beer to take back to their own vessel but Maija's sons had sent word of their suspicions to the priest.

'*You should come no more to the church,*' he had told her after a hushed conversation with Maija. '*You do not go beyond the walls of this house, nor will the boy.*'

Did he think those men had come to take revenge for what had befallen a comrade, to help him gain what had been denied?

'*There is great unrest in Finland, family disagrees with family, friend opposes friend, dissension spreads town to town ever more widely.*'

But why insist she and Alec remain indoors? They had disagreed with no one.

He had fingered the heavy gold cross seeming to search for the right answer and when it came his voice was heavy with sadness.

'*A spark in a hayloft can burn down the barn, the barn can spread fire to the house, from a house through a town. Should those men be what we call "Red" cadres, men intent on overthrowing this country's government, they will use any means of fomenting trouble. I would not have you be the spark that sets Ruotsinpyhtää ablaze.*'

She had of course agreed to his request and though she would miss those moments in the pretty little church, the walks along the river bank, their confinement would ensure Alec continued to rest.

Ann glanced from the window at a sky suddenly darkened with threatening rain clouds but her eyes seemed to see only the lamplit gloom of a small room, a boy lying on a truckle bed to the side of a black iron stove obediently swallowing medicine from a spoon held to his lips by an elderly grey-haired woman, a woman who smiled at a young man entering the room. But the smile was quickly gone. She reached for her bright knitted shawl, answering the young man with brief hurried words, and left the house.

Ann watched herself ask if anything was wrong while the young man, not understanding her words yet obviously reading correctly the anxiety in her eyes, answered by bending his knees, placing his hands together with his eyes closed before straightening and making the sign of the cross to head and chest.

'*She is gone to church*,' Alec laughed, delighted at guessing the object of the performance, '*Lars is saying his mother is gone to church.*'

But why so hastily?

It had remained unsaid. While she took hot water from the stove to wash utensils used in the preparation of poultice and medicine, the young man Lars amused Alec with shadow pictures, animals and birds his hands and fingers created in the glow of the lamp.

Then Lars was no longer in the room, Maija was taking garments from a deep chest, putting some to one side while depositing others on the cleared table, as Alec lay asleep. A peaceful scene yet Ann felt the tension of it throb again in her veins.

The priest, half hidden by the well of shadows, spoke softly to Maija then beckoned to the younger woman at Alec's bedside. He began to speak rapidly, only realising he was doing so in Finnish when Ann shook her head.

'*Forgive ... forgive.*' He shook his own head briefly before he went on. '*Lars comes to warn the strangers in the village are not come for the buying of fish and beer nor are they Finn. The one with the bruised face is Russian but his companions Lars tells are German. They are like to be part of the force supplied by that country to assist our government suppress the revolutionists. This I fear poses danger for us all.*'

'*Danger ... I don't understand!*'

'*Germany and England are at war, should you and the boy be discovered here you could both be taken prisoner and Maija and her family – maybe the whole village – punished for sheltering you.*'

'*But Alec might not be English, we can't be certain.*'

The priest turned momentarily to the sleeping boy and in the dimness it seemed his lips moved in silent prayer.

'*We can be certain he is not Finn. But that I fear might have little relevance; the fact of his being with you, an English woman, will arouse suspicion and seeing what I have of those men leads to the belief interrogation would be far from gentle; the boy . . .*' he glanced again towards the truckle bed, '*the boy would suffer greatly.*'

Ann saw her own reaction, saw herself reach to wake the sleeping Alec, saw the black-robed figure catch her by the arm.

'*Not yet, let him sleep.*'

'*But we wouldn't want Maija or anyone to suffer because of us. We have to leave now, before it is too late.*'

'*No, the risk of being seen is too great. In the hour before dawn Aarno and Berndt will come for you. You and the boy will go with them to the fishing. They will try to get you to England, but the journey will not be easy for there are enemy ships in both the Baltic and the North Sea.*'

Maija's sons came as promised.

Beyond the window sounds drifted on the warm afternoon, clucking hens scratching in the yard, grunts of Betsy and her piglets snuffling at the trough, an occasional moo of cows grazing in the meadow, but Ann stood in a world of blackness, a sharp wind biting at her face.

Maija had sorted clothing for her from the chest: trousers, a thick wool jersey topped by a thicker jacket, a bright knitted cap which completely covered her hair and forehead. She held on tightly to Alec with one hand, her own clothes bundled in a cloth bag gripped in the other. Above them cloud heavy and black scudded across the sky; shafts of pale intermittent moonlight played over streets so quiet it seemed the very earth slept.

'*Hei!*'

Ann seemed to watch a group of figures, their shapes dark silhouettes exposed in the open space stretching between houses and river bank.

'*Hei!*'

With this second 'hello' a man shuffled from a doorway, a flash of moonlight revealing something held in his hand. Was the man holding a gun? Her memory of the episode aboard the ferry made her gasp but Aarno swiftly shushed her as he pushed her behind him. A flash of steel blade glinted in the same brief break in the cloud; he murmured softly to his brother who, catching hold of Alec's free hand, urged them towards the river.

Stumbling after Berndt, dreading every step on that unfamiliar ground would have her fall headlong, a further shout made her nerves scream with fear in case the man's noise woke the village, and brought on to the street the very people they were attempting to avoid. Then, from the well of shadow cast by a building, another figure emerged, weaving drunkenly towards the one now lifting chest-high the object he held.

'*Olut.*' A man's voice laughed, errant moonbeams glistening on the bottle waving above his head. '*Olut ei ... koskenkova kyllä.*'

'*He say no* olut, *no beer,* koskenkova – *vodka* – *is better, no trouble more.*'

Berndt's laboured explanation as the drunken pair turned back in the direction of the houses left a sob of relief in Ann's throat as Aarno rejoined them, a murmur from him bringing a grin to his brother's face, a grin echoed when moments later Lars appeared at their side with an empty bottle in his hand.

Fish! Ann's nose wrinkled at the pungent recollection. They had joined the larger fishing vessel anchored off the mouth of the river, Aarno and Berndt helping herself and Alec on to the deck, Lars carrying her bundle of clothes. Alec had settled immediately, helping with the gutting of fish when preparing meals, working alongside Lars at the nets, comforting her when her stomach rebelled at the sight of food. How many days had it taken for the promised 'sea legs'? She had not counted but at last she had been able to go on deck. As on her journey to Russia to join her parents the very vastness of the sea, the sheer boundless expanse of water marked by nothing but the vessel on which they sailed, held her speechless. Aarno and his brothers had smiled, trying with their limited knowledge of English to tell her this was the way they preferred, that they hoped to meet no ship that was not a fishing boat.

But their hopes had been dashed. Fresh pictures sprang to Ann's mind, pictures of a grey overcast sky, of waves chopping fractiously at the sides of the boat, of Lars rushing Alec below deck, Berndt directing her to sit on a coil of rope beside which was a bucket of freshly caught fish, sharp movements of one hand down chest and stomach indicating she begin to gut them.

What followed had been a nightmare of fear.

A boat grey as the waves it sailed upon, a gun mounted on its deck, had drawn alongside; two men in dark blue clothing and round caps were coming aboard, the rifles in their hands jerking accompaniment to staccato demands. But it was the flag stretched taut in the breeze, a flag portraying a large black cruciform shape whose narrowed inner edges were overlain with a white circle and at whose heart stood a crowned eagle with wings outstretched that had held her gaze: the imperial war flag of the German Kaiser.

'. . . *the eagle is pushed from its nest* . . .'

Maija's muttered words echoed. Was it this flag she had stared at with that strange vacant look? Was this the eagle she had spoken of?

'. . . *its wings are broken* . . .'

The wings of the eagle of that flag were not broken, they were spread powerfully, arrogantly wide, every contour seeming to express challenge.

At the loud insistent bark of an order shouted over the screech of wind Ann's mental vision switched to where Berndt stood beside open and empty fish boxes, the shrug of his shoulders and a nod of the head towards nets still in the water signifying a lack of catch.

Irritation lending force the sailor kicked viciously at the nearest box then strode up to the bucket.

'*Ja!*' he snorted eyeing the fat silver-scaled contents. Then again, '*Ja!*' but in a different tone. Ann shivered with the memory. There was no irritation, only a breathy almost hissed approval followed by a strong hand fastening about her wrist and jerking her roughly to her feet.

'*Nein,*' his companion called, glancing towards their own vessel.

The laughed reply held no meaning but the grip on her wrist as he dragged her towards the hatch had screamed its reason in her brain.

Berndt's cry of protest and his move to help her, were halted by a rifle jabbed to his middle. Her captor had flicked a thumb to his nose adding insult to another coarse laugh, then letting his own rifle fall to the deck had flung her face down across the closed hatch, his hands throwing her heavy jacket up over her shoulders before snatching at the waistband of her trousers.

The buttons snapping off, the slide of cloth!

Ann felt again the sting of her forehead, the pressure of a hand heavy on the back of her head forcing it against the wooden hatch cover, the touch of rough fingers on her waist.

Lars waved a bottle raised in each fist in an attempt to distract the attacker. But welcome as was the proffered vodka the drinking of it was to wait.

She could not see what the man was doing yet the movement at her back suggested the loosening of his clothes. Ann gasped again, a vicious punch to her spine ending the twist to free herself.

He was pulling again at her trousers, inching them further, easing them on to the swell of her hips, his fingers digging forcefully into her flesh, but all of this was as nothing compared to the dread filling her mind.

'*Achtung.*'

The word meant nothing to her but its effect upon the man tearing at her clothes was pronounced. His hands stilled on her body, a ragged intake of breath his only movement.

'*Achtung! Zurück zum Schiff! Achtung! Zurück zum Schiff!*'

Called through a megaphone, it carried across the whine of wind and the slapping of waves.

At the obvious command the sailor guarding Berndt called warningly to the other then with his rifle slung across his shoulder and the bucket of fish clutched in one hand, a bottle snatched from Lars deposited with the fish, he proceeded to lower himself over the side using his free hand to cling to the rope ladder.

'*Gott im Himmel!*'

The words accompanied a savage kick to her rear; the man continued to swear as he turned to follow his mate, grabbing the second bottle before he too scrambled down into the waiting rowing boat.

Trembling, near to tears as she had been during those terrifying minutes, Ann breathed heavily as the scene faded.

Lars had run to her, shielding her with his body while she adjusted trousers and jacket, then helped her to her tiny cabin, but it had been Aarno with his slightly better knowledge of English who had answered the question of how that man had known her to be female.

It has been days after the ordeal. Aarno had stood beside her on the deck, his tall broad frame etched against a setting sun whose touch on his bronze beard made it gleam golden red against weather-bronzed skin. The same golden light made his blue eyes sparkle, eyes which had blazed contempt.

'*He not care; male, female, he not care.*'

Turning from the window Ann's stomach clenched.

'. . . *male or female, woman or boy, either is acceptable.*'

The horror was happening all over again, and this time there would be no one to prevent it.

24

The front door! Thomas Thorpe's nerves screeched. Only one sort of visitor knocked at the front door: the police.

They had found the body. His stomach jolted sickeningly. They had found the body he had thrown into the Devil's Pool, they were here to arrest him. But how could they be certain it was him had killed that man? Had he overlooked something? Dropped some personal item of his own then missed seeing it in the darkness? Thoughts tumbled chaotically but from beneath the tumult another surfaced. The police could not be certain he was home; he must remain still, make no sound, that way they would assume the house empty and leave, then when darkness fell he could get away.

No, they could not know for sure he was here . . . but half of Cross Street would. Like water on a flame it killed the hope. Though he never invited any neighbour into his home they missed little of what went on in the street; they would have seen him arrive from work, they would be watching even now from behind cheap lace curtains. Maybe at this moment one or two were deciding to come ask was everything all right. He grimaced silently. They would be there to stick their noses in, to angle for anything they could gossip over.

A second brisk rap made his pulses race but years of quick thinking, of covering his own back, left his brain cool enough to think lucidly.

He had met only two people apart from the dead man. Enoch Phillips would see nothing amiss in the borrowing of a horse and trap; the vehicle had been returned to him empty as when it had been loaned. He would know nothing of any help to the police. And Ann Spencer? Despite nerves taut as bow strings Thorpe almost smirked. They had met on the street, what was exceptional in that? He would say he had tried to calm her fear by telling it was not unusual for a young lad to lose track of time, that the boy was probably already back at Leah Marshall's house. But of course if that was not so and if the lad did not return in a couple of hours then he would organise a search; she would not deny the truth of this, nor would she make any claim against Thomas Thorpe: his threat that the boy would never again be seen would hold Ann Spencer's tongue very, very still.

Bolstered by his own sense of supremacy he opened the door, his every sense reeling at the sight meeting his eyes.

'*. . . you will never be the recipient of Ann Spencer's love . . .*'

Edward Langley paused in the task of washing down the milking parlour. Much as he tried to prevent it those words cut as deep now as when she had said them. But why on earth should they! He pushed the broom savagely. It was like he had said to her, she meant nothing to him. Then why did he feel like a child who had lost his well-earned penny? He argued with himself as he swept slurry into the yard. She had shown little concern for Leah or for anyone else. His broom stilled as he acknowledged the truth he had tried to deny. The 'anyone' was Edward Langley!

'*. . . I ask you to remember what I do is my own business, it has nothing whatsoever to do with you.*'

There was the crux of his annoyance, of the angry words he had thrown: he wanted to be part of her business, part of her life, he wanted her to turn to him when things went wrong.

'... *you, Miss Spencer, mean nothing to me* ...'

Of all he had said that was the most fallacious; Ann Spencer meant everything to him.

He was in love with Ann Spencer! With a mocking laugh he pushed the broom. Acceptance of that reality had come too late. Watching muddied water seep away into the drain he smiled bitterness at the next thought. He loved Ann Spencer but like the water he brushed away his reluctance to face the truth had swept her from his life.

Leah had accepted that the girl did not wish to remain in Wednesbury, yet deep inside she was hurting too.

He set the broom in its place against the wall of the milking shed and gazed out across the open field towards Leah's house, a dot in the distance.

Leah Marshall had loved him from birth, and he loved her dearly ... but there had been room in his heart for another. Now hope of that was gone and he must live with the heartache of that loss.

He inhaled quickly to pull himself together and was halfway across the yard when a sound arrested him.

Birds calling as they settled for the night, the soft lowing of milked cows, the snicker of the horse in the stable? He was so used to these sounds he had to deliberately concentrate for them to register. No, none of them had caught his attention. Listening for several seconds then hearing nothing he smiled wryly: now he was imagining things.

Almost at the door of the kitchen he stopped abruptly, every sense alert. There it was again! It had not come from the house. Turning slowly taking care his boots did not crunch on the hard-packed earth, he swept the yard with a sharp penetrating gaze as he listened intently.

The stable! He looked towards the low wooden building.

Old Jess could pull a cart, he could nibble at the odd bit of greenery while out on the rounds, he could neigh when the fancy took him but one thing he couldn't do was laugh; and the sound of a laugh had come from that stable.

Had whoever was in there already been inside the house, had his home been rifled for anything a thief might value? Doors were never locked; anyone wanting to enter would have met no deterrent; but why go into the stable? Unless of course the thief meant to steal the horse along with whatever else he had taken. But if that swine wanted Jess he was going to have to fight for him.

'I shall show this to him, but he must ask nicely for it.'

Standing at the door left carelessly ajar Edward listened to the speaker inside.

'I shall tell him it is so easy to do, that he should learn quickly.'

Learn what quickly – how to rob people's houses? Edward flung the door open, only to stare disbelievingly at the intruder.

Thomas Thorpe looked uneasily at the figure on his doorstep. What he had dreaded a night back, that the man approaching from the hedge was Arthur Clews, had proved groundless but the person confronting him now was even more formidable. He stared at grey-streaked brown hair dull as the eyes which looked back at him, at a body strengthened by years of hard work and a face whose determined expression spoke clearly of a matter to be settled.

A matter which should have been settled already, as easily dealt with as Deborah Marshall. Now it was too late.

'I thought as 'ow if I come now I'd catch you in.'

Catch him! That had been the aim all along; the first element of shock giving way to cold anger Thorpe had the

232

overriding desire to strike the face regarding him beneath its dusty bonnet.

'Y' see we reckoned as 'ow you wouldn't want this talked on along of the chapel, it not rightly bein' chapel business.'

Perhaps not. But you will make sure everyone who worships there and many who don't will be treated to every last detail, each one painted with lurid colours.

'I've teken the liberty of callin' to the 'ouse rather than talk along of the street.'

With ears pressed to doors pulled slightly ajar on each side, talking here would be just as public as on the street. Reluctantly Thorpe stood back from the door saying through tight lips, 'Please come in, Mrs Clews.'

He would offer no tea nor ask her to sit down; courtesy had been stretched far enough. Planting himself before the fireplace, as far away from his guest as the small living room would allow, Thorpe watched the quick glances dart in every direction. Was she summing up the home her daughter would be moving into? That had been this woman's plan from the outset. Allowing the daughter to take over the cleaning of Chapel House, the girl's eagerness to lie with him, had been a scheme cooked up with one purpose in mind, to trap him into marriage. Well, there was no ring on Sarah Clews' finger yet.

Hiding the thought behind a forced smile he asked, 'What can I do for you?'

'It be like this.' Ada Clews glanced at a chair but receiving no invitation went on, 'I've been a talkin' . . .'

She had been talking . . . to whom? Fury flicked darts of ice along every vein but Thorpe maintained the false smile.

'That is we been a talkin',' Ada continued, 'it were at the cemetery – you knows all of we teks what flowers we can afford on Sunday afternoons and if pennies don't stretch to that we goes along anyway to tend the graves of family already passed on – well like I says as we was leavin' we got to talkin' about the carry-on between some of we women an' Leah Marshall.'

She was not here to discuss the affair of her daughter!

He turned his back, pretending to clear a cough rising in his throat, then with his handkerchief held to his mouth to disguise a surging sense of release, faced the woman still talking on.

'Well I tells you Mr Thorpe, there got to be quite a bit of argy-bargy, some sayin' it be right not to buy her stuff an' others sayin' it were daft to be refusin' of it seein' how 'ard times be.'

Why bring this to him, to his house? Now that the fear of retribution had eased, his anger began to return.

'Mrs Clews,' he glanced at the clock, 'I really don't see . . .'

'D'ain't none of we deny it be 'ard,' Ada ploughed on ignoring the blatant glance at his clock, 'we all 'as a job findin' enough to feed a family but as Jinny Jinks reminded, that lad livin' along of Leah Marshall is like to be a spy.'

'Mrs Clews . . . Ada, this has all been gone over—'

'Ar it 'as!' Ada interrupted. 'But not the way Ezekial tells it.'

Ezekial Turley – that man again! Thorpe's irritation grew. It would be better all round should that man meet with the same accident as had befallen the one who had come to Chapel House.

'Ezekial reckons that lad be no more a spy than be you or me, reckons he don't be no German neither. We asked 'ow he come by that,' Ada answered the frown before it became a question, 'he said it were summat the lad said. Ezekial 'ad gone across to Leah's place to collect his quart of milk as usual and meetin' the lad comin' from the stable stopped to chat. That were when that young 'un said what he said.'

I don't care what he said, I just want you out of my house!

Ada correctly interpreted the sharp disgruntled sniff. Her glance dropped to the table covered with turkey-red chenille cloth, a luxury she could never hope to afford. Thomas Thorpe was not happy with her being here but she wasn't going to be pushed off before relating all of what had passed on that walk back from the cemetery.

'Conversation 'ad come around to the discussing of the war,' Ada's head lifted determinedly, 'Ezekial sayin' nothin' comes of fightin' 'cept more fightin'; the lad nodded, answerin', "War is never good, Little Father, it robs both parties of life and love." It were them words "little father", Ezekial said, of all the places in the world the Army took him he'd only ever 'eard that spoken in the Crimea by Russian soldiers showing respect for an officer. Seems like so many of 'is kind Ezekial had run from a 'ome with too many mouths to feed then lied about his years so as to join the Army; he'd been no more than thirteen when he went to the Crimea as a boy in the Regiment of Foot. It had been durin' the battle of Kinburn, in all the smoke and noise of the fighting. He got confused and on bein' sent by his sergeant to fetch a bucket of water, lost his way and was captured along of some river bank; he were bein' clouted by his captor when along comes an officer covered in medals who after bein' told of what were goin' on turns to Ezekial and says in plain English, "Soldiers of the Little Father do not fight against children; his Imperial Majesty the Tsar would wish you to be returned safely to your regiment. Perhaps you will convey the compliments of General Mikhail Mikhailevitch to Colonel Halys who is Little Father to that regiment." That says Ezekial be proof to him the lad livin' along of Leah's be more likely to come from Russia than from Germany and with them countries at war wi' one another then that lad won't go a spyin' for Germany.'

'Mr Turley's opinion is a sensible one.'

Though you yourself don't be inclined to it! Ada noted the curtness of the reply but kept the observation to herself saying instead, 'Everybody thought as much, even Jinny Jinks and meself agreein' wi' Ezekial there be no more ill feelin' towards, Leah, that we should all be as we was a buyin' of her dairy.'

The woman had said nothing which could not have been aired in the street or even in the chapel. Much of the same had been said there already so why bring it here? Thorpe's mind raced. Had she truly come to talk of that stupid argument or was it simply bluff, was she lulling him into a false sense of security before finally delivering her blow? He looked at the woman watching him with what might almost be a smile. Knowing he had to answer, he pushed the words through stiff lips.

'It is good to hear the dispute is ended and things are settled.'

'Ar well,' Ada's dull eyes glinted, 'don't everythin' be settled . . .'

It wasn't *almost* a smile, it was the grin of a cobra poised to strike! Hairs on the back of Thorpe's neck stood on end as the woman paused. He could strike her down with the poker, kill her, finish it here and now then vow she had struck him first and in the struggle to take the poker from her it had struck her on the temple; and the reason for her attack? Her misguided and wrongful accusation of abuse of her daughter.

'Y' see . . .'

He clenched his fingers as though already gripping the fire iron. 'It be this way, Mr Thorpe, we all of us women be of the same mind regardin' tekin' custom back to Leah but ain't not one of we be of a mind to go a' tellin' her so and that be what brings me to your door. I be to ask would you talk along of Leah Marshall?'

25

'How long have you been here?'

Edward frowned at the boy standing beside the horse, one hand stroking its shoulder, then before he could reply went on, 'Do you have any idea the worry you've caused going off like that!'

'I'm sorry Edward.' Alec Romney's blue-grey eyes clouded.

'I should think you are sorry. What in the world made you do such a thing!'

Alec took a moment to answer. 'You have heard what the people of the town say of me: I am a foreigner and so cannot be trusted.'

'That's just stupid tittle-tattle, it will have been forgotten in a month.'

His fingers suddenly stilled, his gaze rested on the smooth body of the horse. Alec seemed to enter a different world, one which reflected unhappiness on his young face.

'No Edward,' he said quietly, 'what you call tittle-tattle does not always fade so readily. It can live and grow, spreading its poison, scarring minds and breaking hearts.'

Edward heard the catch of a stifled sob and as the boy's glance lifted again saw in a beam of setting sun the sheen of tears glint in those wide honest eyes.

Alec emerged from a world only he knew. 'Believe me Edward,' he smiled painfully, 'I know . . . I have seen the harm gossip can do, the pain it can inflict, and since coming here to Wednesbury I have seen it again; I have seen the sadness it still brings to Ann's face, the harm it is doing to the livelihood of Grandmother Leah, the wretchedness it is placing in hearts filled only with kindness. Try to understand, I could not let that continue.'

What had happened in this young lad's life, what had caused the grief lying deep in his eyes? Edward chose his words carefully. 'I do understand, Alec,' he smiled briefly, 'I understand you did not want to be the cause of contention, that it was for the sake of Leah and Ann, to give them some measure of peace, but wouldn't it have been kinder to tell them before leaving?'

Alec smiled fleetingly then turned again to the horse, riffling its mane through widespread fingers. 'Kinder, Edward, for whom? For Grandmother Leah maybe, but not I think for Ann. She would have insisted on leaving with me but that could have seen the whole thing start over again; no matter where we went she could have been ostracised, rejected for consorting with a foreigner, for being with me. No Edward, telling Ann of what I planned would not have been a kindness.'

An old head on young shoulders! Appreciation welled in Edward. The lad might have acted wrongly but it had been done for all the right reasons.

'I have only one fear,' Alec was speaking again, 'it is that Ann sees my going as a renunciation of our friendship, and all that we have come to mean to each other.'

'Then you need have no fear!' The swift return came sharper than intended. Edward paused, catching hold of his emotions before adding, 'I hold Ann Spencer to be a better judge of character. It's my belief she would see your going for what it is, a sincere and very loving act of friendship.'

'Would you tell her so? Would you tell her and Grandmother Leah I left only out of love for them?'

Grandmother Leah! Edward let the phrase echo in his mind. There had been no affectation in the term, just a quiet affirmation of love and respect. Listening to his own thoughts Edward stepped across to the stall, the horse immediately nuzzling his hand. Should he say that Ann had spent an entire day searching town and heath, tell of Leah's fainting which was probably helped along by worry over his safety? Edward dismissed the thought. The lad had likely had all he could take for now.

'If that is the way you want it, then I'll tell them though I think they would much rather hear it from you.'

Glancing at the man who too had become a friend Alec shook his head. 'The break is made, Edward, that is the way it must remain. It was wrong of me to come here, to sleep in your barn without obtaining permission.'

'You slept all night in the barn? Why not come to the house?'

'To be seen there would have brought the same troubles to you, the people who refused Grandmother Leah's products would refuse yours. I meant to be gone by daybreak but when I woke you were in the yard. I didn't want you to know I was here so I decided to hide in the hayloft until it got dark. That way I would not be seen leaving but –' he patted the horse's neck – 'I stayed too long talking with Jess, telling him how much he would like Vanka. Vanka is my donkey, Father bought him when he got too old to perform any more in Cinizelli's circus. The tricks he learned there delighted us, especially that of putting his nose into pockets. My sister Tasi would put sugar lumps and sweets in the pocket of her coat then after petting Vanka a while would turn to leave. That was when Vanka would wave his head up and down showing the treats "stolen" from Tasi.'

Seeming of a sudden to realise where he was, he said quickly, 'I'm sorry I disturbed your evening Edward.'

'Hold on.' Edward caught a sleeve as Alec brushed past. 'You are not going anywhere.'

'I have to.'

'No, no you don't have to.' Edward clung on. 'You have no idea of the danger – one wrong step on that heath could find you at the bottom of a mine shaft, or should I say you might never be found. It isn't even known how many there are or where they may be. It would be wiser to stay the night and then if you still feel you have to leave I won't stand in your way, but one thing I ask, let me tell Leah and Ann you are safe, spare them another night of worry.'

'*I be to ask would you talk along of Leah Marshall.*'

Thomas Thorpe secured the white clerical collar about his neck and slowly fastened the row of buttons running the length of a long black gown, his fingers lingering on each one from sheer pleasure.

He had been on the verge of refusing Ada Clews' request. But then a thought had struck him. Going to Leah Marshall's place would provide him with an unexpected treat.

He smiled at himself in the mahogany-framed cheval mirror which his mother had so prized as he smoothed the sleeves of the gown meticulously about the wrists.

Just at the moment of telling the woman to go, he had realised Leah Marshall would not be the only woman in that house; there would be another one also, who a few hours hence would be giving herself to him: Ann Spencer.

To see the fear leap to her eyes, fear of what she knew she could not avoid if she wished to see the boy again, had appealed. He would watch her glance at the older woman without uttering a single word asking for help; Ann Spencer would know that for her there was no going back.

He took a folded white cloth from where he had placed it with almost reverential care on the foot of his bed and draped it about his shoulders, gently shaking the ends until the fringes dropped neatly into place.

Should he wear this to Chapel House, allow Ann Spencer to be the first to see him so dressed? Perhaps she could be granted the privilege, perhaps he could be gracious, permit her the knowledge it was not just plain Thomas Thorpe who stripped and raped her but Reverend Minister Thomas Thorpe.

The idea was titillating. He raised an arm in the attitude of blessing. 'Reverend Minister', he smiled at the reflection silently repeating the words exulting loud on his tongue. Then caution prevailed. To give Ann Spencer the honour of being first to witness him in his ministerial robes might be to rob himself of the longed-for gratification of that first appearance in the chapel. He could not be one hundred per cent certain she would not reveal the secret he wished to keep to himself a while longer, unless . . . he lowered the raised arm in a slow regulated sweep, smiling at the man in the mirror . . . unless once again he borrowed Enoch Phillips' pony and trap.

She had not spoken with Leah. Ann sat on a bench in the park and stared unseeingly at the empty bandstand. She had taken the coward's way out, telling herself it would be less distressing for the woman if she were not called upon to say goodbye. But that had been a lie, to salve her own conscience. She had waited in that upstairs room until she had seen Leah go for her usual afternoon visit to the cow pasture. She would most likely be there for an hour chatting to each animal like it was a personal friend. Ann's insides twisted. Those cows proved truer friends to Leah than ever she herself had. She had watched the dark skirts move deeper into the field, the figure become gradually lost among much the larger shapes of the animals, watched until she was sure any backward glance of Leah's at the house would not show her leaving it.

She had forced herself to walk with head held high, giving no word to the women glancing openly at her as she passed by. They had murmured to one another, murmured and nodded as she crossed the market square stopping at none of its stalls, watching as she turned left along Spring Head no doubt happy in the thought the town might well be seeing the last of her.

And they would. In the very moment Thomas Thorpe's evil was done she would take Alec and they would run and not stop until they dropped from exhaustion.

'Sorry Miss . . . Miss . . .'

An apologetic voice was speaking as though from a distance. Ann looked at the man standing a few feet from the bench.

He spoke again, raising a finger to his smartly peaked cap. 'The park closes at eight, I be 'avin' to ask you to vacate the grounds.'

Still somewhat bemused, Ann stared at the green-uniformed man now taking a large silver watch from a pocket of his coat.

'It be that time now, miss.' He glanced at the watch, 'There y'be, what did I tell you, eight o'clock it is, church clock don't never be wrong.'

Led by the nod of the man's head Ann turned in the direction of the parish church of St Bartholomew, its spire now ebony dark against a sky veiled in the deep grey of late evening.

'Five, six, seven, eight,' he counted the strokes, his glance on the watch. Then returning it with a triumphal flourish to his pocket he went on, 'Church and watch they keeps time together, ain't one fails the other and both now says eight. And seeing that be the time the park gates needs be closed I 'ave to ask you to leave.'

The market square was empty of shoppers, its stalls closed. *'Not like times afore this war started, times was then the market would be busy 'til gone eleven at night, but now wi' food short and folk not 'avin' money enough to pay prices some be askin' then it don't be wondered at the stalls and shops be closin' sooner.'*

Leah's sad words came to her as Ann walked on into Union Street, its shopfronts dark and shuttered, her footsteps echoing eerily along its silent length.

What imp of fate had decided she come to this town? Why had she and Alec not made a home for themselves in Grimsby? The people of that town had shown no animosity, accepting them for two young people displaced by Zeppelin raids they had read of in their newspapers.

It had been such a relief when Aarno had told her they were nearing the English port. It would cause no concern, he explained, fishing boats from Finland used often to land their catch here and still did whenever they evaded German gunboats, but even so it would be better if Alec and herself went ashore in the evening when the dockside would be empty of fish merchants and porters. They had remained below deck all of that day, Aarno pointing out that the boat should be seen to leave the port with the same number of crew as when it had docked.

Evening had seen Alec and herself dressed once more in their own clothes, he manfully hiding his emotion as he shook hands with each of Maija's sons. She had not been so strong; her tears had threaded her words of farewell. Aarno had taken them to the house of a cousin who years before had married an English woman and settled in Grimsby, then he had insisted on giving them English coins accrued from the sale of fish. She and Alec would need money, he had said, then left before she could fully protest.

They had been so kind, Alvar and Maria. They had asked no question of herself or of Alec, Maria answering the attempt at explanation with a simple, 'Aarno has said all that needs be said.'

All that needs be said! Guilt stabbed at her. She had not said all that needed be said to Leah. Ann shrank into the brown wool coat her grandmother's savings had bought for the journey to Russia, hunched her shoulders until the collar touched her ears, but it did not shield against the barbs seeming to prick her skin.

She had told of the events leading to the attack by armed horsemen in that great square in St Petersburg, and of Alec being nursed by a Finnish woman, but she had told nothing of being robbed or of the shooting which had taken place aboard that ferry; she had said nothing of Maija's sons risking their own lives in order to get her and Alec safely to England, nor of the kindness and help Alvar and Maria had shown allowing them to stay in their home for several days. Alvar had seen them on to the train when she had said she wished to return to Darlaston.

Why had she not spoken of those happenings? The reason had many times invaded her dreams, whispering its threat in any off-guard moment.

Had it been the howl of wind, the crash of waves hurled against the ship? The shouts of people being pushed into rowing boats? Did her own fear of what was happening make her imagine dreadful words screeched by a man forced to release his hold on Alec, leaving him to drop awkwardly into the wave-rocked boat? Or had she truly heard?

Ann hugged the coat about her as though to shield her mind from thought, but memory knows no barrier and so it came vivid and alive.

Alec caught in the grip of a man's hand!

In the span of a breath the street with its silent shops was gone and Ann was in a small boat, a relentless wind throwing sheets of freezing spray into her face. She stared upwards at a man shouting down at her from the deck of a ship, his eyes even in the moonless dark glittering fury.

'...*find you* ...'

Alec dropped to her side, men began pulling on the oars, the boat was moving away.

The man was yelling, a raised fist jabbing the night.

'... *take back ... you die* ...'

The wind was snatching at the cries, breaking them apart, tossing fragments into the void then, as if in a moment of regret, the howling whine had ceased and in that moment had come clear across the widening gap the threat which had haunted her every day, had her heart trip with fear at sounds in her every night.

'... *any who hide you shall die.*'

'G'night Bert, g'night Joe, g'night mate.'

A bevy of voices launched on the night swept away visions of choppy seas, of a ferry boat swallowed up in blackness, but even as Ann watched the group of workmen leave the tavern at the end of the street words echoed in her mind, words shouted in language she could understand: '*Any who hide you shall die.*' That was the reason she had been glad to leave the house of Maija, to move on from that of Alvar and Maria, and it was the real underlying cause of her and Alec's need to leave Leah.

They had stayed too long. Ann walked on. Too long the lie of silence. Too long easing her conscience with the thought, It was only imagination.

Now self-delusion was reaping its harvest. As she turned into Queen's Place Ann stared at the chapel, her heart pounding at what she knew waited in the house set at the rear. Rape! A threat dreadful as that hurled at her from that ferry, a threat that was in no way a product of her imagination.

26

'I have made a mistake.' Alec Romney looked at the man seated opposite.

'How's that?' Edward looked up from the newspaper he had been reading.

Alec paused then said firmly, 'I have been selfish. What I told you about my leaving the house of Grandmother Leah, of going secretly so as to cause her less sadness and provide Ann with freedom to live life for herself without having me to consider was I now realise simply a way of less pain for myself, the way of a coward.'

Edward studied the young face drawn with self-reproach. What was his background, who were his parents? Why had he been allowed to travel without one or the other? Why if he had relatives in this country had they not come forward to claim him and last but not least, how had he come to be with Ann Spencer?

'My father said I should always try to be strong, strong enough to face the truth.' Alec smiled fleetingly. 'That is what I am trying to do now, Edward, to face up to what truth tells me. By leaving secretly I was running, not just from my friends, I was running from myself; that is not the way a . . . a man should behave.'

The pause had been brief, the correction sharp. Had the quick dart flashing across his eyes been fear of letting something almost slip from the tongue?

'... *not the way a ... a man should behave.*'

Edward listened again to the words in his mind and behind them others saying Alec Romney had not meant to use the word 'man'. So what had it been substituted for?

'My father he . . . he also taught me to face my responsibilities and not ask others do it for me. Asking you to speak to Ann and Grandmother Leah in my place was shirking that task.'

Seems your father talked a lot about responsibility but where was his own in letting a young lad travel alone! Edward folded the newspaper then setting it aside asked, 'Does that mean what I think it means?'

'That I will speak to them myself? Yes, that is what it means.'

'Then you can come with me in the morning when I take the milk.'

'No.' Alec shook his head. 'I am too much the coward to wait until morning, I might well run away again; it is better I go now.'

There were several ways he might describe this lad but coward was definitely not one. He was ready to confront what he saw as a mistake and to rectify it.

'Wait,' he said as Alec began to rise from the chair. 'If you've made a mistake then I've made one. You thought to spare the feelings of Leah and Ann, I thought to spare yours.'

'Mine?'

'It was my feeling you had enough to deal with so I didn't tell you of Ann being out the whole day searching for you.'

'She is returned!'

'Yes, but Leah said she knew she wouldn't stay, that she would try to find where you were. It's best you be prepared for her already having done that.'

'What have I done!' Alec slumped back into the chair. 'I have been so thoughtless.'

'That's one fault you can't lay claim to, it was thinking of Leah and Ann that had you do as you have. That, my lad, can't be called thoughtless.'

'That is kind of you, Edward, but I fear my father would not agree.'

Damn your father! Anger rose hot in Edward. Had the man been with you as he should have been none of this might have happened.

Shrugging into his coat Alec looked at the man regarding him across the small living room, at a face revealing unspoken emotion. Was that emotion anger felt against him?

'Edward,' he slipped the last button through its button-hole, 'I have seen the regard you have for Grandmother Leah, the love you hold for her, and I know the stupid-ity of my action will have caused her concern. I apologise to you as I will to her and hope your anger will not be long-lasting.'

I have no anger against you, only against a man who could leave you alone to face whatever the world might throw at you. Edward fetched his own coat.

'It isn't anger I'm feeling,' he lied, fastening the jacket across his chest, 'I'm anxious for the tongue-lathering we both be like to get from Leah for waiting so long before going to see her. Make no mistake this time Alec, Leah Marshall is never backward in coming forward when her temper's riled, so if you don't mind I'll come along; two of us facing the music together will mebbe seem like we each get only half a belabouring.'

Leaving the house with the lad at his side, Edward smiled grimly to himself. Half a belabouring . . . was the moon made of green cheese!

★   ★   ★

She had not been there. Seated in the study of Chapel House Thomas Thorpe reviewed his visit to Leah Marshall's place. The woman had not asked him into the house. When she saw him coming along the narrow lane beside the pasture she had waited at the gate, closing it firmly as he reached it.

'*Good evening Leah.*' He had smiled affably. '*I was hoping to find you at home.*'

There had been no answering smile, only the stony glint of displeasure in her eyes. '*Well your 'ope's been answered,*' she had said sharply, making no move to open the gate, '*an' I reckons this visit be on account of you havin' summat to say so say it an' be done.*'

He had let the smile remain on his lips, his glance sweeping the field with its grazing cows then alighting briefly on the house before returning to the woman regarding him with frank animosity.

'*I don't be goin' to stand 'ere while you admires of the scenery, say what it be you've come to say for when them cows be ready to come into the yard they comes givin' of no mind to who might be a'standin' in their path.*'

'*I wonder, could Miss Spencer be asked to join us?*'

'*You wonder all you like!*'

The answer had bitten back at him but he had gone on. '*What I've come to say involves her, it be best you call her.*'

A snort had greeted that, Leah Marshall's arms folding across her chest as her displeasure deepened to anger.

'*It be best do it!*' she had snapped. '*Now I be a tellin' what be best, you get y'self back where you come from while I still be civil enough to say you don't be welcome rather than show it with a pitchfork.*'

'*I told Ada Clews she should come see you herself.*'

'*Ada Clews.*' The folded arms had lowered. '*What be Ada Clews to do with it?*'

'*She brought a message from Jinny Jinks and the rest of the women who've taken their custom away from you . . .*'

'*Oh ar! Then how be it you comes, why d'ain't they come? They knows Leah Marshall's door be open to all 'cept Thomas Thorpe.*'

He had wanted to tell her then, tell her how he had treated her precious Deborah, tell her how he had killed her daughter then thrown her body into the river like so much refuse; he had wanted to use the pain of that knowledge to repay the snub of her words. But the cold voice of reason had cooled the rise of anger. Why use that weapon now when the slash of it could give more satisfaction at another time?

'*I said for them to do that,*' he had answered, taking the advice of reason. '*But when it were made plain none of them would, when I was begged to come in place of them how, as a friend, could I refuse.*'

The look on Leah Marshall's face had said plainly that Thomas Thorpe was friend only to himself, a look echoing in her sharp retort.

'*Then best do what it be you couldn't refuse!*'

'*Ada said the others as well as herself definitely wanted Miss Spencer to hear in person what I've been asked to say.*'

'*Hmmph.*' Leah had sniffed. '*Well sorry though I be to go a disappointin' of Ada and the rest of 'em, Ann don't be here; but don't let that be a worry for I be able as you in passin' on a message.*'

How long had she been gone from that house? Had she decided the boy was no longer her responsibility and so left the town altogether? Had she confided to Leah Marshall the demand he had made? Had saying she was not in the house been a lie, an excuse for not having her come to the gate? No, he could dismiss the idea. Had Leah Marshall been given the faintest inkling of what had been said then the pitchfork would have proved more than a threat.

Ann Spencer had played him for a fool! Thorpe looked at the quietly ticking clock on the mantelpiece. Eight twenty! Anger spurted hot in his veins as he walked into the tiny hallway. That pleading last night when she had run into him, her begging he turn the lad over to her had been playacting, simply a ruse to get herself away. She had no mind to keep to their agreement otherwise she would have been here by this time. Unless! He froze at the sound coming from outside . . . unless she *had* told someone, someone who now stood at the other side of the door.

Who might she have told? Whoever it was out there, why not bang on the door, why not demand to be let in, why not . . . ? Suddenly the answer came to him. Of course! It was an accusation made out of spite; Ann Spencer somehow held him accountable for the fact that she and the boy were unwanted in Wednesbury, so this was her way of taking revenge. What proof did she have of even an unkind word on his part? He would let it lie there leaving a brief shake of the head and a look of sympathy to do the rest.

Words! His would always be accepted over hers. Confidence returned, he opened the door.

'It seems we have something of a misunderstanding.' Thomas Thorpe smiled at the figure he had admitted into Chapel House. 'Please search the house, look in every room, you will find no one there.'

'You said—'

'What I said,' Thorpe interrupted, 'was the person you are looking to find is not in this house, but don't just take my word, look for yourself. The study,' he threw open a door, 'or maybe the living room,' he threw open a second door, standing aside to give a clearer view of an interior lit only by moonlight; 'then of course there is the scullery. But perhaps you would prefer to begin upstairs.'

Begin upstairs! Sick with nerves, Ann watched the spread of his cold sly smile, the unrelenting gleam of his pale eyes. Thomas Thorpe was not referring to any search for Alec.

She clenched trembling fingers together. 'Where is Alec, tell me where he is.'

'All in good time, first there is our agreement to fulfil.'

She had made no agreement, she had been given no option. 'The choice is yours.'

Almost as though reading her mind Thorpe extended a hand to the door leading on to the quiet Queen's Place. 'You may leave now but I should remind you the lad is too well hidden ever to be found.'

He was saying she could go, she need not go through with his demand! The hope died quickly. How would she live with the knowledge she could have saved Alec yet had chosen to turn her back on him?

'You promise . . . you promise you will tell me where . . .'

Gloating at the air of resignation in that unfinished request Thorpe let his hand fall away from the door. 'Where you can find him? But of course I will tell you, a bargain is a bargain.'

As he followed her upstairs Thomas Thorpe resisted the urge to laugh out loud. Ann Spencer's bargain would result in a conclusion very different to that he had just promised.

Perhaps he should have worn that outfit. Watching the slight figure slowly unfasten her coat Thorpe's senses tripped. To have her release the many small buttons of that long gown, to watch the fear grow on her face as each was loosed would have repaid him for the loss of pleasure at not wearing those clothes for the first time in chapel before the entire congregation; but then opportunity was not lost; this evening need not be the one-off affair she expected. Tomorrow night, the night after that and for as many nights as he wanted Ann Spencer would do *exactly* as he wished.

She would remove her own clothing first. He would watch the blush of colour rise in her cheeks, see the tears of degradation sparkle on those long lashes, feel the tremor of her body as he brushed his fingers over tight breasts then slowly down the quivering stomach to that warm moist cleft.

Ann turned away; it was agony enough knowing what awaited her, she did not have to look at him, to see the evil of his mind manifest itself on his lust-filled face.

The laugh as much as the hard jerk swinging her about told Ann the mistake of her thinking.

Help me, help me please to get this over. Ann's prayer stuck in her throat when Thorpe's hands closed over hers, his voice husky as he pulled her close into him.

'No need to be shy . . .'

The murmur slid like a serpent.

'Or could it be that is a pretence, a little trick to liven the appetite.'

Wet lips drooled a trail from earlobe to a corner of her mouth, another lecherous crow in Thorpe's throat showing the pleasure he derived from Ann's shivered sob.

Hands which had held hers moved lightning fast, one to clamp hard on her breast the other threading into her hair and snatching her head back, as his throaty salacious tone hardened to a rasp.

'How thoughtful,' he snarled against her lips, 'but my appetite needs no boost as you be going to find out.'

'I ain't had the seein' of her since afore teatime.' Leah Marshall looked at the man and boy she had berated for the past five minutes. 'Her were upstairs a puttin' away of clothes fresh ironed when I went across to the field to chat along of the girls.'

'What time was that?'

'Hmm!' Leah pondered Edward Langley's question. 'Be 'ard to say . . . I remembers the church clock striking, yes . . . yes it struck four while I were with the girls.'

No use in asking how long she spent with the cows, it was Leah's habit to talk with each one individually, to chat as she might with a woman neighbour. Suppressing worry mounting with every second Edward went on. 'So when did you realise she was not in the house?'

'That I remembers clear. I come in from the pasture and findin' Ann not yet downstairs an' hearing no sound from above thought as how her could be restin'. Lord knows her be a needin' of it. So I reckoned to let her lie until evenin' milking. It were after I settled the girls for the night; I were puzzled as to why her hadn't come along to help in the milkin' parlour nor yet to help with putting the milk into the settling pans, that don't be like her at all: that were my thought so comin' back to this room an' findin' her still not to be here I went upstairs only to find each room empty.'

The evening milking. Edward turned Leah's words over in his mind. Punctual in that as she was in all things to do with her dairying she would have gone to the milking parlour at five. Milking a dozen cows, sponging their udders, seeing them into the barn for the night; then the task of emptying pails of milk into the vats, the scouring of utensils, all would have taken at least two hours, probably much longer.

'There were no sign to tell her 'ad ever been in that bedroom,' Leah was speaking again, 'everythin' were neat an' proper on the wash stand and on the bed.' She paused, swallowing hard.

'On the bed laid careful as any bridal troosoh was clothes, Deborah's clothes I'd asked Ann to keep for herself but her hadn't teken not one thing.'

Half past seven at the earliest, that would have been the time Leah discovered Ann was gone. Edward heard Leah speaking but his brain still mulled over what was already said. If the girl had slipped away when Leah went to the cow field she had been gone – he glanced at the clock on Leah's mantelshelf which showed eight fifteen – more than four hours! Anxiety prickled in every nerve. Ann Spencer had left this house over four hours ago; she could be miles away by now.

'She has gone looking for me.'

'No lad, her ain't.' Leah answered the boy rising from the chair she had insisted he take beside the fireplace. 'Ann told me earlier on, her said her wouldn't go a searchin' of you no more for her be certain you'd gone to be with them relatives of your'n.'

'But why would Ann say that? She had to know I would have gone to them long ago had I been able.'

'Said it be her reckoning you had some idea of where to find your folks and that bein' how it was then weren't no use of her goin' lookin' for you no more.'

'. . . *why would Ann say that? She had to know I would have gone to them long ago . . .*'

Alec's misgivings echoed Edward's own. Why indeed! And if she no longer intended to look for Alec why the abrupt departure? Why leave without a goodbye for Leah?

'I think Ann told you I was gone to my relatives to save you from worry, but . . . I think also she will still be searching so . . .' Alec smiled apologetically, 'forgive me, Grandmother Leah, I must go look for her.'

'What good will that do?' Leah protested. 'It just means the two of you will be out there on the streets. I says it be best you bide where you be least 'til mornin'; won't stand no chance of findin' her in the dark.'

'What Leah says makes sense,' Edward put in, seeing Alec about to argue. 'You can p'raps find your way about the town in the daytime, Alec, but you don't know it well enough to do so at night even supposing you knew her to still be in Wednesbury.'

'You know Ann, Grandmother Leah, you and she cared for me together when I was so sick, you saw her tears, you knew the many times she refused to leave my side. Tell me, do you truly think the darkness of night will prevent my going to look for her?'

Grandmother! Leah's heart tripped. That was something she would never be. Her children were dead and along with them the hopes of holding grandchildren in her arms: the simple pleasures that were the birthright of every woman had been denied her. This lad – she glanced at Alec shrugging into his coat – he was no kin to her, he called her grandmother out of politeness yet the word and the affection she knew to be at back of it pulled at her very soul.

From across the room Edward caught the emotion play-ing over Leah's features. She had faced losing this lad once already; now the same unhappiness stared at her again.

'Wait.'

Sharp, decisive, more an order than a request, it halted Alec as he stepped towards the scullery.

'Nobody questions that you want to go looking for Ann but I think Leah would feel easier in her mind if I were to go along with you.'

27

Leah had looked at him with more than gratitude in her eyes. Edward blessed the night gloom hiding the colour rising in his cheeks. She had divined that he as much as the lad walking by his side wanted to find Ann Spencer.

'Even', Edward lad, weren't lookin' to see you 'ere along o' this time o' night. Don't be summat up wi' Leah do there?'

'No Ezekial, there is nothing wrong with Leah.'

'I d'ain't mean of no pryin',' Ezekial's tone had become tinged with apology, 'I were frettin' of Leah bein' poorly.'

The two had been children together, during their whole lives had known only friendship for one another, so it was natural Ezekial would worry for the health of such a friend. Edward replied with a smile in the darkness. 'Enquiring after the well-being of a friend is never prying, Ezekial; I'll tell Leah you were asking after her.'

'Thank y'lad.' Ezekial turned his glance to Alec. 'An' what of you, young 'un, be you over that illness o' your'n?'

'Quite over it I thank you, Little Father.'

'Ehh.' Ezekial's long-drawn breath sighed in to the night. 'I told Jinny Jinks an' the rest o' they women it were a long time since I'd heard them words, same as I just been talkin' of 'em wi' Samul Bradley. We was in the Crimea along of the same time an' we enjoys a talk over old times. I said to 'im how the lad called me Little Father an' that turned the conversation to

259

him an' the wench 'appenin' to come to this town. Samul said he'd seen the wench not an hour since.'

'Samuel Bradley says he has seen Ann . . . Miss Spencer!'

'That be what I told you.' Ezekial pointed his walking stick in the direction he had come along Meeting Street, 'Back there in the Rising Sun, we enjoys a pint there; Henry Butler keeps a good barrel.'

'Is Samuel still in the pub?'

Ezekial frowned at the brusque interruption. 'Left when I did. Edward lad, be summat up, you seems right agitated.'

'Little Father, did Mr Bradley speak with Ann, did he perhaps ask where she might be heading?'

The question had been polite enough. Ezekial glanced at Alec, his face showing pale in the enveloping greyness. But there had been that same note of anxiety he had heard in Edward Langley's voice. Aware his answer would be disappointing he said gently, 'No lad, Samul said naught of speakin' wi' the wench though he did say as he were puzzled by her turnin' into Queen's Place at such an hour, 'specially seein' there be no service tekin' place in the chapel.'

Samuel Bradley had seen Ann less than an hour ago! Edward had thanked the old man, had heard the tap, tap of his stick fading along the street, but his mind had rung with that one phrase: '*seen the wench not an hour since*'. She had been going to pray, why else go into Queen's Place? But an hour was a long time. Would she still be there?

He must control the urge to run. The lad had spent the night in the barn where he might not have slept well; running to Queen's Place could overtire him after such a recent illness. Edward walked as quickly as he dared, backtracking along Meeting Street then turning left into the narrow almost alley-like School Street, hemmed closely on one side by a ribbon of ebony shapes, each house made darker with the soot and smoke of factory and foundry. Across the passageway they faced the unedifying stern structure that was the National School. But Edward was gazing ahead to where Queen's Place and its chapel stood still robed in darkness at the further end.

'Edward, do you think Ann will still be in the chapel?'

Alec asked the question which had preoccupied Edward since speaking with Ezekial. Trying to keep doubt from his voice he said lightly, 'Probably the peace and quiet of the place has lulled her to sleep, let's go wake her up.'

They had not woken her. Edward closed the door of the chapel behind him. Ann Spencer was not there, no one was; silent, the black shroud of its interior not relieved by a single candle flame, the room had seemed to shrink from the light of the matches he had struck, to draw away, hugging its secrets to itself.

Breathing deeply to contain his disappointment, Edward touched the shoulder of the boy whose own long-drawn breath exhibited that same regret.

'It was a long shot, Alec,' he said, turning towards the street, 'we'll just go look somewhere else.'

His appetite needed no boosting. Thomas Thorpe leered into the face lifted to his by the force of his fingers threaded into thick sherry-gold hair. He was ready now ready to take what he had so often promised himself . . . but not yet. Some deep sense intimated that to rush things was to deny himself the thrill of seeing fear mounting to dread, seeing the tremor of horror ripple through the slender body as the last shred of clothing dropped away; then hear the sob of utter despair as he forced that naked form on to the bed. Yes, it was right he should claim that pleasure; he had earned it by providing a roof for those weeks. She could have given her thanks then, quietly paid the true cost of renting this house yet . . . had Ann Spencer acted willingly then this enjoyment, this extra amusement, would have gone by the board. But she had not acted willingly. He was grateful to her for that, glad of her refusal for this way he could delight in her misery every bit as much as he enjoyed his own gratification.

He clamped his mouth hard on her lips, stifling a plea starkly visible in wide frightened eyes.

After releasing Ann he breathed deeply as she stumbled from his arms. He must control his emotions, keep desire in check or nature would take its own course and while providing ease it would cheat him of the satisfaction of that first delicious moment. But self-denial would be short-lived. Flesh reared hard and demanding. There would be many other moments. He smiled eagerly at Ann as she backed away from him.

'I think we've waited long enough,' then with each syllable dripping lust he added thickly, 'take off your clothes.'

Ann shook her head. 'No.'

In an instant the sensual smile was gone, replaced by cold menace. Thorpe's narrow eyes glittered beneath heavy half-closed lids. 'No? Then I will do it for you.'

'Wait,' Ann's arms crossed protectively over her chest, 'first tell me where Alec is.'

'First!' he sneered. 'Why would I tell you first?'

'You promised if I came here you would tell me where to find Alec.'

'After!' He emphasised the word. 'A sensible businessman doesn't hand over goods until they are paid for; you know my price, the sooner it is paid the sooner you get those goods.'

Ann at once realised that there was nothing to prevent Thomas Thorpe going back on his word, no guarantee he would reveal where he had Alec hidden. Goods. The word stung in her brain. That was all she and Alec were to this man: no more than a paper bag which once used was thrown away. But buying and selling was a two-way operation. Head lifting determinedly she said, 'We both have a price, Mr Thorpe. Mine is that you produce Alec now or the business you hope to engage in is ended.'

'I'm the one to say when it is ended and that won't be for many a day.' Thorpe's screech of anger echoed through the silent house and he struck Ann hard across the cheek, the savagery of it banging her head against the wall. A second blow sent her tumbling to the bed; a laugh rattled in his throat as he reached for her.

'What was that?' Edward Langley paused in mid-stride. 'Did you hear anything?'

'Someone shouting, probably came from the alehouse across the street.'

Maybe. There was nothing unusual in a man's raised voice when leaving that place but the sound which had come with it, the quiet underlying sound of a woman's cry, was not so usual.

'Not the alehouse,' he said, 'much nearer; it could almost have come from the chapel.'

'But there was no one there, you saw for yourself.'

Yes, he had seen – he had also heard. Edward stared at the darkened building; somewhere close by a woman had cried out, a sound alive with fear. Ann? For a moment the thought stunned him. Could the woman be Ann Spencer, had she tripped and fallen in the darkness, was she lying injured?

Edward forced himself to stay calm. A quick search of the grounds would settle matters.

'Best take a look around the back, someone could be hurt.'

He did not want to wait even a minute; that minute could be spent searching for Ann. Alec followed, stopping as his glance caught the gleam of light in a window of Chapel House.

'Samuel Bradley saw Ann coming here.' Edward too was looking at the gleam peeping between curtains not quite closed together. 'Maybe she has been given a night's lodging.'

'She will not be in that house!'

It had come too quickly. Edward looked at the lad already turning away.

'Why, Alec?' He caught the boy's shoulder. 'Why would Ann not be in that house?'

'It . . he held fear for her.'

Edward frowned. 'Fear of what? Does it have rats?'

'I do not think it was an animal caused Ann to be afraid.'

These two, so gossip in town had it, had of their own choosing left that house. But if vermin were not the problem then what had been?

'Alec.' Edward turned the boy to look at him. 'Tell me truthfully, why did you and Miss Spencer leave here, what was she afraid of?'

'You ask for the truth Edward but what I say may not be truth, for Ann did not say what troubled her.'

'But you knew all the same.'

'I can only guess . . . but I think it was to do with the man who came to collect payment for use of the house. It was on those evenings Ann was feared; I asked on each of those occasions should I remain in the room with her but she would not allow me to, so you see I cannot say with truth if it was this man caused her to be frightened.'

Edward stiffened. Just what sort of payment? Leah had said Ann Spencer had come to her with no money to speak of so what had that rent collector asked in lieu?

'This man, do you know who he is, can you tell me his name?'

'I did not see him on either of those evenings but I heard Ann talking with him, she called him Mr Thorpe.'

Thorpe! The one man whom Leah spoke of only with loathing. What had he to do with Ann Spencer?

Another cry, this time cut sharp as though by a blow. Edward ran for the house. If it were not Ann Spencer in there he would apologise; though if a man was using his fist on a woman that apology would be given along with a blow or two to his own head.

Inside the house, at the foot of the stairs, Edward's hand stopped the boy. 'Wait here.'

'But . . .'

'Wait here!' The curt reply brooked no more argument. Alec nodded as Edward took the stairs two at a time.

At the open door of a bedroom he halted at the sight of two figures. Thorpe! But it was not the furious face turning to look at him that Edward saw in that explosive moment; he focused only on the face of a young woman, a scarlet weal vivid across her pale cheek, the nape of her neck gripped in Thorpe's left hand while the other grasped the cloth of a dress ripped open to the waist.

'Get away from her.' Little more than a murmur, it pulsed fury.

Shocked, Thorpe stared into eyes gleaming murder.

'Let her go or I swear I'll kill you where you stand.'

In the seconds it took for Edward to make that threat words of a very different kind came to Thorpe. Langley, they whispered, Langley is in love with the girl. Like warm sunshine it melted the coldness of shock. He could use the knowledge to torment the man as he had, and would continue, to torment the woman. Another blessing! He dropped the cloth still held in his fingers while pushing Ann a step forward.

'But of course I'll let her go,' he smarmed, 'did you think I was holding her against her will?'

Ann couldn't . . . she couldn't have come willingly. Edward looked at the slight figure pulling the torn dress to cover her bare flesh, seeing the rest of that waxen pale face flush scarlet as the weal marking it. He was certain.

Small eyes the colour of slushed ice held Edward's stare; mockery in the voice was loud as an open laugh as Thorpe pushed Ann one more step towards Edward.

'Tell him Ann, tell him did I bring you to this house or did you come of your own choice.'

She had to say she had come looking only for a place to spend the night, that what he had seen had been forced on her. His heart seeming to stand still, Edward waited for Ann's reply. With the whispered, 'It is my choice,' his certainty died.

'Satisfied?'

Like a spark to dry tinder Thorpe's sarcasm ignited the passion of hurt smouldering deep inside Edward, hurling it upwards in a volcanic spurt.

'Not quite!' He spat venom. 'I want to feel the kind you get from striking a woman, except mine will be got from beating you senseless.'

'No Edward, stop, you don't understand.'

Thorpe was already in his grip, he was dangerously close to delivering a blow. Ann's cry halted the strike. Edward answered savagely, 'No I don't understand, I don't understand how you can humiliate yourself like this.'

'I did it for Alec!'

That wasn't the cry of a tuppenny whore! Edward shot a glance at Ann, whose eyes glistened with shame; then his grip on Thorpe tightened.

'Alec,' he snapped, 'you came here on account of Alec! Do you want to tell me why? Or should I ask Thorpe!'

Conscious of the anger throbbing in Edward, afraid his treatment of her attacker would make Thorpe refuse now to say where Alec could be found, Ann hesitated.

'I . . .' A deep breath helped her search for the right words. 'Mr Thorpe and I met yesterday evening. I had been searching for Alec but found no trace of him; Mr Thorpe said he knew where Alec was.'

'But he didn't tell you there and then.'

'No. He . . . he had a very urgent visit to make and could not spare the time it would take to explain.'

Edward looked scathingly at the man he held in an iron grip. 'Couldn't spare the time,' he grated, 'or didn't you want to miss the chance of having a girl who otherwise wouldn't come within a mile?'

'She can leave now but she won't get to know where the boy is.' The words squeezed with difficulty past the barrier of fingers clasped about his throat but Thorpe's eyes screeched dark hatred.

'Edward please go . . . just go.'

'Yes, I'll go,' Edward answered, but his eyes stayed with those blazing hate. 'But first Mr Thorpe is going to answer my question: do I take it you have Alec hidden away somewhere?'

Frantic with fear that Thorpe would take revenge by not disclosing where Alec was, Ann cried out across the room. 'Mr Thorpe was taking care of Alec, he . . . he promised to take me to him.'

'And was that promise made before or after you slapped her face, before or after you tore the clothes from her? Either way you are going to regret both.'

'Do that,' Thorpe snarled as Edward's fist raised again, 'strike me, Langley, and neither you nor the girl will ever see that brat, you'll never find him – never!'

'Is that a fact? Then I must be mistaken. Let's find out shall we?' At last Edward's glance shifted to Ann. 'Miss Spencer, would you be so good as to call my friend? He is waiting downstairs in the hall.'

'I am here, Edward, I could not stay downstairs any longer.'

With a gasp of incredulity Ann stared at the boy in the doorway. 'Alec – oh thank God!'

Alec caught the tilt of Edward's head signalling that he take Ann down to the hallway.

'So!' Edward jerked the figure he held on to. 'You told Ann Spencer the lad she searched for was with you, that she should come get him. That lie was told simply for your own ends and we both know what they were; you didn't like being refused, did you, that hurt your pride, but hitting a woman did no harm to your self-esteem. My guess is it did just the opposite. Well, we all have fancies and right now mine is to beat the daylights out of you.'

Edward stared with disgust into eyes now clearly showing fear but the look raised no pity in him.

'Edward ... please, no more; Alec is safe. Let that be enough.' Ann had refused to be coaxed away.

No! Edward resisted her words. The swine had to be made to suffer for what he'd done.

'Edward, please.' Rushing forward, Ann placed a hand on his arm. Edward struggled to think rationally. Thorpe deserved a beating . . . but what would be the effect upon Ann of witnessing yet more violence?

'Think yourself lucky,' he said as he threw Thorpe from him, glaring down on the sprawling figure, 'you've got away with it this time you filthy swine, but I advise you to listen carefully: should you approach Ann Spencer again, should you even look in her direction, I will break every bone in your miserable body.'

28

She had heard little apart from Ezekial's account of his talk
with Samuel Bradley and how he had seen Ann turning into
Queen's Place. That had been dubious from the start.

Leah stared at the butter muslin she was making into cheese
covers.

Why? she had asked herself. Why would the wench go to
the chapel which had openly displayed rejection of both her
and the lad? And if not the chapel . . .

Leah's needle rested in the cloth.

Samuel Bradley's conversation with Ezekial had revealed
there was no service that evening so the place would have
been closed up. There was only one more building in Queen's
Place and that was Chapel House. But why in God's name
call at the very home she had literally been thrown out of? Yet
that was where Edward and Alec had found her.

She had seen a light from a window, and though she had been
reluctant to disturb whoever was inside she felt she must ask if
they had seen Alec. Was it Alec had come here asking help?

It would take more than a pinch of salt to swallow that!

Oh that might have been the underlying cause of her being in
that house; had the whereabouts of the lad been already known
then, Leah's instinct had told her, Ann Spencer wouldn't have
gone near Chapel House and certainly wouldn't have stayed
conversing with Thomas Thorpe.

But the lad hadn't been there and Thorpe had not met or spoken with him, so why hadn't that sly little toerag told Ann so? Why ask her inside when he knew he couldn't help?

Except to help himself.

It hadn't needed a deal of explanation. Edward's face looked drawn with a fury she had never seen in him before that night; Alec's young face looked pale, his eyes darkened with the unspoken thought that all of what had happened was his fault; while Ann, her face coloured with emerging bruises, had run straight up to the bedroom to change her dress for a skirt and blouse of Deborah's.

Glancing across the hearth to where Ann sat opposite Leah felt sure even though none of the three spoke of it that Thomas Thorpe had assaulted the girl.

She had not asked; if Ann wanted her to know it would be of the girl's own free will.

But she needed no words from Edward nor none from Ann to feel the truth of her own conviction. The sight of a dress being mended told her enough, a dress she had been informed had torn on a bramble protruding from a hedge: brambles scratch but they don't bruise. Bruises were caused by a hand, usually a man's. Lord, she'd seen enough black eyes on women she called on with products from her dairy, seen the scarlet weals on cheeks caused by drunken husbands and sometimes fathers.

Leah's glance returned to her needlework but her fingers remained unmoving, her mind preoccupied.

Had Thorpe been sniffing of the barman's apron . . . had he been drunk as a bob 'owler? So far gone in beer he hadn't known what he was about? No, that wasn't Thorpe's way; he didn't visit the alehouses with other men from his workplace nor, so Ezekial had it, did he frequent the Rising

Sun or put in an appearance at any other public house in the town.

A blind? A deception in order to have the congregation, especially the female congregation, think more highly of him? Was he a man who took his ale in secret, did he think by taking a jug to Chapel House instead of his own in Cross Street it would forever go unnoticed?

Leah's hidden smile was one of gentle sarcasm. Little managed to stay completely unknown in this town; sooner or later Thorpe's 'secret drinking' would have become public knowledge. Gossip was the lifeblood of its womenfolk and it certainly wouldn't have been spared by those not sharing in admiration of the so-pious lay preacher.

So it was safe to say Thorpe had not been drunk and it was safer still to say those marks on Ann Spencer's face had been caused by no bramble.

Coals sighed deeper into the bed of the fire. Leah watched the fountain of brilliant sparks disappear into the blackness of the chimney, just as her own bright lively children had been snatched away into the darkness of death. She had known the manner of Joshua and Daniel's passing, two pieces of paper lying in a drawer in her front parlour had borne the words she had dreaded: 'killed in action'. She had thought that no words could ever again cut so deeply, that nothing on earth could ever again bring such sorrow. Then Deborah had been found dead.

Old hurt deepened to almost physical pain and Leah closed her eyes.

Deborah had fought in no foreign field. Leah breathed hard against her gathering tears. But there were wars of many kinds, some waged silently in the deepest innermost reaches of the heart while others were conflicts of the soul. These were the battles her daughter had fought.

What had been the reason? What had brought about the change which had made Deborah lose that happiness she had previously radiated? She had seen the same in Ann Spencer that evening she had returned from searching for the lad: withdrawn, barely speaking a word yet her eyes had been fearful. Then the very next night she had been brought bruised and half-stripped from Chapel House, and the only other body in that house had been Thomas Thorpe.

No one would convince Leah that man had not struck then tried to rape Ann Spencer just as no one would convince her the death of Deborah had been by suicide.

Leah looked at the young woman quietly sewing cheesecloths.

Two pretty young women, both with a patent dislike of Thomas Thorpe. Assault! Attempted rape! Had both girls suffered the same? Had Thorpe abused Deborah until unable to stand any more of it she had thrown herself into the river? Once more Leah's denial of suicide was absolute. That left one more question. Had Thorpe raped her daughter then murdered her, silenced her to ensure his filth could never be brought to light?

Dear Lord, Leah prayed silently, hold my girl in Your arms, comfort her with Your love as I would have with mine and if she came before You with any mark of sin I pray You forgive; but Lord I ask no forgiveness for what I carry in my heart. Vengeance, says the Holy Book, be Yours to repay but if Deborah's death was at the hands of Thomas Thorpe, then I will steal that vengeance from Your holy hand.

'Should you approach Ann Spencer again, should you even look in her direction I will break every bone in your miserable body.'

Edward Langley's face had been distorted with anger, his whole frame had seemed to vibrate with rage as he spat the words between clenched teeth.

Sleep had refused to come so Ann sat at the bedroom window her gaze travelling over pasture silvered by the high moon, at freckles of light stippling the leaves of trees growing tall in the hedges bordering fields, pinpoints of silver-gold, but the beauty of the night was lost in emotions which had pulled at her since hearing that outburst.

He had made to strike Thomas Thorpe, the tension holding him almost rigid emphasising the fury driving inside him.

Any decent man would have reacted the same in the circumstances yet . . . Ann conjured up vivid pictures of German sailors with guns in hand, of one grinning while another was snatching her clothes. She saw the figure of Berndt, his 'no' a soundless movement of the mouth, prevented from saving her because a rifle was jabbing against his ribs.

Ann shuddered again at the imagined touch of rough callused fingers pressing into her waist, riding quickly over her hips.

The page of memory turned. She watched a man emerge from the cabin, a man waving a vodka bottle in each hand. 'Lars.' She whispered the name even as, soundless as before, the man mouthed words. Lars was calling to her attacker, but the temptation Lars proffered was not so appetising as the sailor held in her attacker's grasp.

Then as though by the hand of the Angel of Mercy the man was gone from her and Lars had supported her as she stumbled across the deck and down to the cabin. Lars' smile was replaced by the pull of anger while his eyes blazed both pity and loathing, pity for her being subjected to such an ordeal and loathing for its perpetrator; a look clear on the faces of all three brothers, etched deep into their wind-bronzed features.

The picture faded back into the past yet memory's book did not close.

Her waking eyes looked on fields pearled by the soft radiance of a white-gold moon, at leaves pirouetting in a whispering breeze, but Ann's inner eyes watched a different scene.

Lamplight shed pallid gleams about a small neatly ordered room where a figure was sent tumbling on to a bed from a blow; a figure then dragged roughly to its feet; a man gripped the back of its neck while at the same time with his free hand ripping its clothing from throat to waist.

Ann tried to blink away the spectacle but it rolled on, showing a woman's cheeks flush scarlet as her glance caught that of a second figure in the doorway.

Edward Langley. Ann felt the heat of shame burn in her cheeks. She had not been swift enough to cover her exposed breasts, to gather the torn cloth together before his glance had swept her naked flesh. Mere seconds were all that look stayed on her, then it flashed to Thomas Thorpe. Incandescent in its rage, it seemed it must consume him in the fires of its fury; but more terrible still, the face turned to Thorpe was contorted like that of an animal ready for the kill. Such rampant need for revenge surpassed all she had seen on the faces of Maija's sons.

But what could have evoked such an almost carnal desire for retribution?

Decency? Regard for a woman? Like Aarno, Berndt and Lars, the friends who had brought her from Finland, Edward Langley had all of those characteristics; yet not once during her time with those brothers did the touch of a helping hand send a lightning bolt along every vein.

He had thrown Thorpe to the ground, stood over the fallen man while snarling a threat. Then he had snatched up her coat to drape it about her shoulders and in so doing drawn her close against himself, his arms clasped about her as if holding someone he loved.

But that was nonsense! Unsettled by the strength of remembered feeling Ann sought refuge in the moon-dappled view from her window. Edward Langley had simply steadied her, his hold had been no more than that.

Why then if she understood the reason could her heart not accept it? Why in every waking moment did her very soul long for what never was nor yet could ever be?

This should have been Ann Spencer lying on the bed, her legs shyly parting to receive him; her breasts pleasuring his hand as her hips lifting to his thrust pleasured his manhood.

But she had been snatched from him.

Langley! He pushed deep into the body spread beneath him, the ferocity of it resulting in a cry of pain. But Thomas Thorpe was deaf to the moan, oblivious to any but the pain of his own bruised pride.

Langley had dared to enter this house, the house of a minister of the chapel . . . his, Thomas Thorpe's house; that was one more action to be avenged. The man might think himself immune from retribution, but Thorpe knew better.

Langley would pay. Langley and the girl both. She would pay with her body; it would be her he would ride, her he would plunge into time and time again.

His body slapped against flesh heaving to meet the frenzied thrusts, a growl erupting in his throat with the eruption that shook his frame.

But it had been no growl of satisfaction.

Away from the bed, pulling on his clothes, his back turned on the girl who no more than scratched the itch of his loins, Thomas Thorpe resumed his thinking.

Ann Spencer would heal the sore of humiliation biting at his heart but what reprisal would wipe away Edward Langley's insults? That he would consider long and carefully; he would revel in those thoughts as he would in ones which had Ann Spencer begging for his mercy.

She was pregnant!

Thomas Thorpe's fingers stilled on the button of his trousers, the voice he had not been listening to now suddenly clanging like a bell in his ears.

The stupid sow was pregnant!

'I can't go hidin' of it much longer, Mother already be askin' about my monthlies.'

Ada Clews was asking questions. Did that imply she had suspicions?

'So you see I'll 'ave to be telling her soon.'

'No!' He turned to the girl, whose own clothing was neatly back in place. 'You must not tell her, you must not tell anyone.'

'But Mother knows I've not seen of a monthly and my excuse of bein' took with cold in the stomach won't satisfy her when I be overdue again next month; 'sides I'll be showin' afore long and I won't be able to claim overeatin' be puttin' a stomach on me, not with food bein' the way it is in our 'ouse. It scarce be markin' the plate for Mother and me, her reckoning Father needs it more cos of work in the iron foundry be so heavy, and the lads he says must have extra what with them labourin' in the coal mine.'

Foundry! Coal mine! Monthlies! Words buzzed like wasps in his head until he wanted to slap the mouth speaking them.

But that would add problem to problem, a cut lip was not easily lied about; and neither would a swollen belly be.

Fastening the last of the buttons, a forced calmness in his face, he looked at the girl now pinning her loosened hair into place.

'You be sure, I mean you might have miscalculated.'

'There be no mistake in my countin' nor there don't be none in Mother's.'

Several hairpins held between her teeth had caused her reply to be mumbled but Thorpe had caught not only the words but the meaning behind them. Once Ada Clews learned of her daughter's condition, she would come looking for the man responsible.

'I knows you wanted to wait, that you said to keep our love a secret for a while longer, but my havin' tumbled puts a different light on things.'

Yes, her becoming pregnant certainly provided a different perspective. But one thing it did not alter: his resolve not to marry Sarah Clews.

29

The woman had looked at Alec so strangely.

Turning cheeses in the cool cellar Ann recalled an event which had occurred during the return from delivering goods to Leah's customers. The task had not been easy, her nerves jumping with every call, but it seemed the women no longer objected to her, each one sparing a minute of their busy day to enquire after Leah's welfare. Yet uneventful as the rounds had proved, she had breathed a sigh of relief when at last she and Alec could make their way home.

They had been halfway along Dale Street, Alec smiling and pointing at a group of brightly painted gypsy caravans on a patch of open ground.

'You've a kind face pretty lady.'

A woman dressed in a tightly knotted shawl and a dark skirt, its voluminous folds caught at one side into the waistband exposing a white cotton petticoat ending several inches above another of red flannel, stepped quickly to the verge.

'Buy a necklace, just two pennies.'

She had held out a bundle of coloured cords each holding a tiny glass bead then when Ann had refused her wares had turned to Alec.

'Buy a necklace from a gypsy young sir, a present for a sweetheart . . . come choose a colour, they all be—'

The words had broken off as Alec came round the side of the cart. The woman's bronzed face paled, her jet black eyes suddenly glazing over as they fastened on him, while her voice, which seconds before had held a jaunty note, became no more than a murmur.

'*Kalo!*'

Her body had trembled.

'*Kalo RAI!*'

Cords had spilled from her shaking fingers, falling to the ground like slivers of rainbow.

'*He comes Kalo RAI . . . he takes the eagle's brood, Raklies . . .*'

She had held up four fingers of her left hand.

'*Mush . . .*'

One finger had lifted on her right hand, staying a moment in the air before both hands dropped to her sides, but her stare had stayed on Alec who had picked up the fallen necklaces and was handing them back to her.

'*The nest lies empty . . .*'

She had droned on. '*. . . but Kalo RAI is not gone, he waits . . . he waits in the shadows.*'

'*Elva.*'

A second woman called from the steps of a caravan painted with flowers, its sides holding a medley of pots and kettles blackened by use.

'*Elva don't mean to be botherin' of you.*'

The woman had moved so swiftly.

Ann paused in the task of turning a large round cheese. She could not recall the woman leaving the steps of the caravan, could not remember her crossing the open ground; one moment she had been a distance away yet it seemed in the next she stood beside the girl she had named Elva. Her eyes were also blackbird bright, her skin the same sun-polished bronze, but the sable hair emerging from beneath a red bandanna was dusted over with a sprinkling of grey.

'*She is not bothering us, she was very kindly offering to sell us a necklace.*'

A smiling Alec was taking coins from his pocket but it was the look in the second woman's eyes that held Ann's inner gaze, one bright with what could almost be fear as they rested on Alec.

'*There be no need o' buyin'* . . .'

Her words to them had been sharp but those muttered to Elva, though unintelligible to Ann, had left no doubt they were a reprimand.

'*Please,*' Alec had said as the younger woman had turned away, '*please, I would like to buy a necklace, they are very pretty.*'

There had been none of that earlier dazed stare; the girl's eyes were now brilliant as black gemstones as her fingers closed hastily on the coin Alec proffered.

'*I be givin' you good day.*'

'*Wait!*' Ann had cried. '*Tell us,*' she had asked as that black-bird stare had met her own, '*tell us what Elva's words meant.*'

There had been long moments of silence, the woman clearly undecided, then as Ann's request was repeated she had said quietly, '*Raklies be girls, mush be boy or man.*'

'*And Kalo RAI?*'

The gypsy's glance had flicked to Alec then returned to Ann with an intensity which seemed to bore into her very soul and when she spoke it was with a voice that seemed strangely not her own.

'*The wings of the eagle be broken, its chicks cry no more . . . Kalo RAI searches for another . . . the dark Lord of Death waits in the shadows.*'

It had been so very like Maija's words as translated by the

priest. But death waited for everyone! With this common sense in mind Ann turned the last of the cheeses then made for the cellar steps, but even as her feet touched the first one she asked the question for which common sense had provided no answer.

What had been meant by an eagle pushed from its nest?

Emerging from the cellar Ann experienced a sudden sense of foreboding.

It made no sense; yet three women whose lives were worlds apart had said the same thing.

'You do love me, Thomas?'

Love Sarah Clews! Thomas Thorpe's face twisted in disgust. He could sooner love a sow! How could she ever think herself a minister's wife . . . if it wasn't so ludicrous he would laugh. But laughter, like his promise to deal with Edward Langley, would have to wait.

'Mother be knowin' my times; when I be over again this next month there'll be no puttin' her off, the band'll bost for sure.'

That part was true enough. Thorpe grimaced again. Ada Clews' anger would shout to the rooftops, the entire town would know who was responsible for her daughter's condition. He could of course deny the whole thing, say it was a lie told to cover the tracks of another who had taken himself away on learning of his lover's pregnancy. But then such a feast of gossip would feed the townsfolk for months.

But that was one junket the townsfolk would be denied.

Thorpe reached for the jacket draped across the back of a chair, smiling at the decision he made at the moment of assuring the girl of his devotion.

Lay preacher! The term stung like an angry wasp. He should be more than that, he *would* be more than that, it was *his* chapel, *he* was its minister . . .

Another thought followed on, one reminding him that scandal was an enemy not easily defeated, folk could be swayed in the wind of it. Its blast could blow Thomas Thorpe clean out of the chapel.

Unless, he mused as he thrust both arms into the sleeves of the coat worn for visiting parishioners, unless another more juicy dish was provided, and of course it would be.

'*You do want to be married in our own faith, in our own chapel.*'
He had laid the ground carefully.

'*Your family, all of our friends, they might not attend should the ceremony be held in some other church; that would spoil your day I know.*'

'*But we don't 'ave no proper minister.*'

Had she seen the look sweep across his face, the pallor of bitterness snatch colour from his cheeks?

'*You does the job good as any,*' she had rushed on, '*but only a minister can marry folk and we don't 'ave one.*'

'*I wrote again last week, someone will come.*'

'*And if he don't, if it be same as before, that there be nobody comes despite your askin', then we'll 'ave to be wed in some other place.*'

'*No my love.*' He had mastered his distaste at taking the lumpy body in his arms, having her sniff against his chest. '*I won't have anything mar our special day, we will be married in this chapel.*'

She had looked up at him, tear-reddened eyes rendering plain features even less attractive, a nasal, '*But how?*' babbling on a fresh tide. He had drawn her head back against his chest. An act of comfort? Thorpe's smile spread a sliver of ice along his mouth. The comfort had been for him, that way he had avoided looking at the girl he had come to despise.

'*There is a chapel in Darlaston,*' he had murmured softly, '*there is a minister there, maybe he will come perform the ceremony here.*'

Leaving the house in Cross Street Thorpe's mind continued to review the events of the previous evening. It would go better if they saw the minister together, he would see for himself the feelings they held for each other. Saying as much had all but stuck in his throat but Sarah, thick stupid Sarah, had taken his choked words to be ones of love, her arms reaching up to embrace him as he had gone on to say the man would not deny them and that very soon they would no longer need hide their love.

She had wanted to rush off, to tell her parents that very night that Thomas Thorpe wished to marry her. Striding quickly along streets grey with the lowering evening Thorpe laughed quietly to himself.

'*Please my love ...*' he had replied, holding her the closer, '*give me a few more hours, a little while longer of having that delight whisper its secret in my heart.*'

The fool had swallowed it as eagerly as a babe sucking its mother's milk and now they were going to Darlaston.

The laugh dissolved, leaving a stone in its place.

Sarah Clews would not be speaking with that minister; Sarah Clews would not be speaking to anyone ever again.

'I wish it could have been splendid as the jewels worn by ...'

'Jewels,' Leah looked up at the hesitation, 'and where might it be you seen "splendid jewels"?'

Ann glanced across from where she had been replacing supper dishes on the dresser and saw the bloom of pink rising in Alec's cheeks. He had obviously made a slip of the tongue, said something he wished he hadn't.

'I . . . it was . . .'

Ann watched the agitation on the young face, echoed in the faltering reply. Was Alec trying to cover his embarrassment at offering a cheap trinket?

'It was at Peterhof.'

Ann smiled at the firmness of the reply yet at the same moment felt remorse that she could have suspected him of speaking anything but the truth.

'Peterhof you says,' Leah frowned, 'now where be that place?'

'It is in St Petersburg, it is the Imperial Palace of the Tsar.'

'Tsar.' Leah's frown changed to a benevolent smile. 'Imperial Palace! You sure you ain't been a dreamin', lad?'

Alec's answer when it came was quiet as the smile curling his mouth, his eyes glistening with pleasure as if looking on a different world.

'Not my dream, Grandmother Leah, but one told to me by a friend of my mother. It was, she said, a ball given in honour of Prince Carol of Romania. It was rumoured he was to ask the Tsar for the hand of the Grand Duchess Olga who, it was also rumoured, did not like him but protocol insisted she attend the ball along with her parents and sisters. My mother's friend told they looked so wonderful, the Tsar in military uniform with golden medals and orders of award gleaming beneath an avenue of amethyst chandeliers, the Tsarina in a white gown that glistened like frost on a winter's morning, great necklaces of diamonds about her throat, jewelled bracelets on her arms flashing fountains of silver fire as she moved. The Grand Duchesses Olga, Tatiana, Marie, were each like their mother dressed in white gowns, but theirs were worn with silk sashes tied about the waist, matching to perfection the colour of gemstones in necklace and tiara. All three looked like delicate white butterflies flitting in a field of brilliant flowers as they danced among the guests, the gowns of the ladies a lovely rainbow of colour: she said it was like watching a fairy tale.'

'It certainly be like listenin' to one.'

'Perhaps one day I might give you a real diamond.'

'No lad.' Leah smiled down at the cord held between her fingers. 'This along of the jewels I already 'ave be more precious than any a queen might wear; mine don't be stones found deep in the earth but gems that lie in the heart: my diamonds be the love given by a husband and children, my rubies be the deep affection I know Edward Langley has ever felt for me and my pearls . . . they be the happiness for the friendship you and Ann 'ave given. These treasures of the soul be the true riches of life, beside which . . .'

Leah laughed lightly but Ann sensed the emotion it tried to cover.

'. . . what would I go a doin' with a real diamond when I 'ave this pretty necklace to wear? I couldn't go a puttin' it on old Betsy, her'd try eatin' of it like her does everythin' else, and for sure I couldn't be drapin' it about the neck of one of the girls for the rest would be so jealous they'd stop givin' milk.'

Alec went quickly to put his arms about her. 'Then you will always wear pearls and rubies for you will always have my friendship and my affection.'

'And you'll always 'ave my love.' Leah returned the kiss planted on her cheek. 'Now get y'self off to bed and I'll fetch you up a nice cup o' cocoa.'

30

'The lad be nigh on asleep afore he finished of his cocoa.' Leah smiled at Edward who at her usual insistence had stayed for 'a bit o' supper'.

'She's really taken to the boy.' Edward Langley's glance followed the dark-skirted figure as it disappeared into the scullery. 'She'll really miss him when he leaves for good but then we must accept that he will want to search for these relations of his.'

He had wanted to ask if Ann would be going with him but not wanting to hear her say yes Edward's glance dropped to his own cup.

'Leah will understand.'

'What be it I'll understand?' Leah emerged from the scullery.

'That when the time comes Alec will go search for his relatives . . . maybe even return to St Petersburg.'

Edward looked up quickly. 'The place you say he talked of. Did you know it?'

'The Peterhof.' Ann nodded. 'I knew of it, I would imagine everyone in St Petersburg did. It is a very beautiful building, the walls are sandy pink with pilasters at each corner reaching to the eaves and the large windows are set in high graceful arches. I only saw it depicted in a watercolour painted I think by my mother. I could not bring . . .' Ann stopped speaking for a moment, fighting tears. 'The embassy would not pay . . . I did not have money enough to ship my parents' belongings home.'

Watching Ann's struggle with emotion Edward's grip tightened fiercely about the stout pottery mug. If he could take her in his arms, comfort her with his love, but the cool politeness she had always shown him had intensified since he found her in Chapel House. It seemed almost she was afraid of friendship, afraid to allow anyone other than Leah and the boy to get close to her. Why? Did some man already hold her heart, had she gone to him on returning home; was that the hurt he sometimes caught reflected in those vivid blue eyes, had some man turned from her, hurt her so deeply she could not trust another? He smiled grimly to himself. Whatever the truth was, why would Ann Spencer take a lame man for a husband?

Feeling Leah's eyes on him he took up the conversation. 'The way Alec described that ballroom, the guests, the clothes they wore, it was pretty impressive. Do you think he saw the inside of that Peterhof place, that maybe he saw the event he spoke about?'

Ann shook her head. 'I very much doubt that. What I learned from reading my father's books supports what Alec said. The Peterhof is one of the imperial palaces of the Tsar, reason enough for not allowing a young boy to wander its rooms much less attend a function, especially one as important as a possible royal engagement.'

'*One* of the palaces!' Edward smiled.

'Tsar be another word for King don't it?' Leah slipped a cup on to its hook on the dresser then glanced at Edward. 'So like our own King George he'll 'ave more'n one palace to his name.'

'My father's books recorded several built by Catherine the Great, she presented them as gifts to various of her lovers;

these of course are not imperial palaces and so not as beautiful as the Peterhof or the larger Winter Palace, though they are
very elegant.'

'Bit much for me, I wouldn't know which room to be in
next.'

'Bit much for all of us.' Edward's smile flipped to Leah
before returning to Ann. 'Alec,' he said, 'has he ever spoken
of any other place, of where he lived, of his parents?' At Ann's
shake of the head he continued, 'Don't you find that odd?
That in all the time you have been together he hasn't once
spoken of where he is from? Of why his parents let him leave
that country alone?'

'There has to be a reason; could the lad be orphaned?'
wondered Leah.

'He spoke of a mother, it was a friend of his mother told
them of that ball.'

' "It was told to *me* by a friend of my mother," ' Ann
corrected, 'Alec said it was told to him, not to his mother.'

'There y'be.' Leah stirred milk into tea Ann poured. 'The
poor woman must be dead and her man along of her, ain't no
other explanation for a lad o' that age bein' sent so far on his
own!'

'There was a man with Alec.' Ann stared down at her own
cup. 'They were together in the Ploschad Morskoy Slavy,
the great square fronting St Petersburg docks, he ... the
man ...' Ann was suddenly back in that moment, her ears
filled with the sounds of horses' hooves pounding on flagstones, the shouts of men, the screams of terrified women
and children running for their lives, the crack of a pistol shot
bouncing from wall to wall of the surrounding buildings, leaping from one to another, reverberating, drumming its deadly
tattoo. 'The man ...' Her voice had become the whisper of a

frightened observer. 'He is asking for help . . . my father . . . he knows my father . . . nooo!'

'Ann.' Edward caught a trembling hand. 'Ann, it's all right!'

'Let 'er be,' Leah said softly. 'Whatever be inside won't never heal lessen it be brought into the open.'

Ann blinked away the scene but not the regret colouring her next words.

'The man said he worked with my father at the embassy, he spoke of a promise; he wanted my help but I didn't listen. I didn't listen and then . . . a soldier on horseback shot him and I grabbed Alec and we ran away.'

'That be a terrible thing for any to witness, more so for a lad young as Alec were, the shock o' that could be cause of his not talkin' of his folk or his whereabouts.'

'Yes.' Edward nodded agreement. 'I've seen the like in men so shocked by what they witnessed on the battlefield they only survived by shutting it completely out of mind.'

'That was not the only thing that happened.'

'You means the robbery on that boat, some no good a stealin' of your money!'

'There was more than that, I . . . I didn't tell you the rest. It happened on that same boat.' Ann talked on as Leah slipped into a chair beside Edward. 'I don't truly know how it happened, I've gone over it so many times; maybe the darkness of that night, the worry of finding myself not as I'd thought on a steamer for England, but on the ferry sailing to Finland has made things unclear in my mind.'

Leah was sympathetic. 'Tek your time Ann wench. It be summat of the same wi' y'self as wi' the lad, your mind most like were numbed by fright.'

'I did not see it happen, he must have been waiting in the shadows . . .'

'Ann, you don't have to—'

'I heard a sound, a sort of gasp.' Ann seemed not to hear Edward's anxious interruption, 'Alec he . . . he was not at my side, I was about to call his name when I saw he was held by a taller figure, a man with one arm across Alec's throat, the other hand holding a club over his head.'

Ann looked down at her fingers twisting in her lap as she recounted the whole experience, finishing with, 'The other figure, the man who . . . who shot Alec's attacker, he said it was not money being demanded but the precious possession I had taken from St Petersburg. But I had taken nothing except the framed photograph of my mother and I can't possibly see anyone thinking of that as precious apart from myself.'

'It be strange and no mistake and though I don't be a lover o' violence I thanks God that second man acted as he did; frightening as it must 'ave been for the pair o' you, at least it meant you bein' safe.'

'I prayed so.' Ann did not look up. 'I kept Alec as close as I could but when we were ordered off the ferry . . . the night was so black and the waves of the sea so whipped by the wind they tossed the rowing boat like a cork.'

'Rowing boat.' Leah's brows drew together. 'Y'means to say that ferry weren't in no dock when you was put off and that in the dead o' night? Whoever were responsible for that should ought to be locked up!'

'People were being pushed to the rail, I could hear voices calling, possibly women separated from children, men anxious to locate their families, but the seamen shoving them into the boats paid no heed. Then I was seized. I grabbed at Alec but somehow we were separated; it was just as the sailors in the boat took up the oars that I saw him, he was half over the side of the ship but then someone made a grab for him, tried to haul him back aboard; I thought the tussle would see him being dropped into the sea but the sailor holding him threw the other figure aside and Alec was beside me and the rowing boat moved off. Then above the crash of waves I heard a shout; words broken apart by the wind: "We will find . . . take what you carry . . . both die and any who help them." '

Leah shook her head in incredulity. 'Lord wench, what in the name of heaven could it be thought you carried?'

'It was enough to have one man commit murder and another threaten to do the same. It was that threat had me so afraid for Maija and her sons.'

Maija . . . sons? Leah met Edward's eyes, and she indicated that she also knew nothing of those people. A slight shake of her head silently advised him not to ask but sit and listen.

'Maija found us next morning wet through and almost frozen with cold . . .'

The only other sound in the small room was that of the clock ticking above the fireplace. Ann continued speaking softly as though to herself, the tension of her body telling clearly the fears she had lived with, but it was Edward Langley Leah watched, the concern on those strong features, anger which had the fine mouth thin to an almost invisible line, the hands bunch to fists clenched so fiercely the knuckles strained white against the tan of his skin when hearing of the German sailor's intended rape. Though her sympathies were with the girl she had given a home to, her heart went out to Edward: he had suffered heartbreak in his life and would suffer it again should Ann Spencer choose to go along of Alec to search for his relatives. Given her feeling for the lad it was certain she wouldn't let him go alone.

'I thought we would live with my grandmother,' Ann went on, 'but she had died a few weeks after my leaving for Russia.

There was not much left of the money Aarno had given us and as I was unable to find employment I knew the little we had would not last long. That was why I was so grateful for being allowed to rent Chapel House, but even then ...' She looked up from staring into her lap, the strain of the past stark in her eyes. 'Careful as I tried to be when buying food it ... it became necessary for us to relinquish that tenancy.'

And it be my belief I don't be needin' of two guesses as to why. My mind says the kind of rent Thomas Thorpe were set on collectin' were refused and it be that reason had you put on the street.

To speak her thoughts would serve only to incense Edward Langley still further; Leah kept them to herself saying simply, 'All o' that be past and done, you and the lad be safe thank the Lord.'

Safe! Ann rose, taking the cup and plate Edward had used into the scullery. Then why the stab of fear whenever the words of the gypsy woman returned to haunt her in the still of the night: '*Kalo RAI searches for another, the dark Lord of Death waits in the shadows.*'

31

'*You have my heartfelt sympathy.*'

Thomas Thorpe smiled as his hands smoothed the long black gown. '*If there is anything I can do you need only to ask.*'

Red-rimmed eyes swollen with weeping had looked up at him, a crumpled scrap of cloth was pressed to quivering lips.

'*It be 'ard for her to say anythin' just now Mr Thorpe, but y'can be sure her'll thank you later.*'

He had knelt in front of the weeping woman taking both of her hands in his. Secretly revelling in the caring picture he made before the assembled group of sympathetic neighbours he had crossed himself, piously murmuring as if for the ears only of the bereaved woman but careful his words were just loud enough to reach the rest.

'*Greater love has no man than he lay down his life for another.*'

He had squeezed her hands gently.

'*Your son has given his life for the good of many, your comfort is in knowing the sacrifice was seen by the Lord who will reward it in heaven.*'

He should have been wearing this when visiting that house. Watching the reflection in the mirror he touched the white dog collar. It would have made such an impression, the women there would have gazed in admiration.

'*It be terrible painful Mr Thorpe, terrible painful for a woman come to know the losin' of a child.*'

Reaching for the white fringed stole laid carefully across his bed Thorpe's smile deepened at the words murmured by Ada Clews as he had risen to his feet.

A pain that woman would know for herself. He draped the stole about his shoulders, placing the fringes in elegant lines. Yes, Ada Clews would soon know the pain of losing a child. The life of Mary Carter's son had been given for his country, he would be spoken of as a hero; and Ada Clews' daughter? Hands together in the attitude of prayer Thorpe watched himself smiling back from the mirror. Hers had been given for a more important reason, the saving of the good name of Thomas Thorpe.

'But your sacrifice my dear,' he laughed full-throatedly, 'your death will not be remembered as that of a heroine. You will be remembered for the whore you were.'

Leah removed her shawl and hung it on a peg set into the scullery door. Then she took a cloth from the line of string stretched from wall to wall and began drying ladles and pans Ann was washing.

'It be a sad business,' she said, 'poor Mary Carter be beside 'erself, young Luke were the apple of 'er eye.'

'I would have liked to call on her but I feel maybe that would not have been the best thing to do with having known the family for such a short time.'

'Mary'll understand, wench.' Leah placed dried ladles on a wooden tray. 'If y'be agreein' then we could stand together outside of the chapel come Sunday; Mary and 'er family will see and appreciate that when they attends the service Thomas Thorpe be holdin' in remembrance of their lad, they'll know we be showin' respect.'

Thorpe. Ann shuddered. How could she be there, how could she look at the man who had almost raped her?

'Won't be no need of waitin' 'til the service be over.' Leah had seen the tremor ripple through the slender figure but knew that breaking off abruptly would disclose the fact and maybe cause Ann embarrassment, so she went on. 'Ain't like there be any coffin to be carried along of the cemetery, like so many more folk robbed of their loved ones by this war, Mary Carter won't never know where it be 'er son lies.'

Like you not knowing where Joshua and Daniel are buried, wanting in your heart to believe a service was held for them, yet fearing deep down the continuous onslaught of battle would have made that virtually impossible.

Ann kept her thoughts to herself.

'Do Alec be back yet?'

Thankful Leah had changed the subject Ann placed the last scrubbed utensil on the draining board. 'No.' She draped the wrung-out dish cloth over the edge of the shallow stone sink. 'Probably got to talking with Mr Langley and forgot the time.'

'He likes Edward, the two of them gets on well together.' The drying finished, Leah returned the damp cloth to the line then as Ann was about to carry the bowl of dishwater to the drain in the yard said, 'Edward an' me talked some time since wi' regard to Hill Rise an' this place being brought together as one. I'd thought of it often after Joshua an' Daniel were killed and then with Deborah . . .'

For a moment it seemed Leah would say nothing more, but with a quick indrawn breath she went on.

'. . . well with my own children gone and Edward being like a son—'

'I understand,' Ann cut in quickly, 'I will speak with Alec as soon as he returns.'

'P'raps you does then again p'raps you don't understand, but I don't be goin' to discuss that over a bowl of dirty water, so you finish up in 'ere an' I'll go brew a pot of tea.'

It was obvious. Empty bowl in hand, Ann stared across the yard to the open field. Leah was ready to join her holding to Hill Rise but while Edward Langley loved and respected her as he would his own mother, he could not be expected to accept Alec and herself.

'Like I was a sayin',' Leah poured tea as Ann entered the living room. 'Edward an' me talked some time back about his place an' mine becomin' one – wait!'

She held up a hand silencing Ann's intervention. 'You hear me out afore you go sayin' any more. I put it to Edward it be sensible but he refused; said right out as he wouldn't tek this place, weren't no surprise to me nor were the next thing he said, that bein' the dairy an' all that be along of it should go to you.'

'Me!' Ann was aghast. 'But that is impossible.'

'Ain't naught impossible about it.'

Ann stared at the flat contradiction. This house, the dairy, it was all of Leah's life, it held her every memory. Resolve settled firm. Her answer must be no – yet it must be given gently.

'Edward . . .' she began tentatively. 'You have known him from birth, you have said yourself he is more son than friend, I . . .' She paused, wanting to find words which would express her feelings while not sounding ungrateful. 'I can only be a friend, a friend who values that relationship far too much ever to take advantage of it. Perhaps Mr Langley does not quite understand or he would never have made such a suggestion.'

Edward Langley understands a lot more than we oftime give him credit for. But then so did Leah Marshall. It were his thinking that to give the dairy to Ann Spencer would be to keep her here in Wednesbury.

'Edward do be like a son,' Leah agreed as she refilled the cups, 'and like a son he be entitled to mek his own choice, if that be to refuse to join his place to mine then so be it, but,' she glanced over the cup with a tender smile, 'like I would to a daughter I says to you think careful wench, not just of today but all the days lyin' ahead.'

'I have thought,' Ann answered quietly, 'I've thought many times but always with the same answer. Once this war is ended Alec will begin to search for his relatives and I shall stay with him until he does.'

Why had Edward Langley said she and not himself should be given Leah's property? Emptying the teapot on to the heap of sleck, coal dust and fine chippings with which the living room fire was banked every night to keep it slumbering until morning, Ann heard the questions in her mind. Was it meant as some kind of test? Did he think her friendship with Leah had some ulterior motive? That she had deliberately worried her way into that woman's affection in order to steal her home and business?

Her gaze wandered beyond the yard, resentment rising swift and hot as it panned across the pasture to rest on the figure striding across the adjoining field.

'Mother were gone to the Carter house, they had word today of their Luke being killed in action, Mother wanted to say her sympathy; I feels sorry for the Carters, o' course I do, but it meant I could slip away without her being any the wiser.'

His cassock hung in the wardrobe his mother had spent half her life polishing, collar and stole were folded carefully and placed in the matching chest. Thomas Thorpe's smile was one of pure satisfaction.

The girl had been waiting in the place he had specified. Waiting for him to take her on to Darlaston to speak with a minister. Fool, he laughed aloud, fool to think a man of Thomas Thorpe's standing would marry a common working-class woman.

'Nobody don't know where I be going; I done exactly like you said, I kept our secret.'

He had forced himself to smile, to take her hands, to say her trust made him happy. They had walked a little way as she gabbled on about the surprise her parents would have on learning their girl was to marry Thomas Thorpe, while he carefully watched that no other person was to be seen. They had drawn level with St Peter's Church, the old building almost entirely surrounded by open heath. He had drawn her into the lee of its high walls holding her close, not, as she giggled, to snatch a kiss and a few moments of cuddle, but to give him the opportunity to further scan the heath. There had been no one. Releasing her, he had adopted a look of regret as he said he had not as yet a ring to place on her finger but for just a little while perhaps this other small gift would serve to mark his love.

She had cried her delight as he took the necklace from his pocket, happily lifting her hair so he could fasten it about her neck.

He had fastened it well and truly, pulling it so hard the pretty bauble had bitten into the flesh of her throat. How long had he held it, twisting its length like a garrotte, how long until she had stopped struggling? He had held her upright, his body supporting the weight slumped against it, waited those few vital seconds with the cord tight about her throat, then he loosed it, stepping away as the limp figure slid to the ground. But he could not leave right away; first he must make sure she was dead. He had touched the hollow at the base of her throat and then had come the thought. It must seem she had been brought here against her will, that she had been the victim of rape. Minutes later he was gone, leaving her clothing half torn away, her legs spread wide apart.

He had felt no sense of urgency, no pressure to hurry from the scene. The body would be found but nothing would link him to the killing. How could it! He smiled. He was heaven-protected, that had been proved over and again with Deborah Marshall, then with the man thrown into the Devil's Pool; and again today when it had led him to find that trinket. He would have passed without seeing it but at that moment the sun's rays had glinted on the small glass beads, a necklace dropped by one of the gypsies who had camped on the patch of open ground. It had gleamed up at him and in that instant he had felt heaven's smile, had known he was being provided with the means whereby to dispose of the problem that was Sarah Clews.

Back in the tiny living room of his cramped terraced home Thorpe's eye lighted on the black leather valise lying open on the table. There had been no comeback from that quarter and there would be none from tonight's activity.

He snapped the clasps of the bag shut and closed his eyes, luxuriating in the glow spreading through his body. The angels of the Almighty had been given guardianship of Thomas Thorpe, they would let no breath of suspicion touch him, not now nor when he dealt the same to Edward Langley and – he took a long deep breath of satisfaction – when he took what was owed by Ann Spencer.

'Why did you tell Leah she should make me heir to her property?' Ann's fury lashed the shadows. 'Was it your way of proving to her and to yourself that I am nothing more than a thief, that I pretend to feel for her in the hope of getting all she owns? Well sorry as I am to prick your balloon, Mr Langley, you are once again entirely wrong in your assumptions. Leah knows and now I am telling you, there is nothing here I want other than the friendship of Leah Marshall, the memory of which will stay with me when I leave with Alec to search for his family.'

'Now you hold on a minute!' Edward grabbed at her as she turned away from him, making the teapot wobble precariously. 'You might feel no more than friendship but Leah's feeling runs deeper than that, she loves you as her own, as she would a daughter. It is for that reason I asked she take you as partner in the dairy; I thought with the home you had with your grandmother now gone you might make a permanent one with Leah, that it would keep her from the bitterness of losing someone she loves. But as you have made very clear, I am wrong. You go your way, Miss Spencer,' he loosed his hold, 'never mind the grief you leave behind.'

'Be a bit late for you don't it lad?' Leah looked up from her sewing as Edward came into the living room, then catching the glint of anger in his eyes asked, 'Be there summat amiss along of Hill Rise, summat wrong with the cows?'

'No.' Edward shook his head. 'There's nothing wrong at Hill Rise.'

'The Lord be thanked for that.' Leah laid aside the cheesecloth she was hemming. 'So why is it you've called? Not that you don't be welcome whatever the hour.'

'I just wanted to be sure Alec was all right.'

At the entrance to the scullery Ann looked towards the man who minutes before had summarily brushed her aside. 'Alec!' she said quickly, 'he went to Hill Rise, he . . . he's supposed to be with you.'

'So he was until a couple of hours ago. We sat talking for a while then I left him reading the evening paper while I went to make a last check on the cows. When I returned some twenty minutes or so later he was gone.'

'You means the lad never wished you goodnight, that he just up and took hisself off? That don't be like Alec.'

Edward saw the sudden leap of fear in Ann's eyes; her hands holding the old brown teapot trembled convulsively. He could go to her, hold her, tell her everything was fine, that it was in every lad's blood to dawdle on the way home, but that would incur another taste of her displeasure.

'I thought the same,' he agreed. 'It is not Alec's way to leave without a word. At first I put it down to the fact he had simply realised the time, that he had stayed longer than was meant and wanted to be back here before either of you got to worrying for him.'

Alec had left Hill Rise two hours ago! Ann stared at the pot clutched in her hands. But he had not returned home.

'. . . *male or female, woman or boy, either is acceptable.*'

With Thomas Thorpe's threat ringing in her mind the pot fell from her hands.

32

'Sit you there wench, rest you a while.' Leah eased Ann into a chair after Edward had caught her from falling, then to the man hovering at her side said, 'I tells her again and again her be workin' too hard.'

It wasn't work alone had this effect, something had frightened Ann Spencer. But what? There had been that confrontation in the yard but she had shown no sign of fright at that yet it was there in her eyes, real visible fear.

'I'm sorry.' Ann smiled weakly. 'I . . . I felt a little dizzy.'

Something of the truth. Edward picked up the fallen pot. Now how about the rest, that which is really troubling you?

'Oh!' Ann was staring at the pot. 'Oh Leah, the teapot, I'm so sorry.'

'No need to be, wench,' Leah chuckled, restoring the lid to the pot before taking it from Edward. 'This here pot's had more knocks than a man's had hot dinners.'

'It isn't broken?'

Leah turned a glance to the rug laid in front of the hearth.

'With three lads rough and tumblin' every minute my back were turned,' she looked fondly at Edward, 'it were needed to 'ave a rug thick enough to save elbows and knees. I pegged that one with every pair of worn-out trousers, every jacket that couldn't no more be seen decent on either of them scoundrels and it's saved many a limb and many a dish.'

'I don't recall wearing a pair of bright red trousers.' Edward's mouth pursed as he looked at the scarlet design worked into the centre of the rug. 'Not Daniel's choice of colour and somehow I don't see Uncle Joseph wearing that shade to the coal mine. Hmmm.' His mouth twisted more wryly. 'Must have been Joshua, I never knew . . .'

'Uncle Joseph would tan your hide were he here, and don't you go a thinkin' I won't do of the same if you keep on wi' your cheek; it'll pay you, Edward Langley, to be rememberin' y'don' be too big to 'ave your arse smacked!'

'Bully.' Edward laughed, closing Leah into the circle of his arms, but there was no laughter in his eyes when he looked at Ann.

'Alec often stays a while in the stable before coming into the house. He is probably in there now, I'll go look.'

Edward answered quickly, 'You stay here, I'll go look in the stable.'

'Y' shouldn't fret so much about the lad, it be as Edward said, young 'uns often dawdles, lads especially; they all seems to suffer the same affliction, they just 'ave to stick their noses into everythin' regardless of what or where.'

'Normally I would agree,' Ann answered, 'but he must have been upset otherwise he would not have left Hill Rise the way he has.'

'Upset y'says.' Leah paused in folding her needlework. 'You surely don't think Edward's been upsettin' of the lad.'

'No . . . not Mr Langley.'

'Then who, weren't nobody else along of Hill Rise.'

'The newspaper.' Ann seemed to be searching in her mind. 'Mr Langley said he left Alec reading the newspaper.'

'He reads of the paper every night.'

'You remember shortly after we came to stay in this house

Alec read a report of the Russian royal family having been arrested, how upset he was by that?'

'I thought that to be strange, I knowed Russia be the country he come from but . . . well, the arrestin' of royalty don't really reflect on 'im.'

'Not on him,' Ann agreed. 'But what of his parents? We know his mother had a friend who worked in the Peterhof Palace . . . what if Alec's parents were similarly employed in some other establishment, either royal or government? Alec saw as I did those mounted soldiers shooting and slashing with swords, saw the indiscriminate slaughter of people unable to defend themselves. It had to be treatment such as this on top of hunger and despair that drove the country to rise against the Tsar.'

'Ar, I can well see that wench but what I don't see be how ordinary folk such as the lad's mother an' father be to blame.'

'They were not but it is easy to see how they were thought to be. We have read reports, seen newspaper photographs of the storming of the Winter Palace, of the Kremlin in Moscow, and many other royal houses and government buildings being invaded, their residents arrested and even killed. The people attacking them were likely driven to the edge by misery and hunger, fired by the promises of the Bolsheviks saying deposing its rulers and giving the country to the people would put an end to their hardship. They would not stop to enquire who was master and who servant.'

'Y' means Alec's folk might 'ave been killed?'

'I think that is Alec's fear.'

'Poor lad.' Leah's slow shake of the head echoed the sympathy in her tone. 'What wi' men a' threatenin' to kill 'im, an' illness that seemed like to do the same, he's suffered enough wi'out havin' that fear hang over his head.'

'What happened tonight . . .' Ann paused, then went on. 'Could it be Alec read something which upset him so much he simply walked away?'

Leah dropped the folded needlework into the ancient sewing basket and gave an exasperated snort. 'Hmm, wouldn't y'know it, the one night we needs look at the *Star* I forgets to buy it! I meant to pick one up after bein' to see Mary Carter but what wi' one thing and another it went clear from my 'ead!'

The one thing and another being Thomas Thorpe. The explanation continued silently in Leah's mind. The man's fawning, his toadying, it was all a sham, a pretence meant to impress Mary and the others. He had glanced up as he knelt in front of that distraught woman. Thorpe's eyes had fastened on hers, reading the revulsion there, the fact that nothing of his deception was lost on her, while his own had laughed their reply, 'There's naught you can do about it.'

'Perhaps Mr Langley will be able to tell us what Alec might have read.'

'Ar wench, p'raps he might.' Leah let the picture slip away. 'This be 'im now, maybe the lad'll be along of 'im.'

The body of the girl had been found. Thomas Thorpe listened to the men grouped outside the chapel.

'Were Tom Bissell an' Charlie Tonks found 'er, said as it looked like her'd bin interfered with.'

'Hey up . . . women 'ere!'

The speaker lowered his voice, saying in a subdued murmur, 'They said as they found 'er on that waste ground up along of St Peter's Church. Seems they goes there every now an' again settin' their ferrets to the rabbit warrens, that old place be overrun wi' rabbits an' a couple o' them makes for a good dinner.'

'Y' said it looked to be the wench'd been interfered with. How come Tom an' Charlie got that idea, what was—' The man broke off, his glance going to Thorpe. 'Sorry Mr Thorpe,' he said, 'I shouldn't ask such wi' you not bein' a married man.'

The minister should not be subjected to such indelicate conversation. Discuss it! He could quote them chapter and verse regarding the most intimate secrets of the bedroom, tell them how many times he had tasted what to him, an unmarried man, should be forbidden fruit.

'No.' He shook his head, 'It is best you keep nothing from me, that way I may avoid speaking out of turn when I visit the Clewses.'

'You speak outta turn!' Another of the group spoke, 'I can't see you a mekin' of no mistake Mr Thorpe.'

Of course he wouldn't see any mistake, neither would anybody else; Thomas Thorpe was much too smart for that to happen. One hand traced the sign of the cross over his breast as Thorpe answered gravely, 'I pray heaven's guidance as in all things. I would not wish a slip of the tongue to add to the unhappiness of that family, therefore I ask you keep nothing back.'

Glancing first at the women huddled a little way off the man relating the discovery put a few more steps between the two groups, then hunched his head low on his chest as he continued. 'Tom, he reckoned the clothes were almost ripped off the wench and . . .' He paused to confirm the women were out of earshot. 'And the legs was spread wide like her'd been . . . well y'knows what Tom were sayin'.'

'He were sayin' some filthy swine raped of 'er.' A voice harsh with anger voiced the thoughts of every man.

'The coppers Tom an' Charlie fetched to the spot d'ain't say as much.'

'Wouldn't need to,' another answered, 'the state of the wench's clothes'd tell that.'

'That be all well an' good, but what do the coppers be doin' about catchin' the swine? I says we band together an' go search that heath.'

Search all you like, Thorpe thought. You won't find him there, in fact you won't ever find him at all.

'Coppers 'ave a good idea who the culprit be . . .'

The police had a good idea! His confidence faltered. Could he possibly have overlooked something? But he had suffered the same doubts after killing the man tipped into the Devil's Pool, and they had proved unfounded. Thorpe breathed deeply. It would be the same this time.

'Charlie said . . .'

Thorpe forced his attention to the man speaking.

'Charlie seen afore the coppers took the body away, he seen a necklace around the neck, nuthin' good mind ya, one o' them cords with a bit o' glass on it, the sort them gypsies was toutin' along of the fair.'

'So they thinks some gypsy done for 'er?'

'That be about the size o' it.'

The police believed the killer to be a gypsy. Thomas Thorpe's glow of confidence burned again. It was going precisely as he planned.

'Seems they don't be the only ones lookin' for that gyppo,' the harsh voice piped up again, 'Arthur Clews also be searchin' and if he finds the varmint afore the coppers does there won't be o' no trial for there won't be enough of him left to 'ang.'

Either way would suit very well. He masked his sense of triumph with a discreet cough and brought his attention to the women, their group calling quiet goodnights as they began to disperse.

After he had spent a moment with each, sharing with them sympathy for the stricken Clews family, Thorpe watched the last of the congregation walk away from Queen's Place.

They would never find out. He glanced at the silent darkened chapel. Thomas Thorpe was the Lord's minister; Thomas Thorpe was heaven's protected.

He had walked home by way of the heath. While cutting freshly churned butter then weighing each block before setting it on a muslin-lined tray, Ann dwelt on her fear of the night before. Edward Langley had gone to the stable to see if Alec had followed his usual routine of spending some time grooming Leah's old horse, but had returned alone. She had been determined to look for him, arguing he could have stumbled in the darkness, have turned an ankle and so be unable to walk unaided; or he was lost on the heath, there were no markers there to guide him. She must have gone through a bevy of reasons but in the minutes it had taken to fetch her coat Edward Langley had gone, leaving Leah to tell her to stay in the house; it was enough searching for the lad without having to do the same for her.

Why should she be ruled by Edward Langley! Why abide by what he had said! Leah had heard the mutiny in the words, simply answering quietly that no one was imposing any restriction but it would ease Leah's own mind if she stayed in the house.

She had watched the clock as she had during the long nights of Alec's illness here and in Finland, and as then felt the weight of fear for him rest heavy in her heart. He was a boy she knew practically nothing about and yet her protective feelings might have been those of a sister. Ann carried the portions of butter to the cool cupboard, placing them neatly in rows. A sister! She returned to the task of patting and weighing. What would it have been like to have a brother or a sister, sharing with them the dangers she had shared with Alec? Could ties of blood be any stronger than those of friendship?

'I thought you might care to see this.'

Ann couldn't repress a swift gasp as she whirled towards the figure standing in the open doorway of the dairy.

Still scared but not for the lad. Edward Langley's thought seared him as he caught the sigh of relief. That toad Thorpe was what this girl feared. She worried that even after the dire warning he had been given still he might try in any way he could to harm her. Don't try it, Thorpe! Edward answered his own mind. Not if you want to go on living!

'It's last night's edition of the *Express and Star*.' He waved the newspaper. 'But if Alec's already said what it was sent him off so quick then I'll put this along of the firewood.'

Alec had made no reference to the newspaper. He had said only that of a sudden he had noticed how late he had left it before setting off back to the house. In order to make up a little of that time he had taken the way of the heath rather than the longer way via the town. But in the darkness he had become confused; it had been Edward's shrewd guess as to the way he had chosen and by calling his name Edward had probably saved him hours of wandering that empty heath.

Edward Langley had probably saved him from falling down some disused mine shaft! The reprimand had remained unsaid. She had seen unhappiness darkening Alec's grey-blue eyes, which had swept away her intention to reproach him. So instead she had thanked Edward Langley for his help while Leah had shooed Alec upstairs to his bed.

'Thank you.' Ann pushed her thoughts away. 'Leah and I both like to read the newspaper. Would you put it in the scullery?' She glanced down at the mound of butter still to be portioned. 'This has to come first I'm afraid.'

'A deal of work.'

'It could be reduced, if the dairy were mine . . .'

'Which you have already refused.' Edward completed the half-finished sentence. 'But supposing this place was yours, how would you cut down on labour?'

She had many times toyed with the idea while working in the dairy, had often wanted to speak of it to Leah but had always held back, not wanting to seem interfering.

'Well?' Edward put the folded newspaper in his jacket pocket.

'I . . .' Ann hesitated. 'Leah's way is best.'

'Best up to now, but who is to say there's not a better way waiting to be tried out? C'mon, tell me what you have in mind.' He smiled. 'I promise not to tell Leah if you don't want me to.'

'It is the patting and weighing.' Ann paused, butter pats in hand. 'It is the time it takes as well as the effort and then there is the task of weighing, each portion has to be of exactly the same amount or the customer would soon complain.'

'And then some!' Edward chuckled. 'But I don't see how to be certain of each being the same unless they are weighed.'

'They would be if the butter were pressed into individual moulds of precisely the same size. This could be four ounces, eight ounces, even one pound, whichever Leah thought preferable.'

'Do no damage to try.'

'You said you wouldn't say anything to Leah!'

'Nor will I . . . at least not until I try the idea out at Hill Rise where Leah won't see, then if it works I'll claim the whole thing came from me. Now while you store the rest of those portions in the cool cupboard I'll take this lot along to the scullery for scrubbing, then perhaps you might offer a man a cup of tea.'

33

She had given Edward Langley his cup of tea. Watching his cart leave the yard Ann felt a twinge of guilt. He had helped with the scouring of dairy utensils, had even returned them to that building while she scalded tea in the pot waiting on the hob. Had it been so obvious she wished to be left alone? He never refused a second cup from Leah. She had tried to be conversational but her mind had continually turned to the question of the newspaper and what it might contain. If she were alone she could snatch a moment to look through its pages. If there was anything of significance she could read it before Leah returned from making deliveries. She had liked to do this for herself a couple of times a week saying it kept her in touch with folk and Alec, as usual, had gone along with her.

Edward Langley had thanked her for the drink and for a moment it had seemed he would say something else, but then he had turned abruptly and left without a backward glance. He thought her rude, her attitude unfriendly. Ann sighed. He could be forgiven for that but who could forgive her?

Back in the living room she took the paper Edward had left and placed it on the table. The title page was filled with news of the offensives being launched by Allied troops, of every hard-won step. Ann briefly closed her eyes, thinking how every victory demanded its price, one paid by the lives of men and the heartbreak of families left behind. Had Alec's parents paid that price? Ann turned page upon page, her glance passing rapidly from headline to headline searching without knowing what she looked for. And then she saw it.

A small paragraph tucked in a corner of the centre page carried the heading; RUSSIAN ROYAL FAMILY, NEW PROCEEDINGS.

Ann's eyes flew over the lines of print.

It is reported the ex-Tsar, his family and a few retainers currently being held in a house in Yekaterinburg are to be tried by the Presidium of the Divisional Council.

A few retainers! Ann stared at the words. No one was named, no indication of who those people were. This latest news to come out of Russia told Alec no more than any of the accounts he had read before.

'What are you reading?'

Ann felt colour rise to her cheeks at Alec's quiet question. How could she tell him she was looking for what he had not shared with herself and Leah the night before?

'Edward ... Mr Langley ...' She hesitated awkwardly. 'Leah forgot to buy her newspaper last night so he brought across his copy.' Then glancing across his shoulder towards the scullery she asked, 'Where is Leah?'

'She decided to spend a little time with Mrs Carter, the death of the woman's son is still of much grievance to her. Grandmother Leah thought sharing that grief might in some way relieve it.'

As she and I might have helped relieve yours had we been given the chance! Ann pulled herself up shortly. This was happening too often; it was not for her to chastise, even mentally, when she could not face up to her own shortcomings such as failing to recognise the friendship offered by Edward Langley.

'No doubt you have seen the report rumoured to have come from Russia.'

'Rumoured?'

'Of course, what is reported there is not the truth.'

It was stated with quiet conviction yet Ann recognised it was said out of a need to believe.

'That council,' Alec went on, 'those people do not have the right, they will not, they cannot put the royal family on trial. The people will never allow that to happen. The Tsar is the Little Father of all the Russians, he is loved by all and would never willingly cause harm to any one of his subjects.'

Yet some in that country held him to blame; why otherwise would the family have been taken away and imprisoned? And the retainers mentioned, were they also blamed, held responsible for the misery and hunger of the common people? Was Alec's worry to do with this? Ann stared at the newspaper. She had never directly questioned Alec about his parents, their reasons for sending him away. Should she do so now? Ann turned to look at him directly, asking firmly, 'Alec, are your parents in the employ of the royal household?'

'No.'

The answer had been quick, with no trace of hesitation. The clear eyes fastening on her own were wide with the candour they always held. Ann's tension eased. Alec's parents were not employed in that household therefore they could not be among the people imprisoned at Yekaterinburg. So what exactly was Alec's worry? As she was about to put the very question which would with luck produce an answer to cast light on the fear she knew haunted the boy—

'Eh wench, what a to do!'

'Leah came bustling in from the scullery, and her breathless exclamation drove all else from Ann's mind.

'Eh, I can't believe of it . . . whatever be the world a comin' to!'

'Leah, what is it, what's wrong?' Ann was at the woman's side.

'A cup o' tea wench,' Leah panted, 'a cup o' tea afore I can bring meself to put tongue to it. Don't need to look so scared lad, be naught amiss wi' me.' She looked at Alec, who had also moved quickly to her side. 'But there will be with old Molly lessen her be took from the cart; be so good as to give her a feed then let her loose in the field for to stretch her legs.'

Leah took several swallows of tea before saying with a shake of the head, 'No, I ain't never knowed the like, not once in all the days the good Lord has allowed I live 'ave I ever knowed the like; I tells you, wench, Gabriel's Hounds was runnin' free in Wednesbury t'other night.'

Gabriel's Hounds. Despite the anxiety of the moment Ann's mind slipped back over the years to when she was a small girl, her nightdress barely reaching small bare feet, her eyes wide with wonder as she listened to her grandmother's tale of the warning of Gabriel's Hounds.

'Were barely on five of the mornin' it 'appened. Your grandfather were on his way to the pit. He had reached the Black Bridge atop of which the aqueduct carries coal barges when he seen a little wench. No bigger than you, her seemed to be lost. Her made no answer to any question and when your grandfather made to pick her up and bring her to this house to be cared for until her folk be found, that little wench turned from him and walked straight through them dark black bricks leavin' not a sign behind. Grandfather knowed he'd been given the warnin' of Gabriel's Hounds and he come

rightways home not goin' to his work at the mine. It were later that same day a collapse of coal underground trapped and killed some thirty miners.'

Superstition! Ann smiled at the memory. Old wives' tales! But Leah had not been given to such talk and as for pit disasters, she had lost her husband to one so what previously 'unknown' occurrence had her so disturbed?

'I'd just left of Mary Carter . . .' Leah held out her cup for a refill, continuing as she stirred the hot milky liquid. 'I was halfway along of Meeting Street when Jinny Jinks comes a wavin' of her arms and a callin' my name. I stops the milk cart thinkin' her be wantin' of extra milk or p'raps another wedge o' cheese, but all her asked was had I 'eard, had Ezekial Turley mentioned of it? I told 'er I'd seen neither hide nor hair o' the man but her up and asked the same thing, had I 'ear of it? I admits I were a mite sharp wi' Jinny but sometimes you needs be if any sense is to be got from 'er, but eh wench, the shock were mine on listenin' to what it were had 'er flappin' like a sheet in the wind.' Pausing to swallow more of the hot refreshing liquid Leah glanced towards the scullery then, assured Alec had not returned, continued in a low voice. 'Young Sarah Clews . . . Jinny said young Sarah Clews had been found dead.'

'Dead!'

'Ar wench,' Leah nodded, 'strangled, but not afore some man had teken of his pleasure, and that weren't come by easy.' Leah finished the last of her tea. 'Tom Bissell and Charlie Tonks – it was them found the body – they reckons the clothes was torn near altogether off the wench which tells what 'appened had no consent of the poor little soul.'

Rape! Ann shuddered at the thought. The girl had been raped and killed. 'But who . . . where?'

'Tom and Charlie found 'er on the 'eath up along of St Peter's Church.' Leah answered. 'And as for who done it, they says the police be huntin' forra gypsy.'

Ann frowned. 'Why would they think the killer was a gypsy?'

'Cos the thing Sarah were strangled with was one of these.' Leah touched the trinket about her neck. 'What could speak more plain.'

'Sarah cleaned at Chapel House but I very rarely saw her; my hours of work did not coincide with the time the girl was there.'

'You understands, Mr Thorpe, we have to speak to everybody who might have had contact, there might just be summat'll help with enquiries.'

'Of course.' Thomas Thorpe nodded.

'The girl were fetched to that house each time by a member of her own family and teken home by the same once her work were done.'

'To the best of my knowledge, yes,' Thorpe answered glibly. 'On the odd occasion I arrived as they were leaving it was a younger brother collected Sarah but I cannot vouch it was always that one member of the family who came to escort her home.'

'No, no, as you say, your work did not permit.' The uniformed policeman wrote laboriously in his notebook then, his glance still running over the page, asked, 'Apart from service in the chapel, did you see Sarah Clews at any time in the last week?'

Take your time, make it look like you're digging deep. Not that you need have any concern.

A suitable moment having elapsed he nodded again. 'Yes.' It came uncertainly, another pause seeming to indicate a mental check. 'Yes, yes I did.' He met the policeman's eye. 'It was the evening before that, I was on my way to visit Jonas Beardsley along of Monway Sidings . . . he is too plagued with the rheumatism to get himself to the chapel so I try to go pray with him and his wife at least once a week. It was that evening I saw Sarah. I admit I did wonder as to the reason she was out on the heath alone and feeling in some way responsible for her safety I offered to turn back and see her home.'

'Did her tek you up on that offer?' The policeman licked his pencil.

Thorpe made a display of fighting self-condemnation. 'No.' The word seemed to force itself through barriers of reproach. 'If only I had insisted.'

'Don't go blamin' yourself Mr Thorpe sir, you wasn't to know.'

'That . . . that doesn't make it any better.'

'I appreciates your feelings, what with you bein' the minister an' all . . .'

Minister! Thorpe's insides glowed like a gas lamp.

'It must 'ave you feeling sort of protective of folk.' The policeman was writing again. 'Did her give any reason for not going home along of you?'

'I . . . I really shouldn't . . . she spoke in confidence.'

Glancing up from the notebook the constable looked Thorpe straight in the eye. 'I be speakin' in confidence when I says it be best you answer all y'can. This be a murder, Mr Thorpe, an' minister or no minister you could be teken in for questionin' along of the station.'

'Yes . . . yes of course.' Thorpe drew a long, suitably aggrieved breath. 'It's difficult to come to terms with breaking a trust . . . but then if it will help find whoever did this terrible thing . . .'

It wouldn't! Of that he was *supremely* confident.

'Sarah,' he went on slowly, every word weighted with pseudo regret, 'she begged me not to say . . . not to divulge her secret to her parents but . . . Oh Lord,' he lifted both hands, cradling his face, 'oh Lord, I wish now I had.'

The constable allowed a few seconds before saying quietly, 'This secret, I 'ave to ask what it were?'

'A . . . a young man.'

Did that appear reluctant enough? Thorpe smirked silently.

'Sarah said she was going away with a young man, she knew her parents would not agree to a courtship between them so they were running away. She begged me not to tell.'

The constable wrote a further note, then asked, 'This young man, did you see him?'

'No. I offered to stay with Sarah until he arrived but she would have none of it, I had a member of the congregation to visit and must not keep them waiting, she said. If only I had ignored her, insisted she return home with me, she would still be alive.'

'We all learns with hindsight.' The pencil was licked again. 'So you didn't see any young man?'

Let the reply wait a little. Unwillingness to answer would lend plausibility to the illusion of regret on betraying a confidence.

'Not,' he paused, letting his glance drop away from the other man, 'not directly.'

'Then indirectly!'

The constable was becoming a little impatient. Thorpe let the reaction pass. Allow the man his moment, it was all he would get.

'I was some distance on towards the houses at Monway Sidings but still averse to leaving Sarah standing alone. I looked back determined to return to wait with her, but I saw someone had joined her so I went on my way.'

'I see, and was the someone you seen with her a man?'

'Yes.'

'Could you see who it was? Did you recognise him, was it someone you know?'

Who would know him better! 'You must understand, I was a distance away, it was dusk . . . I can't be sure.'

'But you 'ave some idea, you've seen the man afore.'

Not a question this time. Thorpe gloated at the way he had led the interview to this point, exactly where he wanted it.

'. . . *should I fail to get what is owed by one then I simply take it from the other, male or female, woman or boy, either is acceptable.*'

His threat made to Ann Spencer sang in his brain, in addition to a joyous chorus in his soul.

'. . . *but taking from both at the same time is infinitely more acceptable.*'

This was the way heaven wanted it; Thomas Thorpe was merely the Lord's instrument.

'I . . .' He swallowed his satisfaction, replacing it with marked disinclination. 'This can't be taken as positive identification but . . . but it looked to be the young man living in the house of Leah Marshall.'

34

'You 'ave to be mekin' of a mistake!' Leah frowned at the two men in her tiny living room.

One of the men answered, polite but firm. 'Possibly, Mrs Marshall, but we have to follow up all information.'

'Information!' Leah snapped. 'An' who be it give that information?'

'I'm sorry.' The man shook his head briefly. 'I am not at liberty to say.'

'But y'be at liberty to question folk, to accuse a young lad.'

The woman was angry, the constable had warned of the likelihood. Detective Inspector John Allingham brushed a finger over the bowler hat held in his hands. 'Nobody is being accused, Mrs Marshall, we simply wish to speak with the young man. Is he here?'

'He be in the stable.' Leah's reply rattled like stones against a roof.

'I'll fetch him,' Ann answered from the other side of the room.

With a brief nod at the uniformed man accompanying him the inspector glanced at Ann. 'Thank you Miss Spencer, the constable here'll go along with you.'

'Her ain't like to tell him to run off!'

A policeman at the door was not the most welcome sight at any time and now with a local murder it had to be more disagreeable.

'I didn't expect she would,' the inspector said patiently, 'but rules are rules, Mrs Marshall, and it is the constable who must request that the lad come for questioning.'

'He'll be like to tell you the same as y've 'eard already from the wench and me.' Leah wasn't going to be overridden easily. 'Don't know what else you expects, that lad wouldn't harm so much as a fly, but I won't go sayin' the same for meself should I find who the one be a tryin' to blacken of his name.'

This woman had lost her own three children. She had taken the young woman and the younger lad into her home after they could no longer pay the rental of chapel property; two young people unrelated by blood. The boy also was not British. Waiting in silence the inspector made a mental review of his research.

'You wish to speak with me.'

The faintest trace of an accent, finely chiselled features, fair almost blond hair, blue-grey eyes: all fitted with the description he had been given; but he had not bargained for the open honesty in that face, the genuineness of the smile. The inspector accepted the chair along with the tea brusquely offered by Leah, smiling to himself as he laid aside his bowler hat. There was many a wealthy home he'd had cause to visit could learn a lesson or two in hospitality from these people; worried as they were at a police visit, it did not permit the teapot to rest on the hob.

'Your name is Alec Romney, is that correct?'

'Yes sir.'

'It is all right to call you Alec?'

Smiling at the ready 'of course, sir', the inspector stirred milk into the hot liquid, sipping from time to time while listening quietly to Alec's account of leaving Russia to arrive eventually in Wednesbury. It accorded perfectly with the account heard earlier from the girl.

'The night before last,' he asked as Alec finished speaking, 'can you tell me where you were let us say between the hours of six and nine in the evening?'

'Yes sir.' Alec's grin was rueful. 'I was at Hill Rise. I stayed later than I should . . . it worried Grandmother Leah.'

'Hill Rise be Edward Langley's farm over towards King's Hill.'

'Thank you,' Allingham acknowledged the constable, then to Alec, 'What time did you leave?'

'Mr Langley's clock showed a few minutes past six.'

'Did Mr Langley accompany you back to this house?'

'No sir, I . . . I rushed off without saying goodnight, it was rude of me.'

'Was time your only reason for leaving so suddenly?'

Alec answered after a brief pause. 'No sir. Not entirely, it . . . it was something I read in Mr Langley's newspaper.'

'A newspaper report?' The inspector echoed.

'Be 'ere . . .' Leah passed a folded newspaper, her finger tapping the relevant section.

'"The Russian Tsar and his family to be put on trial."' The inspector looked up from reading. 'Why would that have you leave the Langley place without a word?'

'The lad be worried,' Leah came in quickly. 'His folks be back there, with all that be goin' on in that country he be feared there'll be neither folk nor home left for him to go back to. Ain't you never took y'self off when it seemed worry were all too much, d'ain't you never fear when you was a lad!'

'War is a bad time when it's nation against nation but civil strife, friend fighting friend, would I imagine be even more dreadful, and news such as what be reported there be bound to set folk at one another's throat. So I understand you being worried for your family. I hope you hear soon that they are safe.'

Leah took back the newspaper, her eyes flashing anger the policeman's words had not appeased. 'Be that all – be you done wi' your questionin'?'

'Not quite.' Inspector Allingham glanced again at the boy. 'Alec, you said you left Hill Rise a few minutes after six, is that correct?' At Alec's nod he went on, 'And you arrived here at this house at what time?'

'I'm sorry, I don't know. I didn't think to look at the clock.'

Evasion? The inspector wondered.

'It were goin' on twenty past eight, least that were the time showed on that there clock and it don't never be more'n a minute or two out. But y'can ask of Edward Langley, the chimes of St Bartholomew's clock can be 'eard clean across the town, and with his bein' out on the heath he couldn't help but hear the quarter-hour soundin'.'

Collusion? They could have worked all of this out between them. When the constable finished writing Allingham said, 'Hill Rise Farm, Constable, how long do you estimate it would take me to walk from there to this house?'

'Hmm!' The constable pondered a minute. 'Depends.'

'On what?'

'Well sir, I means whether y'be walkin' by way of the town or else across the 'eath. Comin' along of the town I would say a man should do it in 'alf an hour, bit longer for a woman her not p'raps 'avin' the stride of y'self.'

'And if I . . . or a woman . . . chose the way of the heath?'

'Then I'd advise against—'

At the other man's irritated, 'Constable!' the uniformed policeman cleared his throat with an embarrassed cough, going on to say, 'The 'eath be riddled with spent coal mines, the shafts covered wi' bracken, that is the ones as be knowed of an' there be many as ain't. That bein' the way of it a body would need watch every step; I'd reckon on puttin' another fifteen minutes on that 'alf-hour.'

'And if the journey is made in the evening?'

Behind the chair occupied by his superior the constable looked across at Leah. He'd grown up with the woman's sons, sat with them in the classroom, shared their horseplay in long summer evenings.

It be all right, I knows you have your duty.

The constable read Leah's silent message. 'By way of the 'eath be a much shorter route but crossin' in the dark . . . I'd say 'alf-hour if you wishes to get across safe.'

'Half an hour.' The inspector echoed.

Leah recognised the tone, the calculation behind it. 'I knows what you be a thinkin', so why did the lad tek so long? You'll get to answer if you does for y'self what he done . . . you be a stranger to these parts same as 'im, you knows as little about the pits an' open shafts as the lad, but like 'im y'knows they be many and every one a waitin' to drag a body deep into the bowels of the earth; to my way of thinkin' that meks the pair of you equal so why not you go y'self now while it be dark, you cross that heath alone and see the time it teks.'

The woman had a point and all power to her elbow for making it, but he still had a job to do. Looking at Leah, at the challenge sharp in her eyes, John Allingham nodded.

'I take your point, a man would indeed need take his time.'

'As would a lad!'

'As would a lad.' He acknowledged the quick retort then reached for his bowler hat, saying as he ran his finger over the domed crown, 'That is a pretty necklace you have, Mrs Marshall.'

Leah smiled at the boy beside Ann. 'It were a present from Alec.'

'He bought—'

'Please,' the inspector held up a restraining hand, 'if you don't mind, Miss Spencer, I would rather Alec answer himself.'

'I got them from a gypsy,' Alec answered at once. 'Their caravans were parked on ground along . . .' He looked at Ann.

'Dale Street.'

'Dale . . . Street.' The constable wrote laboriously, his superior waiting until he finished before nodding to Alec to proceed.

'The caravans were so beautifully painted, I was telling Ann I had never seen the like in Russia when a young woman came across to us asking we buy a trinket. I had money Mr Langley insisted I take for helping with the milk floats. What better to spend it on than a present for a loved one?'

'Them.' Allingham cradled the bowler. 'You said you bought "them"; that implies you purchased more than one.'

Alec smiled a little sheepishly. 'Two,' he said, 'I bought two, one for Grandmother Leah and one for Ann.'

'But you do not wear your gift, Miss Spencer?'

'That is my fault, I draped the necklace over the ears of the horse telling Ann how my sister and I would place strings of beads over the ears of Vanka, my donkey, and how Vanka would trot proudly about the grounds as though he were still in the circus ring.' Alec paused. 'Sorry . . . I should have known.'

'So this second necklace, where is it now?'

'I do not know, sir,' Alec replied quietly. 'Rosie, the horse, must have flicked it off. I did not notice until I brought her into the stable; the necklace could have been anywhere along any one of those streets leading here.'

'Mmm.' The inspector mused a moment then, 'This second necklace, the one which was lost, did it have the same colour of stone as Mrs Marshall's has?'

'No. I chose colours I thought to complement their eyes; Grandmother Leah's eyes are the colour of ripe chestnuts so for her I chose amber while for Ann I took azure because her eyes are that lovely gentian blue of perfect summer sky.'

The scratch of the constable's pencil fell silent. Inspector John Allingham rose to his feet.

'Alec Romney,' he looked up from smoothing the crown of the bowler hat, 'I must ask you to accompany me to the station there to give a formal statement.'

'Why?'

'What for, the lad ain't done nothin'!'

Leah's hot protest joined Ann's question.

Allingham was sober-faced as he replied. 'We have a witness placing Alec Romney at the scene of a murder. We have the body of a girl who was strangled with a necklace, a necklace such as that Alec Romney states he purchased from a gypsy, but subsequently lost: a necklace with a blue glass bead.'

'So your young friend has been arrested.'

Ann's breath caught as a figure stepped from the shadows to bar her way.

'Alec is not arrested, he is simply giving the police a statement.'

'Statement you say.' A thick chuckle erupted in the darkness. 'So if it is only a statement they want why is he not returning home with you? How come they haven't released him?'

Thomas Thorpe! She did not need to see the face of the man blocking her path; the sound of the voice was something she would forever remember. She sidestepped but on the instant a hand fastened on her arm, the fingers biting with savage pressure.

'Let me tell you why he is being kept locked up. He is a murderer, he strangled Sarah Clews.'

'No!' Ann screamed, trying at the same time to shake off the hand.

'Oh but yes.' It slid smooth as a serpent. 'There was a witness, a witness who will swear on oath to seeing him with her on the heath.'

Ann's senses jarred at the gloating so evident in the voice. Thomas Thorpe was glad Alec had been taken into custody, grateful for the awful predicament he was in.

'That witness . . .' Ann tried again to pull free of the clutching hand. 'Whoever it might be is wrong. It was not Alec with Sarah Clews, he didn't even know her.'

Thorpe treated himself to a low abrasive laugh. 'A murderer doesn't need to know his victim.'

'Alec is not a murderer! He would never harm anyone!'

'That must needs be proved; can he prove he didn't strangle the girl, can he prove he wasn't out on the heath on the night of her killing? If it be he can't then . . . well, we all know the penalty for murder and young as he is now the time will come when he is given over to the hangman.'

'He didn't do it . . . you have to know he didn't do it.'

The strangled sob gratified Thorpe. This time he would get what had until now slipped from his grasp.

'I know he did not kill Sarah Clews,' he said.

'The witness, they have a witness!'

'A witness can change his mind, retract the statement, say

334

he is no longer sure of who it was he saw with Sarah; it was already dusk, light on the heath is deceptive.'

Hope surged in Ann as she looked at the face in the shadows. 'This witness, will he . . . do you think he will withdraw the statement?'

Thorpe pulled sharply on her arm, drawing her close against his throbbing flesh. 'He could be persuaded . . . and you know how.'

'It was you!' Ann twisted away from the mouth seeking hers. 'You told the police it was Alec with that girl!'

'And I can say I made a mistake, I can save your friend's life – but such a generous act needs be paid for.'

He must have waited for her. Ann's whole body contracted with abhorrence for the man pressing his mouth to the base of her throat, his hand pawing at her breast. He had known she would stay with Alec at the police station for as long as she was allowed but, uncertain whether she would return to Leah's house by way of the town or the more direct route along the Holyhead Road, he had waited here at the small opening leading off that main highway. Regardless of the rest of her journey, she must take this path in order to reach the house.

'So,' Thorpe breathed against her throat, 'do you pay or does your friend go to the gallows?'

Would he keep his word? Stand by a promise to tell the police his identification of the figure he had seen with Sarah was a mistake? Thoughts raced in Ann's brain. He had told so many lies before, how could she trust him now? But how could she not if Alec were to be saved? Forcing herself to answer she said quietly, 'I . . . I will do whatever you ask but first we must go to the police.'

She thought to fool him. Thorpe's mind shouted silent laughter. Go to the station, tell the police a mistake had been made. The only mistake was Ann Spencer's believing he would fall for such a trick.

'There'll be no goin' to the station 'til payment be made nor will that debt be settled in Chapel House.' The hand clasping her breast moved swiftly to her throat, one savage tug ripping open a blouse gleaming white in a sudden shaft of brilliant moonlight. Another rip revealed small high breasts. He stared at the moonlit mounds, the flesh between his legs pounding its insistence. 'Your fee,' he said hoarsely, 'will be paid here and now.'

35

'You are with him from choice . . . of your own free will. Lord, how stupid can a man be! You certainly made a fool out of me. I'm sorry I've spoiled your evening; rest assured I won't do so again.'

In the silence of her bedroom the words of Edward Langley rang in Ann's head. He had come to Leah's house to enquire further after Alec and on being told she was still at the station, had set off for there to walk her home. It must have been her cry as Thomas Thorpe pushed her to the ground, Thorpe almost leaping on to her, that alerted Edward to the fact someone was being assaulted.

With one hand he had hauled Thorpe halfway to his feet then seeing the face as he twisted the man round had snarled, *'You again! I warned you, I told you what I'd do if you came anywhere near her again. It seems you didn't understand, but you'll understand well enough by the time your bones be mended.'*

His free hand had crashed into the face staring up at him then as it lifted for a second blow she had grabbed his arm.

'No! It isn't what you think.'

'No?' he had grated, *'Then what is it?'*

She must not let him beat Thomas Thorpe. It had raced through her brain like an onrushing tide, washing away thought of anything except Thorpe's promise to tell the police he had been mistaken in identifying Alec as the person with Sarah Clews. *'I . . .'* She had stumbled on words she knew had

337

to be spoken yet burned on her tongue. '*We ... Thomas and I...*'

A flash of eyes caught in a strong moonbeam had warned she was not convincing Edward Langley, but she had to – for Alec's sake she must make him believe. Her next words had come almost on a cry.

'*I am with Thomas because I want to be with him.*'

It had seemed an age before he had answered and when he did his voice had been laced with disgust.

'*You are with him from choice ...*'

Ann's eyelids pressed down hard but the attempt to block out the consequence of what she had said failed totally, Edward Langley's scathing remarks echoing relentlessly.

'*I'm sorry I've spoiled your evening ...*'

There had been contempt in the reply, his glance following the way Thorpe had fled the very second Edward's grip had been released.

'*... rest assured I won't do so again!*'

He had turned from her, becoming rapidly lost among merging shadow. She had not moved. Ann opened her eyes and stared sightlessly at a window showing nothing but the sable dark of night yet at the same time filled with the picture of a young woman standing alone, listening to the fading sound of dying footsteps.

But had it been Edward Langley's steps she had listened so intently to or was she on the alert for those of Thomas Thorpe, returning to carry out his intention?

Ann moved to the bed. She had waited, shame at what she was about to do stinging like acid in her veins. She would not do as he asked; she had even turned to follow along the way he had gone, to tell him of her decision, but then filling her mind's eye had come the picture of a young boy with tousled fair hair, eyes dark with incomprehension, a boy who asked, '*You do believe me, don't you Ann? You do believe I did not kill that girl?*'

And so she had waited, trembling but resolution strong and steady as a rock. She would lie with Thomas Thorpe, suffer his assault of her body, lose the respect of Edward Langley, even the love and friendship of Leah; she would forgo all of these if it meant Alec's freedom. Each of those actions would bring her pain. Ann slipped into bed, the sheets cool against a body hot with shame. But of them all the thought of Edward Langley's contempt hurt most.

Ann sought sleep but none would come.

She had waited there on that dark secluded path, waited for Thomas Thorpe to return, but he had not come back.

'*Don't you go a tellin' me I be wrong . . .*'

Etched on the shadowed ceiling, the scene played clearly as if in daylight. Leah had taken one look at the clothing Ann held together across her chest. '*It be that filthy toerag Thorpe, I'll pull his gizzard out through his earhole!*'

Leah's eyes had glistened with reproof as she dismissed Ann's confession of being with Thorpe because she wished to be.

'*. . . I knows that blackguard better'n he thinks; he can pull the wool over the eyes of Ada Clews and the like but he can't do it with me. Be my guess he stood waitin' of you and it all be to do with the lad. Tell me that don't be the truth.*'

More lies! Ann watched herself turn away from the other then swing quickly back to the woman tying the corners of her shawl beneath her breasts saying as she did so,

'*You refuse to say so I'll just go get it from Thorpe. He knows Leah Marshall be no mullock, her don't be ignorant of the fact he be naught but a roarin' ranter spoutin' the Scriptures, actin' like he*

339

be the Lord's true disciple when there be folk to impress. But when there ain't he sheds the role like a snake sheds its skin, but like the snake the poison inside of him remains deadly.'

'No Leah please you can't, he might refuse to ...'

'What might Thomas Thorpe refuse?'

The question had placed Ann in a quandary, seeming to rob her of the ability to think clearly. Was it best to confide in Leah or to lie yet again?

Impatient at receiving no answer Leah had begun sharply, *'Keep it to yourself if you will but that won't keep it from me, not if I have to squeeze every word from his lying ...'*

The flow had halted as she frowned, intensifying the tightness of her face, her anger-brightened eyes boring into Ann's.

'That be it don't it?' Sudden perception had kept her voice low. *'That no good fossack's promised summat as'll see the lad freed, but first you was meant to pay and we both knows it weren't money he were askin'.'*

Ann had recognised it would do no good continuing to lie. Quietly, brokenly it had all come out.

'You truly thought he would tell that inspector it were a mistake, that it weren't Alec he'd seen along of Sarah.' Leah had shaken her head in disbelief. *'You could believe that knowin' the lies he's told! Lord, wench, that man be so crooked he can't lie straight in bed; hadn't it been for Edward comin' along as he did Thorpe would have teken what he wanted and laughed all the way 'ome; as for goin' along of the police it'll snow in hell afore he does that.'*

'Then I will have to tell them.'

'Won't mek no odds, they'll think it be one more con on your part to get the lad out.'

'But I can't just leave him there.' Ann heard the desperation in her own voice and the common sense in Leah's down-to-earth answer.

'Alec be best off where he is. Arthur Clews be driven half mad by his wench's murder, I wouldn't answer for what he might do to the lad. No, I says let things lie as they be; it'll be frightenin' for the lad bein' locked up but he'll be safe there 'til the real killer be found.'

Ann watched the pictures fade leaving the ceiling a tiny sea of shadows while thoughts buzzed in her brain.

What if the real killer was never found?

What if Alec was judged a murderer?

What if the law hanged him?

Ann closed her eyes and sobbed.

The body had been found!

Thomas Thorpe's veins drummed.

'Found floatin' in the Devil's Pool.'

It couldn't have been! Thorpe refused to accept what he heard. The body would have been sucked down, pulled into underground mine workings.

'Arthur Clews come upon it, he were out searchin' o' them gypsies.'

Clews! Thorpe's brain clicked to normal. The man was deranged at the loss of a daughter; in that crazed state, wanting as badly as he did to catch the person responsible, might he not have thought whoever it was in that flooded shaft had first killed the girl then drowned himself out of remorse? It would make a decent argument against Alec Romney being guilty, a case Thomas Thorpe must prevent being put.

'But the police already got the one who done for that wench.'

'Ar, but 'ave they got the right one?'

'He be naught but a striplin' of a lad and Clews' wench were well built and strong from workin' along of a factory all day; I for one don't see he could 'ave overcome 'er.'

'You be right, Joby, the wench would 'ave been more'n capable of throwin' him off.'

He for one did not believe Romney was the culprit. How many more thought the same, or more importantly how many yet might be swayed if this line of talk was allowed to go on?

They would not him pass by without first listening to this latest piece of news. That would be his chance. Thorpe stepped closer to the group of men.

' 'Old up a minute, Pastor, what be your tek on all o' this?'

Pastor! Thorpe swelled with pride. These men valued his judgement; it would not be difficult leading them to think in any way he desired.

'All of what?' he asked innocently, then as the man Joby finished his explanation waited a moment as if giving the matter deep thought.

'There is certainly truth in what Joby says, the girl was taller and heavier than the boy but . . .' He drew a long breath as if reluctant to continue. 'On the other hand with the attack coming from behind, the cord pulled tight across the throat would have prevented her breathing so she would very quickly have lost the strength to fight off even a boy.'

'Pastor Thorpe be right.' A voice spoke from the rear. 'It don't matter as to height or strength, once there be a cord a throttlin' o' somebody they can't fight back.'

'So who be it Arthur Clews pulled from the Devil's Pool, how do it be he got in there?'

'Was any identification found on this unfortunate man?'

The voice at the edge of the group replied to Thorpe's question. 'Clews said no. Said as there were naught in his pockets.'

Of course there was nothing in the pockets. Thorpe smiled to himself.

'Police found nothin' to say who it be lyin' in the morgue, naught to say where he be from nor the reason of his bein' in Wednesbury.'

'... *naught to say where he be from ...*'

In his small living room Thorpe let the conversation run again in his mind.

'... *nor the reason of his bein' in Wednesbury.*'

He looked across to the black leather valise lying on the table.

Nobody would ever discover the reason for that man being here.

He had not offered to walk with the wench along of the police station. Leah watched Edward Langley's milk float merge with the purpling grey of approaching night. He stayed less and less each time he came; this evening only long enough to reload his freshly scrubbed churns back on to the cart. What had gone on between him and Ann? Their strict avoidance of each other shouted the fact it was something serious. It had been going on since that business with Thorpe. Leah stared at the small shape black against the gathering night. Had Edward Langley heard something or, worse, seen something, a sight that both disgusted and hurt? She could tell him what Ann had told her, that what had taken place was done for the lad; to get Thorpe to say he was not convinced it had been Alec on the heath with the Clews girl. But that would be to break not only a confidence but the promise she had made to Ann not to say a word of any of it to Edward. You must not interfere, she had reminded herself as he had hugged her goodnight. You, Leah Marshall, have led your life; you must leave others to lead theirs.

'*Would you ask Miss Spencer to tell Alec I will go see him tomorrow.*'

His reply when she had remarked Ann was about to visit the lad remained with her as she closed the doors of the dairy. Not offering to walk her there then see her safely home was out of character for Edward Langley. At the scullery door she cast one more backward look across the fields. The knife of disappointment had stabbed deep into Edward Langley's heart; the wound might never heal.

36

Leah would not leave Ann Spencer, she would not turn her back while a friend came and went from the police station alone at night; Leah would not act the way he was acting, which was petty and . . . and what?

Back at Hill Rise, the horse fed and stabled for the night, the cart with its load of empty churns placed ready for the morning milking, Edward Langley paced restlessly about his small living room.

Petty. Halfway home the truth had smacked him in the face, a truth he had fought the rest of the way to Hill Rise. It was not anger or annoyance which was making him avoid Ann Spencer, but jealousy; he was jealous of her relationship with Thorpe. He kicked savagely at the stone hearth. How in God's name had he let himself come to this! He was behaving like a child sulking because he hadn't won some game; and now he had allowed that resentment to affect his treatment of Leah. He had known even before he passed through the gate of Leah's yard that she would go along to the station rather than have that girl make the visit alone, yet even that had not made him turn back.

And what if Thorpe should be waiting! The thought brought him up sharply. Leah would not tolerate the man, she would strike out – and Thorpe? A new fear ran like a cold tide in Edward. Thorpe would strike back.

'Touch her, touch either of them, and I swear to God I'll kill you!'

Snatching up his jacket, Edward raced from the house.

Sarah was beautiful of spirit.

Blossoming in the gentle innocence of girlhood her nature was that of true kindness.

Like the Good Samaritan our Lord spoke of, she would not pass by any who needed help.

Though we would not have her taken from us, we know that grace and spirit, that sweet tenderness that is the essence of purity has found for her a place in the Kingdom of God.

Innocence of girlhood. Thomas Thorpe read again the words he had penned. If only they knew, if only those people who would sit listening as he spoke that eulogy knew as he did the real nature of Sarah Clews. But he must take care no trace of his true feelings showed in his reading. He took up the paper, reading aloud. That wouldn't do. Something was not quite right, something didn't fit. Frowning, he stared at the tribute he had compiled. It lauded the girl, it showed none of her faults, but summed up, albeit wrongly, her virginal qualities . . . so what was it lacking?

Beginning again to read aloud he stopped suddenly. Of course! The fault lay not in what was written but in the reciting of it. He was reading the whole in a flat monotone, with no inflection, no intonation. There was no pause to allow blinding tears to be surreptitiously wiped from the eyes, no small delay for choking sobs to be brought under control by means of a pretended cough, those little theatrical touches that would have the entire funeral party weeping openly and more importantly have them applaud him as their caring minister.

That was how it must appear on the day Sarah Clews was laid to rest. It had to seem the words came spontaneously, each one from the heart. For that the piece must be learned, practised over and over until it was word perfect.

Just one thing more would have made the day one of consummate joy. He glanced at the leather valise across the table. That would have been to wear the garments he had taken from that case, to conduct the ceremony in full ministerial robes. But every pleasure was attended by a little pain. There was nothing to prevent him wearing them in private.

Thomas Thorpe took the paper from the table and walked slowly upstairs.

As on the occasion of the service held in memory of George and Mary Carter's son killed in action she had come with Leah now to show respect for the daughter of the Clews family. How painful it was to part with loved ones. As Ann stood beside Leah, her thoughts whipped back to a cemetery in Moscow on a grey day with snow flurries falling. Just one mourner stood at a graveside, just one small posy of flowers adorned a plain wooden coffin. In reality it had taken no more than minutes for the black-robed Russian Orthodox priest to say the words commending her father to the mercies of God, to lift high the heavy cross lying on his chest and with a kiss to the cold metal turn and leave, yet in memory it seemed she stood there for an eternity. Just one young girl alone with her father. Ann's chest tightened with the remembered pain of knowing the father had no love for the girl standing at his grave.

But no love was preferable to no respect, which was what Edward Langley felt for her now. He came as he always had to help at Leah's dairy, he even shared a cup of tea with Leah and each evening he walked them both to the police station and back to the house, yet in all of that time he spoke not one word to herself. She watched him now walk across to the group coming out of the chapel, seeing him take the grieving mother's hand. Tears stung the back of her eyes. She had at one time dreamt Edward Langley might feel tenderness for her, that somehow his feelings might bloom into something deeper.

Dreams! She watched him, his raven dark hair tipped blue by the touch of sunlight, and though not close enough to see his face she knew his clear chestnut eyes would be smiling in friendship at the others leaving the chapel, but when Edward Langley rejoined Leah and herself his smile would touch only Leah.

Like so much in her life the dream of friendship with Edward Langley had been a daytime fantasy and a pleasant illusion some nights in the interlude between wakefulness and sleep.

'How be things wi' you wench?'

Deep in her own thoughts, taking a moment to realise the question was for her, Ann answered falteringly, 'They ... things ... everything is well thank you, Mr Turley.'

'Mmm!' Ezekial's response indicated her answer wasn't all truth.

'How are you keeping, Mr Turley?'

'I be fine lad, I thanks you.' Ezekial smiled at Edward and Leah, who had come to join them. 'I were just askin' o' the same of Ann and were glad to hear everythin' be well along of 'er.'

Had she seen Edward glance at her? Had a look of misery flashed briefly across his face?

No more! Ann snapped sharply to herself. There would be no more daydreams; anything she may secretly have hoped to grow between herself and Edward Langley was irretrievably broken.

'I'd 'oped the business of that body found floatin' in the Devil's Pool might 'ave connection to the killin' o' young Sarah, that it would somehow prove it don't be the lad that done it, but it ain't showed none.'

'Ann and me shared that same hope,' Leah answered Ezekial, 'but so far as be knowed there were naught found could link one to the other. That man's death be a mystery. He be knowed by nobody in the town, he weren't never seen in any street, there were naught along of him in that water might throw light on where it be he come from, but same as I knows Alec don't be no murderer, I feels that man d'ain't go killin' of himself.'

'That will be for the coroner to decide.'

'Ar Edward, y'be right in that,' Ezekial nodded, 'and followin' on the poor soul will suffer a pauper's burial, but today at least prayer was said for 'im.'

'Prayer?' Edward asked.

'Ar lad, Thorpe led the congregation in a prayer askin' the dead man's soul be taken by the Lord, that were a thoughtful act.'

Thoughtful! Leah snorted inwardly. As in everything Thorpe did, a prayer for an unknown man was designed to have everyone in that chapel think him a caring, godly man.

'This is where I bid you good afternoon, Mr Turley.'

Despite the dressing down she had given herself earlier Ann felt the sharp drop of her stomach. Was Edward saying goodbye to Ezekial?

'I'll be across later with the evening milk yield.'

It was answer enough. Edward Langley was going home. Ann turned along the path leading to Leah's house.

★   ★   ★

'As if he don't 'ave enough to put up with.' Leah lowered the newspaper she had been reading. 'This'll set him off worryin' all over again though why he sets such store by what be goin' on I don't know. True, he cares what be happenin' but it don't be like it can 'ave any effect on him.'

Replacing the teapot on the trivet near the fire Ann fetched a jug of milk from the scullery cold cupboard before asking who would be set worrying and by what?

Leah's clipped reply sounded slightly exasperated. 'Alec, it be Alec'll be worryin' . . . here,' she pushed the newspaper across the table, 'read that and you'll see for y'self what I be talkin' of.'

Ann read silently.

An announcement reported from Moscow earlier this month stating the ex Tsar and his family currently detained in the town of Yekaterinburg were to be put on trial was today followed by the further announcement the ex Tsar shall be shot . . .

'Shot!' Ann's horrified eyes stared over the newspaper. 'They can't shoot him, he is their king, the Russian people will surely never allow him to be executed.'

Leah said quietly, 'Read on wench, read the full piece.'

Ann's eyes sped over the official declaration.

The Presidium of the Divisional Council in pursuance of the will of the people have decided the ex Tsar is to be shot. The decision of the Council was carried into execution on the night of July sixteenth.

'The lad didn't seem to be himself.'

'If he's bin hurt!'

'He hasn't Mrs Marshall, you know me better than to allow any harm to befall the lad while he be in my keeping.'

'Yes.' Leah nodded. 'Yes I knows that, William lad, I be sorry for sayin' what I did.'

From his regulation six-foot height Constable William Price smiled down at the woman he had known from boyhood. 'That be all right, Mrs Marshall, we all gets a bit edgy from time to time.'

Leah had spoken sharply out of worry for Alex and now Ann's nerves also quickened. Why was he not here? Had he perhaps stumbled against a table or chair, knocked an arm or a leg? Could he have had a fall and be bleeding beneath the skin as he had before? Questions sharp as wasp stings jabbed again and again until Ann blurted, 'Constable what did you mean by saying Alec did not seem to be himself. Has he said he is not feeling well?'

Formalities did not permit the use of first names when dealing with people at the station, but it did not forbid a smile and the one William Price directed towards Ann was generous. 'That be it Miss Spencer, the lad didn't say anything, least he didn't after reading of the evening newspaper.'

Ann's mind fled to those other times Alec had searched for news coming out of Russia, searched for news of his family. This time had he found what he looked for – was Alec's family dead?

'Can we see him please?'

William Price shuffled a little uncomfortably, his eyes avoiding those of Ann and Leah.

'Well!' Leah demanded. 'Like Ann says, can we see the lad?'

He had to reply. Leah Marshall's shout would wake the town if he didn't. The constable coughed. 'He don't be here, Mrs Marshall.'

'Don't be 'ere! What d'you mean he don't be here!'

Stuck for a suitable answer, the constable breathed his relief when the inspector walked into the station. He was the boss, let him take Leah Marshall's ire. Quickly he reported the proceedings so far then walked to the back of the small counter.

'Mrs Marshall,' Inspector John Allingham said, ushering the two women into a tiny office. 'The boy is no longer here.'

'Be this the parrot home at the zoo!' Leah snapped. 'I've 'eard that three times already; what I want to know is why . . . why ain't he here and where do he be?'

'Allow me to explain.' Ready to launch into a long preamble John Allingham changed his mind as Leah's frown became a scowl 'The fact of this being a case of suspected murder means the suspect cannot be kept here but has to be transferred to Stafford Prison. Alec Romney was taken there this morning.'

37

'*The decision of the Council was carried into execution on the night of July sixteenth.*'

Lying in bed staring at the moon-kissed shadows drifting across the walls Ann recollected the rest of the article she had read in Leah's newspaper.

'*... The great Russian Eagle, proud banner of the Romanov Dynasty, was torn down and trampled beneath the feet of the people surging through the massive wrought-iron gates, a restless moving tide leaving death in its wake.*'

Suddenly out of the silence it seemed a voice murmured in Ann's ear, '*The eagle is pulled from its nest.*'

Maija's words translated for her by the priest.

'*... restlessness breathes over the land, death ... death waits in the shadows ... its hand moves, the light of Russia is gone.*'

Could Maija have 'seen' the tragedy which only now had fallen over that land? Did her trance reveal the death of the Tsar and his whole family?

And the gypsies! Ann's nerves twanged as the words returned.

'*The wings of the eagle be broken, its chicks cry no more ... Kalo RAI searches for another ... the dark Lord of Death waits in the shadows.*'

The eagle is pulled from its nest. Ann stared at the walls. The Tsar had been forced to abdicate!

'*The wings of the eagle be broken.*'The Tsar had been executed!
'*Its chicks cry no more.*' The Tsar's children too had been killed!

It all seemed to fit, except . . . Ann shivered.

'*Kalo RAI searches for another.*' Death searched for another!

Alec had heard those words, he had read that same newspaper article; he was a bright, intelligent boy, could he, like herself, have fitted those puzzling words together and let himself be frightened by them?

'*Its hand moves, the light of Russia is gone.*'

The words seemed to hover among the shadows.

That again could only refer to the Tsar. She had been a very short time in St Petersburg but it had been long enough for her to realise that to the peasant folk their Tsar *was* the light of Russia.

But what of the gypsy's final words?

Again the whisper in the darkness.

'*Death waits in the shadows.*'

Did Alec think that referred to his parents? That even now it waited to claim them?

Would it have helped to have told Leah of Maija's strange words, of those of the gypsy? Ann closed her eyes. She had wanted to speak of them on the way home, longed for the reassurance the older woman always gave, but the prospect of Edward Langley thinking her foolish had kept her silent.

That was unfair to Edward! Edward Langley might not like her, he might even resent her, but he would never be rude to her.

A fleeting moonbeam lit the tiny room. Just like Edward's smile lit the room whenever it beamed on Leah.

Heartache strong and real twisted in her chest. Edward Langley's smile would never again beam on her.

★   ★   ★

'That be a coincidence.' Ada Clews looked across to her husband finishing his evening meal.

'What do?' Arthur asked, chewing on a pork chop.

Laying the evening paper on the table Ada poked a finger at a passage headed MYSTERY MAN IN DEVIL'S POOL NAMED.

Arthur leaned forward to read the close-typed print, saying as he finished, 'What be a coincidence about that?'

'The name.' Ada frowned. 'I seen that name afore. I remember cos it struck me as bein' lah-di-dah, certainly there ain't nobody in Wednesbury wi' a name fancy as that.'

' "Tristan Reue Gaylord," ' Arthur read aloud. 'That ain't a name I've come across. Tristan Reue Gaylord,' he repeated, sucking the chop bone. 'A name as arty-farty as that would bring a few ripe remarks from men in the foundry. But last we 'eard the police had nuthin' to go on, nuthin' to say who he be or what he be doin' in Wednesbury.'

'Maybe the police advertised; you knows, askin' in the newspapers did anybody know of a man gone missin'.'

'Well.' Arthur sniffed, running a finger around his plate to scrape up the last remnants of tasty gravy. 'Seems somebody did if they've got a name, shame it weren't known when Thorpe said a prayer forrim.'

Thorpe! Ada's senses tightened. Why when she had read that report, why each time she scanned it again did the name Thorpe sing in her mind?

'That be it.' She slapped a hand hard on the table, setting Arthur's knife and fork clattering on the plate. 'That be where I seen it.'

'Seen what?' Arthur reached for his tobacco-stained pipe.

Tutting impatiently Ada retorted, 'The name, y'fool, it were in Thorpe's house. It were when I went to talk to 'im about Leah teken up sellin' her butter and cheese to the women.

355

There were a black leather bag lyin' open on his table and that name were wrote clear: bold black letters . . . they stood out plain on the biscuit coloured inside of the flap.'

'So what?'

'So what!' Ada's patience snapped. 'What were it doin' in Thorpe's 'ouse? He never once mentioned anythin' about it . . . and then in the chapel when he prayed for the dead man's soul he d'ain't once speak that name; strikes me there be summat as don't meet the eye in that, same as with our Sarah. Thorpe's tongue stilled mighty quick when I tried to talk to 'im about her, and her were the same whenever I brought him into the conversation. I couldn't never rid meself of the feelin' summat was bein' kept very close to the chest wi' the pair of 'em. Oh Lord!' She stopped suddenly, eyes wide. 'Y'don't think . . . I means could it be . . . ?'

Arthur stared back at his wife, his work-weary eyes filled with the same enquiry. Could Thorpe have made Sarah pregnant?

'He wouldn't,' he said, 'he be a man o' God.'

'Man o' God!' Ada spat contemptuously. 'Since when did bein' a man o' God stop any man gettin' between a wench's legs, an' if any man 'ad the chance wi' our Sarah, it were Thorpe, her thought the sun shone out of his arse.'

'But Matthew went to the Chapel House along of her and then walked her 'ome again.'

'Ar, so he did,' Ada returned. 'But he d'ain't stay in that Chapel House so he's told me since, he left Sarah there on her own, so the lad wouldn't know had Thorpe been there all along. You knows our Sarah . . . God rest her . . . and while I don't wish to speak ill o' the dead, I 'ave to say that wench could be a dark 'orse when it suited her.'

'So you thinks. . . .'

'Can't see it bein' no other, that house be the only place her were on her own an' nobody other than Thorpe were ever allowed in there since them lodgers o' Leah Marshall's left.'

Putting aside his pipe Arthur tied a scarf about his neck then reached for his jacket, saying as he slipped his arms into it, 'I be goin' to 'ave a word wi' Thomas Thorpe.'

'Y' don't think as he be goin' to own to it, supposin' he do be the one put our Sarah up the stick, he ain't a'goin' to tell you.'

'Not voluntary.' Arthur buttoned his jacket. 'But then I only says "please" one time.'

'*You was stubborn as a young lad but now you be a man y'be even more stubborn.*'

Leah Marshall's words as she walked with him to the gate closing off the path to her house from the one leading to the road rang in Edward's mind.

'*You two be 'urtin' of yourselves when there be no call forrit.*'

She had scolded as if he were still ten years old. Edward smiled despite the ache inside of him.

'*Would tek no more'n a word to put things right.*'

No Leah. This time you are wrong, a word . . . many words . . . would not cure the pain in my heart. You did not see what I saw! His eyes closed in an attempt to shut out the picture of Ann spread-eagled on the ground with Thomas Thorpe on top of her. You did not hear what I heard! She was with him because she wanted to be.

Each to his own! But the slimy Thorpe was the last man he would have thought Ann Spencer to want. Shows how wrong you can be, Edward Langley!

'Hey up lad!' In the darkness a man caught at Edward's elbow as they collided.

'Sorry ... wasn't looking where I was going,' Edward apologised then, 'You be going the wrong way, the Rising Sun is in that direction.'

'I'll be goin' there later, I 'ave a bone to pick first.'

'Oh.' Edward laughed. 'That doesn't bode well for somebody.'

'That'll depend on the way I be answered, but either way Thorpe'll be answerin'.'

Thorpe! Edward listened intently as Arthur related what Ada had said regarding the drowned man's name.

It was no surprise. Thorpe was a roaring ranter when preaching in chapel but when talk turned to himself, he was sparing with words ... he told very few truths.

'Would y'mind comin' along o' me, Edward, I knows I loses me temper sometimes so it might be best I don't see Thorpe on my own.'

I wouldn't put it past that toerag to claim you'd assaulted him when you'd merely looked at him. Edward kept the thought to himself, and fell into step beside the older man.

Knocking at the door of number twenty-three Cross Street and for the second time receiving no reply, Arthur Clews shuffled irritably. 'There be somebody in.' He glanced at the living-room window from which a gleam of anaemic yellow light spilled through a gap in the closed curtains. 'Thorpe don't be one to go a wastin' o' money on lamp oil when he don't be 'ome; that one would skin a fart for 'apenny and sell the skin for tuppence! Well Arthur Clews also be a man who be mean, I ain't goin' to 'ave no wasted journey.'

So saying he marched round to the back of the house. He was through the scullery and into the living room before Edward caught up to him.

'Lord God Almighty!'

Taken aback by the exclamation, Edward looked over Arthur's shoulder into the tiny living room, his own astonishment making him gasp. What in the world was Thorpe playing at!

Thorpe's face was the picture of fury. 'What do you think you are doing coming into my house!'

'What do *we* be doin'?' Arthur Clews laughed outright. 'What the bloody 'ell be *you* doin' dressed up like a tart in a brothel?'

'Whose robes are those?' Edward ran a slow glance over the black cassock, its tiny cloth-covered buttons reaching to the ankles, the white silk stola draped round Thorpe's shoulders, the prayer book held reverently in both hands.

One eyebrow arched high as Thorpe sniggered disparagingly. 'They are mine, whose else would they be?'

Clews' reply flashed out before Edward had time to think. 'Try Tristan Reuel Gaylord.'

Obviously stunned, Thorpe stared for a moment but as quickly pulled his thoughts together. These men had no proof, therefore there was no need for him to answer.

'That be who them robes belongs to!' Clews answered the silence. 'Was it you found 'em and decided to keep 'em for y'self?'

Watching the sneer slide across Thorpe's face, watching it settle on his thin lips, Arthur felt the thunderclouds of anger begin to gather. Ada and many like her had trusted this man, followed his words as they would those of a saint but that sly smirk, that cunning glint in the narrowed eyes, were proof enough for him Thomas Thorpe was no saint.

Not caring whether he was right or wrong, his anger augmented by a fast-growing suspicion, Arthur Clews stepped further into the room. 'You stole that there gown and the scarf wrapped 'round your shoulders . . .'

'Cassock,' Thomas Thorpe corrected him. 'This,' he touched the black cloth, 'is known as a cassock and this,' he ran a finger over the white silk, 'is a stola but then you are too ignorant to know that.'

Sensing the tremor of rage run up Clews' spine Edward placed a restraining hand on the man's arm.

'Ar, I don't be clever as some or as quick wi' words, but I be smart enough to know *you* be naught but a liar. If them things be your'n how come you ain't never worn 'em to chapel? I'll tell y' why . . . cos they ain't your'n, you took 'em from the chap you killed then tipped into Devil's Pool.'

'Arthur, you can't go saying such!' Edward's hand tightened as he spoke the warning but it was the look on Thorpe's face that grabbed his attention. Sheer arrogance burned like fire in eyes which had dropped their guard.

'He thought to take my place.' Thorpe stared at the men in his living room. 'The fool thought to be pastor but the chapel is *mine*. It is decreed by heaven only Thomas Thorpe may serve there, *he* is the Chosen, the man called by God Himself to minister there, to conduct His divine service, so you see . . . he had to die.'

Thorpe had murdered that man! Edward's mind reeled. He had killed him in cold blood and now he was parading in the clerical robes he had stolen from him.

'The Lord's word has to be obeyed.' Thorpe raised the prayer book to his lips, his eyes glittering fanatically. 'It was His will, nothing must stand in the way of that.'

'My God Arthur, did you hear what he said?' Edward's incredulous question was clear yet all that Clews heard was a whisper, a murmur soft in his mind: Sarah . . . Sarah.

Across the room Thorpe laughed, a high-pitched manic screech which seemed to bounce from wall to wall. 'That slut!'

he screamed at the murmured name slipping from Arthur Clews' tongue. 'Stupid bitch thought to become the minister's wife, thought that opening her legs would put a ring on her finger! Marry ...' He laughed again, a piercing half-crazed laugh that rang in his listeners' ears. 'Thomas Thorpe would not stoop to marry among the lowest of the low, a common foundryman's daughter.'

'Y' wouldn't marry her but you'd tek her to bed often as chance were given!'

'A whore who hoped to better herself by marrying the minister,' Thorpe raved on, not hearing Arthur, 'she thought we were going to Darlaston to talk with the minister there, to ask would he perform the wedding ceremony, but that could not be allowed, the trollop had to die before she could make trouble.'

'Wait, Arthur!' Edward held Clews securely then looked across to Thorpe, saying quietly, 'Sarah Clews had to die.' At Thorpe's nod he asked, 'Who killed her?'

Eyelids closed, the prayer book pressed again to his lips, Thorpe stood for a long moment like a soul in rapture. Then lifting his face as if to the sky he said exultantly, 'The Lord's Chosen ... the instrument of heaven: Thomas Thorpe was granted that privilege.'

Edward looked at the man still floating on a cloud of ecstasy. Thorpe saw murdering the girl as some sort of reward. Christ, he must be insane!

'Let go o' me Edward, I'll kill the filthy swine.' Arthur Clews struggled to throw off Edward's grip.

'Tristan Reuel Gaylord ...' Mindless of the other two men Thomas Thorpe laughed dementedly. 'He thought to steal my place as minister, to take my chapel, he thought to blacken my name as did the other two ...'

Three! Edward's brain rocked at this new information. Thorpe had killed *three* times: Gaylord, Sarah Clews . . . but who was the third victim?

'The other two.' He tried to sound matter-of-fact. 'You said Sarah so who is the other, was it a man?'

Thorpe fingered the fringes of the stola, straightening each until they lay in perfect symmetry each side of his chest, then turned towards the door. 'I think I'll go see her now; tell Leah Marshall I killed her daughter.'

'You go get the constable, I'll wait here and don't go a worryin', Edward, I be more'n a match for Holy Joe.' Arthur Clews pulled savagely at the arm twisted behind Thomas Thorpe's back.

'I don't know Arthur, he's a sly one.'

'He be welcome to try puttin' one over on me if'n he be daft enough but I tells him clear, should I see so much as the bat of an eye I'll lay him out cold.'

Edward smiled grimly to himself. Chalk and cheese, that was these two: Thorpe small, almost weedy in stature while Clews was strongly built, his arms bulging with muscle gained from years of heavy foundry work. No, Thorpe stood no chance of getting away.

He waited until Thorpe's hands were securely tied with the string drying line snatched down from the scullery.

'Edward,' Arthur Clews called as Edward was leaving. 'Go to Leah Marshall first. Better for her to be told by you what this tripehound done to her wench than hear it from the police.'

Two minutes later, once all sound of Edward's leaving had died away, Arthur Clews hauled Thorpe to his feet.

'You ain't goin' to meet no coppers,' he breathed, 'you ain't goin' to see no doctor neither, there's gonna be no let off for balance o' mind bein' disturbed. You killed my wench and you be goin' to answer forrit.'

Outside the house Arthur Clews breathed a prayer of thanks that the sky was dark with promised rain clouds and for the fact Leah's house backed on to cow pasture beyond which lay derelict ground. Going that way there would be next to no chance of meeting anyone.

Glad he had thought to gag Thorpe, he half dragged, half carried his reluctant prisoner. As he had guessed they met no other person. Coming to the edge of Devil's Pool he glanced at the water, its viscous surface moving sinuously in the breeze like some huge black serpent.

Thorpe also stared a moment at the dark mass then began to struggle.

'Won't do you no good.' Clews snarled, grabbing a piece of fallen rock and smashing it against the other man's head. Working quickly he removed the thin rope from Thorpe's wrists, wrapping it first about a larger heavier rock which he then tied round the neck of the unconscious Thorpe.

He glanced at the scudding clouds. It would take a minute or so more before Thorpe regained consciousness. He must not act before then. Arthur Clews' mouth set determinedly. Thorpe must be awake so he could hear his sentence.

A groan told him his waiting was over. Clews scooped up a handful of water, throwing it in Thorpe's face.

'Y'be awake now.' He snatched the befuddled man to his feet. 'I wanted you to be awake afore I left you.'

Fully aware now, Thorpe felt the weight of the stone drag at his neck. 'What . . . what do you think you are doing?' His voice trembled. 'Take this thing off my neck at once.'

'Oh I ain't thinkin' any more, my decision already be med.'

Forcing Thorpe closer to the rim of the pool he hissed against the terrified man's ear.

'You put my wench in there, now you be goin' to follow 'er, you gonna be given a taste o' what it be like in that black hole.'

'No . . . Clews, no . . . you can't!'

'Best leave that to us.' The reply was firm. 'I'm sure the inspector will ask should he feel we need help.'

After bidding William Price goodnight at the corner of Cross Street, watching him stride purposefully on along Holyhead Road, Edward said quietly, 'You know where Thorpe is, don't you?'

Beside him, cloaked in night's darkness, Arthur Clews laughed briefly. 'Ar I knows, but I don't be goin' to tell you lad. Be it enough for you to know that he got his dues.'

Arthur Clews had taken his revenge, of that he was certain. But what of Leah? On his way home to Hill Rise, Edward's thoughts returned to his friend. There had been no gasp of surprise when she was told, no cry of shock; Leah had simply nodded. Why? He frowned at the answer which came. Leah Marshall already knew!

'It were always in my heart you died of no accident nor would you 'ave teken the path o' suicide.' Leah Marshall touched the face of the photograph smiling from the mantelpiece. 'Now the truth be out and the one who harmed you will be brought to justice in my world and in yours. Rest happy now my darlings,' she smiled at each photograph in turn, 'rest in God's peace.'

At a sound on the stairs she left the neat front parlour, glancing concernedly at Ann coming into the living room.

'I still thinks y' should let me or Edward come along of you.'

'No.' Ann shook her head, 'neither of you can spare the time away from the farm.'

'But Stafford be so far away – too far for a young wench to go on her own.'

Ann smiled. 'Leah,' she said gently, 'Russia is a long way but Alec and I managed so I'm confident I can manage a train journey.'

'Well if y' must, but you will both come back here?'

'You know we would not leave just like that, you mean too much to both of us.'

'Off y' go then wench, the lad'll be more than anxious for you to collect him. I just thanks God the whole thing be cleared up.'

Thomas Thorpe had not yet been found. Ann walked briskly towards the police station, as she did so reviewing the events of the past few days. Edward Langley and Arthur Clews had both made sworn statements that Thorpe had confessed to three murders, but without the confession of the man himself it was strange Alec was being set free.

But he was and that was all she cared about. The thought added a spring to her step as she walked into the small yet imposing police station. Inspector Allingham had said he would furnish her with a letter which would ease the process at Stafford Prison.

Constable Price handed her the sealed envelope but Ann was prevented from leaving by the inspector's quick, 'Miss Spencer, would you give me a minute in my office please?'

'Good morning.' A man dressed in grey pinstripe trousers paired with a knee-length grey overcoat, a high white wing collar and a dark tie rose to his feet. 'My name is Sir Hugh Gresham. I have been sent to accompany you, that is if you will allow.'

The inspector answered Ann's dubious look. 'Everything is quite all right I assure you, Miss Spencer. Things will be resolved much more easily if Sir Hugh is with you.'

Deciding this must be usual or the police would not advise her to accompany this man, Ann allowed herself to be ushered out to the waiting automobile. The strangeness of being in a motor car for the first time kept her virtually silent as it sped along.

How far was it to Stafford Prison? It seemed they had been on the move for hours; the scenery had long changed from the jumbled buildings of town to peaceful countryside. She bit back the question as the car swept between high-pillared gates leading up to a large gracious house, its tall windows framed in cream stone.

Speechless, Ann stared at the huge entrance hall, its tiled floor set off with exquisite tables and voluptuous statuary. But it was the sitting room she was led into that made her catch the breath in her throat.

Silver-blue damask draped each window, the folds touching a vast carpet of the same colour. Set around a large ornamental fireplace settees and deep armchairs echoed the same beautiful shade of blue.

This couldn't be Stafford Prison! Dazed and not a little afraid Ann watched Sir Hugh Gresham pull a tapestry cord hanging beside the fireplace.

'I'm sure you would like some tea, Miss Spencer.' He smiled affably then ordered tea and sandwiches from the manservant who answered the summons.

The cup felt like paper in her hands. China this fine must cost a fortune. Ann's hands trembled as she accepted the tea.

'Miss Spencer,' Gresham said, settling into an armchair. 'Would you be kind enough to tell me everything you know about Alec Romney, how you came to meet him. Was he alone or with someone else? Please, I ask you to think carefully, try not to leave out any detail no matter how insignificant it might seem to you.'

'Is Alec here . . . can I see him?'

'All in good time. Now, if you would do as I asked.'

'It was in St Petersburg, the Ploschad Morskoy Slavy . . .' Speaking clearly and calmly she related every moment of the time she and Alec had spent together finishing with, 'And that was when Alec was arrested.'

He had listened without interruption then as Ann finished speaking said quietly, 'That accords perfectly with what Alec himself has told us. Now I think you should see him.'

'Alec.' Ann was on her feet as the door opened and Alec entered the room. 'Oh Alec, are you all right?'

'Of course,' he laughed, gripping her in a hug, 'and you and Grandmother Leah, you are both well?'

'Both happy you are coming home.'

'Miss Spencer, there is something you have to know.'

'Let me tell her.'

Was there the air of an order in Alec's words? Ann frowned at the deferential way the older man retook his seat.

'Ann,' Alec sat beside her, his hand holding hers, 'I have not been honest with you. I am sorry for that but circum-stances forbade it. You see before I left my home my father swore me to secrecy. He felt the nearness of the country's revolt and feared for our safety, so it was decided the family would leave one by one, each of us at intervals and in disguise as peasants. That way the Bolsheviks would pay no attention; it was the upper classes their sights were set on. I was to be the first followed by my youngest sister Stasie who would go via a different port. But it seems someone, probably a British embassy employee, got wind of my leaving from the Square of Maritime Glory, hence what took place there. The man chosen to see me safe to England was your father but with his death that had to be changed.'

'*They trusted me, they trusted me as they would no other man . . . they asked I take into my keeping their most precious possession.*'

The dying words of her father returned to Ann.

'You have to be wrong,' she said, 'my father was asked to carry a most precious possession but though I searched his home and even enquired at the British embassy if he had left anything there, I found nothing. Yet on that ferry it was demanded I hand over what I had taken from St Petersburg; but you know I had nothing of value.'

Alec glanced at the older man then back to Ann. 'It is you who are wrong, Ann, you had with you the whole time Russia's most valued treasure.'

'Alec, how can you say that! You must know I would gladly have given anything rather than have your life threatened the way it was.'

'That was why I could not tell you,' Alec said quietly. 'You see, Ann, my name is not Alec Romney, it is Alexai Nicolaïevitch, son of Nicholas Alexandrovitch Tsar of all the Russias.'

'The . . . the son of the Tsar!'

'Indeed he is.' It was Gresham who answered. 'He is His Imperial Highness Alexai Nicolaïevitch, Tsarevitch and heir to the Romanov dynasty.'

Ann frowned confusedly. 'The newspaper reports, they said the entire royal family had been assassinated.'

For a moment Alec held his breath as though struggling against overriding emotion, then with a supreme effort said, 'All of the people taken to Yekaterinburg were as reported shot dead, but the one they thought was me was Mikhail

Derevenko, the son of Dr Vladimir Derevenko who together with Professor Fiodrof was doctor to the royal family. They lived with us in the royal palaces of St Petersburg and Moscow; they accompanied us in the summers we spent at the royal residence of Tsarskoïe Selo. Mikhail and I were of the same age, we shared the same colouring and stature, so much so that often when I was bleeding or too ill to stand with my father at some official function Mikhail would take my place. He took it when I left to go with your father and as a result gave his life for me. Had I known ...' Alex paused, emotion once more threatening to overcome him. 'Had I known what would happen I would never have left my family.'

'The same ruse was used for Stasie,' Alec went on. 'Mikhail's sister Anya exchanged places with her. Brother and sister for brother and sister. We thought it a grand game, better than we played in any of the royal palaces, this was a *real* adventure, one to tell the family about when we returned home. I know my father would not have allowed the children of Dr Derevenko to substitute for us had he the slightest notion things would turn out as they have.'

'And your sister Stasie?' Ann asked the question gently.

'Is safe.' Gresham smiled. 'Her Imperial Highness the Grand Duchess Anastasia Nicolaïevna was brought safely to this country several months ago.'

'But I still don't understand.' Ann shook her head. 'How come you are here and not in prison?'

'Sir Hugh?' Alec looked at the man seated opposite.

'The governor of that establishment is a close acquaintance of the Prime Minister,' Gresham explained. 'One evening while dining together he told the PM about a young lad held on suspicion of murder, a lad who claimed to be Russian. The PM confided the same to the highest man in the land.'

The King! Ann's insides tightened. The King had been told about Alec!

'He ordered an immediate release adding that the boy must be brought here in strict secrecy where he could be questioned thoroughly; and to every question put to him he replied with instinctive accuracy, even details that could be known to none but the closest and most trusted family relatives. His Majesty is therefore convinced of the truth of his identity.'

'I'm sorry I could not confide in you,' Alec smiled, 'but the risk to yourself was too great.'

'*We will find them, take what she carries and both will die ...*'

The words screamed above the shrieking wind by a man trying to snatch Alec from the rowing boat lowered from the ferry returned to Ann as did the final words of the gypsy.

'*Kalo RAI, the Dark Lord searches for another ...*'

It could only mean Alec! But this time the Dark Lord would be cheated of his prey. Looking at the boy with whom she had shared so many dangers Ann thought, I did what you asked, Father, I kept your promise for you.

'Miss Spencer,' Sir Hugh Gresham intervened, 'what you have heard in this house must never be told to a living soul. There are still factions in Russia who would stop at nothing to see the Tsarevitch dead.'

'Ann can be trusted completely,' Alec put in. 'She would never betray the friendship we have.'

Ann squeezed the hand which held hers, the movement saying what words could not.

'As you may understand,' Gresham went on, 'the Tsarevitch cannot return with you to the home of the woman he calls Grandmother Leah. He must stay now with his relations here in England where he will be guarded day and night. Suffice to tell that lady and any who ask after Alec that during his time in Stafford Prison he was claimed by his relations.'

'But why did they not look for him sooner?'

'The answer to that,' Gresham went on, 'lies in the fact that he was not aboard the steamer bound for England. When that was discovered it was thought he might have somehow mistakenly boarded the ferry plying between St Petersburg and Finland. But when that ferry sank in mid-channel leaving no survivors the trail went cold.'

Taking Ann's other hand Alec said quickly, 'I hope this clears up the situation and though any hope of being with you and Grandmother Leah must be abandoned I know that the bond of friendship that we share will never be broken.'

38

On the journey to Wednesbury in the motor car with Sir Hugh Gresham, Ann silently went over all that had transpired.

Alec had said he wanted only to be an ordinary boy. She had smiled at this, saying he could never be an ordinary boy. He was Alexai Nicolaïevitch, heir to the Romanov dynasty.

'You are Russia,' she had said, 'and when the bitterness is past and the wounds healed and the sorrows of that great nation are assuaged, then Russia will open her arms to you and carry you home.'

As she alighted from the car at the path leading to Leah's smallholding, Ann's heart flipped when she passed the spot where Thomas Thorpe had thrown her to the ground and attempted to rape her. But the horror of that was over; never again would she come face to face with him. At the same time she must come face to face with Edward Langley. She must explain to him that what he thought of her was not true. She had not of her own wish lain with Thomas Thorpe. Chances were Edward would not believe her, would not even wait to listen to her explanation. Nevertheless she would try.

She proceeded along the narrow path and yards from the gate of Leah's house stopped at the sight of the tall figure. Daylight glinted on hair the colour of ebony.

Edward. She stood as if rooted to the spot but he was already running to meet her.

'Edward,' she said, 'I have to tell you—'

'No.' Edward cut her short. 'There is only one thing I want to hear from you. Do you love me? Will you be my wife?'

Caught in his arms Ann knew her journey was truly ended.

From now on she would live in the love of Edward, of Leah and of the young lad she had left behind in that grand house; she would be content in the knowledge friendship's bond would never be broken.